The Car Thief

The Car Thief

by *Theodore Weesner*

GROVE PRESS NEW YORK

Originally published in 1972 by Random House, Inc., New York

Portions of this book appeared originally in *The New Yorker, Esquire, The Atlantic Monthly, Audience,* and *Works in Progress.*

Published simultaneously in Canada
Printed in the United States of America

FIRST GROVE PRESS EDITION

Library of Congress Cataloging-in-Publication Data

Weesner, Theodore.
    The car thief / by Theodore Weesner.
      p.   cm.
    ISBN 0-8021-3763-6
    1. Automobile thieves—Fiction. 2. Children of alcoholics—Fiction. 3. Fathers and sons—Fiction. 4. Teenage boys—Fiction. I. Title.

PS3573.E36 C3 2001
813'.54—dc21   00-063651

Grove Press
841 Broadway
New York, NY 10003

01 02 03 04   10 9 8 7 6 5 4 3 2 1

For my father, a man not remembered

And for Sharon, a woman not celebrated

In remembrance and celebration

Book One
The Arrest

One

Again today Alex Housman drove the Buick Riviera. The Buick, coppertone, white sidewalls, was the model of the year, a '59, although the 1960 models were already out. Its upholstery was black, its windshield was tinted a thin color of motor oil. The car's heater was issuing a stale and odorous warmth, but Alex remained chilled. He had walked several blocks through snow and slush, wearing neither hat nor gloves nor boots, to where he had left the car the night before. The steering wheel was icy in his hands, and he felt icy within, throughout his veins and bones. Alex was sixteen; the Buick was his fourteenth car.

The storm, the falling snow, had come early to Michigan's Thumb, for it was not yet November. The previous day had been predictably autumn, drizzling steadily, leaves still hanging apple-colored overhead among the city's black wires. But by evening a chilling breeze had begun moving through the city, blowing over the wide by-passes and elevated freeways. Now in the morning the snow-covering was overall. It was four or five inches deep, as wet as a blanket soaked in water, as gray and full in the sky as smoke from the city's concentrations of automobile factories.

A cigarette Alex had not wanted so early in the morning was wedged in the teeth of the ashtray drawer. He could not remember having lighted it, and he thought about snuffing it out but made no move to do so. The dry smoke reached over the dashboard like a girl's hair in water. Picking up the cigarette, discovering either weakness or nervousness in his fingers, he drew his lungs full and replaced it in the teeth of the drawer. The smoke burned his eyes, as if from within, and he squinted as they watered.

He drove with his back not quite touching the seat. His shoulders and arms, down to his hands on the steering wheel, kept shivering lightly. The windshield wipers slapped back and forth quietly before him, slapping the melting snow to streams trailing to the sides. The only color within the ashen storm was an occasional diamond sparkling of oncoming headlight beams. He kept shivering. For a second he looked at himself, at his maze of trouble. Immediately he felt bound to the driver's position, bound to the steering wheel and accelerator and to the view ahead through the windshield. The act of driving became tedious.

At Chevrolet Avenue, near home, near where in their

apartment his father was sleeping at that moment, he turned toward downtown, entering heavy traffic. The line of cars, taillights flaring red and receding in domino lines, moved slowly. He turned on the radio, and turned the dial. No music. News. News of the storm, of traffic, of snow-removal equipment. With an outstretched arm he kept the dial moving as he drove along. Still he could not find any music. If the clock was right, it was just past eight. Unable to find music, he desired it all the more, as if on its sensations he might float away from the tediousness of driving.

He drove on. The cars before him were moving as carefully as ships in fog. Less carefully, he followed. He glanced at his rear-view mirror and saw the headlights of a car close behind. Raising a little higher in the seat, he glanced at his face in the dark mirror. He settled and returned his fingers to the radio dial. He searched again for music. He had been surprised at the anger and fear he had seen on his face, but he knew of nothing to do about it. He knew of nothing to do but to keep driving.

At last, at a point where the slow trainline of cars overlapped a sidestreet, he suddenly spun the steering wheel and nosed the Buick from the line. He pressed the accelerator and the rear of the heavy car came sliding sideways, trying to catch pavement, and catching, burned a brief squeal, squirting momentary rainbows of slush.

He began driving slowly. He turned corners here and there. He had no plan now of going anywhere, nor was he much aware that he had no plan. He turned into a driveway once to turn around, but backing out again, in a confusion of changing his mind, he continued the same way. The tediousness of driving kept building in him. It was as if the car held only a cup of gasoline but would not stop rolling on and on.

He turned the radio dial again. He found music now but it was too thin to allow him to float anywhere. Letting the dial go, he tried to escape into a fantasy. He imagined someone being sentenced to death on a challenge of no one in the crowd being willing to drive through the city at a hundred miles an hour and he was raising his hand, stepping forward. But the fantasy did not work. The ordeal of driving did not go away. As if allowing him a moment's diversion, the tediousness slipped back into him, stirring through his chest and stomach.

He saw, in time, that he was on Court Street, on an outer edge of the city. Buses were separating and gathering on the other side of the street, exhausting sprays of diesel pepper into the snow. The buses were filled with downtown office workers and high school students, perhaps a few stray and way-late factory workers. Alex imagined the bus aisles with melting snow underfoot, with books on girls' warm knees. He saw himself as if in a distant past, hanging by a loose arm, reading concave advertisements as the bus swayed along.

Still the tediousness of driving did not go away. The pressure kept growing until he felt it in his jaws, and he began losing his strength of grip on the steering wheel. His stomach was drawing tighter. It was a pressure, an anguish, which had overtaken him before, but he did not think of that, nor very clearly of anything. He closed his eyes against the feeling and opened them. His jaws felt chilled. He removed his foot from the accelerator, and as the sensation was seizing him, he slammed his palms against the steering wheel, jarring it, as if a violent striking there might cancel an explosion elsewhere.

No explosion came. In only a moment, coasting almost to a stop, the feeling turned from its peak and began to ease. He guided the car toward the curb, where it rolled to a stop in the deeper snow. Pushing a chrome tab, he hummed the window down. He realized how hot and dry the car had become. He turned his head to the open space for better air. The snow falling by and the sharp moist air were refreshing. When he had rested a moment and his stomach and breathing were closer to normal, he pressed the accelerator lightly, not to spin the wheels, and drove on again. He gave little thought to what had happened. Shivering, feeling chilled once more, he pushed the tab and the window rose beside him.

At a red light, turning a corner onto Court Street in front of him, was a black police cruiser. Two uniformed policemen were in the front seat, and Alex's eyes and the eyes of the driver glanced at each other. Alex looked away, as if casually. His heart seemed to pause. He felt the body of the cruiser pass before him and beside him, as long as a submarine. His eyes and the eyes of the driver had spoken to each other. He wondered how the policeman could not have helped seeing that he was guilty. When the light changed, he pulled away carefully. He did not look back.

After a moment he had still not looked back. Always before when he saw a police car he used both mirrors, moved little more than his eyes, in case the cruiser's taillights flared and he had to go. Now he imagined the cruiser U-turning to come after him, quickly this moment approaching the side of the Buick. But checking his mirror, he saw an empty snow-blown street. He felt disappointed. For a moment, only a moment, he felt a fear of never being caught.

He pressed the accelerator, and the heavy Buick moved out faster. He had switched license plates the first night he took the Buick, but he had been driving it ten or twelve days now, too long, he knew, to keep a car so easily identified. He knew he should trade the Buick for a Chevrolet, if only to save on gas money. He knew it every day, but he did not trade it. His father left him a dollar bill on their kitchen table each morning for his lunch and bus fare, and he suffered through giving up the dollar—for gas, never oil—as he suffered through other things he had given up, other things he was leaving undone.

A moment later, for the first time, he had a notion of

something pleasant lying at the end of the Buick's inevitable road. Perhaps it was a notion that the Buick was
going to an inevitable end. At other times on the thought
of where he was going, the seizure began in his stomach
and he would steel himself as if to have his toes or fingers
axed off. Now he felt a relaxation, a promise of rest, of
sleep.

He had the radio dial going again, and hearing a voice
say, "Here comes a big hit from last year," he centered
the dial on the song's tone, and raised the volume, and
removed his hand. The music came over the speaker and
he hummed along.

> *I fall to pieces*
> *Each time I see you again*
> *I fall to pieces . . .*

The music filled the dark interior of the car. Within a
fantasy, within a complicated response to the song—it
was one, like many others, that his father had played
deep into past alcoholic nights—Alex imagined someone,
some young girl, being sentenced to death on a challenge
of no one in the crowd knowing the exact words to the
song, and he was raising his hand, reaching out his hand
and stepping forward.

He was floating now, lightly delivering the words.

The Buick moved along, sheet-spraying from
both sides like a motorboat. As if by habit, Alex was
driving in the direction of Shiawassee, a small town
where he knew a girl named Eugenia Rodgers. He was
doing forty through the slushy snow, sliding to the side
occasionally when the rear wheels seemed to miss catching. The cars across the median, moving toward the city,
were doing no more than twenty or twenty-five, their
headlights approaching gradually in the storm, one after
another. Other days, driving on the divided highway at

off hours, he had cruised at eighty or ninety, sometimes
flooring the accelerator for a mile or two, raising the
speedometer to a buoyant hundred and four, five, six miles
an hour. He was fairly calm in those moments, more
frightened in the aftermath than in the moment itself.
He did not like driving fast. He had no idea why he did
it, because he liked to do things different from others. He
slowed down now, to thirty-five, to a careful thirty.

His brother, Howard, also lived in this direction.
Howard, who was three years younger, lived with their
mother and her second husband some twenty-five miles
from the city where they operated a lakeside tavern. Alex
was thinking of Howard now, trying to call up images of
him, trying to make the images stand still as he drove.
What would Howard think if he saw him in the Buick?
The thought of seeing Howard, of actually seeing him,
made Alex shudder.

He leaned closer over the steering wheel, to concentrate on the on-again, off-again view presented by the
wipers. In the weeks that he had been driving to Shiawassee he had thought of Howard a few times, but he had
never considered going there, to Lake Nepinsing. Nor did
he plan on going there now. He had not seen Howard
since an August day, three years before, when their
mother, a stranger—it was her first visit in five or six
years—came and took Howard away in her car, carrying
his possessions and clothes in cardboard boxes. It was a
miserable time to recall, and Alex looked away from thinking about it.

He thought of Eugenia Rodgers. She was his age, sixteen, although he had told her he was nineteen. Nineteen
seemed a proud age to his mind; sixteen possessed no
such quality. He had met Eugenia, or picked her up, several weeks before, and now, even if it was no more than
nine or nine-thirty and she would be in school, her town
and her country school were a place to drive to, rather
than nowhere.

He had been driving to the country schools since September. He had discovered the first one by accident, merely driving one day when he should have been in his own school; thereafter he searched them out intentionally. In easy fantasies, imagining he was the owner of the car, he drove around the corners and fronts of the strange schools during their lunch hours, to let himself be seen. Riding a coppertone stallion. He returned to one school or another for several days running, picking out a girl and looking for her, and partially following her, almost never speaking or approaching. Then, frightened by the 4-H football-type boys in threes and fours who always began to stare at him and say things to each other, he went on to another school, to Flushing and Linden and Grand Blanc and Atlas and Montrose. They were schools only an eighth or tenth the size of his city high school—two or three hundred students to three thousand—but there had been a wonder and excitement those fall days of discovering that the students were, incredibly, always fifteen and sixteen and seventeen, with recognizable bodies and backs and postures, except, when they turned, for their faces, which were unknown and unknowing. He drove among them and walked among them. He intentionally parked his Chevrolet Bel Air or his Buick Riviera under their eyes, left the car and re-entered the car under their eyes. He was able to see himself in these moments as he imagined he was seen by them, as a figure from a movie, a stranger, some newcomer come to town, some new cock of the walk with a new car, with a plume of city hair.

Twenty miles from the city he took the ramp off the highway and continued right on the road to Shiawassee. He passed the side road down which Eugenia Rodgers lived, down which she had walked several times to meet him, for she was not allowed to have boys pick her up at her house. After another mile or so he came into Shiawassee. It was a town of five or six blocks of stores, with a movie theater, with new parking meters, the street-lights lighted today under the dark sky. He drove past the high school. It was on Main Street, set back from the street, with a couple of dairy bars directly opposite. The two floors of windows in the brick school building were lighted, and looked warm inside, and as he drove by, slowly, he saw a woman teacher's back close to a window on the second floor. He turned a corner, to park where he always parked to wait for Eugenia. He did not know what he was going to do and did not think much about it; it was not a new problem. He buttoned his coat as he walked along through the slush, aiming for one of the eating places.

If he saw Eugenia he might apologize, after a fashion. He had picked her up two days before, during her lunch hour, and when they drove into the country, to a lake, and the lunch hour was ending, he had refused to take her back. It had been autumn then, two days ago. They had gone to a lakeside park which was deserted in October. She wanted to go back, because if she missed again, the teacher was going to call her mother again, and her mother, who had remarried not long ago, was going to confine her. But he had refused to take her back, even when she begged, even when she let him feel her breasts, even when she became angry and started walking. He followed her with the car, and stopped before her on the shoulder of the road, watching her through the rear-view mirror as she bent forward to begin running, pressing the accelerator as she came close. He convinced her twice more that he was stopping to pick her up, and left her both times. The next time he stopped, she walked past the car and did not look at him, and he let her walk perhaps a quarter of a mile before he went after her again. When she finally got into the car, it was nearly two o'clock. She sat still and said nothing, and he looked at her now and then as he drove. In town, when he stopped at a corner, she left the car without looking at him and he had not seen her since. He felt like a fool, remembering, but he knew that if he told her some story, that he had killed someone, had hit them with the car, or that he had killed his father, she would listen and would not believe him, but would, in her way, forgive him.

The eating place was an old grocery store with a large open space immediately inside. It was so poorly lighted that it looked closed from the sidewalk, but as he approached he saw a group of faces through the glass, a group of truant boys around one of the pinball machines. The boys looked up as he entered, and he glanced at them as he turned the other way. As always, he sensed the possibility of an open fight, of being hit for being a stranger. Around the rest of the dark store, along the walls, were shelves of canned goods and jars and bread and cookies, and some chest-high stand-up counters where students could eat their lunch. He removed a bottle of Pepsi-Cola from an old red tub cooler, let the water drip, and at the counter where an old woman sat simply staring toward the front windows, he laid a packaged pineapple pie next to the bottle and removed his wallet, thinking he did not want the pie or the pop, nor did he want to be there, but thinking little beyond this. Before him in his wallet was a thickness of money and he felt a chill of terror. The money; he had forgotten. He removed a dollar bill and returned the wallet to his pocket.

For change the woman thumbed off a pile of nickels. He put them in his coat pocket and carried the pie and pop over to the row of pinball machines. He had had no intention of playing, but he placed the pie and bottle on the glass and reached into his pocket. The woman shouted behind him, "Can't you read?" He knew she was calling to him and he felt as if his face had been slapped. "I mean you!" she called. "You there!"

He turned on her, seeing red, too confused and enraged to speak.

One of the boys down the row said, "Awh, ma, when

you gonna stop bitching?" and the other boys tittered.

Alex turned back. There was a sign: KEEP BOTTLES OFF GLASS. He took the bottle and placed it on the floor beside a leg of the machine.

He had a nickel in his fingers now but he had no desire to play the pinball machine, no more than he wanted to be there. Still, he worked the nickel flatways into the slot, pushed the handle in, held it as the balls fell, pulled the handle out. The machine lighted and clicked itself back to zero, alive under his hands. But he stood mute. His mind's voice was telling him, trying to tell him, that he did not want to play it. Nor did he want the packaged pie he had bought, or the Pepsi-Cola. He saw everything going this way, the way of this morning, driving here, driving there, doing things he did not want to do.

He left. A moment later he was back in the snow, feeling relief in the colder air, walking. He decided to go ahead and drive to Lake Nepinsing. He even laughed some, and raised his hand, a habit of his laughing, to blur the exposure of his teeth.

Lake Nepinsing was both a lake and village, east on a winding road off the highway, north of Shiawassee. The tavern was several miles past the village, but the school was in town. He passed houses here and there along the winding road, then there were houses along both sides, and then a sign: LAKE NEPINSING/SPEED LIMIT/25. He drove slowly, beginning to feel nervous again.

On the right there was a bait shop, and on the left, the center of town no more than fifty yards ahead, he saw part of the lake where it touched a side of the village. The lake surface was smoothly black, absorbing the snow as it touched down.

Driving slowly, creeping, he entered the town. An orange Rexall drugstore was ahead on the corner on one side, on the other side was an old red brick dry-goods store. The school was closed. Its windows were as black as the lake water, glistening. No one was about and there were no tire tracks on the drive. He had slowed to a stop to look, and although he did not want to turn around in the school driveway—for fear of getting stuck, because the police were always cruising around school buildings—he turned the Buick onto the untouched snow anyway, and rolled along as slowly as a police cruiser himself, all the way to the rear of the building. He paused, and shifting to R, backed around and drove out again, trying to re-cover the zipper lines he had made entering. From the interior of the car, in the surrounding whiteness, he began to fantasize that there had been a catastrophe, that a war had come home, that he and Howard were two who were lost and all they needed in the world was to find each other. With their ratlike cunning they would survive, they would effect a new life. Automobiles, schools, families, all would vanish. They would effect life itself.

He turned back and drove in the direction of the tavern. Driving through the town, he noticed a woman leaving a car, keeping her head down as she stepped over to the sidewalk, and he wondered if she might be his mother. He wondered, given all the times he had walked on sidewalks in the city, if she had ever passed him. Had she known she was passing him? It did not matter if she did; he felt neither love nor hate for her. If he felt anything it was a distant curiosity. He did not want to talk to her; but he'd like to see her, to look her over without being seen.

The tavern had not opened yet for the day. The front windows were dark and there were no cars or tire marks in the parking lot in front. The neon sign LAKEVIEW TAVERN was unlighted and hardly visible inside one of the windows, although some small neon beer signs along the window sill were lighted, Blatz and Falstaff, red and yellow. He had all but stopped on the highway, and now he pulled over, into the parking lot. He knew he should not be stopping there; if his mother or her husband happened to drive out or in on the road, they could not help seeing him. Still he stopped. He sat in the car with the motor running and looked around. He felt as nervous as he had the first time he took a car. Then, as if climbing farther into the thin branches of a tree, he opened the door, leaving the motor running, and stepped out into the snow and damp air. He heard a car coming on the highway behind him, and he stood still, without looking, as it passed.

At the dark glass of the tavern he held his hands like blinders. He had never seen the inside of the tavern. Empty of people it looked disappointingly worn and threadbare. The lights over a shuffleboard were out, but behind the bar, among mirrors and bottles and glasses, a Miller's Highlife clock was lighted. For no reason he tapped the window lightly with his fingers. However loud the tapping seemed, no one appeared, nothing happened. There was his reflection in the dark glass, in the gray air, and it occurred to him that the figure he saw was lost in a way he could not understand.

Against the rising of nervousness he walked around the end of the tavern, stepping through the unmarked slush. A T-shaped dock was in the water, and an old red gas pump stood on the bank. A rowboat was in the water, moving slightly, lifting a little toward shore and out again on a slack rope. Walking out on the dock, he stopped and looked down into the water; it appeared more green here than black. Crouching to see better, he felt the snow fall on the back of his neck. The sky reflected its gray colors on the surface, and as he leaned forward his face and shoulders reflected darkly. The shreds of snow parachuted onto the water, shriveled gray and disappeared; his mind was ranging off as if in judgment of things the size of life itself, and of himself, but of nothing he could see in particular.

Turning his neck down, looking directly into his re-

flection, he found he could see through his face into the
water. He worked his reflection to reveal the bottom. It
was still autumn down there, brown and green, the sand
blond, moss hair wavering black from green stones, from
the dock piles. Two nearly translucent fish, no thicker
or longer than a finger, hovered unconcerned. He glimpsed
the sweep of his trouble and it was so wide and unknown
that his head began trembling while his mind told him
nothing.

In Shiawassee he parked where he could see the
door of Eugenia Rodgers' school. He sat in the car a long
time, smoking and looking around. He yawned, yawned
within the yawn, and his eyes watered from exhaustion.
He had not known he was so tired. He considered lying
over on his side in the front seat, to sleep, but did not. It
was dangerous, inviting to strolling policemen. He
slumped in the seat, and his head bobbed; he was waiting
for Eugenia to come out, and not waiting for her either,
just waiting.

He heard no bells ring, but at last, as he was watching, the main door opened and two boys came out. Then a
girl came out, alone, and he was not sure at first that
it was Eugenia. He looked at the door again, which did
not close all the way as one student after another kept it
swinging open. Then he looked at the girl again and
realized it was Eugenia. She walked with her face down
against the snow, without a hat, her coat collar turned up
and her shoulders high against her neck.

The coat; she was wearing the coat he had given her.
It had been in the back seat of the Buick, a lady's camel's-
hair coat with a small chain sewn inside the collar. He
had forgotten about the coat. It was too large for her, too
long, and she walked with her hands drawn into the sleeves.
He imagined her fuzzed and ratted sweater, her thickness of lipstick, the odors of her neck and hair, her large

and firm breasts, and he felt aroused to see her. If he touched the horn for the slightest beep he knew she would look over at him, and she would turn away from her bearing across the street and walk to the car as she had before, without looking at him on the way. In the car she might pause before looking at him; she might ask for a cigarette and conceal herself with a search for matches, or she might ask for a light and conceal herself in a search for a cigarette, or she might close her eyes and lean over to kiss his ear, to use her tongue, or in their game of profanity she might say, "You son of a bitch," and smile her shy and uncertain smile.

He did not touch the horn. He watched her walk along. She, like himself, had not worn boots. He knew she was on her way to the pinball-machine lunchroom, and he thought of taking her off somewhere to buy her some warm hamburgers. She usually bought cigarettes with the few coins she scraped or stole from her mother, and she loved hamburgers and French fries. But he watched her pass from view. It was like the playing of a thin song, and he was relieved when it was over.

Driving among the students, passing the dim windows of the store, he glanced to see if she might see him, and he saw bodies and faces inside the glass, and the gold-flecked backside of one of the machines. He imagined she had seen him; he had never driven away like this from anyone and it gave him a little strength, as if something were finally passing, finally ending.

For a moment, driving through Shiawassee, he saw a clarity in his life. His troubles seemed to fade for the moment. What if he mailed the money to the school, with an apology? *Here is the money. I am sorry I took it.* And if they did not actually catch him driving a car, how could they prove it? If the cars were all recovered, would they care? It was a soothing idea. It seemed if he could begin, if he could follow the idea to its end, he could secretly step into a new version of himself.

The moment passed. He knew that sending the money back would make no difference. He considered throwing it out the window, or burning it in the ashtray. Or he could hide it, and someday, a year from now, he could return and retrieve it. No—he was afraid to hide it. It would be there to worry about, to be found, to be traced. What if the gang of them forced him to tell? What if they came to his house? They might drag him from his bed, drag him outside in his underwear. Or they might beat him up in the house—or take things to make up their loss, or break things, break him and leave him there. And what if his father was home when they came? It would not matter—they would fight his father, jump him, however strong his father might be. A man, a powerful, red-faced man called Big Mike, the father of some bride at some hall—Alex had seen him beaten in a flurry by Cricket Alan, beaten so quickly and so thoroughly he was left sitting down and bleeding like an old half-conscious heavyweight. They would do the same to his father. Afterward in streetcorner conversations one would tell the story of how Alex Housman's old man had been taken—*"You should see this dumb son of a bitch, here he is, see, in his undershirt, see, and Cricket, Cricket says . . ."*

He was on US 21 again, driving toward the city, staring ahead. Looking at himself, he saw that there was no way out. He released his grip on the steering wheel, and tried to will his heart to settle down. He reached for the radio dial, to search for music.

When they caught him, he knew, they would walk him somewhere, or drive him somewhere, in a caravan of cars. In a field, or in a parking lot, or behind the school, someone would toe-kick him from the rear, in the ass, in the spine, and they would push him across a circle. Blood, split lips, closed eyes, rattled ears and skull, all at once or one at a time or one alone—*"You should see this dumb son of a bitch, here he is, see, and Cricket, Cricket says . . ."* He feared the girls of the school watching. He feared the crushing of his pride. Whatever he possessed of that substance, he feared that unlike his eyes or nose or lips, it might not heal again.

———

Two

One previous day in October, two men, two old rummies, had appeared on the expanse of dairy-bar sidewalk opposite Central High School. They were passing out leaflets for a political party, a labor-socialist party which used a rolled-sleeve worker's muscle in a V as its insignia. The two wore threadbare overcoats, in spite of the balmy weather, which reached below their knees. They stood around smiling, unshaven, sallow, offering the leaflets, and when a boy, a student, began asking them questions, a small crowd gathered. In a moment a word caught and moved like a flame in a dry field: "Communist."

"No, no, you kids, we just passing these flyers out, you don't want 'em, don't take 'em."

The crowd grew and thickened quickly, pressing closer, trying to see and hear. The two men edged away somewhat, one of them throwing his stack of papers in a barrel smoldering with lunch bags. "See, don't mean nothing to me, I just trying to make a buck, is all."

"Are you a Communist or not?"

"Son, I'm a drinker, that's all I am."

But the dairy bars were emptying a couple of hundred more high school students, and the parked cars and barber shops were emptying, and the crowd was soon so large that it was spilling over the curb into the street, and running fifty or sixty feet down the wide sidewalk. Few could see anything, but the word still flew. When the beating began, the crowd heaved back a little at first at the center, and then retightened and continued to grow. Occasionally a football hero or two went pushing and charging to the center, to get in some licks, and others followed. Boys and girls on the edges tiptoed and toe-jumped like dancers, trying to see, and there were attempts here and there at wit and humor. When the first police cruiser pulled up, nosing the crowd, rocking as two policemen jumped out with their night sticks, there were perhaps a thousand students and adults around the two men, and the crowd had spilled far enough into the street to block traffic. As the policemen edged their way into the crowd, girls pointed with head nods and wild eyes and screamed so the policemen would not misunderstand, "Communist! Communist!"

Alex parked the Buick three blocks from the school, where he had parked the day before, and walked back. The snow had turned to rain by now and the leather of his shoes was quickly soaked black. He had considered clearing the car of evidence, to wipe away fingerprints and to empty the ashtray, but for no clear reason he parked it and let it stand. About ten minutes remained in the lunch hour, and as he walked back, the feeling of drawing nearer to the school moved through him with the sensation of a wind rising and falling, rising again.

Ahead, before the dairy bars, there were only a few students about, and they were walking with their faces down against the damp snow. Alex walked past the parked cars, cars which were full, their windows steamed over. The windows of the dairy bars across the street were also steamed over. He did not cross the street. He was growing vaguely weak in his joints, fluid in his muscles. He imagined a car door being thrown open, or the door of one of the dairy bars being thrown open, and someone running—

he would not run himself—and grabbing his arm, calling back to the others following, as if they could not see, *"I got him, here he is, I got him,"* the others strung out, walking, trotting, smiling, without their coats. Teachers could see from the second- and third-floor windows across the street, men teachers whispering afterward as Mr. Burke had once, after a fight, whispered to him, "Hey, who got his clock cleaned down there?"

He did not look toward the steamed windows of the dairy bars across the street. He walked by and crossed over to the sidewalk leading to the school. He was thinking he might as well try to hit one of them, maybe feign submission, for there would be words, and come up, come around, with all he had—he might as well try for Cricket Alan, close his eye, break his nose bone, maybe knock him out, cold-cock him. But no one came running after him, and he walked along, rubbery. Just as he reached the heavy double door, the other side came swinging open and startled him. It was a girl, nameless, a familiar and pudgy face. She wrinkled her face and turned it down immediately against the weather, and went on, and he forced a weak smile over the jumping of his heart.

Within the warm air he foolishly stomped his feet on the link-metal mat, splashing the water the mat lay in on his pants legs. He walked on into the first-floor corridor. In spite of all else there was a faint feeling of coming home after having been away. Here was the tile floor, the familiar hallways lined with dark-green lockers, the whiskey-colored varnished molding, the globes hanging from the ceiling. Except for two girls walking away on the right, the corridor was empty. Far off, also to the right, music was playing, record music from the noon-hour dance in the girls' gym, which, because he had never learned to dance, he always avoided.

His locker was to the left, in the basement near his homeroom. He walked along. Here he was, he had come back, the object, he believed, of a morning of corridor conversations. But the first student he saw, Barry Fagan, coming down the stairway ahead, walking fast, looked at him as he passed, nodded, walked on. Alex tried not to walk too fast, or too slow, and it was difficult to coordinate himself.

Going down the stairs to the basement, he met his homeroom teacher, Mr. Hewitt, coming up. Mr. Hewitt, besides teaching history, was the varsity baseball coach, and a quiet man, neither popular nor unpopular. He nodded lightly at Alex as they passed. Then, behind him, Alex heard Mr. Hewitt say, "Alex, were you here this morning?"

Pausing, Alex said, "No."

"Where were you?"

Rather than condemnation, there was some kindness in the man's voice, and Alex, stopped on the steps, was affected and weakened by it. He found it hard to look up at Mr. Hewitt, who stood waiting. At last, glancing up, Alex said, "I'm back to school now."

Mr. Hewitt was amused. "You're back. Good, I'm glad to hear that. Where have you been?"

"Nowhere," Alex said. "Just messing around." He stood where he was, looking down again, knowing that Mr. Hewitt was standing there looking at him.

"You have a minute?" Mr. Hewitt said. "I'd like to talk with you."

Alex hunched his shoulders, to say yes, and walked along slightly to the rear of the man. They went past Alex's locker and into the homeroom, and Alex still found it hard to look up. It seemed that if he did, something like whimpering would spread from his chest to his throat. He glanced up enough to see that Karen Parker was sitting at a desk in the homeroom, reading, and looked away as Mr. Hewitt said to her, "Karen, would you excuse us a minute, please?"

She did not quite understand, and Mr. Hewitt added after a pause, "We'd like to have a talk in private for a minute."

whipped his shoulder to shake off the hand. The hand did not return. Nor did Alex look back. He continued staring down, hardly seeing the face of the lock.

In a moment he knew, decided in the knowing, that he was not going to the afternoon classes. What was he doing there? How could he have thought of coming to school? Sitting at a desk, sitting there, sitting there, sitting there. He closed his eyes for a moment, still facing the wall. But he could not see what he seemed to have been trying to see.

At last he let the lock drop. He turned to leave, making his way as calmly as he could through the confusion of corridor movement, aiming for the side door on the landing, fifty feet away, aiming for the gray and cold air outside. He experienced a slight shivering of panic as he walked, panic against the ringing of the second bell, a fear of being collared by some teacher, being led to a classroom and turned over to another teacher like an errant Tom Sawyer when he was of a range of mind this moment to go for the teacher's head, or eyes, or throat.

Outside, moving down the steps and walking away, he felt the school itself was watching his back, and he felt diminished being watched. He hurried along. Some relief came when he made it around a corner and out of sight of the buildings. His feet were so wet by now they were squishing water inside his shoes. He thought of going home, to undress and put on dry clothes, but he would have to wait until his father had left for work. He walked on. Water was dripping from his hair by now, down his neck and down his forehead, and from his sideburns. Clear water was gathering in the slush over the sidewalk, small pools in the nickel-colored footmarks. He walked along at a good pace, thinking he had never been so wet, but it was not until he was among the stores and buildings of downtown that it occurred to him that he had left the Buick behind. He had forgotten it completely. Not sure if it was funny or crazy, he tried again, again with little success, to laugh at himself.

In the men's room of the Fox Theater he used paper

towels to wipe his hair and neck and face. Downstairs at the curtained aisle entrance he removed his coat and walked in. An orange-tinted advertisement for a dry cleaner's was on the screen, but the lights were not yet completely dark. Perhaps fifteen people were scattered about the cavern, and he took a seat as removed from any of them as possible, on the right, the second seat in, opening his coat over the back of the third to dry. He never felt at ease until a theater was completely dark—the worst moment was when a movie ended and the lights came on, a moment he usually avoided by turning to watch the end as he walked up the hill of the aisle, slipping out and away before the lights came on. Now his timing was lucky. Just as he slouched some into the cushioned seat, to conceal himself, the remaining overhead lights dimmed to darkness and "Preview of Coming Attractions" was fanning over the screen.

Three

When the telephone rang, Alex was asleep on the couch in the living room. He was in his underwear, wrapped in an old Indian blanket he and his father kept on the couch, his clothes on the floor beside him where he had pulled them off. The only light in the room came from the opened door to the bathroom, off the living room at the end of a short hallway.

In the blur of his sleep—it had been short but long enough to thicken his response—he made his way into the kitchen, to the ringing phone, and took up the receiver. As he answered, holding his forehead with his other hand, someone began half whispering in a hurry and it was a moment before he realized it was Eugenia Rodgers. She was in a state of some kind, but he hardly had voice enough yet for talking and asked no questions. Even when he began to understand what had happened and why she had called, he did not want to appear frightened in her eyes and said little. More or less whispering, because she was whispering, he said, "Oh," and "They found the coat?" She carried on like a child, no longer bluffing, saying something of hating her stepfather for his promise not to tell if she told, and of his telling just the same.

He stood, cold in his underwear, and closed his eyes for a moment. Then he opened them. The call seemed to have taken place in a dream from which he had awakened a moment ago. Off in the dream Eugenia Rodgers said she had told them "everything" and they had "called the police."

Stepping over to feel the wall for the light switch, he discovered that his hand was weak. The fluorescent lights came faltering on. He squinted. By the wall clock it was nine or ten minutes after ten. The day was refusing to die. He stood still a moment, not knowing what to do. He remembered the call again as if he had already forgotten. They had found the coat. He was thinking she should have said they had found her wearing the coat, and he was thinking he should have thanked her for calling—he had not—and he should have apologized for the other day. A yawn took him then and made his eyes water with exhaustion. He exhaled to nearly collapsing, envisioned the blue-uniformed police, and felt far too tired to fight, or to run, or to think, felt no more than a thought away from anything.

In the bathroom he looked at himself in the mirror. Except for the fact that he had no need of shaving, there was a resemblance to his father when his father got up from sleeping after drinking. His hair, extra thick like his father's hair, was pressed high on the right, as were the veins on that side of his face from sleeping. He felt another, stranger resemblance on the inside—felt gummed and swollen—and he was beginning to tremble. He tried to decide what to do. Should he run or should he stay? The idea of running, out in the rain, hitchhiking, taking another car, was like something from a movie. He hardly had energy enough to think about it. It only meant more trouble, more fear. He would stay. His decision was easy. Whatever might happen, he would stay.

He sat on the toilet stool as a place to sit. With his elbows on his knees he rested his eye sockets and head on the heels of his hands. He had not forgotten the call, but still he kept remembering. His father. The thought of his father was different now. It made his heart wince slightly. He knew at last what his father would feel. He would not feel anger, nor would he have any strong words. His father would feel as he felt now.

He drew bath water. He did not like baths and usually did his washing at school in the showers. But he had not showered for several days, and besides, a bath was a way to get warm, to wake up. He drew the tub half full, wadded his underclothes and laid them on the floor, and stepped into the water. He did not wash at first, but lay soaking. The telephone call kept returning to his thoughts, like something he could still not quite remember, or believe, or forget. Of all the places of disclosure—his teachers, the basketball team, Mr. Hewitt, students—only one frightened him now, his father.

The police? Would they actually come here, rap on the door, take him away? Were they coming here now? He moved along more quickly on the idea, not to be caught in the tub, to be dressed. He wondered if the police would be impressed with his ingenuity of switching license plates, impressed with his cooperative answers, impressed with him. How could such an intelligent young man, a fine young man, a basketball player, get into such a mess? No, he thought, they would not see it that way.

In his bedroom he put on clean underwear and socks, and a pair of clean khaki pants, and for its little flair of style, his only white shirt. He had grown some since his father gave him money to buy the shirt, together with a tie and a jacket. They were for his ninth-grade graduation dance, which he walked to, dateless, to spend the evening in the corner with some other boys who did not know how to dance, telling jokes, less angered or nervous in their presence, leaving the corner only once, when everyone circled Miss Long, the music teacher, dancing with Mr. Fulton, the metal-shop teacher. The shirt cuffs were high on his wrists now. He had worn the shirt once since then, one night when he dressed up in the same outfit, went to the movies, shot pool in a pool hall which was empty that summer night, and came home to hang the clothes back in his closet.

Startled, he thought of the money. He had to get it out of his wallet, get rid of it, before the police came. In the bathroom he removed the thickness of bills, but he thought if he flushed them away, they might come floating up somewhere and his fingerprints would be traced. He thought about burning the money and flushing away the ashes. Then he thought about hiding it where he could find it later. This seemed a better idea now, together with a notion of someone else finding it if he could not. He found a place immediately. The roll of bills fit easily inside one of the clawed feet of the bathtub. But once he was in the living room he imagined a policeman, looking nowhere else, crouching down to reach in and retrieve the roll. In the bathroom again, the bills on the floor beside him, he struck a match, took up a dollar bill and lit the corner. It burned slowly, smoking like a green leaf. He held the burning edge down, then up, then down. When the flames came close to licking at his fingers, he dropped it. It hit, a triangle, on the damp porcelain above the water line and stuck, continuing to smoke. Then, before he could worry or think much about it, he dropped the full thickness of bills into the water and pressed the handle. The water swirled, washed the burning

piece with it, and sucked the stack away. The bowl refilled.
None floated up. But there was the yellow burn stain. He
flushed again. But he had not waited long enough and the
bowl only gasped and resettled. He wiped the stain away
with a piece of toilet paper and stood waiting again, and
waiting. When he flushed now, the bowl swallowed. It refilled clean. He waved his arm through the air against the
lingering odor of smoke.

Before the mirror, he combed his hair. He looked better
now; he was shiny-faced, combed, in a clean shirt. Something was over; he felt leaner than he had in weeks. And
he began to feel hungry. He had drunk water and pop, but
he could not remember having eaten all day. The feeling
of hunger was pleasant but tenuous, and he tried to sustain
it. He tried to believe that something was in fact over.

He fixed an elaborate meal: bacon and eggs, chopped
onion and green pepper in the eggs, scrambled, rye bread
toasted, cold milk. It was a meal he and his father had
often, although separately nowadays, and not for breakfast but for supper. It was the only meal Alex knew how to
cook for himself, and his dinner was usually a choice between this or a slab of rubbery cheese on dry bread, or peanut butter, stuffing the sandwich home on his way back
down the stairs and down the sidewalk, clearing his throat
at a gas station with a bottle of pop.

He ate until he remembered again. He had eaten a
little more than half. As he remembered, his stomach filled
and his appetite immediately disappeared. He sat at the
table holding his fork aloft, and a moment later he was
moving to the bathroom, taking the first dribbles in his
hand on the way, losing his meal in an explosion the moment he raised the toilet seat. He stood several minutes
over the toilet, bending as if to work a snake from his
throat, resting his hand against the wall, and bending
down again. He flushed away the bacon and eggs and toast
and acid. He wiped the water from his eyes, and he tried
to tongue-sever the irritable yellow saliva from his mouth,

and blew burning bacon and egg bits from his nose into folds of toilet paper. He placed his hand against the wall again, trying to even his breath. He believed it now. Sitting on the stool, his stomach cramping but with nothing there to be released, he shivered with goose bumps. He felt as able as a six-year-old; he was afraid.

By the clock in the kitchen it was ten minutes to twelve. His father was out of work by now. But his father seldom came home before twelve-thirty, or one, or sometime in the night after the bars closed at two-thirty. He had no thought of telling his father, but like a child alone in a house, he longed for his father to be there.

There were the dirty dishes. They had a pact always to wash their dishes and wipe the table and counter. It was only when things went bad for his father that the dishes began to stack—a mess which started at the start of a binge, so Alex failed as well and the sink soon filled with dishes and cloudy water and bits of egg and bread and cigarette butts floating. When the binge ended, the kitchen was cleaned. It would be shining some afternoon when Alex came home from school, peace floating comfortably throughout the apartment. Or they would do the job together on a weekend morning, washing the dishes and scalding them with water from the teakettle, cleaning the refrigerator, mopping the floor, beginning another string of fixing separate meals, washing separate sets of dishes, one leaving it clean for the other.

He left the mess. In the living room he looked down at Chevrolet Avenue from the window, thinking of the police, thinking it might be better if they came first, or at the same time, to counter his having to face his father.

He was in the kitchen again when he heard someone outside. It was still no more than twenty to one, and if it was his father, he was probably sober. He heard the several sounds, the car, the car door slamming, and in a moment, footsteps on the stairway, coming up. He stepped from the kitchen, and re-entered as his father was coming through the door. His father looked pleased to see him, and spoke quietly, said, "You're still up," as he was closing the door.

The sweep of cold air he had admitted passed over the room. Alex felt chilled, anyway. His father placed his lunch pail on the table and removed his coat, a blue denim finger-tip-length work coat. He was clearly sober, and in a calm mood. He rubbed his hands together. "Whatcha doing up so late? Schoolwork?"

Alex nodded.

"Why so glum, chum? Everything okay?"

"Sure."

His father was turning back his cuffs. The odor he carried of the factory was in the kitchen now, a smell of oil, of machines. He turned to the sink to wash his hands. He wore a khaki shirt, from the army, and blue denim work pants. Alex thought about telling him now, of saying, when he turned back, that something was wrong, that he had done something awful, that he was in trouble. But he did not tell him. Always before when he wanted something, some dollars, or permission, or a baseball glove or a white shirt and tie, he approached his father when he was drinking, when he was flushed with love or generosity or something.

Drying his hands, his father said, "You hungry? How about some bacon and eggs?"

"I already ate."

His father was at the refrigerator, removing the carton of eggs and the bacon. Alex began picking up his dirty dishes, but his father said, "Don't worry about those. I'll do them with mine."

"I guess I'll go to bed," Alex said.

"You tired?"

"Oh, a little."

For a moment then, as his father was working at the counter, neither of them spoke. Then Alex said, "I guess I'll go to bed then."

"Sure you won't have a bite to eat?" His father was looking at him now.

"No, I'm pretty tired," Alex said, looking away from looking at his father. He paused a moment, aware that his father was watching him, and then he walked from the kitchen, saying no more.

In his bedroom, not turning on his light, he sat on the edge of his bed to remove his socks, and when they were off, he still sat on the bed. At last, standing, he removed his shirt and pants. He knew his father knew something was wrong, and he knew this was the time to talk to him, but he still could not do it.

Then his father came to the door. Alex was turning down his covers, straightening the pillow of his unmade bed. His father half whispered from the doorway, "You going to bed now?"

"Yes."

"Well—okay. You have yourself a good sleep now, son."

"I will."

"Good night now."

Still his father paused. Then he said, "You want your door closed?"

"Okay."

"Goodnight now, son. Have a good sleep." His father closed the door softly, as if not to disturb something.

Pushing in between the cold sheets, pulling up the covers, Alex lay on his side and kept his eyes open. In a moment he recognized the sound of the rain on his window, and then he could see more clearly the light which came around his shade from the lights in the street outside. His place in bed grew a little warmer and it was almost comfortable lying there, more comfortable than otherwise with his father there, and sober, and a little worried about him. Nor could he help seeing the reversal of things. The misery was usually in those outer rooms, the old records playing, perhaps a sudden smashing of something, a dish, a cup, a fist against a wall or door, or a sudden laugh, or perhaps the throwing open of his bedroom door, the black silhouette in the harsh light of the doorway—"Son, hey son, old pal, wake up a minute"—perhaps nothing but the music and his father's silent presence throughout the night.

Alex lay sleepless. He remembered a time, a morning, when he went to the bathroom and found his father collapsed from the toilet stool, his pants around his knees, exposed, hairy, in an odor, not having flushed the toilet, a cigarette burned its full length in a charred groove on the linoleum. It was a warm summer morning, and when he turned off the phonograph, and watching for the rise and fall of his father's breathing, had affirmed that his father was alive, he left the apartment and walked down Chevrolet Avenue past the factories, and along the river and railroad tracks into town. It was no more than five o'clock in the morning, the sun still low and red, reaching in near-horizontal shafts between the city buildings and into alleyways, and he discovered a routine he followed other mornings, a soothing pastime, walking from one closed and caged movie theater to another, to look over the color posters, the glossy black-and-white pictures behind glass, trying to determine, for the afternoon, the most promising movie.

━━━━━━━

Four

He was arrested the next day, but not until school had nearly ended. With no more than five minutes remaining in his last class, a girl from the principal's office entered the room with a white slip of paper.

It had been a day of questions and answers, of failures to answer. In homeroom that morning, Mr. Hewitt had leaned over his desk and whispered, "What happened to you yesterday? I looked for you."

"I guess I forgot," Alex had whispered back. "Everything's okay now."

Mr. Hewitt had looked at him as he straightened up, as if asking with his eyebrows if Alex was sure, and Alex had signaled with a small nod that he was.

During lunch hour he had walked on the sidewalk past the parked Buick. It stood as he had left it, but looked somewhat larger. He did not turn his eyes to it as he passed, but looked ahead, as if both he and the car were being watched. He circled the block not to pass the Buick again, and this time he crossed the street and entered the dairy bar on the corner. It was filled with bodies and noise, cigarette smoke layering toward the ceiling, the jukebox playing. Entering, not knowing just where to go or stand, he overheard someone say something about the noon-hour dance being about to start, and something grated within him, as always.

In the school building, with lunch hour about to end, he had stopped a girl he hardly knew. It was Irene Sheaffer, whose house and bus stop he had driven by often in the cars, although they had never exchanged a word. Seeing her, passing her on the landing, and feeling a momentary fearlessness, he stopped her by saying, "Can I talk to you?"

She looked at him, without understanding.

"Can I talk to you?" he said again.

". . . Yes." She appeared mystified, perhaps frightened.

"Not right here."

"You mean right now?"

"Yes." He noticed some of the small details of her, her eyelashes, her neck, her lips not lipsticked, not granuled, a flesh color.

"I have a class right now," she said.

"Just for a minute."

"But what is it?"

"Here, come out here." He moved a step toward the door.

She did not move. "Where are you going?" she said.

"Out here."

"But I can't. I have to go to class. Couldn't you—"

"Just for a minute."

"I can't, really. I have to go to my class."

He moved another step toward the door. He saw that he did not know quite what he was trying to do, and he made an expression of its not mattering anyway and nodded, and committed, pushed the door open and stepped outside himself.

He stood there. Almost at once the door opened behind him. She stepped out, letting the door close again. Looking at her, he was worried already over her being late, getting wet, cold, over not knowing what to say.

"Is something wrong?" she said.

He said nothing; his feeling was to grab her, to embrace her, wrap her close to him.

"Are you all right?" she said.

He nodded. He looked at her. Suddenly, inflamed with himself and embarrassed even before he spoke, he said, "I love you."

She said nothing. They stood looking at each other.

Then, kindly, she said, "You don't even know me."

He laughed, suddenly, lightly, glancing down against the exposure of his teeth. It was funny, but he felt relieved and pleased that he had said it. "No—no, I don't know you," he said. "I'm sorry. I'm crazy—that's all. I'm sorry. You better get back."

Smiling, as if to say it was a joke, and not to be embarrassed, she turned to the door. As she shifted her books he reached and opened the heavy door for her, and let it close again behind her. A moment later, when he let himself in, she was out of sight.

He recognized the girl entering the room as one who worked in the principal's office. When the teacher, Mrs.

Scholls, read the note and looked in his direction, he was not surprised. But he may have been stunned in a way, for he could not quite recall afterward how the next minute or two passed. Mrs. Scholls came to his desk and said softly, "You're to report to the principal's office," and as if transferred by magic, a moment later he was in the corridor, and he knew also, however vaguely, that he had visited the boys' lavatory, but he could recall only the dirty-white marble air of the room.

Behind the wooden counter in the office, four or five girls and women were working at desks. He knew Mr. Spencer's office was to the left, but as a girl looked at him for his question, he said, his voice quite clear, "I'm supposed to see the principal." The girl directed him but he hardly heard her words. In an outer office a lady at a desk said from a distance, "Alex Housman?" and he nodded that he was.

He stopped at the doorway to the principal's office. Mr. Spencer, at his desk, and two men, standing, in suits and unbuttoned topcoats, had their faces turned to the door. Alex had never met Mr. Spencer, but the man said, "Come in, Alex."

He walked two or three steps into the office, and Mr. Spencer rose and came around his desk as if to shake hands, but went past him to close the door.

One of the men was walking over to him, reaching inside his topcoat to remove his wallet, which he flopped open. Alex glimpsed an intricate gold badge, some blue on it, then it was gone. Mr. Spencer was behind his desk again, standing, although Alex had not seen him return. The man introduced himself, Lieutenant Somebody, and the other man, Detective Somebody, but Alex did not listen carefully enough to register their names. He saw their faces looking at him. The lieutenant said, "I guess you know why we're here?"

"Yes," Alex said.

A moment later they were in the corridor, and the first

students, the fast-walkers, were already in motion, although Alex had not heard the bell ring. But classroom
doors were opened, or opening, classes were on their feet,
and the day was ending.

They had to go to the basement for Alex to get his coat
from his locker. Both detectives walked with him. He laid
his books on the shelf and slipped his coat on, and locked
up again. Returning the way they had come, the corridor
had thickened to a slow herding. Alex was not between the
two men, both were on his right, but he noticed passing
students glancing from him to them and back again, and
he tried then to walk without looking into faces. Just before they reached the outside door, the men both slipped on
porkpie rain hats. The man who had done the talking, the
lieutenant, held the door for them, and when he came up he
was on the other side so Alex was in the middle. He thought
for the first time about running. It was one thing he could
somehow do well.

Their car was parked in the No Parking space where
the sidewalk met the street, half blocking the crossway to
the bus stops and dairy bars. It was a black car, unmarked
except for a small antenna coming from the roof. The mass
of students was passing around the car as water passes
around a boulder. The lieutenant opened the rear door for
Alex, and when he had stepped in and sat down, the door
was slammed behind him. The lieutenant took the seat in
front of him, and the other detective, a younger man, went
around to the driver's side. The car was dirty, cigarette
ashes all around, the floor ribbed metal without carpet;
the engine was as noisy and loose as a truck's motor. They
nosed through the flow of students, the faces, the turned
necks, those oblivious altogether, in a J-turn, and headed
downtown.

The city police headquarters was in a wing of the new
civic center, a concentration of manilla-colored brick
buildings with much glass in rows. Entering from the rear,
going down into a wide car-filled parking lot, they passed

young trees all around held upright by staked wires and pieces of bicycle tire, and drove in and under the building, into an open garage which was filled with black police cars. Here the younger detective came around quickly to open the door, to take Alex's arm as he was getting out. He kept Alex just a half-step ahead of him as they passed among other policemen in uniform, and detectives, and mechanics in overalls.

They walked directly into an open and lighted elevator. The door closed—it had a small window crosshatched with chicken wire—and they rose. The man did not release his arm. The doors opened then and they entered an over-lighted new corridor. They walked along and turned a couple of times, and at last, where there was a small bench outside an opened office door, the detective pushed him down and said, "You stay put now."

His waiting began. The two detectives went on and he never saw them again. He sat there. After a few minutes a uniformed policeman, wearing a powder-blue shirt with three dark stripes on his sleeve, walked by with papers in his hand but barely glanced at Alex. Alex thought again about slipping away. But he imagined a maze of yellow corridors; he imagined he was being watched.

He spent several hours in the police station, from about three-thirty until eight or eight-thirty or nine, getting stranded in a shift change and in the dinner hour. A man finally came from the first office, folded handcuffs hanging from his belt, catching Alex smoking, and said, "That's all right—don't put it out. Come on in."

The man was conversational. He asked Alex how he was doing, how school was and who was going to win the Pontiac game, and he asked many questions about full name and date of birth, and address, and then if Alex had a girl friend, and what he wanted to be when he grew up. Alex cooperated. He said he sort of had a girl friend, thinking warmly of Irene Sheaffer, but that he did not know what he wanted to be when he grew up. They talked about drafting and apprenticeships in the factories and the General Motors Institute of Technology, and at last the man said, "What about the cars? Let's talk about them. When did you take the first one?"

"You mean the exact date?"

"Sure. Do you remember it?"

"It was a Friday. The first Friday in September. After school started."

"What was the car?"

"A Chevrolet, a Bel Air. Green, two-door."

"You got a good memory. Where did you find it? How long did you keep it? Where did you leave it?"

"I just kept it one night. I found it out at Lakeside Park, and I left it down on east Kearsley Street, about two in the morning."

"Who was with you?"

"Nobody."

"Come on. Who was with you?"

"Nobody."

"You took these cars alone?"

"Yes."

The man eyed him. Then he said, "Okay—keep your memory going. What was the next car? All the details."

Alex's memory remained clear. He could remember all but the numbers of the license plates he had switched. He talked for about an hour, told of smashing one car into a parked truck, and of trading the spare tire of another for three dollars in gas, up to and including the coppertone Buick Riviera, telling where they could pick it up. When he finished, the man said, "Go on."

"That's it," Alex said.

"You sure?"

"Yes."

The man took up a sheet of paper. "What about the Olds Eighty-Eight you took on September twenty-seventh? Why'd you leave that off the list?"

"I didn't take it," Alex said.

"Let's see your wallet."

Alex laid his wallet over on the desk, and thinking of the thickness of bills he had carried in it the day before, looked away. The man took it up and examined it.

"This your phone number?" he said.

"Must be."

"Who's home?"

"Nobody."

"Your mother's not home? She work?"

"I just live with my father."

"Aah so. Where's he?"

"At work."

"Where?"

"Chevrolet."

"What shift does he work?"

"Second."

"You and your old man get along okay?"

"Sure."

The man was shaking his head, looking at him. "Why?" he said. "It makes no sense."

Alex said nothing; he knew no answer.

The man, rising, said, "What you doing in a mess like this? You nuts? Don't you know this is for real?"

Alex said nothing.

"Well, let's go," the man said. "I'm gonna have to put you in the detention home."

Alex was taken to another part of the police station. He was left sitting on another bench, not far from the main door and opposite the complaint desk, a crescent-shaped counter with openings like those at a bank. He was waiting for the "ID Clerk" to come on duty. The blue-shirted policemen behind the counter paid little attention to him, much less than he paid to them. He listened to their radio and telephone conversations and orders and questions. He smoked. He stood up several times to relieve the numb pain growing on his tail bone from sitting, and he stepped over several times to press a swig of water from a cooler. The fact that he was waiting to be taken to the detention home hazed over his thoughts as coolly as an impending basketball game, or an impending fight between others. He did not quite believe it.

At last a young man came hurrying in, wearing civilian clothes, popular, for it seemed all the policemen behind the counter called something: "Hey, DJ, where the hell you been?" "DJ, how's the duck hunting?" "Hey, old Murphy's hot after your ass." And: "You got a customer there."

The young man was already past Alex, but he looked back and said, "Be with you in a minute." He went on through a door, and lights came on all along the upper half of a corrugated plastic wall. Alex saw his shadow move across the room, then disappear. Ten minutes later he opened the door and said, "Okay, let's go."

Alex was photographed in an alcove marked with heights—look to the right, *flash*, chin up, *flash*—and his fingers were separated, rolled over an ink pad and then over a white card. The young man moved very fast. He wore a white shirt and tie, but with his sleeves rolled above his elbows, a cigarette behind one ear. He asked questions and clicked at a typewriter as Alex answered, spun the card out, and Alex was soon left sitting at another bench, within the ID room this time, to wait.

Two men passed through while he sat there, each accompanied by a uniformed policeman—one a tough, mean-looking man of about thirty who had been in a fight, little more than his eyelash visible from one swollen eye, and blood on his face, neck and shirt, the other an egg-shaped old man dressed in a mismatched coat and tie and pants. Later Alex heard DJ on the phone: "Where the hell is Watt? I got a prisoner over here . . . No, no, juvenile."

Alex sat smoking, reaching out to throw matches and flick ashes into a wastebasket beside a desk. In time a uniformed policeman walked in, with a card in his hand. "Housman?" he said to Alex. Alex nodded. "Let's take a ride," he said. Alex rose. He put out his cigarette against the inside of the wastebasket.

Outside, it was dark. They went down to the garage in one of the elevators, and out into the cold air. It was shivering cold to Alex, for all this time he had not removed his coat. Nor had he eaten, had barely eaten all day, but he was not hungry. He did not know the time. He felt it must have been past eight, perhaps close to nine. He and the policeman walked across the low-ceilinged garage, which was quiet now, and coming to a marked police cruiser, the policeman told him to get in front. They pulled out from under the building and across the lighted parking lot. Alex sat with his hands in his coat pockets, still shivering. The policeman said almost nothing. The rain had stopped and there were only wet spots left, with traces of snow in the gutters.

They drove through the city, for a time in the direction of Alex's house, then they turned east. They passed close to the factories along the river where his father worked, and was probably working at the time. Alex remained cold. As they left the larger buildings of the city and came nearer those streets lined with houses, he noticed something unusual. There were orange lights around. He saw some small children on the sidewalk in costumes and masks, skeleton and pirate suits bulky over winter coats. Then they left the city.

Some ten minutes later, in the country, going along a dark paved road, the policeman suddenly put on his blinker—it flashed green on the dashboard—then braked and turned to enter a long driveway. The buildings were there, but they were poorly lighted and just visible in the sweep of headlights. Alex saw the brick wall to the right, with blacker spaces in the receding darkness where the windows must have been. He could not see how high the brick went, for there were small outdoor lights on the corners of the building, and blackness above. To the left in a glimpse the headlights flashed over part of a wire fence about eight feet high. The policeman said, "Let's go," and Alex realized the man had automatically disliked him.

The policeman came around from the driver's side, leav-

ing the motor running, tall with his hat, his leather gear
squeaking, and walked beside Alex to a door. Alex could
see now that the building went on perhaps another hundred
feet, that the other end was not lighted and disappeared in
darkness. He glanced up and saw that the building was
even higher than he had imagined, not two stories but
three, perhaps four. From the darkness overhead, not very
loud in the stillness, a Negro voice said, "Hey, you, new
man—poleece catch yo ass?" Barely audible laughter came
from within.

The policeman said nothing. At the doorway he pressed
a button and they stood waiting. A faint clicking came
from inside the door, then it opened and a man was standing there. The policeman handed him the card he had
carried. He said, "Here's a new one for you."

The man, who was short, said, "Give you any trouble?"

"No," the policeman said.

The policeman did not go in. The man nodded for Alex
to enter, and Alex stepped inside. The man said something
to the policeman and then closed the door. It caught cleanly
and locked, a heavy door.

Ahead there was a light from a side corridor, but the
inside of the building was mainly dark. "Right along here,"
the man said. He waited so that Alex walked about a step
ahead of him. This corridor was old, the paint on the walls
granulated, the red tile floor worn. "Right here to the left,"
the man said.

Alex stepped into an unlighted room, but the man
turned on a switch inside the door immediately. The light
was dim, and caged, hardly lighting the room well enough
to see. It was a room about ten feet square, the walls lined
from floor to ceiling with small green lockers, with a length
of bench in the center.

"Strip," the man said. "All but shoes, socks and underwear."

Alex removed his coat. He could not help glimpsing
himself again as he least liked to see himself, as a punk,

his hair and clothes stylized and cheap, his teeth crooked. He pulled his white shirt from his pants and unbuttoned it down the front. He partially turned his back on the man to unbuckle and unbutton his pants. The man stepped from the room then, but only for a moment. As Alex was holding his leg to pull his pants over his shoe, the man laid a manilla envelope on the bench beside him. "Put your valuables here," he said.

Alex, standing in his undershorts, removed his wallet and keys and change and put them in the envelope. It was a used envelope, with ten or twelve names down one side, all but the last name, *Curtis*, crossed out.

From behind him the man threw a pair of faded blue jeans to the bench, then, on top of the blue jeans, an old flannel shirt. As Alex was removing his shirt he realized his cigarettes and matches were there in his pocket. He glanced over his shoulder—the man was sticking a wire basket of clothes into an opened locker—and got the cigarettes and matches into his hand before he slipped the shirt sleeve over his arm. He dropped the shirt on the bench and took up the blue jeans with his free hand. As he held them to step in, he began slipping the cigarettes into a hip pocket, and suddenly, however awkwardly, the man had his arm in a grip, spinning him around, immediately slapping his face in a flurry, slap-whipping his face so that he was knocked back against the wall of lockers, his cheeks stinging. "Pick them up!" the man said.

Alex reached down, picked up the cigarettes, the matches, the blue jeans.

"Here, give them here!" The man took the package, crushed it in his hand and held it.

He said no more and Alex continued dressing, feeling angry and afraid, trembling. The faded blue jeans were small in the waist, and the middle seam was crotch-tight. He put on the flannel shirt. The cloth was comfortably warm on his arms, but it was also small, and odorous, a laundered smell. He reached to take his belt from his pants and the man said, "No belt. Leave the belt alone. Tuck the shirt in."

Alex pushed the shirttail in around his waist. He saw how high the blue jeans were above his shoes, perhaps six inches, and felt foolish. Then, as ordered, he folded his clothes over and pressed them into one of the lockers. The man picked up the envelope, reached his hand to the light switch, and nodded Alex out.

They crossed directly to a small office where the man sat down behind a desk, and Alex, as directed, sat in a straight-back chair. The man looked at his card. Without looking up, as if commenting to himself, he shook his head. For the first time Alex felt accused, and guilty.

The man gave him a brief talk. He said his name was Mr. Kelly and that he was in charge. He had no idea how long Alex would be there, it might be two weeks or two months. If he wanted to get along, there was one thing he was never to forget—they had rules and regulations and they were to be obeyed without exception. All infractions would be punished without exception. At last he told Alex to get on his feet.

In the corridor he told Alex to walk ahead. Alex walked ahead of him to where the corridor ended, where the door on the left was made of metal. Mr. Kelly, with a key extracted from a ring on his belt, unlocked the door. He reached in to switch on another light, and he said, "Up you go."

Alex went up a circular metal stairway ahead of the man. Overhead somewhere he thought he heard something, voices, or the creaking of beds, within the sound of their footsteps on the metal. At the top, at a landing, there was another metal door, one with a hole about four inches wide in the center. The light switch here was on the outside. The man flipped the switch and looked in before he unlocked the door. Alex entered first. It was another corridor, not much wider than the door itself, lined with doors on one side some six or seven feet apart. Both walls were marked the full length with initials and messages and drawings dug and scratched into the white plaster. Two of three caged lights along the runway were lighted. Mr. Kelly closed the door behind him before he continued. Alex felt the sense now of confinement, of being cornered.

"Go on," Mr. Kelly said.

Each door along the way had a hole like that in the main door, with numbers stenciled over the holes, several of the numbers rubbed and scratched as if from within, but still readable. A urine smell was in the air.

"Right here," Mr. Kelly said.

It was number 11. Alex stood waiting while Mr. Kelly found another key to unlock the door. He pushed it open but did not go in himself. "In you go," he said.

Alex stepped into the room. For just a moment, from the light around his shadow, he saw more marked walls, a cot, a seatless commode against the wall. The door was pulled shut at once behind him and there was only the circle of light from the hole in the door. Then the door was being locked, the key was working, and he looked back. There was nothing to see but the hole. A moment later he heard the door at the other end of the runway being opened. Immediately he was in full darkness, although he had not heard the click of the light switch. The sound of footsteps on the metal stairway followed, and fainter, the opening, closing and locking of the door at the bottom of the stairs.

He realized the room had a window.

Someone spoke, calmly and softly. "Hey, man, what you in for?"

Alex looked toward the door again but did not answer.

Someone else said, "Hey, how you like the service in this hotel?" A high-pitched *hee-hee-hee* followed, and other laughter, but it settled quickly. Another voice said, "Go to sleep, fuckstick. Go back to flaggin' yo liddle biddy dummy."

Alex stood waiting, listening. He thought he also heard the sound of steady breathing, someone asleep. There was also a light hissing sound of steam. He recalled visiting the dog pound once, years ago, with Howard, when the two men working there let them stand and watch as they removed dogs from wire pens, and placing them in a small concrete oven of some kind, either gassed or electrocuted them, two or three at a time when the dogs were small, removing their silent and warm furred bodies with shovels and placing them in peach baskets to be carried away. There had been an odor of steam there, and odors of urine, and of scorched hair.

The lighter color of the window was visible now, and he stepped over. The window was not barred, but it was covered on the outside with heavy mesh wire. The wire crossed at right angles in squares of about an inch, and was not quite as thick as a pencil.

There was little to see, except that it must have been the back of the building, away from the road. There were no lights. Nor were there any stars visible in the dark sky. But then, far off, perhaps a mile away, he saw lights which seemed to come from a house.

He stood by the window. He was not very tired; it could not be much later than nine-thirty. And his insides were excited—he was in jail, he was locked up. There was a cooler temperature near the window from the night air. Then, far off, near the lighted house, he saw a single orange light moving along, swinging, out of view, then in view again.

He could see the shape of the cot now and he sat on the edge. He had no desire to lie down. He sat quite a long time this way, thinking but barely following his thoughts. The excitement of being in jail, the notoriety, had already faded. He thought he had been there for about an hour but was not sure. It may have been no more than fifteen or twenty minutes. He sat thinking, scanning his life as if to see what it was that had brought him there, and unable at the same time to see anything very clearly.

He stood at the window again, leaning to the side. He

wondered if there was any talk of him at the football game over in the city, any talk of the detectives taking him from school. Probably not, for not many would know where he had been taken, and if they did, it did not much matter. He remembered the years he had sold popcorn at the stadium, for both football and baseball games. He had made one cent on each ten he collected, and on a good night, besides his admission, he made about two dollars. He had worked at the stadium until he went to high school, before he made the move up to hot dogs; he quit because he had grown ashamed of wearing the white cap and jacket, because he wanted to join the spectators sitting in the stands.

Right now his father was probably working at Plant 4, across the river from the lighted stadium. From there as well as from their apartment, the big plays and the touchdowns could be heard. He wondered if his father, hearing the crowd tonight, would think of him and think he was within the crowd. Or would his father know by now? He doubted it. He doubted the police would have notified him at the factory. His father would probably go home and find the apartment empty and think he was out late. Would he think he was at a party, a dance? It was something they never talked about.

He thought of Irene Sheaffer and winced, remembering what he had said. He imagined her sitting at the football game with a well-dressed young-man-type boy. He had never seen her in a gang of girls. She was not that kind of girl, but he did not know why, nor did he know what kind of girl she was. He wondered again if she had told anyone what he had said to her. He felt pleased now that he had said it, on the idea that she might never forget.

Football games; he had always felt depressed during and after football games. He never liked simply to go back home, and he was afraid to go to the dances. He usually left and walked into town, walked for a time with the lines of cars moving bumper to bumper beside him, the policemen waving red flashlights. But in town the procession

soon passed. The people who stopped there were always
older people who parked and disappeared into the cocktail
bars, and he continued walking along, looking in store
windows, never in a mood at those times to go to a late
movie, sometimes trying to pick up a stray girl at a bus
stop, inviting her to milk shakes, or to walk, but with
little luck. He usually shot a few games of pool somewhere
and walked home again. It was only that first night, and
the nights after, when he had a car, that he did not go
home early.

He left the window and sat on the cot again. He was not
sleepy but he felt tired now, and he had become chilled. A
radiator had started to hammer lightly somewhere and he
thought the heat had either just been turned on, or turned
off. He lay over on the cot on his side, on the stiff blanket,
but did not remove his shoes. He let his feet hang over the
edge.

The fear, and then the excitement, and then the calm
he had felt since being locked up, were gone now, replaced
by a small sickness of self-pity in his stomach. He pulled
his knees up closer to relieve the pressure. He did not want
to move, wanted just to lie still. It seemed movement might
set something loose, something hard to control. The blanket
was wool, hard and bare, grained, with a smell like that of
the clothes he wore. His pants were too tight for him to feel
comfortable. They squeezed his genitals. He lay with his
head on both hands, with his eyes open.

Later, waking up, he remembered having grown cold
but did not remember growing sleepy. He seemed to wake
from the cold. But he did not move to undress, or to cover
himself. He curled up tighter for warmth, drawing his
shoes onto the blanket. He had no idea of the time, or of
how long he had slept, but on waking he needed only a
moment to recall where he was.

He stood next to the window again. There was no light
in the sky, but a changing color, a spreading overhead of
purple. He guessed it might be about four o'clock. He saw

a strand of smoke, far off, tailing to one side. Turning his head slightly to see around a line of wire, he saw the smoke was coming from about where he had seen the house lights earlier. Then, for the first time, he saw the ground, just visible, thirty-five or forty feet below, through the lines of wire.

He continued to shiver. In time he thought he recognized a ragged ball diamond lying out behind the building, a small screen backstop, worn base paths. He stared. The warmth of work and life in a factory seemed now, over the field and sky, all the richness one wanted to ask for under the sun. Life in school, with books and dreams and romance —they seemed the private, far-off world of the privileged, lying safe over there, sleeping well now after a night out.

He remembered the night at Lakeside Park, when he had stood looking as he stood now, shivering without being cold. He stood at the edge of the dark gymnasium floor that night, and all the time he was there, he hardly moved a foot. The backboards had been raised, unseen in the overhead darkness, to make room for the dance, and colored lights, reds and greens, blues and violets, revolved overhead, overall, over his face where he stood, over the shadowed bodies of those dancing on the floor. Music was furnished by boys from his school he had not known were musicians. He had taken two buses, the second to the end of the line, and walked another three quarters of a mile to get there; it was the first time he had ever gone to a school dance. And he thought he had been the last to have the back of his hand stamped at the door—where two girls had to check his name in a book to be sure he was from Central High School—but after a time the victorious football team came in and a brief uproar passed through the half-dark room. He still did not move. The uproar settled quickly, was absorbed quickly, as if by the darkness and the music, and the dancers continued to dance, and he stood watching. Occasionally, passing, the brighter red or yellow light caught someone's upturned face, and when it caught his own, he stiffened and did not change his expression. He did not stay long. When he left, on his way to the door, side-stepping politely through the dancers, he had to pause once to let a couple not looking avoid bumping into him. He smiled lightly over this, as if over something cute, something youthful, but if they had bumped into him, and if he had had a knife, he could have ripped their throats with it. Out in the parking lot he took his first car, a Chevrolet Bel Air with keys hanging in the ignition.

Book Two

Detention

One

A buzzer started the day. It must have buzzed for a full thirty seconds. As it ended, Alex was sitting on the side of his cot, still partially asleep. The buzz was continuing, lightly, in his head, and as he was coming around, he began to shiver.

The sky remained nearly dark but there was light enough now to mark the new day, to reveal the room, to reveal the sudden foreign world. The walls were marked with scratches, names, dates, pictures, dug with holes, and the floor was covered with a transparent carpet of dust and dirt and hair. A brown towel hung at the foot of the cot. His shivering continued as he sat there, and he started to stand, but sat down again, feeling weak. He raised his hands to his forehead, to cradle the weight of his head, and his fingers and arm muscles, short of strength, hardly obeyed. He saw a simple difference between freedom and confinement: he could not go, he had to wait to be taken. Someone coughed, not far away, and the sound was startling.

Lights came on in the hallway, yellow-lighting the hole in his door. Then came the key sound of the metal-stairwell door being unlocked, then locked again, and then footsteps. Close-by, perhaps next door, there came without warning a loud and sudden *knuk-knuk-knuk-knuk-knuk-knuk-knuk-knuk,* on and on, as if never to stop. Then the man's familiar voice, just as insistent, "Let's go! Let's go! Let's go!"

He stood waiting, shivering less now. Immediately his door was being banged, *KNUK-KNUK-KNUK-KNUK-KNUK-KNUK-KNUK-KNUK,* as if never to stop, each rap jarring him as he stood there. The door was quickly unlocked and thrown open. There was the man. "Good!" he said. "Good! You got your bed made. Let's go now. Five minutes to wash up. Let's go!"

He was gone. The noise started again at once nearby. Alex stood in place, afraid to enter the corridor. A Negro boy passed his open door, looking in as he passed. Alex stood there. The knocking continued down the hall. In a minute the man was looking in his room again. "Come on, let's go!" he said, and he looked to be enjoying himself shouting. He held a wooden paddle in his hand Alex had not noticed before.

Taking up the towel from the foot of his cot, Alex stepped into the corridor. The small boy was not in sight. He looked back and saw that the man was not in sight either, although the door at the end was closed and he had not heard it open. He walked along—water was running somewhere ahead—glancing through the opened doors himself. Passing the doors, he thought he saw three or four boys, all but one of them black, putting on shoes and socks, buttoning flannel shirts like his own, making beds. They looked about his age, or younger, fourteen or fifteen, although the small boy had looked no more than eleven or twelve.

The last room on the right was the bathroom. It was doorless, the walls inside more marked and scratched than those in the corridor or in his room. The small boy was over the only sink, with the faucet running. A shower nozzle was on the rear wall, with a drain on the floor, and a rusty toilet was opposite the shower. The room was about five by five. The boy was washing elaborately, bent over the sink, lathering his neck and ears in white suds. A piece of yellow lint showed clearly on his nearly bald, purplish-black head. Alex stood waiting, still shivering some. In a moment another boy came into the small room with a towel, another Negro, bigger, cobwebbed himself with sleep, but he only glanced at Alex as Alex glanced at him, and stood silent and sleepy. But then, as the small boy stepped away from the sink, the second boy stepped in quickly ahead of Alex. Alex felt a flare of anger, and humiliation, but he merely stepped over to block the path of anyone else trying to do the same.

The small boy was looking him over. He stood toweling off the water which hung in full drops from his head and face. Then he smiled, his gums suddenly bright pink above his small teeth. He said, "You got soap an' stuff, man?"

Alex shook his head and did not quite say no.

"Here," the boy said. "Use The King's!" He held out a thin, wet piece of soap.

Alex took the soap and said nothing. He knew the boy was standing there looking at him but he did not look back. Then the older boy left the sink, and he stepped over. He had just washed his hands a little with the soap when he heard the man shout, "Okay, line it up! Let's go! Line it up!"

He splashed some water on his face and hurried out. At the end of the corridor, at the door, three or four boys were standing in a line. He realized the man was standing at his own doorway, and it frightened him. "Come on," the man said. "Let's *go!*" Alex went past him into the room, draped the towel over the bed rail again, stuck the boy's soap on top, and came back out. The man closed his door sharply behind him and locked it. Going to the line, Alex heard the man say behind him, "Get that shirttail tucked in." Alex reached back and pushed the short shirttail into his tight blue jeans.

They filed in a line of footsteps down the metal stairway. At the bottom the man unlocked the door and left it unlocked, leading the line into the hallway. There were five of them altogether, with Alex the last in line. It had been cool upstairs and in the stairwell, and was suddenly warmer here in the hallway. There was an odor of food cooking, a steamy odor perhaps of oatmeal, of toast. They walked along in a sloppy line, hangdog and sleepy. Alex still felt weak; it must have been five-thirty or six o'clock.

The line turned right, through a double door which had been closed the night before, into a large dining room. It was filled with children, even, to his surprise, with some girls, sitting quietly at long picnic tables with attached benches. Dimly burning yellow-lighted globes hung from the ceiling. Alex self-consciously followed the line across the room, feeling that everyone was looking him over. They had been the last to enter and the others seemed to be waiting for them. Some of the girls looked as old as fourteen or fifteen, some of the children as young as four or five. At one table there was a man in work clothes and some women in white uniforms. Some of the children were toying with their silverware, but they were mainly still and silent. At an empty table across the room, next to some large steamed-over windows, following the others, Alex sat down. No one spoke, nor did they touch anything on the table, and neither did he.

He sat waiting. Across the room, where part of a kitchen was visible through a doorway, the man was now the only one standing. There may have been fifty or sixty children altogether, and it was as if he had seen them somewhere before in photographs. The girls wore plain sacky dresses and resembled girls in photographs of child laborers in history books, photographs of large tenant-farmer families at their dinner tables.

The man was nodding toward a table of small girls, and he said, "Oh, let's see. Claudia. Claudia."

Glancing to the side, Alex saw a girl of seven or eight retrieve her legs from under a table to stand. She hardly moved her head, as if studying the downward fall of her beltless dress.

The man said, "Let us bow our heads."

The girl, Claudia, spoke in a sparrow-sized voice:

"Be present—at our table—Lord
Be here—and everywhere—adored . . ."

Alex was looking down at the oilcloth fixed tightly to the table, at the heavy bowl and saucer before him, at the heavy spoon with gold knicks. The oilcloth, patterned with red and yellow and green sea horses, was faintly gray and threadbare. He had only bent his head a little and he raised his eyes. He felt no hunger.

Everyone at the table was lifting the saucer from the bowl and he did the same. The saucer bottom was bubbled with steam. It was not oatmeal, but Cream of Wheat. He had not eaten any hot cereal in years. The boy who called himself The King was handing him a dented stainless-steel pitcher. Alex took it, saw that it was milk, and passed it to the next boy. Then The King passed him a bowl of sugar, and he passed that along as well. The food sickened him a little, however hollow his stomach felt. Then a small girl approached and placed a platter with half a loaf of stacked toast at the end of their table. The toast came around; he took one slice, although everyone else had taken two, and passed it on. The next man grabbed three slices, and immediately, from across the table, the boy who had cut in front of him at the sink, whispered, "You gonna eat that?," nodding in the direction of Alex's bowl of Cream of Wheat. Alex handed him the bowl.

He bit into the slice of toast. It was an uneven slice, as if cut with a saw. He discovered no hunger. He chewed and forced himself to swallow. His stomach took the toast reluctantly. To his right, filtering through the steam over the windows, through the haze over the ground, was the first cold and orange color of morning. The sun must have just reached the horizon. He looked back, as if not to see.

Upstairs, through most of the morning, they sat or lay around without talking much to each other. Alex spoke to no one. He sat on the floor in the corridor, frightened some by the others, disliking them. The rooms with their cots were locked. They had the narrow runway of the corridor, the doorless bathroom at the far end, and another doorless room at the near end, next to the metal stairwell door. This room was almost filled by an old wooden picnic table with fixed benches. Occasionally two or three sat at the table and talked, or one or two stood at the window at the end of the corridor, but most of the time most of them stretched out somewhere on the corridor floor, using an arm for a pillow, to sleep. When they talked, Alex did not look at them, and when someone walked past him he did not look up. He lay over on his side most of the time as if to sleep, and he was tired, but he was too afraid to doze off very far. When he did, within seconds some realization brought him back.

From their talk he learned that there was a better world downstairs, that upstairs was used for punishment, and that the detention home, after the highway passing outside, was called The Lincoln Hotel.

Later in the morning, when the others were stretched out asleep, he walked down quietly to use the bathroom. On his way back he went into the room with the picnic table and stood at the window. This window was also covered with heavy-mesh wire, and now in daylight he could see a wire fence, eight or ten feet high, enclosing the field which spread out behind the building. The fence was perhaps two or three hundred yards away. From the window he envisioned school, far off in the city, and he thought of his father, and wondered where he was. He also thought of his brother, Howard, imagining him safe in school, in that white building.

As he stood looking from the window, children from downstairs appeared on the ground below, streaming onto the field. Mr. Kelly came walking among them. They wore odd coats and mackinaws against the cold, and they were either very quiet or Alex was too high above the ground, too sealed in, to hear much. A softball game got under way, and jump rope, and much standing around. He heard some shouts now and then. He stood and watched for the full thirty minutes or so they were out, and stood watching after they had disappeared back into the building, leaving the windblown field empty.

He sat on the floor in the corridor, his forehead resting on his arms crossed over his knees, knowing that nothing had ever filled minutes or hours as slowly as this, as idle confinement. He saw the days stretching on and on, with no known number to pass, and for a moment it seemed their only end could be some infinite horror or explosion. The idea made him weak with fear; he seemed already in movement down a long incline. Looking up, noticing some of the others had also raised their heads or were sitting up, he heard the footsteps on the metal stairway. Perhaps it was lunchtime. Then the key was in the metal door, and the door swung open. His neck twitched once involuntarily. The man looked in, and looking at him, said, "You, Housman, let's go."

The boy who called himself The King called out, "Mista Kelly, let me go downstairs today, please, can't ah go downstairs?"

Mr. Kelly ignored this. He held the door as Alex, on his feet, stepped through to the stairwell landing. He locked the door, and stepping past Alex, said, "Let's go. You got a visitor."

Alex followed him, terrified all over again, feeling without strength as he waited for the unlocking and locking of the door at the bottom, as he followed into the hallway. Another door stood open near the door to Mr. Kelly's office, and as they came to it, Mr. Kelly said, "Right here."

Alex knew who the visitor was, and did not want to go in. He also knew he had no choice. Glancing up, he saw his father standing inside, in his topcoat, looking at the doorway.

Mr. Kelly did not come into the room. Alex stepped in. He felt as young as the other young children in the home, and as shy as a five-year-old. His father stood in place, looking at him. He tried to smile, it seemed, and seemed almost to sniffle, and said, whispered, "Ohh, son," and Alex knew they were far beyond anger.

His father squeezed his arm, quite hard, and Alex only glanced at his face and had to look down. He smelled the familiar wool odor of his father's topcoat, of his being dressed up.

Kindly, still whispering, his father said, "You okay?"

Alex nodded, and again it was like the sympathetic voice from Mr. Hewitt. His cheeks began to wrinkle, and he looked down, trying to steel his jaws.

"Are you sure?" his father said.

Alex moved, nodded his head again. They stood silent for a moment.

"I brought you some things," his father said.

A paper bag lay on the table there, but neither of them made any move for it.

"Your toothbrush, and other things," his father said. "What they told me . . ." But he let it go, and whispered, "Ohh, son, whatever happened?"

Alex did not know what to say. Nor was it easy for him to speak. "I'm sorry—" he started.

"No, no, don't say that," his father said. "Don't even think it. Oh, listen, it's more my fault than it is yours. Don't be sorry—no, no."

Again, for a moment, they stood silent.

Stepping closer, his father whispered, "Listen to me now, son, 'cause I can only say this once. I want you to be very careful what you say to people, 'cause they're not going to like it that we don't have a mother. Do you understand? You tell them we do fine—we do just fine. They might try to take my boy away from me. Do you understand what I mean?"

Alex thought he understood, but he gave no sign. He was looking down again, embarrassed by his father's words, and not thinking, but seeing his father, dressed in suit and tie and white shirt, and in his brown-and-cream checked overcoat and his blood-colored scarf, and already a little juiced.

"Don't forget now," his father whispered. "I'm with you, I won't let you down."

Alex nodded, and looked up again, and felt angry that he could find neither voice nor words.

"They can get to you in a place like this," his father whispered. "That's one thing you're gonna have to watch out for. You're gonna have to keep your mouth shut and take whatever it is they have to hand out. You understand me, son? Don't try to fight these birds. 'Cause, boy, they'll just bust your ass. And they can do it, too."

Over a distance Alex saw his father looking at him for a response, and he finally gave a slight nod, and made a slight glance away, to avoid his father's eyes.

"Listen, son, if they think your old dad's not been a very good father, they're liable to ship you off somewhere for a couple years. Do you see what I mean? Anybody asks you, you say I take a little snort now and then and that's about all. We're gonna have to keep our stories straight. Do you understand?"

Alex nodded again, to the floor.

"And there's something else you're gonna have to do. And it's not gonna be at all easy. You remember this now —you're gonna have to come out of here a better man than when you went in. In spite of me. Do you understand? You see, what you did, it's not such a bad thing—only don't ever tell any of these pricks I said that. But don't let them make you think it is bad, either. I mean, you tell them you're sorry and all, but don't let them make you think something's wrong with you, 'cause it's not the case. Are you with me? This is the most important thing you have to remember. You just be calm and quiet, see, and let them do the talking, and be sorry, and when you get outta here, then you can show the cocksuckers the kind of stuff you're made of."

His father straightened his neck then, and paused, and Alex still saw him over a distance, his face slightly flushed, his eyes red.

"A deal?" his father said.

Alex looked at him.

"I'll tell you something," his father said. "Just between the two of us. It takes some guts to do what you did. Don't you ever do anything like that again—but don't you ever worry about it, either. It's over. In the past. A deal?"

His father was smiling, as if with pride. It was like those nights when his father came home from work and woke him, when he had a good glow on, and carried home doughnuts or hot dogs, and told him stories, cuffed his eleven- or twelve- or thirteen-year-old head of hair, and had Alex hit his brick-sized arm muscle, or his tightened stomach, to show how tough and hard he was at forty-nine or fifty or fifty-one.

Looking up at him now, Alex felt as if he had heard nothing of what he had said, and saw him not through tears, but through a film of confusion. And over the distance he heard his father saying to him, "Are you sure you're all right, son?" and felt himself wrapped into his father's arm against the wool of his coat, and heard him saying, "If you're not, goddammit, I'll get you out of here, I'll find some way if I have to tear this fucking place apart myself."

The afternoon upstairs passed as sleepily as the morning. Now for Alex it was a world less removed from the world he knew. He was, by a layer, less afraid. Exhausted, yawning often, he was able to sleep for perhaps an hour after lunch. He lay on his side on the floor, facing the corridor wall, his knees raised and his head on his arm muscle.

Later, sitting up against the wall, he saw that The King was the only other inmate not lying down. The King was at the far end of the hall. He sat facing the radiator and in a moment Alex realized he was masturbating. His elbow and arm were fluttering. The others lay along the corridor like lifeless bodies.

Alex got up, and without looking to see if his standing had disturbed The King, went into the room with the picnic table. He stood for a time at the window there, staring out over the field and the sky. Sitting at the table, reading over its names, dates and messages, he saw the name of a boy he had once known, had gone to school with and run the streets with, when they were ten or twelve years old. Joey Hyde. He was now in a reformatory up north somewhere. Under his name on the table was a list of five different dates, raggedly aligned. Alex imagined him being

locked up here, three years ago, four years ago, when he
had been safely, ignorantly it seemed, in school himself.

Others walked in and out of the room now and then,
stood at the window for a time, but said very little. Alex
remained shy of them, afraid of them. He heard the boy
who had cut in front of him at the sink, out in the corridor,
say to The King, "Man, you so uncool, you know! You jack
off so much. You jack me off, here, man! Come on, do me!
Come on, man, do me!"

Another of the Negroes, a very thin boy, seemed to talk
to himself as continuously as The King masturbated,
walking, muttering *mahfuck* often, seeming angry over
being locked up, angry over something. The other white
boy, whose sand-colored hair grew raggedly around his
neck and ears, whose face, his skin grimed, looked crushed,
said hardly a word. Alex, going to the bathroom once,
found him lying over the floor drain, facing the wall,
asleep, within spattering distance of the commode. He
waited, and later, hearing the boy speak, discovered that
his voice was Negroid-thick, and Southern.

The evening, after supper, was less quiet, as if they
had rested enough for the day and had found their energy.
Alex remained tired; he had eaten about half of his evening meal, so he had some food on his stomach, but he still
had not slept much in some three or four days. He remained
afraid. He stood at the corridor window, while the others
were at the table talking, and with the sun going down, the
sky growing darker, the only changeable scene to watch, a
reminiscence of being other places at the same time rose
naturally, came in naturally with the colder evening air
around the window. The evening hours were longer here
than they had ever been elsewhere. During the day he
missed mainly school, but now he envisioned the city, and
its lights, and the people, moving within their air of ig-
norant freedom.

At red darkness, at about seven o'clock, when they
could just see each other in the corridor, Mr. Kelly came

upstairs and turned on the lights. As he unlocked their doors, The King followed him, begging again to go downstairs. Mr. Kelly paid no attention. It was shower night; everyone had to shower. They undressed in their rooms and lined up with their towels, naked, in the cool corridor, wearing shoes but not socks. Alex handed The King his sliver of soap and said, "Thanks." Except for answering a question, it was his first word to any of them. He unwrapped the new bar of Lux his father had brought him in the bag. The other white boy came from the shower first, dripping and no cleaner-looking. Undressed, he looked more shrunken than before; his ribs were visible turning their curves, and his skin from the neck down was as white as the skin of an old man. The King, like boys in the shower at school, did not stop glancing down at the others, turning around in the line, glancing down, talking, glancing down, turning back. While The King was in the shower, the older Negro boy, ahead of Alex, who was last in line, said to The King, "Man, stop playin wid yo fuckin self. Leave yo fuckin weenie alone. You gonna get silly in the fuckin headbone, man."

When Mr. Kelly had left, thirty or forty minutes later, leaving them locked in their rooms in the dark again, the same boy called out, "Hey, who's beatin his meat besides me?" In a moment he called out, "Everybody is who didn't answer. Heh-heh-heh. Hey, King, you beatin yo little biddy dummy again?"

The King did not answer.

"You better, you dumb fuckstick," the boy called out. "You never gonna get no broad, man. You hear? You get Miss Rosy Palm all yo life, man. You hear? You get nothin but the *dregs*, man. 'Cause that all you *is*."

The floor was silent for a moment, and then the boy began to sing, or chant, roughly, in a wail:

> "Sendin my ass to BVS
> Ain't no snatch to lay

> Nothin but my hand to play
> Sendin me
> Bendin me
> Bustin me
> Rustin me.
> Ain't no doors
> Ain't no hoes
> No scratch!
> No snatch!
> Bustin my ass wid two-by-fours
> Bustin my ass wid scrubbin floors . . ."

Silence followed, and continued, interrupted only by an occasional cough, or a squeak of bedsprings.

The night was clear. Moonlight came raggedly through the window, through the wire, the film of dirt on the glass. The moon was still low, more yellow than white, and the far-off house was lighted again. Alex had seen the house less than a day ago and this had been the longest day he had ever known. Dressed in his underwear, barefooted, cold from the shower, he stood at the window. After a while he removed the hard-grained blanket from over the pillow and laid it, folded double, over the cover blanket. He sat on the side of the cot again. After a moment, to get them warm, he lifted his feet from the floor and lay back on top of the blankets. He lay still, watching.

Waking, trembling from the cold, he rose from the cot and pulled the covers and top sheet from where they were tucked under the mattress. He slipped in between the sheets now, which were clean, warm where he had lain, icy on the edges, and pulled the covers and extra blanket around his neck for warmth. The pillow was odorous, the air alive and sharp on his face. He lay waiting for sleep again, which seemed no more than a moment away. Off in the darkness, over the cold night, a dog was barking. Alex was close to the unconscious passage into sleep when he glimpsed himself lying there in a cot, in a locked and screened room. The air seemed to stop. He glimpsed himself as clearly as if he were Joey Hyde, who must have been lying in another cot, in another locked room, across the state. An idea came to mind: a simple wish to be a person other than the person he was. The idea rose quietly; he did not move in the cot. As if it were actually possible, the idea became lucid, until he knew, in sudden disappointment, that it was not possible at all.

Two

Just faintly Alex remembered Mrs. Komarek. She was a lady who lived in the house next door and looked after him and Howard back at the beginning of his memory. Mrs. Komarek had an ashen mole on the side of her chin where hairs sprouted, and a mustache, frosted gray, and she had an odor like dill pickles, but not an unpleasant odor. Mornings, as early as sunrise, while their mother slept behind a closed door, Mrs. Komarek came across the yard and into their house, and into their bedroom, and led them, carrying Howard and carrying their clothes, downstairs, to dress in the kitchen, and then walked them across the yard and driveway to the kitchen in her house to eat breakfast. Just as many nights as they slept at home they slept in a large bed upstairs in Mrs. Komarek's house, a bed whose sheets were crisp as paper and whose quilted covers smelled like bread.

Afternoons, on her way to work, their mother stopped to see them. Her fingernails were painted red mirrors, her lips shining red, and rich with an aroma of cologne, she usually knelt, rustling with the grain of nylon, to give them cheek kisses before she left, sometimes slipping into the back seat of a taxi pulling up at the end of the driveway, sometimes walking away on the sidewalk, waving before going out of view of Mrs. Komarek's yard.

After supper in the evenings, Mrs. Komarek bathed them in her bathtub and put them in the large bed upstairs, and played the radio downstairs, or she bathed them in their own bathtub and rocked Howard in her arms in a straight-back chair, and she said to them too many times for it ever to be forgotten, "I've got a crush on you little shitasses," after which she always laughed happily.

She washed clothes. Her washing machine was going and her tubs were full every morning by the time they got up for breakfast. She had lines all across her backyard which she took down and put up again in the basement in bad weather, and a car or two drove up every afternoon, to exchange baskets of dirty clothes for baskets of clean ironed clothes, to give her dollar bills, which she folded and put in her apron pocket. When she fed clothes through the wringer of her washing machine, from one tub to another, Alex often stood guard against something falling over the side to the floor, lifting the outpouring, twisting wet fabric on its way into the tub. With clothespins in her mouth, she hung the clothes in the backyard, and throughout the afternoons she ironed at her ironing board, or sitting at her mangle, using her foot, while they played on the floor. She hummed when she ironed. She hummed so softly that at times she hardly emitted any of what she must have been singing in her mind, and most of what she hummed wandered on an endless road as if composed slightly after delivery. She seldom talked when she ironed, and seldom turned on the lights, and turned on the radio only for short times, to listen to sleepy afternoon programs which began and ended with organ music. And she said something else to them often, besides her other remark. She said, "If I had a thousand dollars I'd buy you two," and she laughed happily over this as well.

When Howard napped and Mrs. Komarek was washing or hanging out clothes, Alex played behind the garage, which stood at the end of the driveway between the two houses. It was a place not completely out of sight of her yard, but it was out of sight of the driveway, a partial hiding place where there was some dirt to dig into, and a tree whose erupting roots he had skinned, to pull off sticky blond wooden hairs. Bushes and brush blocked most of the way to the yard behind his own house, but it was there one day that he heard something and looked up to see a man watching him from among the leaves and branches, a man in a uniform, and a hat, with Mrs. Komarek standing behind him, near his shoulder. In a moment the man had him by the waist, holding him overhead, looking up at him, asking him if he knew who he was, telling him, when he shook his head no, that he was his father.

Days passed. They lay about the corridor, sat at the table, stood at the windows. In a semidream one morning Alex saw his father in the kitchen of their apartment, dressed as he dressed on weekends. His music, his records, were playing on the phonograph, sad country songs of separation and divorce and cold and cheating hearts, and in a strange dream-flash Alex saw his father not losing himself at all in the music as he always seemed to, but shedding himself and re-emerging as another person, more as an unknown creature, an unseen body behind an animal's orange highlighted eyes. Then he appeared in the dream himself, coming from his bedroom and finding his father asleep in a chair, on the couch, on the floor, and he quietly lifted the arm from the sailing phonograph record, not to disturb his father to waking, but to put an end to the night. His father, rising, visored his eyes as he moved in a stagger to close himself in his bedroom.

In a dream which on waking he did not forget for some time, the large breasts of Eugenia Rodgers appeared on the slight body of Irene Sheaffer. They appeared in a richness of glistening veal, the nipples as pink and firm as oversized pencil erasers. But before any sensation was complete, the eye of the dream withdrew, like the eye of a camera. He felt a love and yearning painful enough to wake him, but he woke to a strain of suffering more intense, and finding himself on the dirty corridor floor, rising from the floor, standing at the window, sitting at the table, the feeling lingered.

In another dream, lying again on the floor, there arose a cafeteria air of heavy steam from stainless-steel beds of water, and odors of meat loaf or noodles or macaroni-and-cheese or tuna-fish casserole, or some combination of all these odors. They were from junior high school, from the cafeteria where he had eaten his lunch. Then he was moving quickly through the school corridor, and as he was passing through the locker-room door he was already un-buttoning his shirt, then he was unbuttoning his pants with one hand and simultaneously working his lock combi-nation with the other, pulling off his clothes and kicking off his shoes, pulling his socks inside out, and slipping quickly into the straps, finger-straightening them, of a manilla-colored jockstrap, and into white wool socks, and trunks, and white basketball shoes, grabbing a green sleeveless jersey and slamming the tinny locker door, and moving, goose-bumped, slipping into the jersey on the way, through the cool tile tunnel entrance which opened into the expanse of cool gym, walking under the netting, the high, wire-covered windows, over the glaring honey-colored floor, among the hollow *thud-thud-thud* of so many basketballs, the squeak of rubber soles, walking and checking an urge somehow to flash, to roar.

Then he was stepping back and forth over benches in aisles, searching out locks hung to give the impression of being locked, lifting the handles and opening the doors, removing wallets from draping pants pockets and from among keys and watches and rings on shelves, and in the janitor's wire cage, pulling the dollar bills out and stuffing the leather wallets into a bed of damp and wadded paper towels, looking around and looking around until, waking, he sat up, and leaned once more against the marked wall.

His father—Alex was not sure if the memory of his father appearing behind the garage was entirely his own. It was a scene his father liked to recall. Alex did remember clearly the confusion which followed; his mother, as if going to work one day and not returning, disappeared, and some days later, with their father, loading their belongings into the trunk of a taxi, Mrs. Komarek squeezing them so hard in farewell that it hurt, they moved across town to Mrs. Cushman's. Mrs. Cushman's was a house filled with children like themselves. They moved in, and time passed, and one day, just faintly, when a car turned into the yard and stopped, and the man, the familiar stranger, wearing a civilian overcoat now, came walking toward them, came walking to where he was playing with four or five other children—just faintly he could remember that he was the man who had picked him up by the waist and held him overhead, and told him he was his father.

It had been a Sunday and the car itself was the occasion. His father took him for an afternoon drive. They drove through the city, and into the country, where, on a gravel road, he sat on his father's knees and steered the large round steering wheel, weaving the car down the road. Back at Mrs. Cushman's he was sorry the day was ending, sorry the cold afternoon darkness was falling, sorry that this man, his father, who bought him hamburgers and ice cream cones, who let him drive his car, who liked him, had to go away, and anxious as well to go back into the house of children, as if to display himself. They sat in the car

for a time. His father wrote a telephone number on a slip
of paper, where Alex could reach him if he needed anything, and his father gave him a dollar bill and some
change to keep in his pocket, all of which Alex took, saying
nothing, and put in his pockets. He sat there, feeling
pleased. His father told him he'd try to get back as soon as
he could to see him again, and they'd have lunch together
again one of these days soon, and Alex still sat there,
smiling. It had already grown leg-cold in the car with the
motor turned off, and he had smiled so much that his
cheeks ached, but there was his father next to him, this
man who liked him, who talked to him and asked him
questions: How was he getting along in school? Did he
sleep okay? Did he get enough to eat? Did he have enough
clothes to wear? He sat through a short silence, sat still,
smiling a little, until his father told him he was sure glad
he could get out to see him like this, until his father
straightened his leg to the floor and the car's motor
coughed and whined into the vibration of running, until
his father told him he thought he had better go on in the
house now, when Alex finally understood and felt foolish
and left the car too quickly, and then, around the front of
the car, hearing his father unroll his window, stepped all
the way back from his line of going to the house and his
father only told him to go on, said he'd wait until he was
inside; and wanting to do nothing more than please, he
turned and walked quickly back over to the porch steps and
turned again and called " 'Bye" to his father, and from the
car his father called " 'Bye," his voice coming from the
window frame of shadows across the cold air of the yard.
On the porch, which was littered with broken toys, Alex
turned and looked back again. But it was too dark and too
far to see or hear very well, and he opened the door as if
to go in but stepped only inside the storm door, and
squeezed himself there, and closed the storm door, and
waited until he saw the car begin to move away, and stepping back to the porch to watch, saw the two red taillights,

the exhaust flying like a scarf, going out of sight, on its way back into the world.

Warmer weather came in one day, air warm and windless enough so it looked from the sealed windows that one would sweat walking through the brown fields, through the distant rectangular patterns of dried corn stalks and stubble. They saw Mr. Kelly go off once in a hunting vest and cap, carrying a shotgun, but did not see him return. The King said, "See! See! Wha'd I say? You go foe that fence, they go *BOOM! BOOM! BOOM!* Blow yo ass off."

Still at night under the clear sky it turned cold enough for frost, and the trees near the small white house were thinning to webs of branches. The freak snowstorm seemed from another year, not another week. For Alex, as it must have been for the others, the sense of having no voice to anyone outside only became stronger as the season made its turn. If anyone ever spoke for him or of him, it had to be without him. He wondered if he was remembered, and worried that he had been forgotten.

Every message or call was a surprise of a kind, and every one of them but the other white boy, whose name was Billy, stopped and turned his head at the sound of footsteps on the stairway, the noise of the key in the metal door, which was never opened without a particular reason.

The man himself almost never spoke directly to any of them unless it was to give an order. He seemed to feel neither dislike nor any special interest. He hardly looked at a face. Like The King, who was always begging to be transferred downstairs, Alex also wished to be recognized by the man. More and more he felt the desire of a ten- or eleven-year-old to be noticed.

Occasionally now he sat with some of the others at the picnic table, all but Billy, who sat by himself most of the time, or slept, and seldom spoke. Nor did Alex speak very often; he answered questions. The boy who had cut in front of him in the washroom was called Red Eye, and besides The King, the other two were named Leonard and Thomas, but he did not know if these were first names or last. Once when he sat at the table, Red Eye said, "Who you, man?" and nodded when Alex gave his name, and said, "Yeah, yeah, I see you somewhere, I don't know where."

The King, Alex learned, was there for not going to school and because "my old man's in the can, my old lady done cut out." This was The King's fifth time upstairs, and Alex learned later that it was not school this year The King had not gone to, but school last year. Over the summer, into the fall. The King had been in the detention home for seven months now, since April. And he had been in before, on and off since he was six, twenty-some months altogether. Red Eye was in for breaking and entering, but it was his third arrest, and he said he was headed for BVS, the Boys Vocational School in Lansing. Leonard and Thomas, who had been arrested for breaking into a dry cleaner's on Leith Street, were younger than they looked. Both were thirteen. They said they were "aces." Red Eye was fifteen. Alex, the oldest, felt as young as any of them.

One evening, sitting at the table, Red Eye called out something about growing warts to The King, who was masturbating in the corridor again, and Billy smiled, laughed enough to show that his teeth were rotten between one another, his gums more brown than pink. His hair looked as if unwashed for months, perhaps years, large thread-sized hairs, and up this close he looked as if he had been cooked, somehow shrunken to less than a former size. Red Eye, in his high-pitched, singing voice, finally said to him, "How old *you* anyway, man?"

"Me?" Billy said.

"Yeah."

Billy hunched and seemed to say, "Doe know."

They all laughed. But Billy also laughed, and looked more or less happy.

"Man—where you from?"

Billy did not say.

"You don't know how old you are?"

Billy grinned.

"Humh!" Red Eye said to himself. *"Yeah? Where's yo daddy?"*

"Doe know," Billy said, laughing again.

"How come you here?"

"Just pick me up."

"Humh!" Red Eye said. *"Yeah?* How about that! What's yo name? Billy what?"

Billy did not say.

"You doe know yo name?"

Billy did not say.

"Man, you gotta have *two* names, you know!"

Billy just hunched and shook his head.

The King came walking in then, and Red Eye said to him, "Say, man, this cat's name Billy Noname," and they all laughed again, Billy Noname among them.

The King told of a man, a Mr. Hocker, who had been "the chief" prior to Mr. Kelly. In Mr. Hocker's time they were not only locked upstairs but they were locked in their rooms, and not for a few days but sometimes for weeks, let out twice a week for showers, with meals carried up on trays. "The man was always beatin yo ass off wid a paddle," The King said.

Alex, speaking for almost the first time, told of being slapped by Mr. Kelly over the package of cigarettes. He told the story not for itself, but merely to talk, and The King all but jumped. "Say *what?*" he said. "That cat give you some stuff? He get *mean?* Oh, man! Man! We hang his ass! Ohhh-weee—we hang that mother! This poleeceman sayta tell him right off some cat get *mean!* Wha'd he do, he *punch* you?"

"Nah, just slapped me. He didn't do nothing."

"Ah, man, come on—he punch you nor not?"

"Nah. He just slapped me, that's all."

"Awh, man, you uncool. The King see that cat's ass hanged!"

Red Eye said, "You dumb fuck, can't you hear? He say he didn't punch him."

"Shoot!" The King said. "Shoot! I get that mother's me! I hang that dimeass mother! Shoot! *Hang his ass!*"

On Monday, Alex had another visitor. He met the man in the same room where he had met his father. Closing the door, the man, who was about forty, told him to have a seat, and sat down across from him at the small table. He said his name was Mr. Quinn, and explained that he was not a police officer, but a probation officer, and added that he had spent a "season" of his own childhood here in the detention home, and that he had gone on to "graduate school," to BVS in Lansing. The first question he asked was, "How do you get along with your father?"

"Okay," Alex said.

"You ever have any arguments? Disagreements? Money? Staying out late? Haven't you ever had a good fight?"

"Nothing much like that," Alex said.

"Does your father ever bring anyone home? Any friends?"

"No, not much."

"Ever?"

"No."

"How about women? Any women?"

"No," Alex said, a lie.

"You seen your mother lately?"

"No."

"You ever see her?"

"No."

"When's the last time?"

"About three years ago."

"Your father drink much?"

"Oh, sometimes. A little."

"He ever drink a lot?"

"Oh, well, once he did. A long time ago."

"What did he do?"

"Nothing. He just drank a lot."

"So what did he do?"

"Fell asleep on the couch."

"He passed out?"

"No, he just fell asleep, is all."

"What did you do?"

"Nothing."

"How about meals and clothes and so on? Who cooks the meals? How do you get your washing done? Things like that? Tell me about your general life."

Alex said they both did the cooking. He bought his lunch at school, but his father always left him something to eat for supper in the refrigerator, some hamburger to cook, some bacon and eggs, something like that. Only—he was supposed to eat his good meal for lunch. Then on weekends his father usually did the cooking. He did the laundry himself. The landlady had a washing machine in the basement she let them use, and some lines to hang up the stuff down there, except for dress shirts and things like that, that had to be ironed, which his father took over to the Chinaman on Third Avenue. And his father cleaned the house. Picked it up, stuff like that. Except that he took care of his own bedroom. And each of them washed his own dishes.

"Sounds like you do okay."

"Yeah. I guess we do."

"That's an accomplishment, you know."

"I guess so."

"You been happy at home?"

"Sure."

"How happy?"

"Happy enough."

"What you doing here, then?"

Alex said nothing.

"You got an answer?" the man said.

"I'm here," Alex said. "I don't know."

"Didn't you know you were doing something wrong? Something you could be punished for?"

"I was nervous all the time, if that's what you mean."

"You didn't have a good time?"

"Nah, not really."

"That's too bad. Why did you do it? It take fourteen cars to figure that out?"

"I don't know."

"Well, come on, then—let's figure it out. I'll tell you something. You figure out why you made a mistake and you probably won't make it again. That's what I'm concerned with. I'm on your side, you understand? I'm with you. So lay it on me. Don't sweat it. I'm all ears."

"Just for joy rides, I guess," Alex said.

Mr. Quinn sat still for a moment. Then he said, "Okay. You're not going to do it again, are you?"

"No, I'm afraid not."

"Okay. Fine. I'll tell you what's going to happen. Roughly. Sooner or later you'll come up for a hearing, before a judge. He'll do one of two things, depending on who he is and depending on you, on your behavior at the present time and whether or not he thinks you've learned a lesson. And your case might be a difficult one, too, so you should be ready for it. He'll put you on probation or he'll send you over to the Boys Vocational School in Lansing. It's a good thing it's a first offense, believe me. But then, it's no small offense either. The important thing is that you keep your nose clean in the meantime. Okay? And I want you to take a little test for me. You can do it right now, and Mr. Kelly will pick it up in a few minutes."

"Do I have to stay here until then?" Alex said.

"Until when?"

"The trial?"

"The hearing. I don't know. We don't want you home right now while your father's working a night shift. Not for a while. Why, is it tough on you here?"

"I'd sure like to go home."

Mr. Quinn laid a booklet and a half pencil before him on the table. "Listen," he said. "You should have seen this place when I was here." He zipped his leather case. Alex said nothing. "You be careful now," Mr. Quinn said.

He left, closing the door again behind him.

Alex took up the pencil. He had liked Mr. Quinn and was sorry now he had lied, if only for whatever information the truth might have drawn from the man. He did seem tough, Alex thought. But then, he probably did this all the time. And he had lied to him. Lies made a difference in how tough a person acted. He was sure of one thing: his father would dislike the man and the man would dislike his father in the same way. He had an idea Mr. Quinn would be neither kind nor quiet about his father's drinking.

Sample Question: Would you rather be

> a) an airplane pilot
> b) a first-grade schoolteacher
> c) operate a gas station?

He read the question again. It raised an air of being in school, in the sixth or seventh grade, years ago, and it raised a sense of loss. He saw himself, himself and Howard, walking down Chevrolet Avenue and over the bridge, over the odorous river, or climbing down under the bridge, early and still mornings when their father was asleep on the couch, or on the floor, and a record was sailing around and around on the phonograph.

He decided on a) and moved on.

The King sometimes made music by crouching and slapping his hands together and off his thighs in a rhythm which gave the impression of a drummer working. He was good and they were all impressed. Red Eye invented a game of shuffleboard with shoes, sliding them from one end of the corridor to the other, and it caught on so that even Billy Noname played. In this way some hours passed uncounted.

After supper one evening, they became six. A new boy, a Negro, was let into the corridor by Mr. Kelly and locked in with them. He looked older, as old as Alex. He was charred-black, and although he was not very tall, perhaps five-eight, his arms and shoulders were developed into muscular curves and veins, and he had either the head of an infant or the neck of a giant, for one became the other with little change in size.

The King said to him, "Say, new man—come in. Tell us yo name. What you in foe?"

The new man, just in the corridor, turned his head, his head alone, to The King. He squinted. *"Talkin me?"* he said. His voice sang on a wire higher than Red Eye's.

"What's yo name?" The King said.

The new man stared a moment. Then he said, *"Who you, punk? Talkin me!"*

The King said nothing.

"Huh? What you talkin me foe?"

Nothing.

"Huh? Man? Don't you talk to me! I don't want you talk to me!"

After a while the new man sat on the floor. No one suggested shuffleboard that evening. The new man said nothing more, from then until they were locked in their rooms for the night. But a few minutes before Mr. Kelly came up to bed them down, the new man, walking along the corridor, weaved his shoulders and shadow-boxed for several steps.

In the morning, just out of bed and sleepy, Alex heard The King, next door, whisper fiercely, *"Please, Mista Kelly, please, I gotta move downstairs today."*

"Not today," Mr. Kelly said.

"I got to," The King whispered. *"I got to. They gonna get me. They say they gonna whup me. They kill me!"*

Alex, standing next to his door, heard Mr. Kelly half whisper, "Who said that?"

"*Oh, Mista Kelly, I cain't tell you that! You know I cain't tell...*"

"Who said what, Herrick?"

"*Oh, man—don't make me tell you that. Those boys gonna whup me for sure. They mean, Mista Kelly. They really mean. They gonna whup—*"

"Okay, okay, Herrick, slow down now. Nobody's going to hurt nobody. Just tell me exactly what was said."

"*Oh, Mista Kelly, I don't wanna do that! You know I cain't do that!*"

"Herrick, either you tell me what's going on up here, or you're the one I'm going to punish."

In a moment The King was whispering again, more softly, and Alex, his ear close to the hole in his door, heard only a word here and there. Then, after a pause, Mr. Kelly said, "Okay, Herrick, you just stop worrying now. No one's going to hurt you. Come on now, get your room shaped up."

Mr. Kelly came along then, knocking and unlocking the doors, shouting "Let's go!" as always. In and out of the washroom the others looked at The King, silently, and The King kept his eyes elsewhere. The new man was last in line.

Downstairs, when they filed over to the upstairs table, Mr. Kelly kept The King back and directed him to a seat at another table. Then, when they were settled and all was silent, Mr. Kelly called on The King to give the blessing. The King, withdrawing his legs from under the table and standing, did not look down as the others had, he looked up, almost straight up at the ceiling, and placed his hands together under his chin. He said:

> "For every cup and plateful,
> God make us truly grateful."

Red Eye snorted, in order not to laugh; Alex and Leonard and Thomas laughed just slightly, and Alex, looking down at his bowl, bit his lip and sat shaking through most of the breakfast, and shed tears, so as not to laugh out loud.

At the end of the meal Mr. Kelly was standing at the end of their table. He pointed at Red Eye, Alex and Billy Noname, and said, "You, you, and you. Let's go."

In the kitchen he put them to work washing the baseboards under the stainless-steel sinks and counters. The steamy air of the kitchen, the people working there, the sweat and labor—these were no small change after the dirt and sloth of upstairs; the noise alone of pots and pans and faucets running was exciting. On their hands and knees they saw the other three boys led out of the dining room, and they looked at one another. They also looked at one another and looked at a pair of raw legs coming from a beltless cotton dress, knowing they belonged to a big-boned girl of about thirteen. In a few minutes, when Mr. Kelly came back and called them from under the counters, Alex could hardly stop thinking of what was up under the sack dress, however homely the girl, however sweaty, however stringy her hair over her ears. With the others, trying to look at the girl, he followed Mr. Kelly into the hall. Going along, Mr. Kelly said, "I got a nice dirty job for you boys." Looking at one another now, they knew what had happened.

Still, there was something a little joyous about the break in routine. Whatever it was, it was different, a small adventure. They were also spending some time with Mr. Kelly himself, like pupils with the teacher. In the familiar locker room, Mr. Kelly rummaged through a cardboard box, coming up with three jackets, laundered but greatly wrinkled, which he gave them to put on. Alex recalled that Mr. Kelly had whipped his face in this room over the cigarettes, but it seemed now to have happened long ago, in a past year, to another person.

Wearing the jackets, they followed Mr. Kelly along a hallway in a direction they had never taken before. Red Eye, first in line behind Mr. Kelly, gave a middle finger to the ceiling, and Alex and Billy smiled with the excitement of the adventure.

They marched down a flight of stairs, passing part of the laundry works—there was the odor of the sheets—and entered a cool tunnel-shaped corridor, which grew darker along its length. At the other end Mr. Kelly, in almost full darkness, unlocked a door and opened it, and there was the light, a sudden air on their faces, in their noses, the chill of outdoors. A gray spreading of chrome was over the sky, spreading into gray-blue. The breeze raised a little tuft of Mr. Kelly's hair, as he told them to come along. They followed. It was cold this morning. It must have been six or six-fifteen by now. The air was startling and Red Eye raised no fingers.

They crossed an open space of thirty or forty feet, walking near the red brick wall of a building, and came to a smaller brick building, windowless, from whose rear a red brick chimney rose, narrowing far into the sky. Mr. Kelly opened a green, copper-looking door with a small wire-meshed window in its upper half, and they entered. The building was partially dark and instantly warm. They were on a metal landing, and below, hollowing down, was a space twice as deep as the above-ground part of the building. Mr. Kelly said, "Down we go," and they filed down metal stairs, turned at a landing and followed down another flight, where they saw two black furnaces which filled one side of the room, shedding orange-white light downward from their door edges.

A man in khaki pants and shirt appeared from under the stairs. Standing before him, Mr. Kelly outlined their job. They were first to clean up the coal and coal dust which lay along a coal chute, then, when the coal trucks came, they were to push the coal back into the bins—there were two bins, like large stalls—filling the space to the ceiling, then they were to sweep up whatever coal had been spilled, and then they were to help load the ashes, and finally they were to sweep and swab down the furnace room, furnaces, walls and the steps. If they worked fast, they could finish by lunch. They were to work without talking, and they were to obey "this gentleman, Mr. Hamson."

Mr. Kelly climbed the stairs then and left. Mr. Hamson said, "Don't make no difference to me if you boys talk, just so you keep it down."

They stood waiting. Mr. Hamson, a man in his fifties, partially bald and paunchy, said, "Fact, you might as well take it easy for a while. Those boys won't be here with the coal anyway before seven or later, and it don't take but twenty, thirty minutes at the most to clear that chute there. You fellas keep a secret?"

He looked at them. "Smoke?" he said.

They all three took cigarettes, Pall Malls—which Alex's father smoked—and lit up. Mr. Hamson said, "Heck, I like to get along with the boys they send me over here to work. No reason not to, is there? That's the way I see it. What you boys in here for?"

They stood smoking, as if waiting for someone else to answer.

"Well, I guess you don't much care to talk about it. That's okay. I generally don't ask the boys anyway, ya know."

They stood smoking the long cigarettes, the smoke as strange and as strong as cigar smoke. Alex was feeling a little whoozy.

Mr. Hamson said, "Well. I'm going to sit at my place over here. You fellas take it easy for a while. Unless," he whispered, "that door up there opens. You get on the brooms and get to looking busy if it does."

He returned to the space under the stairway where there was a table and a chair, and removed a newspaper from a wastebasket. A lunch bucket was on the table, next to a thermos bottle and cup, and a lighted light bulb hung from a heavy wire overhead. On the wall above the desk, behind a glass face and wire mask, was a large clock with a sweeping second hand.

Red Eye lowered to a seat on the floor first, then Alex and Billy Noname followed. They had sat there only a moment when Mr. Hamson said, "Well, fellas, ya know, maybe you better not sit down. Case somebody comes in."

They stood up; he returned to his paper.

When they began to talk, speaking of The King, laughing a little loudly over really whooping his ass, Mr. Hamson said, "Ya know, fellas, I think I'd keep it down pretty much if I was you. No telling if somebody ain't listening, ya know, like the man said."

And after only a couple more minutes, when they were coming to the ends of their cigarettes, he rose and stepped over and said, "Shoot, boys. I guess you might as well get started cleaning up the coal there. No telling who ain't gonna just walk in here on us, ya know? Might as well be working, anyway. That's the way I look at it. Get it done now, don't have to do it later, ya know?" He looked at them, and added, "Don't have to kill yourselves now. Just work along steady like, and you better flip your butts in that bucket there."

They did so, stepped over to a black bucket near the glowing furnace doors, dropped their cigarette butts in black water, and glanced at one another again, worried over this man who seemed afraid of everything, including themselves.

Pointing to Alex and Billy Noname, Mr. Hamson said, "You two work the chute here. Throw the coal back into the bins. And you," he said to Red Eye. "I guess you better get back in the bin there and when they throw the coal in, you get it and pile it as high back there as you can, 'cause we got a lot of coal coming and we'll need all the room we've got."

Alex and Billy worked along under the chute. The job was easy. They scooped the coal into coal shovels and pitched it back into the bin, where Red Eye had to shovel it up again and carry it several steps to the rear of the bin. Mr. Hamson whispered, puckering his lips to keep a straight face, "Hope you can see that black boy back there not to hit him."

Still he could not check himself, and laughed as he returned to his chair and newspaper. And a moment later, when Red Eye called to them to throw it to one side where it was easier to scoop, the man said, "Keep it down now, boys. Like the man said."

Mr. Hamson seemed part of the punishment. He had spoiled whatever remained of the adventure, and now the work was becoming work. Alex felt remotely sour over the arrangement, but it was Billy Noname who moved. Saying nothing, he edged along the chute back into the bin, where two of the three should have been stationed in the first place. Alex felt left in the taint of Mr. Hamson, and disliked the man all the more. He heard Billy Noname laugh over something Red Eye had said, and wished he could join them.

It was impossible to finish in four hours. The first coal truck did not come until after eight and at ten o'clock and eleven o'clock they were still driving up, one every hour or so. Much of the coal tumbling and sliding down the chute kicked over onto the floor, and several times through each unloading the coal filled the chute and stopped sliding, so Alex had to reach with his shovel to unclog it and push it down as Red Eye worked to clean the end of the chute. Billy Noname tried to maintain room by shoveling the coal to the rear of the bin, piling it up.

The coal dust rose and fell with each release from above, three or four clankings of the truck's mechanism for each load, and they were all three soon black with coal dust, their nostrils full, squinting and turning away when the clouds rose from the tumblings down. Alex coughed often, trying to clear his throat, and spat peppered saliva into the coal itself. Simple breathing made his throat wheeze, and he tried before long to do most of his breathing through his nose, until the insides of his nose, at the roof of his nostrils, also began to feel the irritation. He felt an urge, whatever it might cost him, to simply quit. He felt he was going to suffocate from inhalation of coal dust. But the others kept working inside the bin, and he kept hoping this load, this tumbling of coal down the chute, this braying of the truck's motor, was the last. He was hit a good many times by flying pieces of coal—they were no larger than wood chips—but this was nothing next to the difficulty of breathing. He worked on, shoveling, walking shovelfuls over to pitch them in, clearing the chute, playing games of looking and not looking at the clock, of believing this load had to be the last load, for the time was running on, then not glancing at the clock for another twenty or thirty minutes, until the end of another load.

Close to noon, he thought they had to be near the end. Mr. Kelly could not have been that far off in the hours, and he could not really deny them their lunch. He must have known in the first place that they were innocent. Still he did not show. Alex seemed to pick up a second wind, but every time he thought they were cleaning up the last of the load, another truck pulled up, braying again, raising its rear, and the coal came tumbling and sliding down.

They worked through the lunch hour. Alex kept looking at the clock now, thinking they would still be called to lunch before the food was put away and the kitchen closed. Then, at one o'clock, Mr. Kelly appeared in the furnace room, but fifteen minutes later, after eating a lunch of remains in the cafeteria, they were back in their places shoveling coal, several truckloads still tumbling down the long chute.

When they finished, when they had the chute completely cleared again and still no truck came, when they had swept up the spilled chunks and the dust, and there was no room left to stand in either bin, and still no truck came, it was exactly twenty-one minutes to three. They paused, their chins on their broom and shovel handles.

Mr. Hamson had been in and out during the morning, had eaten his wax-papered lunch and his two apples from his lunch pail at the table, and now, as they stood leaning, he came over, sucking a toothpick.

They did not move.

As if blind to their accomplishment, and to their finishing, and to their exhaustion, to the chute which had been swept clean enough to reveal its scratched steel surface, to the coal stacked ceiling-high in the bins, he said that he'd move the chute back himself but they had better get the rest of the dust by the edge of the bins. Red Eye pivoted around on his handle away from the man, rocked his head back and forth, and did not look at him.

Then as they swept up the black dust, no more than a cup on one of the shovels, Red Eye sang:

> "Bustin my ass wid two-by-fours
> Bustin my ass wid scrubbin floors
> Ain't no doors, ain't no hoes . . ."

And he called out, "Hey, man! Hey, you got any more cigarettes?" He seemed loose enough to use his shovel broadside on the man's head.

They met in the center of the room and the man threw up Pall Malls again in his package. He avoided looking at them. Alex felt bold himself, felt an absence of fear, a presence of humorous cruelty. He laughed for no reason as he accepted a light from Mr. Hamson's hand. Then the man retreated to his table, left them smoking, and Alex's feeling settled.

For the ashes job, Alex worked on the truck outside, as instructed, and Red Eye and Billy Noname worked inside. Alex went up the metal stairway and outside again, carrying a shovel, and walked around the building to a lower side. He was alone for the passage of perhaps fifty feet, and coughing as an excuse to stop, bending over to spit peppered gobs of saliva, he scrutinized the fence, some two hundred feet away, along Lincoln Road. He had no real intention of trying to escape, but as if the role had been forced upon him, he acted it out in part, assumed the sense of a prisoner in a penitentiary movie, where escape was nearly always the issue.

The truck stood, braked, on a steep ramp with walls close on both sides. The man behind the wheel was asleep. His head was slumped to one side, his ear on his shoulder, his mouth slightly open. Feeling high and angry and sad, Alex kicked the tire under the cab to wake the man, but it made no noise. So he pitched up his shovel, clanging, into the bed of the truck, and climbed up as noisily as he could, kicking and stomping, then stomping the bed of the truck as if to clean his shoes. He saw Red Eye's face at a small window overhead, almost filling the window. Although Red Eye probably could not hear him through the glass, Alex roared, "LET'S GO! LET'S GO! LET'S GO!" in imitation of Mr. Kelly, feeling crazy enough to run or to sit down and cry.

The door of the cab opened then and the man stood on the running board to look around at him. "Hey, what's going on?" he said.

"We're loading this truck, man!" Alex shouted at him, laughing, feeling mean. "We're loading this truck. Let's go! Let's go!"

The man stared at him for a moment, then withdrew into the cab again, closed the door.

Ashes. They came sliding down an outside chute. The coal had been coated with dust, but the ashes, with the exception of occasional clinkers, were entirely dust. The chute, apparently loaded inside, overhead, by Red Eye and Billy Noname, directed the ashes into the rear of the truck bed, and it was Alex's job to spread them around so they would continue to flow. He pushed the ashes forward at first, but the wind was wrong and a cloud of gray rose immediately and he stepped to the front himself where the air was more clear. But then the hill of ashes around the chute became so high that it covered the end, spilling over the sides, and blocked the flow. He closed his mouth, squinted his eyes nearly closed, and stepped back into the

side of the loose hill to push the ashes around. Now, perhaps from the break and from the change to cold air, his
muscles seemed wound tight, and he shoveled more slowly,
with less strength.

Before long the powder cloud had puffed up overall,
and there was no way to escape but to try for footing on
the ashes at the side of the truck, to stick his head out of
the cloud. When he had gotten some air into his lungs, and
blinked his eyes a few times, he tightened his face again
and waded back in.

The ashes kept flowing. He worked with his mouth and
eyes completely shut now, as a blind man, and finally, when
all at once it seemed he was losing his breath, in anger and
in something of a panic, he quit. He dropped his shovel over
the side, climbed blindly over the side himself, feeling his
way, and dropped to the ground. He moved up the ramp
past the front of the truck, into the clear air, bending his
head and neck as low as his waist, trying to contain the
gritting irritation in his eyes. His eyes watered and as he
forced them open, he saw only a blur of liquid. Stopping,
he blew his nose, coughed the powder from his throat. He
was before the truck in the clear air this way for some time,
a full four or five minutes, getting his eyes to where he
could see shapes and colors through the blur, when the
truck driver called out, "Hey—you! Where you going?
You better get back here!"

Alex gave him a wild finger, coming up from the waist,
although he barely saw the man. He looked down again,
fingering the water and grit from the corners of his eyes.
The man said no more and Alex did not look to see if he
had moved or not. He was sure he was in trouble, and did
not care.

He stood there. After a couple of minutes, in less of a
blur, he saw Mr. Kelly, without his coat, half running
toward him from the main building. He looked down, continued working on his eyes.

"What are you doing?" Mr. Kelly said. "Why aren't
you working?"

"I couldn't see," Alex said. "I was blinded. I couldn't see."

Mr. Kelly said nothing for a moment.

Then, edging toward concern, he said, "Are you all right?"

"Yeah, I'll be all right," Alex said.

"What happened to you?"

"Nothing. I was just pushing the ashes around and the stuff got in my eyes. I couldn't breathe."

Mr. Kelly stood by him for a moment without speaking. Then he left, walking quickly over to the truck, and Alex heard him call up to the driver, "Didn't you know you're supposed to hose these ashes?"

Alex did not hear the man's answer. Mr. Kelly was mad, and that was a surprise. Squinting in that direction, he saw Mr. Kelly walking around the truck to the ramp, pointing, still talking to the man.

Then Mr. Kelly came back to him, "You sure you're all right?" he said.

"Yeah, I'll be okay," Alex said.

"Well, brush yourself off," Mr. Kelly said.

Alex slapped himself, turning away from the puffing dust.

"You better come with me," Mr. Kelly said, starting away.

Alex followed, pleased. He walked behind Mr. Kelly back across the open space, into the building and through the tunnel and upstairs to the first floor again. Mr. Kelly spoke once, when they were on the first floor. "I wanted to punish you," he said. "But I didn't intend to torture you."

Alex followed him through a pair of swinging doors, into rooms he had never seen before. There, suddenly, on the right, in the rest of a large warm room they were passing through, were two or three dozen children. The younger ones, up to seven or eight, were playing as children play in a kindergarten room, with blocks and games and torn books, a couple scratching on a black chalk slate which covered four or five feet of wall space. The scene, the children, passed like a horrible and wonderful moment in a dream. Alex wanted to stop and look, and watch, for it seemed he was about to see something—but he walked on, drawn by Mr. Kelly through another set of double swinging doors and turning left, into a bathroom.

There was not just one single sink here, but a line of seven or eight basins. And these were shining clean, the chrome polished, and there was a mirror on the wall. Mr. Kelly told him to rinse his eyes with water, so he bent over, cupping water in his hand from the running faucet and splashing it into one eye at a time. But the children's room he had just seen remained with him, moved through him, and he did not wish to open his eyes.

"Is that better?" Mr. Kelly said.

Alex nodded that it was, although his eyes felt cold but not much better.

"Here, let's have a look," Mr. Kelly said.

Alex held his head up and Mr. Kelly used his hands and fingers to spread open his eyelids to look in. "You still got specks in there," he said. "Does it hurt?"

"Not too much," Alex said.

"You can see all right?"

"Yes."

"I think you'll be all right. You go back now and finish up. I don't have to take you back, do I?"

"No," Alex said.

He walked back through the room of children, still behind Mr. Kelly, and he glanced again as he had before, and again it was as if he had come close to seeing something. But he was no longer sure if he wanted to see it. In the corridor Mr. Kelly went on, and Alex turned down the stairs and walked back across the open space alone. For the first time since coming there he felt a desire, a child's desire, to see his father, to be with his father and not to be alone.

The driver was on the bank opposite the truck, spraying water from a hose over the ashes in the truck. There was little dust now, only that which escaped when the coating of wet muck was peeled off in shoveling. Alex felt no fear of the man and did not look at him as he worked. Nor did he feel much strength. He shoveled, one shovel after another, slipping them to the front. Another truck had pulled up to wait its turn.

They worked through what was left of the afternoon and then through the dinner hour. Mr. Kelly did not come this time to take them to the cafeteria. While Alex worked outside on the trucks, Mr. Hamson had been replaced by a man coming on another shift, a man whose name he did not learn and who said little to them. They slacked off when they saw they had missed supper. Then, inside again, under the dim hanging lights, when they had finished sweeping and washing down the walls and the furnaces and it was dark outside, they hosed the floor and swept the water into a drain in the center, and hosed it again, and then again, until the water began to wash partially clean. The floor dried quickly in spots from the heat of the furnace. Then, once again, they stood waiting on their broom handles while the new man telephoned Mr. Kelly. They were too tired to talk very much. By the wall clock, it was past their bedtime; it was five minutes past eight.

Mr. Kelly wore a navy-blue pea jacket. Going back, they crossed ahead of him through the darkness, through the chilling air, and back into the warm building. Mr. Kelly seemed sleepy, and said nothing. But then, in the quiet and nearly dark first-floor hallway, he asked them, "Tired?"

They were, but no one spoke.

"Want something to eat? You hungry?"

They nodded, surprised, and he told them to go wash up and he'd see if he could find something. Alex led them through the swinging doors to the shining bathroom he had used earlier, which was lighted, as if for night use, with a single light. In the mirror they looked like coal miners. Red Eye said to the mirror, softly, "Who is that? I don't know him." Strangely happy, they combed their hair with their

hands, and whispered when they talked as if close to someone sleeping. Alex said, "I think that's the boys' dormitory," pointing toward the unknown end of the building.

One door to the dining room stood opened. Inside, a
couple of overhead globes were lighted. They walked in
cautiously. A half-gallon tin tub without a label was on the
table nearest the kitchen opening, under one of the lights.
Mr. Kelly was in the kitchen, standing, slicing bread with
a knife. They stood waiting until he came in, carrying a
tray with the sliced bread in one hand and one of the metal
pitchers in the other, and told them to sit down. They
reached their legs in under the table and sat down. As
always in the dining room, they did not speak.

In a moment Mr. Kelly returned with a table knife and
four of the clear plastic glasses, which always looked dirty.
"Okay, dig in," he said, slipping into a seat on the bench
himself.

He poured himself a glass of milk and passed the
pitcher on. The tin tub, whose top he unscrewed, was half
filled with peanut butter, with oil puddles in its knifed
terrain. They followed Mr. Kelly, taking up two slices of
bread, spreading on a thickness of oily peanut butter, bit-
ing through their sandwiches, swallowing milk, reaching
for the pitcher again.

Mr. Kelly said, "Go ahead, drink all you want. There's
plenty of milk, plenty of bread."

Alex was surprised that Mr. Kelly was eating with
them. Then it occurred to him, with a small shock, that Mr.
Kelly lived there, that this was his home, that he seemed
never to leave.

They sat together as a momentary family. Almost
nothing was said. Mr. Kelly, as always, was distant.
But he sat there; he was present. At one point he said,
"You eat like you've been working," and they laughed
immediately, and with pride, and the man could not help
smiling himself. Alex saw his reflection, distorted, in the

tin tub. But he felt completely safe for the moment, safe
from something outside the lighted table itself, something
as large and as complicated as the city, which lay as if in
waiting, beyond the cold fields.

Three

The next morning the buzzer sang through his
mind as if in a dream, and he came close to waking, and
then fell away into a sea of sleep again. He was asleep
when Mr. Kelly rapped on the door, and his feet had just
touched the floor as Mr. Kelly entered. But Mr. Kelly gave
him no whacks; the man said, "Come on, Housman. Let's
go." And it was just as well that Alex had not dressed,
for Mr. Kelly threw some clean clothes on the cot, and
holding a cloth bag with a drawstring, told Alex to throw
in his dirty clothes, which Alex did, through the cobwebs
of his sleep, and Mr. Kelly moved on.

Alex pulled his bed together and dressed. The blue
jeans and the shirt, an ex-navy work shirt faded bluish
white, were larger than the others and fit more comfortably. He hurried to the sink to give his teeth a quick brush,
and to get some cold water on his face, to push his un-
cooperative thickness of hair into place. But with the exchange of clothes everyone was late, and he stood waiting
at the door ahead of the others. He had forgotten until
now that The King had moved downstairs.

From the window in the end room he looked out behind
the building. The sky was still dark except for a gray line

around the horizon. The air looked even colder. Red Eye joined him at the window, and yawning deeply beside him, said, "Man, I ever sleep."

A moment later, in a spontaneous move of arm-flexing, they began slap-boxing, feinting, stepping and weaving. Mr. Kelly, coming to the doorway, stopped them with his presence.

Standing in the corridor then, waiting for the others to line up, an unusual thought came to Alex: he was feeling good, he was feeling an energy he had not felt, it seemed, since he was a small boy. But beside him, leaning against the wall as if hanging from a hook, Red Eye suddenly said, softly, "Say, would I ever like to go home," and his voice sounded so unhappy that Mr. Kelly said in a bluff voice, "Oh, come on, cheer up."

After breakfast they did not return immediately upstairs but followed Mr. Kelly to his office. There on the floor was a long wooden crate filled with books, and Mr. Kelly was saying that someone had donated them to the home and they could have them upstairs if they liked, as long as the books were not mistreated, were not torn or mutilated. No one said much of anything. They carried the box upstairs, Red Eye taking one end, Billy Noname the other. Placing it on the picnic table, they waited without touching for Mr. Kelly to leave, to see what they had.

Their disappointment was calm. They expected little. There were no photographs, no drawings, nothing but words packed on each fanned page as thickly as leaves on a tree. The first book grabbed—it had the only dust jacket, the only color—was called *The Egyptian*. It was dropped at once, by Leonard, and picked up by Thomas, who said, "The *what?*" Red Eye said, "Oh, man, the *Egyptian*, mummy stuff—man, you so dumb!"

The other books were old novels, books with pale and faded covers by authors named A. J. Cronin, Hans Hellmut Kirst, Virgil Scott, Jan Struther, Vincent Carr.

Alex was the only one who read, perhaps the only one

who could read, although Thomas sat with *The Egyptian* for a while before he pitched it back into the box. Billy No-name and the new man did not even bother looking, and the others, after scanning and fanning the pages, went back to the routine of standing at the window, sleeping on the floor. The new man had stretched out there again; and again, no one suggested shuffleboard.

Alex started to read a book called *Gunner Asch*, starting it mainly because he knew how to read, although he was intimidated by the mass of words. He had never read anything but the lessons in schoolbooks—assignments in history or science spaced with water colors of Washington crossing the Delaware or Thomas Edison working under candlelight. But the novel was simply written and fairly easy to understand, anl he soon became interested enough in what was happening to stop reminding himself page after page that he was reading a book, to turn the pages to see what was going to happen next.

He sat on the floor reading until he grew sleepy. When his eyelids began to slide down and his head began to cloud, he lay over on his side on the floor to sleep awhile, pulling up his knees, resting his head on his arm. When he woke he got up and carried the book with him to the bathroom. Billy Noname was standing at the corridor window, and the others seemed to be asleep, so there was no sound but that of their breathing. Alex, wondering how long he had slept, asked Billy Noname, "They been outside yet?" Billy made no move, said nothing, as if no one had spoken. Alex said no more. He went into the bathroom thinking Billy was off wherever he had come from, thinking they were all crazy in this place, which for a moment was not as if this were a violation.

Sitting in the bathroom, reading the book again, he became so involved in the story that his legs fell asleep. He kept reading, intending to get up at the end of this page, then at the end of this page, if only because he would feel more comfortable with his pants up and buttoned, but he read on. He rose finally at the end of a chapter, although he read a little into the next chapter before he made himself stop. His legs were buoyant with saws and needles as he buttoned up, and he had to hold a hand against the wall not to sway from balance. Then he checked the thickness of pages he had read between his fingers, and experienced something he had never experienced before. Some of it was pride—he was reading a book—and some of it was a preciousness the book had assumed. Feeling relaxed, unthreatened, he wanted to keep the book in his hands, for what it offered. He did not want to turn the pages, for then they would be gone and spent; nor did he want to do anything but turn the pages.

He stepped over legs again and sat down to read, as far from anyone as he could get, some fifteen feet, to be alone with the book. He read on. Something was happening to him, something as pleasantly strange as the feeling he had had for Irene Sheaffer. By now, if he knew a way, he would prolong the book the distance his mind could see, and he rose again, quietly, to sustain the pleasant sensation, the escape he seemed already to have made from the scarred and unlighted corridor. Within this shadowed space there were now other things—war and food and a worry over cigarettes and rations, leaving and returning, dying and escaping. The corridor itself, and his own life, were less present.

He sat alone at the picnic table, for the light from the screened window. His heart rose to the bottom of his throat occasionally, and he stopped reading occasionally, to let his feelings settle and to enjoy an afterglow, and if he looked up, if he looked at the window, his eyes did not accurately focus on anything but took pleasure only from those things which moved within. It may have been war, which made large things small and small things large for those in the book, and for himself as well, and for the melding of the two. Mr. Kelly could not have known, nor did Alex have any idea himself, how ripe he had been to be taken by a book. Confinement and quiet. It was so pleasant that he feared he would be caught for doing something wrong, as if it were not only the life in the pages of the book which had taken breath in the reading, but his own, as if this were a violation.

After lunch, when they filed from the dining room to return upstairs, Mr. Kelly handed Alex an envelope, saying only, "Letter for you." Alex took the letter as if it were something that happened every day, noted with alarm that it was from his father and pushed it into his hip pocket. He had never received a letter before. Upstairs, he sat on the floor and used his opened book as a prop and as concealment, feeling embarrassed that his father was there, if only by letter. He read this:

> *Dear Alex,*
>
> *I won't be able to see you for a while now, so they tell me, and I don't suppose you have a private phone in your room, so here is a note from your old dad to tell you where we stand.*

("*Your old dad.*" He'd had a few when he wrote.)

> *I talked to Johny Boyle the lawyer and told him they had my boy over there and he says there is not much we can do now until they let you come back home. I am not going to hire any lawyer for I think that might just make some old judge want to show how tough he can be. And they got all the cards in their hand. The smart thing to do is to be patient and to do as I told you before. I won't let you down on this end no matter what happens. So don't you worry.*
>
> *Listen son, I want you to know how sorry I am this has happened. It's like I said before. It's more my fault than it is yours and if we are smart we can make it turn out for the better and not the worse. And I mean the better. I'm sorry it came to this but living alone now as I am I come to see a few things I guess I should have*

seen before. I guess I just took my boy for granted right along and thought you would always just be here when I came home. I guess I've managed most of my life to mess up the things around me. I know your mother had about every reason to leave me as she did. I wasn't much good for her with the old jug and all before I was called up and she wasn't much good for me either and I knew the first day I left if I ever saw her again it wouldn't be for long. I don't suppose I ever told you but we didn't write more than a half dozen letters to each other all the time I was in. I knew what she was up to and it was about all I ever thought about and am lucky I didn't get my rear end shot off. All I thought about was catching her. I never thought about her in any other way. And I know now if I didn't know it then that I just wanted to catch her so I could blame her and not myself. Now here I've messed up again what I care for the most. And I don't know what to do. I know it is not enough to be sorry. If I thought it would do any good I would gladly blow my brains out. Only that might just make things worse for you than they are.

What we have got to do is not going to be easy. We got to get our house together here so that judge will let you come back home to live. This means we have got to be pretty tough and smart. We can't feel sorry for ourselves for a minute. Listen son even if everything went real bad and they decided to send you over to Lansing you are going to have to be real tough because that will only be for a short time and then when you get out you will still have your whole life before you. I won't mention that again and lets hope it never comes to that but if it does we don't want to fall to pieces just because we are not ready for it. I don't want to scare you and I don't want you to think I won't do whatever I can but like I say they got just about all the cards and all we got left is to be tough. If we can do that then we will make it okay no matter what they do to us.

Boy oh boy do I ever miss having you at home. To know every night when I come in that your room is empty and you are not here is pretty rough. I remember when I went to pick up you and Howard and we set up housekeeping here and the good times we had then. We made out okay then and I know we can do it again when you come home.

Don't forget what I told you now. I mean before. Because I couldn't stand to lose my old pal.

Love, Pop

He sat for a moment looking at the letter before he folded it and put it in his shirt pocket. He sat back against the wall. The letter made him think of Howard, and of his leaving. It seemed now that everything had started its fading when his mother took Howard away. He had been too ashamed at the time, or since, to tell anyone, hardly himself, how badly it had hurt. He thought of it only as a bad time, a bad day.

He and Howard on the run—there was a daydream possibility. And suddenly, leaning against the wall, for the first time ever, he felt an urge to give up school. He had always seen quitting school as something terrible and stupid, and now, all at once, leaving school looked as rich to his mind as life itself—to join the army, the navy, the merchant marine, to go away, he and Howard on the run.

There in his lap was the book. He felt little desire to read it now, as if he could not sit still, as if he were nervous again, or afraid. It seemed incredible that only an hour ago he had been so taken by the book that he had felt close to making a turn in his life, close to seeing something, to beginning something simple and important. Now he felt like himself again; he felt like a punk. Still, taking up the book, he tried. But the interference remained. At the end of a few sentences, a paragraph, he had no idea what he had read. He started over, and tried again, and still it did not work. Then, and he had not heard him, the new man

was stepping over his legs, and as he instinctively pulled
them up to give room, the new man's foot caught on his
knee and he stumbled to catch his balance, and immediately, six or eight feet down the corridor, he was facing Alex and spitting words Alex hardly understood,
screaming wildly, *"WATCHOUTTAMAWAYMUHFUCK
—STOMPMUHFUCKINASSMAN!"*

By its corner, backhanded, enraged suddenly with the
book and with himself as much as with the new man, Alex
fired the book at him—it sailed past his side—and threw
a wild finger at him. Alex said nothing. He looked at the
new man from where he sat. Nor did the new man speak;
he stood there. Then, raising his chin as if to spit the
words, he said, *"Shit! Man!"* and he turned and walked on,
moving his shoulders very high, picking up his feet clearly
one at a time.

Alex sat still, growing quickly frightened. His heart
was beating faster and there seemed no place to look with
his eyes. A pressure rose in his bowels; it was too small a
place to have an enemy and he could not believe it was so
easily over. He sat, trying to sit still, trying to answer some
question which would not shape itself—but then, in a
moment, it seemed to be answered for him. He was getting
to his feet, mainly to show himself, and anyone who might
notice, that he was not at all afraid, although he was
trembling, and it happened that the new man came walking
from the room then, down the corridor, and without a
word, hardly a look, he raised his fists like a boxer coming
from his corner, and Alex, who could also imitate a boxer,
raised his own fists.

The new man came on, walking, weaving his fists. They
traded an immediate exchange, girlishly high, neither of
them hitting anything more than the other's tightly sprung
forearms and wrists and hands. Both drew back a step or
two, both were dancing from foot to foot, revolving their
fists. Leonard appeared in the doorway of the room and
said to the others within, "Hey, fight—fight." The others

pushed at once into the end of the corridor, as Alex and the new man danced before each other, each in his own rhythmic pattern of bob and weave, the new man feinting with his head as if ducking punches, as if waiting for the audience to settle, as if boxing before a mirror.

"Comeownman!" the new man said, but he stayed a distance back.

Alex moved after him, dancing, and the new man danced back just as far, a step or two. Alex moved another step closer. He was less afraid now, seeing fear in the other boy. He jumped at him then, going high, swinging more than punching, and clipped the new man once, just over his forehead, and received no blows, no swings, in return. The fight ended, or turned, at this moment for Alex. Frightened to trembling a moment before, he was feeling in control of himself, and the new man was clearly going the other way. The new man was hardly moving his hands or head by now, but holding them nearly stiff, moving his feet some, keeping his hands high as if to protect his head.

Alex moved after him again and the new man backed away again. This time he backed into the others as they were edging around him to leave room, and deciding in quite a clear strategy to go for his head, to hit his head, to really hit it as much as he could, Alex moved after him, or into him, quickly, backing him against the door, swinging and punching with both fists at the new man's head in a flurry of slaps and thumps of hits and misses—but then, as if becoming more frightened, the new man only pressed to the door with his side, trying to keep his head covered with his hands and arms, moving but not fighting back. Alex hit him several times, on his temples, his forehead, but mainly he hit his arms and hands. The new man withdrew into the corner beside the door, where he was stopped altogether, but Alex did not stop hitting him, or hitting at him, thumping his arms, running out of breath. He stopped swinging then and the new man suddenly grabbed into him, getting a grip partway around one of Alex's arms, and around his waist, as Alex was trying to pull back to pull himself free. The man stunk—it was the familiar odor of childhood wrestling fights on dirt driveways and playgrounds, an odor of yellow earwax, of perspiration. Breaking his grip by pushing him down, pulling his arm free, Alex stepped back, and the new man remained on the floor.

Alex stepped back farther, breathing fast and watching. But the new man remained on the floor. The others also moved back as Alex moved back. He stopped then and stood panting to catch his breath, beginning to tremble some again, concealing it by shaking his arms and moving them as if to shake himself loose. The others came up, and stood there, and no one seemed to know what to say or do.

The new man sat up then, and leaned over slightly against the wall, but he made no move to stand and he did not look in their direction. He began touching the tips of his fingers to one eyebrow, then looking at his fingers. But there was no blood; he was not hurt. Nor had the fight been fierce enough to raise any general tension. Leonard said, behind Alex, "Man, you a tiger, I ain't messin wid yo ass."

Alex laughed some in a giddy way, still trembling, but he felt no satisfaction of having won anything. The others were talking now, moving about, ignoring the new man except in glances, and Alex went on down the corridor to urinate. He was still trying to understand why the new man had acted so tough, had acted so tough with The King, and looked so tough—but he could not understand and it frightened him some, especially with the boy still sitting there, still silent. Alex had thoughts of knives, of razors and throats and darkness.

In the corridor again he looked at the new man but he still sat feeling his eyebrow, looking at his fingers. Walking past him, carefully but trying not to show it, Alex picked up the book and walked back, and sat down again, some fifteen feet from him. He was trying again to show that he was calm, while he was trembling lightly. Only Billy Noname remained in the corridor, at the end by the window. Alex glanced at the new boy again. Now he was weaving his head around some, as if he were dizzy, but he still did not look up. Alex called to him, "Hey, man, you okay?"

The boy looked up sharply, and stared at him, but did not speak.

In spite of himself, wishing he had not spoken in the first place, Alex said again, "You okay?"

Making a face, the boy said suddenly, "Ah know you."

Alex said nothing.

"You play basketball! Ah see you play basketball!"

Alex still said nothing.

"Yeah!" the boy said.

Alex said, "Man, you're fucking crazy."

The boy took a second to weigh this and then he splurted a sudden, hard nose laugh, showing his gums and teeth, and Alex felt the network of tension leave him. He also laughed, or snorted, and he said, "You're crazy as a fucking loon, man."

The boy jellied with laughter.

Alex, still sitting, leaning against the wall, carried on, in relief. He said, "You're crazy as a fruitfucking cake, man." Then he said, "You're crazy as a poppinfucking jay, man. You're crazy as a nest of bumblefuckingbees, man."

The boy, weeping tears of laughter, began calling out, "Hey! You mah man! You mah man!" Alex, exhausted, sweated, leaning against the wall, was laughing with him, descending as if around and around in a whirlpool, until he was also laughing tears slightly mad, until his stomach ached, and his cheeks, the tears running to drops on his cheekbones, also ached, until, for a moment, he washed away into a sea faintly insane.

Two boys, both white, were committed, one at a time. Leonard and Thomas were moved downstairs and no longer sat with them in the dining room. Alex did no more reading; the conditions never became right again.

He went back to standing at the window, sitting occasionally at the table, lying on the floor, talking a couple of times with Red Eye about the Golden Gloves fighters and halfbacks whose names they knew. He daydreamed and fantasized often over his own past, pleasant times when he and Howard were together, their escapades, their running, climbing, stealing. Odd moments also rose, the two of them merely walking to school on frosty fall mornings, on winter mornings, playing football as darkness fell on a dog-dung-smelling grassy field. It seemed to Alex that he had never looked back before, and there was a reservoir of moments there to see, if he tried to see them. Still the days continued long—a day at The Lincoln Hotel lasted a full twenty-four hours—and at times, often in the evening, or in bed, as if obsessed with the past, he seemed a child in the present, unable to understand, to see very clearly, his physical surroundings.

As he was dressing one morning, Mr. Kelly, carrying sheets and pillowcases under his arm, gave him the news: he was to strip and remake his bed, he was moving downstairs.

Packing his toothbrush, his comb and soap and extra clothes into his paper bag, remaking his bed, he grew weak with the news. In the hall, waiting for the line to form to go downstairs, he felt that some move or smile or gesture might cancel his fortune, and like a child again, he stood still and looked around constantly without looking directly at much of anything. Then Red Eye and Billy Noname came with their possessions in hand, and he knew it was true.

Downstairs the three of them were separated from the line at the dining-room door and led by Mr. Kelly past the bathroom where they had washed off the coal dust and into a room called the Boys' Dormitory. It was a long room with a row of large screened windows, with two rows of cots, perhaps forty altogether, a couple of feet apart. The cots upstairs had been covered with ex-navy blankets, and these were covered with ex-army blankets, greenish brown and also hard-grained. The three of them were assigned cots in different places throughout the room. Each cot had a small wooden chest pushed underneath, where Mr. Kelly told them to store their things. Lining them up to go to breakfast, he told them if they caused any trouble of any kind it was back upstairs at once. Marching to the kitchen, Red Eye, tickled to have made it downstairs, first in line, raised his arms and exaggerated his shoulders and muscles in a marching pose behind Mr. Kelly. Billy Noname, as always, and like Alex, gave no sign more than gleeful smiling.

They were directed to a table among the younger children, near the girls and the staff. The King himself was one table over, and the three who had remained upstairs were across the room at the upstairs table. By their separation they already appeared meaner and more criminal; the muscular black boy looked like a small-eyed bull again.

Mr. Kelly called on a girl named Wanda to say grace, and close now, Alex watched the girl. She was frightened, shaking all over as she withdrew her legs from under the table. Not once did she look at anyone, or anywhere but at an unmoving space just below eye level. She was about ten, and thin, her arms looking little larger than pool cues coming from the large sleeves of her dress, and she was both sad and pretty in her thinness.

Mr. Kelly said, "Let us bow our heads," and she closed her eyes tight.

Alex watched her from an angle. He glanced, moving his eyes, at the others, the five- and six-year-olds, the eight-, nine-, ten-year-olds, those nearly his own age. They looked less like children this close. The girls in their sack dresses, their rough and unbrushed, unshining hair, the boys in their flannel shirts, some with eyes opened, as vacant as fish, some with eyes closed. They might have been missing an eighth or a quarter or a third of something hard to name or measure. And so he had to wonder if he was missing anything himself, and knew that he could not know. He thought of the fight he'd had with the new man upstairs, whose odor had made him think of himself at seven and eight and nine, and he suddenly remembered a time, wrestling on the school playground, when a boy, quitting, had said to him, "You smell."

After breakfast the three of them were assigned to one of the women in white who worked in the kitchen. She was a short two-hundred-pounder who looked like a washing machine. Red Eye and Billy Noname were given jobs in the dining room wiping tables, centering the salt and pepper shakers, and Alex was led to the kitchen and given a job washing pots and pans, the cylindrical metal oatmeal tubs, the milk pitchers. It was a dirtier job, but there in the kitchen were some of the older girls, the twelve- and thirteen-year-olds, and almost immediately, and by accident, he turned around with two pitchers in each fist, and his right elbow, his sleeve rolled high, struck a girl passing behind him in the breast so hard into her sponginess that it hurt her, and at once he said, "Oh—I'm sorry."

She smiled, embarrassed, smiled more, and went on, and he looked after her. He looked at her legs where they were exposed, her ankles, imagining her body within the hanging dress. She was perhaps thirteen and something in her added smile seemed to say that if they were alone, and if he asked her gently and directly, they would each remove their clothes and go to bed and love each other all day. Washing and rinsing the pots and pans, he kept facing the sink to conceal himself, side-stepping to the adjoining sink, turning back across the aisle to retrieve more dirty pans and pitchers only when no one was nearby, looking for the girl. Then she was coming by again as before and they smiled at each other lightly as she passed. It was clear that she had no small appetite for this herself. He had slept well, the work had raised his energy, and looking after her, he felt something he had never felt in the corridors of Central High School: he felt protective of her, he desired her mere presence, she allowed him to feel his strength.

She had gone to the pantry at the end of the long kitchen; in a moment she was coming back again. They played the game with their eyes as they had before, smiling lightly, in strange happiness. As she passed she looked back at him over her shoulder. He was looking after her, his hands in the suds, as she went around the corner.

In just a moment she came back again. She smiled as before, looking at him continuously, until she passed behind him again, and she glanced back at him on her way to the pantry. Then, returning from the pantry, it was she and not he who did the brushing. She passed close enough for her arm and the side of her dress, and some of her side within, to touch his back and side in passing, and he looked after her, and even as it occurred to him that she was in some way a little crazy (unless his elbow striking her breast had set loose something uncontrollable), the fact that she so clearly wanted him just as he wanted her made him think he would just as soon stay there and wash pots and pans all day if only to sustain the pleasant sensation, made him vow to himself that when he got out of there he'd have himself a girl like that if he had nothing else, made him think that he might prepare a note to slip her tomorrow to arrange a meeting when they both got out, made him think that he could love her not for an hour or an evening or even a night or a day, but on and on, without end. But when he turned back again, there was Mr. Kelly, wiggling a finger for him to follow.

He tried to get another look at the girl as he left the kitchen, but she had not come back yet. He followed Mr. Kelly, and joining Red Eye and Billy Noname, they went down the stairway again to the basement. Alex was assigned to the laundry, left with a man in white shirt and white pants who, like the man in the furnace room, did not eat any meals at the staff table in the dining room. The man, rheumy-looking, half bald, talked to Alex without looking at his face, instructing him to fold and stack several bins of fluffed towels and sheets and pillowcases.

Alex went to work, whipping the towels, folding them in half, folding them over twice more, and placing them in stacks. It was extra warm in the laundry area, a large yellow cylindrical dryer humming and tumbling steadily, giving off heat, concealing him there somehow with its noise, and before long he was off into a world of working and daydreaming of the girl from the kitchen, folding one towel after another, walking with the girl, living with her, touching her, dreams in which she smiled as continuously as she had upstairs. When he heard the man's voice call, *"Hey, you,"* he was a moment returning from his dream of the girl, and turning, as the man yelled, much louder, "YOU THERE, KID," facing him, he returned too far, came up glaring at the man all at once as if to cut him with his eyes. But he frightened himself more, finally, than he did the man. Going on to obey the man's orders, to push a button, to empty the dryer, he was trembling over the gulf in the moment.

The longest part of the day followed. They went to school. Mr. Kelly came back with Red Eye and Billy Noname, and they walked in a marching line upstairs again. From the recreation room, where all the boys were now gathered, they were given a few minutes to use the bathroom. Returning, they stood about the room until Mr. Kelly announced, "Let's go to school now. Time to go to school."

They followed into a connecting room which was lined with rows of old school desks, desks with black iron scrollwork on their sides, a row of windows across the back, a section of blackboard in front. It was like an old one-room schoolhouse. The children went on to take their seats and Mr. Kelly assigned the three new boys desks separated from one another. The others were all withdrawing books and notebooks and pencils from their desk openings. One came up with a zippered Scotch-plaid pencil purse, another with a six-inch plastic ruler with a pencil sharpener on one end. The familiar milk globes hung overhead, unlighted this overcast day, and in the absence of light it was a pathetic imitation of a classroom.

To Alex the room was a room from the past. The air was like that in a dream, dreaming of a place or moment he had not known he even remembered. There was a quality as well in the dim room of knowing-then-what-he-knew-now, as if he had in fact returned to take a seat in the second or third or fourth grade, as if around him was the simple evidence of himself he had been unable to see at the time. A boy of eight or so sat next to him, underfed, his hair thick, uncombed, his neck dark with the grime of his life, and Alex's childhood flared before his mind's eye now as nothing. He did not know what he had missed. But he knew now that he had been cheated in a way he could still not quite understand. The children there, himself included —they were the wards of the city, the strays.

Mr. Kelly sat with Billy Noname at his desk. He whispered to Billy and removed books from his desk which he opened and pointed to. The children horseplayed some, behind Mr. Kelly's back, but only a little, and quietly. When Billy had been put to work, Mr. Kelly walked over to sit with Red Eye for a few minutes, and then he came and sat down on the edge of Alex's seat. He whispered, so close that Alex could smell his breath, asking, What grade was he in, in school? Did he know how to spell? Could he read well enough? Did he have any problems with numbers? Since Alex was perhaps the oldest boy there, Mr. Kelly did not have much to help him with. He explained to Alex, whispering, that this was not a regular class, they just worked at their desks reading and writing, and he left Alex at last with a confusing assignment, roughly to look over the books in his desk as a review, to use paper from the green book to write and figure on, to show some examples of his penmanship, and to write out his times tables from 2 to 12.

Alex removed the books. One was called *Our Country,* and the other looked like the remains of a legal-sized ledger. He had seen others like it around the recreation room. Two thirds of its pages had been torn out, but the remainder, a quarter of an inch, was clean and heavy, green-tinted, green-lined.

"Put your name in your book," Mr. Kelly said, and Alex looked up to see that Mr. Kelly was standing behind him.

He wrote his name with the stub of pencil, and Mr. Kelly, watching, said, "Well—your penmanship is good."

Alex opened *Our Country.* The first story started:

> One evening Mr. Harris said to his family, "This summer we are going to take a trip."
>
> "Where are we going?" asked Tommy and Sally.
>
> "Where would my family like to go?" laughed Mr. Harris.
>
> "Maine!" said the children, who had never been to Maine.
>
> "Maine!" said Mrs. Harris, who had been there only once.

Alex closed the book.

He wrote out his times tables from 2 to 12, two times, three times, four times, just as he had in the fifth grade. They came back to him with ease and with a nostalgia which made his heart fill with air. At the time, in arithmetic, taught by the most feared and brutal teacher in the school, Mrs. Hess, they had been disciplined by ruler slaps on the palms of their hands, and bribed by ten-minute readings at the end of each hour of *Huckleberry Finn,* whose drunken old man, whose adventures, had thrilled and educated Alex in a way he had never known.

When Mr. Kelly came by to look, Alex whispered, "May I write a letter?" before Mr. Kelly could suggest something else.

After a moment, nodding his head, Mr. Kelly gave him permission and moved on.

Alex turned to a fresh page in the ledger. Concealing the page with his shoulders, he tried to think of something to write to Howard. But afraid that what he wrote would be read by Mr. Kelly, he did more daydreaming than writing. He wanted to tell Howard some of the thoughts he had had these past days, but thinking them at the time, and writing them down now, were quite different. He could think of no words. The image of the dog pound came to mind again—the pens full of stray dogs, the yelping, the sickness, the smell of their droppings and urine, the smell of their scorched hair when they were put to death, their warm and lifeless bodies filling and overhanging the peach baskets. Although he knew why the thought came to mind, saw the simple comparison between the pens of the dog pound and these rooms of The Lincoln Hotel, still he saw little more, glimpsed no wisdom. Letting the memory slip off, he looked at the ledger again. At last, pressing the lead into the paper, he wrote:

Dear Howard,

I drove by your school the other day, only it was closed. I drove by the lake but did not see you or anybody around anywhere. I saw some kids on the road and thought you might be one of them, but you weren't.

You must be surprised getting a letter from me. I'll tell you I sure wish I could see you so we could talk instead of me writing in a letter. So we could do some things together. I'm in all kinds of trouble with John Law. To tell the truth that is sort of the reason I'm writing this letter. If I was not where I am at I probably would not be writing a letter. I'm in the juvenile home now and they said I could write a letter. It is not too bad here. I get along okay. The other guys here are okay. Only sometimes I can't even remember why I am here. You know what I mean. It would not be so bad if . we were in it together.

How you doing in school? You playing basketball anymore. You should be pretty good by now because of the good coach you had. Me. I could make the team at Central easy if I tried. Remember all the things we used to do. Remember how we used to go up to Hurley hospital to look in that ventilator at the stiffs in that room with a blue light. Or maybe it was yellow. I don't know. I know it sure used to scare me even if I didn't admit it at the time. We sure had a good time then. I wish it was like that now. Remember all the watermelons we used to steal from the train cars. And the hobos sleeping under the bridges. Remember that one guy we thought was dead with the bugs all over him. The worst time was those times we went to the dog pound. Remember that, how they kept putting those dogs in that little oven or whatever it was. I remember they put a wire on the dogs but I don't know if they were gassed or electrocuted. Boy that sure made me sick. Didn't it you?

I don't know why we never see each other anymore. I know one thing I really learned is when you get in trouble you sure wish you had a brother or something. If they send me away somewhere I'll write you a letter. They might send me to some training school or something. They might have me busting up rocks or something. If they do at least I'll get a good build out of it. I might not even mail this but if I do you write me a letter. Okay. So long for now.

Alexander's Ragtime Band

After school and before lunch, from eleven to twelve, they played outside. It was cool this first day, windy and overcast, football weather, but the boys played softball. Alex did not play. He wished to play, wished it as much as he ever had, but he was in a mood—it may have been the letter—and he sat on the side, the collar of his wrinkled jacket turned up, feeling like a convict. It was the first time he had ever watched a game of any kind when he could have joined, and he felt an urge to show off, to win, to be the best, but he also felt sad, or melancholy, and he wished to be alone, to neither talk nor move. He glanced several times at the windows where he had stood until now looking down, but he could see only the wire, nothing more than some white reflection from the sky on the glass, a whitish gray. He also glanced over at the girls' games for the girl from the kitchen, but she was not there. She may have been inside, locked in on the girls' side. He felt no desire now to talk to her, or to be with her, but it would have been pleasant to see her there. He thought of the dog pound again. Something about the dog pound always frightened him, and now he felt a chill, a sound passing in his ears. He worried over having given Mr. Kelly the letter to mail. Rising after a few minutes to file back into the building, he had an awareness of where he was, and the same sensation, the chill and the sound, came to him.

The afternoon was divided nearly the same as the morning. But something seemed to have happened to the girl from the kitchen. She was not in the dining room for lunch, and afterward, as he again washed the pots and pans, a longer, harder, dirtier job this time, he kept looking around for her, but she did not show.

Then, rather than working in the laundry room, he and Red Eye waxed and polished the woodwork and floor of a small room, using rags made of T-shirts and undershorts and wax from a five-gallon tub. Then they returned to the sad schoolroom, although the afternoon session was less than an hour long. Mr. Kelly spent as much time out of the room as in—Alex sat daydreaming, starting and crossing out dramatic love letters to Irene Sheaffer (*Dear Irene/I'm*

*thinking of you now, behind bars ... Dear Irene/If I never
see you again ...*), and then Mr. Kelly told them to clear
their desks, to line up to go outside.

The girl was still not among the girls who came outside
to play, and Alex stayed by himself again. The sky continued overcast, the air windy, and he was cold sitting on
the ground. When he looked up at the wire-covered windows this time, where he knew someone was probably looking down, the windows were already vague, as if he had
been downstairs more than just a few hours. Pulling grass,
he thought of Irene Sheaffer and felt like a convict again,
one who sits on the ground in the yard on a windy day,
thinking. He chewed some of the grass. In a moment he
saw that his time there, or his time anywhere, amounted
to almost nothing. The same was true, he saw, of his
dreams, and even of his thoughts. They amounted to nothing. He was nothing. A peculiar truth in the idea disturbed
him and confirmed itself, rendering him weak for a moment where he should have had arm muscles and strength
in his fingers, and in his neck.

At suppertime the girl was there. She sat at one of the
girls' tables, but with her back facing him. After the meal,
when she had walked by his sinks only once, to smile again
as before, one of the women in white shouted at her, called
to her, "You!" and said, "What are you doing? Where are
you going?" and the girl left, cowering, looking down, and
did not walk by again.

Alex washed the pots and pans. They were worse now
than at lunchtime, stuck with scabs and crusts of macaroni.
He scratched and scraped over the hot sinks until he must
have lost a pound in perspiration, a quarter pound off his
forehead and down his sideburns. Now that he had seen
the girl again, he loved her less.

From the kitchen Mr. Kelly led them back to the recreation room, where he sat in the corner, in the room's only
easy chair, and read a newspaper. It was already fully
dark outside, and the ceiling lights, and the lamp over his

chair, were lighted. Otherwise the room was dim, as were all the rooms in the building, lighted to twenty-five watts, perhaps forty. Mr. Kelly held the newspaper sheets up as he read so that they covered his face, but he was there, and now and then one of the boys rose from the confusion of comic books and jigsaw puzzles to ask him a question. He lowered his paper to answer. Then he raised it again, flagging it a little. When another boy stepped up to him he lowered it again; he showed no irritation over the interruptions. This was a *free hour*. Alex stood around, looked around, not knowing what to do. He wanted to go over and ask Mr. Kelly a question but could think of nothing to ask.

Red Eye was talking to The King. Red Eye showed no anger, in spite of their intentions upstairs to *get* The King. Nor did Alex feel any anger. Now that they had also made it downstairs, it seemed a joke the way The King had used them to make the move himself. Alex wished to approach them, too, but felt excluded for the moment by their color.

Some of the boys here were silent and looked dejected, others looked mean, if free, and others looked afraid of their own shadows, fear on their faces even if there seemed nothing nearby to be afraid of. It was a look Alex recognized as occasionally one of his own, as the expression he had worn his first days upstairs. He thought again of the years he and Howard had lived with Mrs. Cushman. The confusion of children there was similar to the confusion of children here.

At Mr. Kelly's side he waited a moment for the man to sense his presence, to lower his newspaper.

His voice vibrated as he spoke. "Is it okay to write a letter in here?"

"To do what?"

"I just wondered is it okay to write a letter in here?"

"Yess. It's a free hour."

Mr. Kelly looked at him, not unkindly, and Alex, turning to walk back, felt foolish, felt as uncertain as a five-year-old. He made no move to write a letter.

.   .   .

Mr. Kelly read them a bedtime story that night.
When they had showered and brushed their teeth, and were
in their cots, and the lights were turned out, Mr. Kelly
placed a straight-back chair in the doorway. Light came
over his shoulder from the bathroom, enough to light the
book's pages, and he appeared as a speaking silhouette
from within the darkened space of the dormitory.

Alex lay listening. The story was similar to the story he
had read that morning. But he was enjoying this story,
perhaps enjoying it too much, for he barely listened to the
words. Mr. Kelly's voice delivered the words at a distance,
and remotely the story was about a lost treasure on an
island, where Polly and Billy happened to land in their
floataway rowboat, somewhere off a coast. Alex seemed to
sail along, upon air and water, with them. Polly and Billy
found the corner of a chest sticking out of the sand, and
when they had managed to dig it out, and had managed to
get it unlocked—an old seaman who lived on the island
had come along and was helping them by now—they found
it was empty. (Alex sank with a child's disappointment
over the empty chest.) Then it started to rain, and the old
seaman, whose name was Captain Jones, loaded them, rowboat and all, into his fishing boat, to return them to the
mainland. Rain fell, salt water splashed into the air. The
old seaman gave them rain hats and coats to put on, the
big yellow rain clothes fishermen wear on stormy days,
and when they had the coats on, he told them to look in the
pockets. They looked and found they had gifts—books.
Polly's book was called *All About Ships,* and Billy's was
called *All About Pirates.* And Captain Jones said, "That's
real treasure. You will get more from books than from all
the gold in the world."

The voice stopped then; Mr. Kelly said no more. Alex
lay looking at the ceiling. In a moment he heard the chair
being moved. Then the light which had filled the door and

covered the ceiling went out, leaving the room dark. In a moment, as if waking from a dream, from a journey back into his childhood, Alex returned to where he was lying on this odorous cot, locked in this building.

There were no curtains or shades on the windows, and before long, light from the sky, powdered light from stars and moon, illuminated the room clearly enough to reveal the faintly visible shadow of the crosshatched wire from the windows. Alex lay awake. Sounds were clearly audible through the large room—breathing, turning, bedsprings, light coughs, muffled whimpering (someone cried, lightly, almost every night in the dormitory), faint snores, whistles of exhaling. Still, it sounded as if most of the children were already sleeping, however free or constricted their breathing. Alex lay still. He no longer felt as a child in this children's world. He felt overgrown on the cot, felt foolish being in bed so early. Bedtime stories. He wished suddenly that he was upstairs again, up where it was meaner, where he seemed to belong, where the unfairness was somehow fair.

For a moment, trying, he could not recall or understand why he was there in the first place. What had he done? Why was he locked up? He felt guilty, and his childhood kept flaring, as if to give some answer, but he could not see quite what it was. A startling thought came to mind —the thought again that of those years, of the years of his life, he had grasped nothing. He seemed to be no one any more. He was no longer the person he had been, nor had he become another person.

He had not heard Mr. Kelly walk into the room, but then he heard his voice, near where the boy was whimpering, saying, "Oh now now now, it can't be that bad—let's go to sleep now."

Four

On days following, new boys, mostly black, filed into the dining room to sit at the upstairs table. Others moved downstairs, and occasionally someone disappeared, as if released and sent home, or sent on, under cover. One day Alex realized The King had not been there since either the noon or the evening meal of the day before, and some days later, Leonard and Thomas also disappeared.

In school, Mr. Kelly gave him no new assignments, and not to attract any, Alex tried to keep busy, tried to appear busy. He started and never finished more letters to Howard; he wrote another love letter to Irene Sheaffer, a letter he tore to pieces and deposited in the wastebasket.

Time passed. One day at The Lincoln Hotel duplicated another as if traced not quite accurately. Much of the time, in class, at recess, on work details, during the free evening hour, Alex devoted to daydreaming. There was little else to do. Perhaps because the future was uncertain, he looked mostly to the past.

One evening in the kitchen, the girl returned. He had not seen her coming, but felt her, for she brushed into him on passing, and glancing up, he saw her looking at him over her shoulder as she went on to the pantry. She did not pull the light cord in the small room, and partially concealed by the cross slats of the door, she seemed to stand looking at him, and he, his hands in the suds, stood looking at her, and at the dining-room doorway, and at her. For a moment, half concealed, she looked to be holding herself, embracing herself, in her own arms.

Coming from the pantry again, she walked directly toward him. He stayed facing the sinks, but turned, angled, somewhat toward her, and no longer looked or thought to look to see if anyone was watching. She walked almost directly into him, brushed over his side, brushed her breasts hard over his arm, over his roll of shirt sleeve, going by. Neither of them said anything, but it was as close as he had been to her face, close enough to see the unpainted color of her lips, her stringy and slightly wavy hair, her crazy eyes, a small red pimple at the corner of her mouth.

He watched her go around the corner. He moved against the sink, pressed himself up against the rolled lip of steel.

She came back. He had not thought that she would. He looked at her face as she approached; she brushed over his back in passing, so the bones of her arm and hip pressed against him, and she glanced back over her shoulder again as she walked to the pantry. She stood embracing herself again, and Alex, watching, was too much within his own growth of passion to understand.

This time, returning, approaching, she looked somewhat sleepy-eyed, once turning her head nearly to her shoulder and nearly closing her eyes. She walked into his side again, more directly, just barely pausing, as he raised his arm and felt the bottom of her breast against his arm muscle, felt the weight and the sheathing of brassiere within the loose dress, the heft, the sensation precious and flowing of a balloon not entirely filled with water, and almost immediately, violently, from behind him, he knew she had been grabbed, and turning, he saw her thrown by the shoulder by a tall woman in white, thrown some five or six feet, and then pushed, but not falling, followed through the dining-room door by the woman, and out of sight, and turning back to the sink, he loved the girl again, and despaired over his inability to help her.

Ten or fifteen minutes later, by accident, or by coincidence, a radio was turned on somewhere, music suddenly came on as if an orchestra were no more than fifteen or twenty feet away, and in the moment before the radio was turned off he was caught by the music and brought back to himself, astounded this time with a sudden awareness of his washing pots and pans, with the fact, which he seemed to have forgotten entirely, that out across those fields, across the city, music was playing continuously throughout the night, with the fact that he was a sixteen-year-old boy, strong, he believed, healthy, quick, he believed, locked up there, and for the first time he felt an absolute fear of being sent to the Boys Vocational School, to BVS in Lansing, a fear of being locked up until he was eighteen, or nineteen, or twenty years old.

Working in the laundry one morning, he recalled a time when Howard had gotten lost, or had run away. Howard was too young at the time to go to school, and had fallen into a habit of walking from Mrs. Cushman's house down to the corner of Fenton Road to wait for Alex to come by on his way home from school. Fenton Road, a busy street with stoplights and stores and buses, was three blocks from Mrs. Cushman's, and once Howard started walking there, he was on the corner every lunch hour and every afternoon when school let out. He was three and a half or four years old at the time, dirty and sticky, underfed and thin. One day, to trick Howard, Alex sneaked behind Goebel's Market, past a rusty incinerator, and came out on the sidewalk behind him. When Howard finally looked back and started running, Alex tried to make him believe he had walked by him just a minute before. Didn't he see him? What was he doing, daydreaming?

Another time he circled around Howard in the other direction, taking a different route from school to Fenton Road, and sneaked up behind him again, and tapped him on the shoulder. Was he going blind? Why didn't he keep his eyes peeled? And another time he circled around him, ran on to Mrs. Cushman's, ate his bowl of soup quickly, said when asked that Howard was on his way, and back at the corner told Howard he'd already had his lunch and was on his way back to school. Why hadn't he come with him when he passed before? Had he been standing here all this time? Could he see okay? Howard looked as if he was going to cry. Alex went on; but when he looked back and saw Howard walking away, looking small, he wanted to go after him, or call out that it was all right, he was just fooling. He did neither; he watched Howard for a moment and went on to school.

Alex should have known, from the way he felt, not to trick Howard again. But a day or two later, in the afternoon after school, he sneaked around Goebel's Market again and went on to Mrs. Cushman's as Howard stood on the corner staring the other way. Once there, although he did not forget Howard, he did not remember him either after a while, and he fell into a game of some kind and an hour or an hour and a half soon passed, from three-thirty until five or so, when it was time to eat.

Where was Howard? Alex was at the table with the others, and Howard's chair was empty. They looked at Alex and asked him. Where was Howard? Alex felt at once both chilled and burning. He said he knew where he was, hoping he knew, and left the table. Outside, taking someone's bike, he rode nervously and quickly down to the corner, hurting his crotch on the bar of the bike which was too large for him, hoping to see Howard standing there as always, thinking he would tease him as before, for waiting so long. But Howard was not there, not in view, nor was he anywhere around the corner. The store had crates of fruit and vegetables on the sidewalk under its awning, and quite a few people were coming and going, unloading from buses, factory workers with lunch pails ducking out of cars, and he looked all around in this confusion, even behind the crates, and his eyes seemed to be seeing differently already, but well enough to see that Howard was not there. He turned and twisted and pedaled around on the

bike, then parked it, and then boarded it again and pedaled across the street and down a side street to the school.
Pedaling along, he was thinking of the places he might
take Howard, of the possessions of his he might give him
when they were back at Mrs. Cushman's again. But the
school was closed and quiet, and now during the dinner
hour, no one was around.

Back on Fenton Road he pedaled along the sidewalk
six or seven blocks in the direction of downtown. Wheeling
the bike across the street at a light, he pedaled back. He
went along slowly, looking all round, but he still did not
see Howard, and his fear and his brotherly love were
ascending. He asked a man in a bloody white apron in
Goebel's Market if they had seen a little kid around, but
the man was busy, shook his head no. Alex finally headed
back to Mrs. Cushman's. He did not believe it was true,
believed that Howard would be there, as always, when he
got back, and on another terrifying plane, knew he was
fooling himself. Howard was not there. Some of the children were outside around the porch, and they were not
alarmed, nor was Mrs. Cushman, who was still at the table,
until he told them he could not find Howard.

Mrs. Cushman did not call the police. She called the
factory where Alex's father was working. Alex heard her
say that they couldn't seem to find little Howard, and she
thought they'd better get ahold of him first . . . When she
hung up, turning to them, she said he'd be right there, and
they went back to looking around the house for Howard,
or eating, or talking in the usual and general confusion,
suggesting that Howard was one place or another. Alex
felt no relief. He did not know his father very well, knew
mainly that the man was his father, and did not know
what to expect.

Twenty or thirty minutes later shouts came from the
front yard and from the porch through the screen door—
"Here he is!"; "Here he comes!"—and Alex went out to see
the Chevrolet just pulling up in front, his father there

behind the wheel. He parked the car quickly, near the ditch, and came across the yard quickly, with Alex and some of the other children, and into the house. He was not dressed in suit and vest and tie as usual, but in his factory clothes, denim pants and khaki shirt. He was grease-stained and gave off the smell of the factory, and when he told them to calm down, to take it easy, there was a feeling that here at last was the doctor.

He asked who had seen Howard last, and when and where, and how he was dressed, and as Alex answered most of the questions, the other children stood around excited, trying to answer as well. Alex said nothing to show his guilt, nor did his father press any guilt upon him, and when they were through talking, his father used the phone to call the police. They stood mainly silent, listening, as he explained and gave times and addresses, and names and descriptions, and when he hung up and went outside, they all followed again. Near the car, his father asked Alex what Howard had been doing that far away, and Alex told him that sometimes Howard walked down there to meet him after school.

A black police cruiser came down the road sometime later and pulled over to stop beside them. Two uniformed policemen got out of the car, leaving the motor running. The two seemed as large as the sky in their visored hats, their blue-black uniforms, their revolvers and rows of brass bullets, their squeaking leather. But they spoke softly, matter-of-factly, talking with Alex's father. In the process, as one of the policemen wrote several things down, Alex's father explained that he did not live there himself, he lived across town and the children boarded here. The policeman asked if he thought Howard had started on his way to where he lived. He did not, his father said, but the policeman still asked for and wrote down his address. Where was the boy's mother? Where did she live? Could he have tried to go there? Was there any reason she might have picked him up without telling anyone? Had she ever done that? His father knew her address—which surprised Alex, for she had never visited—but doubted that Howard had gone there, or that she had picked him up, although he was not completely sure.

One of the policemen asked Alex if his brother had ever run away or gotten lost before. Alex said no. Had his brother been upset about anything? Alex said he did not think so. Had any of them seen any strangers around? Several were suggested by the children, several of these refuted by other children, and although they made some notes, none of the suggested strangers seemed to catch the policemen's imagination.

They asked again about Howard's size, and his age, and what he was wearing, and Alex, saying he was so tall, and so big, and was wearing short pants, finally started to sob as he talked. His father put a hand over his shoulder and held him close to his side, and told him to take it easy, not to get upset; they'd find him, all right . . .

The policemen agreed. They said not to worry, he'd probably show up before long, children that age were always wandering off and forgetting how to get back, it happened all the time. They said they'd look for him in the meantime, and if he came back or they heard anything, to give them a call, and returning to their car, one of them waving to the children, they drove off.

Alex went with his father in his car to look. He showed his father where Howard had waited on the corner, but his father still did not ask how it happened that Alex had not seen Howard if Howard was waiting for him. They cruised in the car where Alex had cruised on the bicycle. Then they cruised all the streets nearby, driving as slowly, it seemed, as Alex had pedaled, searching the sidewalks and drive-ways with their eyes. Returning to Fenton Road, where in the dusk the streetlights had just come on, they drove most of the way downtown, but turned off before they were there, to drive down among the factories by the river, and across the bridge to his father's rooming house.

Alex had not seen where his father lived before this. He was surprised that it was no more than a bedroom in a house. Howard, of course, was not there. Downstairs, his father knocked on a door just inside the front door. No, they had not seen any four-year-old boy.

Going back along Fenton Road, they cruised, but faster this time, and stopped once beside a small boy, although Alex knew right away that it was not Howard. Howard was not that tall, and he was wearing short pants. When they came down the road again to Mrs. Cushman's, the porch light was on. But no one was on the porch. And as they walked through the front door they were greeted with shouts of *"He's back!"*; *"He came back!"*; *"He was down in the woods!"*

Howard was in the dining room, together with the other children, with Mrs. Cushman in her rocking chair, in the confusion. When Alex and his father entered, Howard was looking down and he did not look up or look at Alex for some time. He was still wearing the same short pants, and a short-sleeved striped shirt, both of which were dirty, and his stockings without elastic were piled around the tops of his shoes. His father knelt to talk to him, to ask if he was all right, and although Howard said a few things shyly, he still did not look up at Alex.

It was only when his father had stood up and stepped over to the phone that Howard looked at Alex. It was a quick glance; he turned his head back at once.

Within ten or fifteen minutes the incident seemed to be forgotten, but throughout the evening Alex and Howard were kind and grown-up with each other. Their father, with an authority they had never been exposed to before —a simple freedom to go somewhere, to buy something— did not return to work that night but drove them into town, took them to the Coney Island diner, in the neon-lighted heart of the city, to buy Howard the meal he had missed, to buy the three of them the meals they had missed —a table of hot dogs and French fries. They sat in a booth, and when his father said to him, "You look out for Howard from now on," Alex saw the knowledge in his eyes. Later, when his father said, "What a crew we'd make, the three of us," Alex sensed something as large and promising as the maze of neon-lighted downtown itself.

Sundays were special days at Mrs. Cushman's. It was nothing religious, nor did they know anything of Sunday school or church—it was a sense of something exciting, something impending in the air itself, for occasionally, bearing gifts and seldom having called or promised beforehand, one parent or another came driving down the oiled dirt road, as if to remind them of their names, of other possibilities, and then to drive off again.

Alex's father, in time, became the only regular visitor to Mrs. Cushman's. There was a girl whose mother came as often, but she was there no more than six or eight months before her mother took her away for good.

His father took him and Howard in the car for rides into the country, or into the heart of quiet downtown, to stop at the Coney Island for lunch, where he might tell the man at the counter that these were his boys. Sometimes Alex and Howard waited in the car while he went into a tavern to throw off a drink or two, and at other times the three of them walked along the streets downtown and looked in store windows, or they spent a couple of hours at the amusement park, riding the rollercoaster or the bumper cars or churning through the chilling fun house; and stopping to talk to some old man along the street or flirting with some waitress at a midway lunch counter, their father might say that these were his boys.

They came to expect him on Sundays. Sometimes he came driving down the road six or seven or eight Sundays in a row, and other times, for two Sundays in a row, occasionally three, he did not. The weekends he missed were usually in the winter, cold and snow-blown Sundays when with some of the others, Alex and Howard made the long walk down Fenton Road to the Star Theater, and at gray dusk walked home again. The time passed this way.

Most evenings they sat around the living-room floor listening to the radio, the brown cabinet's amber smile glowing small and bright, its voice in control of their bedtime, so they did not go to bed at seven-thirty or at eight o'clock, but at the end of *The Lone Ranger*, or of *Baby Snooks*, or of *The FBI in Peace and War*, or of *Inner Sanctum*.

Then, one day a few days before school let out for the summer, an afternoon when the temperature was in the eighties or nineties, when electric fans were running everywhere, Alex, coming from the school building among the crowd of children, saw his father standing on the sidewalk, waiting. He was working days now, the first shift, and he had just gotten off work—he wore his denim pants and khaki shirt, his factory badge on his belt, his shirt damp under his arms and across his back, his face, and the hair under his throat, perspiring, dirty with work. He stood there smiling; he asked Alex if he and Howard would like to go out to the lake and take a swim, and he waited while Alex ran wildly to find Howard, to bring him back. By the time they had driven back to Mrs. Cushman's, picking up a few more children boarders on the way, searching among their things for something to swim in, they were all invited and all were going. The trip became unforgettable—not only the swimming in the lake water, but the ride to the lake, with the warm air blowing in the opened car windows, but above all, the time after, when they were like wolves with shivering hunger and were treated to hamburgers and frosted malts at a yellow-lighted lakeside stand, Alex glowing with pride when the other children called his father "Mr. Housman," for he had never heard his own name so identified.

His father surprised them a second time. A couple of days later he picked them up after school again and they went to the lake again, although they returned to Mrs. Cushman's in time for supper. This time they made a place for him at the table, and he joined them and answered all their questions, and told little stories and talked, so they all stayed at the table fifteen or twenty minutes longer than usual. When he left they all thanked him in an unusually polite way for taking them swimming, and he thanked them for having him to dinner.

Throughout the summer, perhaps three times a week at about three-fifteen, his car appeared, coming down the road, and the children ran screaming, into the house and across the yard, "Mr. Housman's here! Mr. Housman's here!" Then, at the lake, after a couple of hours in the water, when they were chilled and blued, they refilled the car, with towels over their shoulders, and drove back to Mrs. Cushman's, and he ate occasionally with them, and smoked his cigarette at the end of the meal, and several times he sat for a while to listen to a radio program.

He came on Sundays as well, but dressed in suit and tie and white shirt. But he usually had a bottle in the glove box, and he seldom joined them for Sunday dinners. Nor did he take any of the other children along—just the three of them, Curley Housman, and Alex and Howard. Their lives continued this way until one afternoon in late August, when, at a booth in the Coney Island, he told them he had rented an apartment. He said they were going to gamble on life, the three of them, they were going to set up house-keeping. Later that afternoon they spent an hour filling boxes and carrying their possessions out to the car; then they drove away from Mrs. Cushman's, where they had spent the past five years.

Five

On Wednesday before Thanksgiving a barber spent the day at The Lincoln Hotel. He cut the younger boys' hair in the morning, ate lunch at the staff table like a distinguished visitor, and cut the older boys' hair in the early afternoon. They were five-minute haircuts, up the back of the neck with an electric shaver and over the top of the head. Enough hair fell from Billy Noname and Alex, together with the black wool from Red Eye, to stuff a small pillow. The haircutting was a break in routine which became joyous, lining up, waiting, making faces, being watched and made faces at, trying to sit still, and during their afternoon session outdoors, heads freezing—Billy Noname looked like an inmate of a concentration camp— they played a clown's game of cold softball, throwing left-handed, running bases backward.

Thanksgiving Day was also a break in routine, marked by a heavy rainfall. There had been other rainy days, but on a holiday, with free time to stand and look, the rain and the brown view of field and sky, and of other things, were noticeable through the windows. There were no work assignments, or school classes, and the air within the recreation room and without was woven with melancholy. At midmorning a boy of about ten was suddenly seized with sobbing, collapsed crying he wanted to go home, he wanted to go home. Mr. Kelly picked him up bodily, under his legs and shoulders, so the boy wailed against his chest, and carried him from the room. Alex sat most of the morning doing nothing, or stood at the windows looking out, almost seized several times himself.

They had a religious service after breakfast that morning, but it was brief, cut short by an incident involving a new boy from upstairs. All the upstairs boys were new by now, new to Alex, and they seemed to look tougher and meaner all the time. They seemed to carry an odor and face of the outside, of the city, as people coming in red-faced from the cold give off an outside temperature for a time.

Mr. Kelly started the service by reading an account of the Pilgrims' meal, of their gathering to give thanks. Then he did an unusual thing—perhaps he was affected himself by the heavy rain through the windows—he asked them to join him in a song. They had never done any singing before. But he was in a happy mood, smiling as he talked. "Bless This House." He was sure they had heard it enough to know some of the words. Would they join in? If they didn't know the words, would they please just hum along? He paused. Bracing himself, he began:

> "Bless this house,
> O Lord, we pray—"

Hardly a voice joined. One or two, beginning, left off when no one else began. Pausing again, Mr. Kelly said, "No singers today?" He looked around. "Come on, now," he said. "Let's sing. Let's hum. Let's be happy and thankful." He started once more, deeper in voice:

> "Bless this house,
> O Lord, we pray
> Keep it safe
> By night and day—"

Again he stopped, laughing lightly. He was enjoying himself and they sat looking at him. But when he said, "Do I have to finish it myself," evenly, from the rear, in a whisper, someone said, "Go, man."

Mr. Kelly looked embarrassed by the remark. It had

been one of the new boys from upstairs, a white boy of about sixteen. In a high school classroom the remark might have drawn an eruption of laughter from the pupils, and perhaps from the teacher as well, but no one laughed here. Some of them glanced around at the boy. Alex sat expecting, with a combination of fear and pride, to see the boy punished. He felt embarrassed himself; he had enjoyed Mr. Kelly enjoying himself .

The silence continued. Mr. Kelly stood staring, his face red. Heads kept turning from him in the front to the boy in the rear. Then, and it was unusual as the song itself, Mr. Kelly said, "I'm going to try to forgive that."

He paused. Then he said, "Let us bow our heads," which meant the end of the service.

That evening, in the recreation room, Alex stood at the windows. The city, off across the wet fields, down rows of houses, rows of naked shade trees, seemed as remote as a city in another state, or in another country. Alex felt no sense now of missing the Thanksgiving Day football game, or the brawls following, or the city itself, the carloads cruising from one end of the city to the other, the scattered fights here and there all day, into the night. He did not miss them, but he thought about them. He felt a desire to be there, to be in the city, but only to look. He wished he could walk along the streets this rainy day and look around, as a stranger in a city on a Sunday afternoon, an observer, as if he were going to learn something important, walking the streets and looking at the people passing, the cars, watching them from a distance.

Once, after one of the football games, a man of fifty or so had managed to climb up one of the goal posts to the crossbar so only his feet were held in the grabbing hands below. Then someone caught his pants cuffs, and his pants broke loose at the waist and began, as he struggled with his legs to hold them, to slide down his legs. The full stadium, those waiting to file out, roared with laughter, for the man was wearing red long johns, the kind with a

flap in the seat. Then the long johns were caught by the
cuffs and pulled down, as he tried to hold the crossbar with
one hand and tried to hold up his red underwear with the
other. Then he lost the long johns and they were pulled immediately to his ankles, and he hung there for a moment
with bare ass, white and hairy, before all the hands pulling
at his ankles and at the pants and underwear around his
ankles broke his grip, and it might still have been funny,
but as he fell he was already being hit, and before he even
reached the ground a fist rapped his face and blood rushed
from his nose.

Another time, walking on the stadium field just after
the game, Alex had seen a white man with a red-and-black
ribboned badge on his jacket, flushed and very drunk—he
might have said something—wiped out in seconds by a
black handkerchief-head in a red-and-gray jacket, wearing
leather gloves. The black kid, a bullet, suddenly danced and
struck, hit the man in the jaw and knocked him bodily from
where he had been walking. The man, fleshy and middle-
aged, stumbled back a few feet, and the black kid moved
after him, his leather fists flashing, hitting the man's face
as if throwing a flurry at a body bag, splattering blood
from the man's mouth and nose, until the man, as if already out and only needing room to fall, collapsed from the
knees to the ground, as the black kid slipped away.

The city. Alex felt little desire to go there any more.

Red Eye disappeared. Alex missed him first in the
classroom one afternoon. Glancing toward Red Eye's desk,
he saw that he was not there—the desk was empty. He
looked around the room, over his shoulders, saw that Billy
Noname was still at his desk, but Red Eye was gone. He
had been at the table at lunch. BVS. Alex wondered if Red
Eye had been giving them a story about being on his way
to BVS. He imagined him loose over on the city streets, but
knew somehow that it was not true. Red Eye's hearing had

probably come up, was probably being held that very moment in the courthouse in town, or perhaps he was already in a car on his way to Lansing. Still, in a moment it was not Red Eye's disappearance at all which bothered him, but his own confinement, a glimpse again of time passing.

Outside, after the class, he went up to Billy Noname and asked if he knew what had happened to Red Eye. He had been anxious to talk to Billy Noname, as if the three of them had had a pact of a kind, but Billy Noname only said, "He gone?" and looked around at the others himself.

One afternoon in December, when he was working in the laundry, Mr. Kelly came along and said, "Housman, you got a visitor."

It was his father. Alex's self-consciousness over his uniform was less this time, but still it returned. He walked into the visiting room shyly.

His father stood where he had the other time. But he was entirely different now. He was dressed in his work clothes, as if he had driven out there on his way to work, and Alex could tell at a glance that he was sober, that he had been sober, as in past and near-forgotten times, for at least a couple of days in a row. He greeted Alex by making a happy face, by saying, "Hey, you're looking fine."

Alex was smiling, happy to see him.

"They treating you okay?"

"Yeah."

His father removed his cigarettes from his inside shirt pocket then, inside his denim work coat, and offered one to Alex.

"I better not," Alex said.

His father took back the package, and looking around, as if seeing that there was no ashtray, returned the package to his pocket.

"I had a hell of a time getting out here to see you," he said. "They just called this noon to say I could stop by."

"Maybe that means they're gonna keep me for a while," Alex said.

"Well," his father said. "I don't know. Let's hope not."

Neither of them spoke for a moment, until his father said, "They're about as easy to crack down there as a bank vault. Unless you got a load of money. Then they knock each other down trying to be nice to you. Anyway, I'll tell you something. You're not looking bad at all. In fact, you're looking pretty good. You were sure a sorry little man the last time I was out here."

Alex smiled, embarrassed.

"I'll tell you something I've been thinking about," his father said. "I don't know if I can buy the gas and oil for it, but I was thinking maybe when you get out of here we can manage an old jalopy of some kind for you. What do you think? I mean, something that's in pretty fair shape. Nothing too fancy, just so it's sound and runs pretty good. I was thinking if you could look around and pick yourself up a little part-time job of some kind so you could take care of your own gas and oil, then I'd look after the insurance. That way you'd have yourself a little something to buzz around in. That is, you know, if they say it's okay for you to have a car."

Alex did not know what to say. He was surprised. He had had no thoughts of having a car of his own; he had been seeing himself differently.

"Anyway," his father said. "We'll see."

In the kitchen now following meals Alex cleaned tables and swept the floor rather than washing pots and pans. Billy Noname remained, and so did the kitchen girl. Alex still looked for, and looked at her, every mealtime, but at a distance. At times she looked as crazy as he often thought she was, but on the occasions when, across the dining room, he caught her eye, there seemed to be a light there which said that she was fine.

One night, just before bedtime, Mr. Kelly had Alex and several of the older boys go with him to a small room next to the bathroom, where each took an armload of heavy hard-grained army blankets, and walking down the aisle of the dormitory, laid one on each bed. Cool air came over the room that night, but the extra blanket made three for each bed, and one or two of these could be folded double, as Alex folded his. It made a heavy load, but it kept him warm. This same night, as if to remind them of the season, for it was not otherwise mentioned, Mr. Kelly read a Christmas story.

Snow fell. Alex noticed it for the first time when he was sweeping near the windows after breakfast one morning, when it was just getting light enough to see outside. The storm looked cold, he could feel its bite just by being close to the windows. It had begun during the night and was falling now and blowing over the field of the playground, which was partially covered, bare in spots high and low, from the wind. It snowed throughout the day and they spent the outdoor periods in the recreation room. It was the first heavy snow since the early freak storm, and it made him remember some things he had nearly forgotten. Sweeping the floor, he saw himself at the time, driving the Buick, and it was hard to believe the person flashing in his mind's eye.

Another morning, just after breakfast, when he was sweeping the floor in the dim dining room, Mr. Kelly stopped by and told him to report to his office when he finished in the kitchen. When Alex reported, he stood in the office doorway and waited until Mr. Kelly looked up from writing something and told him to come in. Alex stepped in and stood before the man's desk, and as the idea of what was happening came to him, he shivered.

Matter-of-factly, turning a piece of paper toward him, Mr. Kelly said, "Here, I want you to sign this. You'll be going home this morning."

It was a form of some kind, and Alex was unable to

understand it. His eyes had dilated and he had trouble getting the pen right in his fingers. He did not want to let his trembling be seen, but could not help it. He roughed out his name.

It had to be true. But he did not feel as he had thought he would feel—happy, excited—he felt dizzy and strange. He felt one moment as if he would break into wailing like a fool, and the next moment he seemed to be standing in someone else's body, his eyes glossy. His thoughts came sharply, and ran off before he had a chance to look at them.

Now he was walking in the hallway with Mr. Kelly, and he knew that this was Mr. Kelly's method of releasing them. He knew he would not see the others again.

Mr. Kelly left him in the dormitory for a moment, but said nothing to him, and Alex did not know what to do. Then Mr. Kelly walked in again with clean sheets and a pillowcase, and told Alex to change and remake his bed. Alex went to work changing the bed, but his timing or coordination seemed off, and at the same time he could not quite see if he had done a neat job or not. Mr. Kelly came back and picked up the dirty linen. "Get your things together now," he said kindly.

Alex knelt and pulled out the chest. But he did not feel well. He felt as he had once when he ran at full speed into a face-high wire across someone's yard, and caught it above his lip and under his nose, when he was left feeling dizzy and seeing double the rest of the day. But he got his things together. He used the same paper bag his father had used in the first place. He pushed in his clean set of underwear, a pair of socks. He unstuck his piece of soap from the spot where he always placed it. He tried to wipe the spot clean with his fingers, but it only waxed over and he stopped trying. He added his toothbrush and paste, and his comb.

Mr. Kelly came to the room again and Alex walked with him, back along the hallway. He was thinking that the others were all on their morning work assignments, and felt that he was doing something wrong. He followed Mr. Kelly into the locker room, where Mr. Kelly turned on the light. Mr. Kelly opened one of the lockers and removed the wire basket with his street clothes, his khaki pants, his white shirt, his jacket. Alex removed his uniform, the blue jeans and flannel shirt, and put on his street clothes. Except for the belt he had around his waist for the first time in a long time, the clothes felt loose and light and flowing next to the uniform. And now that he had them on, it was as if he could not remember having just that moment undressed and dressed again. Mr. Kelly handed him a manilla envelope. Alex removed his wallet and keys and some change.

Mr. Kelly left him in the dormitory again. For a moment he stood next to the bed which had been his, then he walked over and stood at a window between beds. He had been in the room so seldom during daylight hours that he did not know the view through the windows was mainly of trees. The branches were bare now, and snow-covered ground was visible beyond and through them. The sky was an ashen winter color.

He was both frightened and thrilled at leaving. He felt again like a ten- or twelve-year-old, nervous and skittish; he even felt reduced in size in these looser clothes. Standing there, looking out the windows, he saw himself as he had been a year ago, six months ago, with his plume of hair, standing around with Cricket Alan, laughing too much— saw himself as another person, and as a fool, and was embarrassed now over the fool he saw.

He actually saw his father's car on the highway. But seeing it made him feel and think so strangely again that when he had watched it a moment, when, coming steadily on, he was certain it was his father, he turned and walked back to the side of his old cot, and stood making believe he had not seen it. He stood waiting, knowing in a moment that the car must have reached the driveway to the detention home, knowing in another moment that his father must have been leaving the car, and then walking, and then entering the building. Still he stood there, and what seemed a long time later, Mr. Kelly came in the door and said, "Okay, Alex," and he knew it was time to go, and knew his father was there, within hearing, because Mr. Kelly had never before called him by his first name. But still feeling skittish, and jumpy, he reserved seeing his father as a surprise—put on his coat, picked up his paper bag—as if to act out surprise over a Christmas package when he already knew the contents.

His father stood waiting in the hall, stood as someone might stand in the hall of a hospital, his overcoat on, hanging unbuttoned. He wore suit and tie and white shirt, and his face was a little flushed. He nodded, smiling continuously, and Alex felt himself smiling foolishly.

He walked out with his father. Mr. Kelly and his father said a couple of things to each other, but Alex still only seemed to smile foolishly and seemed hardly to hear. He carried the paper bag. Then they were outside in the cold air, and then they were walking on the shoveled sidewalk. He wondered who had the job of shoveling the snow from the sidewalk, for here in front of the building, with no fences blocking the highway, it was a good job. He walked along with a feeling of having forgotten something, but with one feeling entwined with another. He wanted his stomach to calm down. There in the maintenance building was the window through which Red Eye had looked at him when he was on the ashes truck and Red Eye and Billy Noname were inside. He wanted to say good-bye to Mr. Kelly. Still, his feelings and movements were entwining as if some of them were held by threads and could not disentangle themselves.

"So long, Alex," Mr. Kelly said.

Alex turned his head back and waved his hand once, and smiled.

Then they were in the car, within the suddenly familiar

ashtray odor of the car. He had begun to shiver, and his
father, looking at him from the driver's side as he was
setting up the combination of hands and key and feet to
start the car, said, "Let me get the heater going."

On the highway, leaving the driveway, his father
reached down under the seat beside his leg and came up
with his bottle, a pint in a paper bag. He uncapped the
bottle with one hand, holding it between his legs, checked
the rear-view mirror, threw off a shot so the hot-sweet
odor of whiskey moved in the car, and wheezed and blinked,
and smacked his damp lips, which were the color of earth-
worms. Alex saw the drink, and he saw his father, from a
distance.

"I think we better get you a new winter coat," his
father said.

Alex was remembering, as if he had forgotten, and he
turned to look through the rear window without giving a
response. He glimpsed mainly the upper part of the red
brick building, above and through the tree line. It was
there, going away itself. In a moment he looked to the
front.

The heart of the city was still several miles away, but
it sprawled like a fried egg and they were soon at its wide
edge. Alex watched ahead through the windshield and
through his side window, and he saw the city, as he was
seeing his father, from a distance. There were houses,
scattered, barren in the winter air, the snow-covered
ground, smoke rising from the chimneys. Before long, on
crossroads, there were rows of four or five houses, and
sidewalks, or paths in the snow, and parked cars along
roadsides and in driveways, telephone poles with lines of
black wire, and occasionally people—a man in his shirt
sleeves, sweeping a porch, a woman in a long coat and a
scarf over her head, walking. At a bus stop some boys his
age were swinging gym bags around at one another. A
mailman was walking, reading addresses on letters. Alex
remembered that school was out for the Christmas vaca-

tion, and he felt again that something was entwined within him and wanted to break free, something held by mere threads.

They were passing through the city streets now, where telephone wires were running out of sight down every side street, and Alex had the feeling of coming in on a plane to land, or in a train, passing quickly and just above, with no one even bothering to turn and look. Simple things, a house color, a porch dirty with snow, a sidewalk shoveled clean, did not seem simple at all.

They turned and now they were driving on a smaller but busier street, going deeper into the city. A car was ahead of them, and cars were passing going the other way. The pavement here was shining wet from the traffic. They drove along. Within a mile or a mile and a half mainly of houses and apartment buildings, they were entering the city's greater thickness, the congestion at the edge of downtown.

There was more traffic here, several lanes of cars among the streets of stores and gas stations, and quite a few people on the sidewalks, and taxicabs and city buses, and then, turning right, they moved along Third Avenue. Still within the congestion, they were approaching home, on the edge of the heart of downtown. All this time his father had asked him only how he was feeling and if he was hungry, and now he said, "Do you think we'll make it?" and Alex realized he'd had more than a few drinks.

At last, turning at the corner of Chevrolet Avenue, then turning between two parked cars, they passed over the familiar bump and entered the driveway between the close and familiar wooden walls, and came into the opening behind the apartment house. There was the row of garages, some of the doors closed, some opened, some cars parked outside in the dirt and snow and gravel. Alex's feeling of something being about to break free subsided; he felt dulled now, vaguely disappointed to be home again. He heard his father say, "Here we are," and he saw his father retrieve his paper bag from under the front seat and slip it into his coat pocket.

The stairway up to their apartment had not been shoveled or swept. There was a path up the center but snow still lay untouched on the ends, peppered with soot. Inside, the apartment's familiar odor played on the air and for a moment Alex had a suffocating feeling of being let into some upstairs corridor again, as if in a dream.

His father was having a drink. He had not taken off his coat either. He looked flushed red now and he was talking, holding the sacked bottle, telling Alex over that distance that he should go buy himself some new duds, explaining that whenever you got divorced, or got out of jail, or lost your job, or whenever you got your heart broken, or—lighting a cigarette, flicking the match in the sink—got your ass busted, what you should do is go out and get yourself some new duds.

His father reached back under his topcoat and came up with his wallet. His wallet was stuffed with bills. It was his habit, once every few months, to remove whatever money he had in the bank and carry it in his wallet, and it was a bad sign, the sign of a binge. Still from a distance, Alex knew his father wanted him to leave, but he did not know if his father sensed his disappointment and suffocation in the apartment or if he merely wanted to be alone to drink. His father was telling him to get himself a new winter coat, and some new shirts and pants, and some new socks and underwear, and a new pair of shoes, and to get good stuff, no cheap junk, and he began handing Alex twenty-dollar bills, one at a time, taking them from his wallet one at a time, giving him five or six, then two or three together, in a gesture, closing his wallet and returning it to his hip pocket. And he was to have a good time, enjoy himself and have a good time, his father told him.

Alex was still not hearing quite right or quite completely, including his own words—yes, yes, he'd have a good time, he told his father. A moment later, not having removed his coat, he was passing between the two house walls again, and it was as if he were still not free from the detention home, could not possibly be free so quickly and suddenly, as if all this were taking place in a dream on the floor along the upstairs corridor. He walked along Chevrolet Avenue feeling partially blinded.

By a clock in a coffee-shop window, he saw it was only ten minutes after nine and he was startled by the time in a way he could not understand. His stomach became skittish and overactive again .

Then he was downtown, walking along a wide snow-dirty sidewalk which was partially crowded with Christmas shoppers. He passed before dime stores, taverns, clothing stores, diners, among the odors familiar on the cold city air of Karamelkorn, roasting peanuts, diesel exhaust from starting and stopping buses, among people, the jingle of Salvation Army booths on corners, in the overcast winter air.

In an excessively warm and large men's store called Gards, he stepped along on a thick carpet looking over the line of winter coats. It was an expensive store, but crowded, and no one questioned him. He found a coat he liked. The price tag on the cuff said "$55," with a single bar crossing the S of the dollar sign, but he still removed it from its hanger and laid it on a table while he removed his old $14.95 coat. He slipped on the new coat and stepped into the prism angles of a triple mirror. The coat caught his attention for only a moment, for there was his face and he did not care to see his face from three angles here in this store. He was surprised at his raggedly short hair. He looked from the coat to himself, from himself to the coat. His hair fuzzed down the back of his neck, the fuzz nearly as long as the hair on the sides and top, from the barber's near-shaving of his head. His skull looked misshapen and his eyes looked small, rat-small, from the sides in profile.

He stepped away from the mirrors. Working awkwardly with his arms in the puffy sleeves, he got the staple out with his fingernails and removed the price tag and label from the cuff. A saleman was watching him and he was sure the salesman thought he was trying to steal the coat. The salesman wore a vest and blazer and was a clean-cut young man. Alex worked his puffy arm up under the coat to remove his wallet. He handed the salesman three twenties and the price tag and looked away from looking at the salesman's face as he did so, as the salesman made change. In a minute, his old coat and a receipt in a large paper bag, he walked from the warm store back into the cold air, thinking he should buy a hat to conceal his head.

He walked among the people like a shopper, carrying his paper sack from Gards. He had never been a shopper before and he sensed he was impersonating someone, that he was—he wasn't sure, perhaps a prisoner on the loose—wearing a disguise. He walked along, and then, before him, coming his way, disappearing from view and returning into view among people on the sidewalk, were two boys he knew from high school, Joey Turner and Franklin Cash.

They all three stopped for a moment, making a rough triangle on the sidewalk, but there was no handshaking, no hello's, no asking when he had gotten out. Joey Turner had started talking at once, and Alex, still from a distance, heard him say, "Hey, my old man told me to stay away from your ass, man. Old Joe thinks you will get his little boy in trouble. Old Joe says to—" Alex was smiling slightly, looking down at the sidewalk, feeling both foolish and embarrassed. Glancing up again, he saw Joey still talking on, waving a black-gloved hand, emitting rapid white breath, vaguely aware that the Big Sara he was talking about was his mother, the Little Joey himself. Glancing over then, Alex saw that Franklin Cash was staring openly at him, studying him coldly, and the world of high school, a frightening world he had somehow forgotten, came back to him.

He looked back to Joey, who was still rattling on, but heard little now of what he was saying. He was startled and surprised by the look on Cash's face. He glanced down at the sidewalk again, but then, quickly, he looked up, for Cash had started walking away. Joey Turner, before him, stopped talking, stopped moving his hands, looked at Alex and looked around at Cash's back moving away. He hunched his shoulders, made a face to Alex of not understanding, and turned to go, to catch up with Cash.

Alex, left standing, needed a moment to start going himself. He angled over to the store side of the sidewalk, and into a doorway, and stopping there before a wall of glass, he saw shoes on pedestals, saw small signs: *$12.95, $14.95, $9.95.*

In a moment he was walking on the sidewalk again. He kept his eyes to the front and somewhat high, to avoid looking at another face. The wallets, the money—they flashed into his mind for the first time in weeks. But he had never considered being shunned, or considered anyone being ashamed to stand with him on the street. He thought of his hair, and thought that he must look like an ex-convict; he must look like a car thief.

After a moment, he stopped. Stepping from the sidewalk traffic, he stood with his back near but not touching the shiny gray marble of a bank front. He stood again as if he were a shopper, as if he were waiting for a bus, stood there for one minute after another, looking to the air just above the heads of people passing. Here he was, wearing a new coat, holding his old coat in a paper sack. No, this is not a dream, he told himself. He looked at the stream of his breath, to see it diffuse. More than seven weeks had passed, from Halloween to Christmas. He was out now. Then, and he did not understand altogether why it happened or where it came from, a feeling of relief began to fill him. His chest filled with the feeling, and the threads there broke now, and his eyes dilated again. In a moment, turning to walk on the sidewalk, walking because he could not stand there laughing out loud and weeping, he turned his head up and down, and looked here and there as he walked, to conceal his irregular face.

Book Three

The Beating

One

     At Christmas, in their rooms at school, Alex and Howard had always volunteered to take the collected nickels to buy trees and carry them to school the next day. At a gas station on Third Avenue, after dark, Howard would stand as lookout while Alex sneaked in from behind the station to pick off two trees and drag them away. The teachers always congratulated them on the large size they managed to find for only a dollar and a half, or a dollar seventy-five, on what good little shoppers they were.

When there was fresh snow they used to shovel sidewalks, very quickly, to see how much money they could
make. Or they went every day to the YMCA to play basketball, to box, to swim, or they sneaked into movie theaters
in the afternoons, or hung around downtown, or did all of
these. In the evenings they often went shoplifting in the
crowded department stores in town, or they made fudge
which never formed a ball in water, or they hopped car
bumpers on dark side streets for heel-scratching, exhaust-
fumed rides across the city. Or, perhaps for the second
time in the same day, occasionally for the same movie, they
sneaked into a movie theater, and walked home again at
midnight on the dark and frozen streets.

On Christmas Eve their father would wake them when
he came home from work, or call them, for they would be
lying awake, and they celebrated their Christmas in the
living room. They opened their gifts, their baseball gloves,
footballs, boxing gloves, Monopoly sets, and their father
opened his leather gloves, scarf, necktie, a deck of cards,
a package of cigarettes, some gifts shoplifted, some pur-
chased.

On Christmas Day itself, while their father slept off
his night's drinking, or dressed and said he'd be back in a
while and drove away in the car, they would walk into
town and go to the movies, and spend their remaining coins
late in the day on rifle and bazooka shots, aiming for the
glass shoulder holes in jerky mechanical Nazis, and although the air of the city, with nearly everything closed
for Christmas, nearly everyone elsewhere, was haunting,
they did not call any attention to the day's strange quality,
and they did not count their time as unenjoyable, for they
did not count their time.

On Christmas Eve day, Alex bought a small
Christmas tree at the same gas station on Third Avenue
and carried it home over his shoulder. Earlier, at Kohl's

drugstore, studying through a glass counter, he had picked out a gift for his father, a Zippo cigarette lighter. From a closet in the living room he took out a box which held some old lights and bulbs and ropes of tinsel, and an old tree stand, and at dusk that evening he set up the tree before the living-room window, added a glass of water at the base of the tree, and added the decorations to the fragrant, prickly branches. He went out and downstairs and across Chevrolet Avenue to look up at the window. He saw red lights, green lights, blurred colors through the filmed glass. At first darkness, from the cold and dusky street, it looked warm up there.

He washed the dishes, swept the floors, picked up in the apartment. He wrapped the Zippo and put it under the tree. When he ran out of things to do, he sat down on the couch in the living room. He thought what a fool he used to be, what an idiot, and he knew that his time in the detention home had changed him. He weighed, cautiously, a reservoir of wisdom he believed he had tapped within. Or was it peace? He thought how wise it would be not to distinguish between the two, and so he did not.

He thought of calling Irene Sheaffer on the telephone, even as he knew he would not call. He would call her someday, when he was more sure of himself. He wished he had thought to send her a Christmas card. He could have signed it *Merry Christmas, Alex Housman.* Or he might have signed it *Love, Alex Housman.* It would have been his second presentation of the word to her. He imagined her feeling the same when she saw the word as he felt thinking of it.

Later, his neck began to bow and he lay down on his side of the couch. Then, in one of the rare shivering moments, he remembered sleeping in the same position on the corridor floor and he returned for an instant to facing the dirty wall. He tried to replace the slight fear by recalling pleasant thoughts of Howard, of Irene Sheaffer, but neither of them came forward in his mind.

Waking, finding himself on the couch, chilled, he felt afraid again but had little idea what it was that frightened him. The apartment was quiet and empty. He went to the kitchen and stood there for a moment. It was several minutes after two o'clock. He looked behind him. Then—it was an old habit—he checked the space behind the refrigerator, and the space under the table. He did not know what it was he was looking for, or what frightened him. He checked throughout the apartment, behind doors, under beds, in closets, and finding no beasts or murderers, he went through the rooms again and turned off all the lights but those on the tree and one in the kitchen, and undressed in the dark in his bedroom.

The cold sheets seemed to wake him. Lying there, his eyes open, sleep moved farther from his reach. The air still possessed something which continued to frighten him. He felt no sureness of himself now. He had been denied things. Perhaps a telephone call, perhaps a word on a Christmas card. He had no freedom to give such things. He imagined someone having Irene Sheaffer in a bed like this at this moment, holding her small naked body; he imagined her small breasts, her small seat, her small patch of fur, the ribbed snake of her spine. He saw how completely impossible it was for that person to be himself. He felt a prisoner of this place. Lying there, he became conscious of the sound, at least of the interior sensation, of his heart beating. He was alive, he was lying there this Christmas Eve.

Kohl's Pharmacy, on the corner of Chevrolet Avenue, was less than a hundred yards from the apartment. Alex left the apartment often these cold days of Christmas vacation and walked to Kohl's—mornings, afternoons, evenings. He bought a *Life* magazine the first time, and read the entire magazine, peacefully, at the counter.

He began reading paperback novels. He scanned the revolving wire rack once or twice a day for twenty or thirty minutes at a time, looking over the covers, and reading the opening and ending paragraphs. When he believed he had glimpsed himself in the pages, or had glimpsed a world he either believed he knew or believed he desired, he stepped over to the cash register to pay for the book. He often sat at the counter for as long as an hour at a time, over a cup of coffee, over one of the novels, and then upstairs in the apartment—while his father slept in the morning, or after he had left for work in the afternoon—he often sat at the wooden kitchen table and read for another hour, or two, and he read in the bathroom, sometimes in the bathtub, and lying in bed at night, waiting to grow sleepy.

The books, finished, accumulated on the overhead shelf in his closet, to the rear and out of sight. It was not that the covers revealed torn blouses which revealed flesh, but that occasionally the words on the pages had disappeared as words and he had appeared there himself, and his own uncounted life had become counted for a moment, and exposed, and he felt the need to conceal the exposure in his closet.

He stayed away from downtown. The streets and stores would be crowded with shoppers and with students and he had no wish to go there again. He read one or two, sometimes three books a day. He came to accept and find satisfaction from the companionship of the books, and from the companionship of himself. Reading allowed him to feel slightly experienced and intelligent. Several nights, leaving the drugstore counter as they turned out window lights and prepared to close at ten o'clock, he walked down the Chevrolet Avenue hill, along the factories and railroad tracks and yards there, the taverns and cafeterias beyond (sad country music broadcasting from their doors, from their red-neon-bordered windows) and he believed as he walked that he was doing a lot of thinking, and that he was growing sure of himself. He was ready now, he thought, to go to school. He was starting a new life for himself; he was starting a new self for his life. (Included, although he did not confess them quite aloud to himself, were Irene Sheaffer, and basketball, and some fusing of warmth and pleasure he sensed might be there in the lighted classrooms these coming winter days.) Calmly, he thought, he was going to show them.

Mr. Quinn asked routinely how his Christmas had been and Alex told him routinely that it had been fine. He mentioned nothing of Christmas Eve, or of his father's failing to come home that night, and had no intention of doing so. They talked of other things. It was their first Saturday meeting and Mr. Quinn had some forms to fill in, some questions to ask, some instructions to give. He told Alex to stop by every Saturday at that time, at ten o'clock, until the hearing came up, and if he had any problems or questions that couldn't wait until Saturday, or if something happened so he couldn't make it on time, he should use the phone. "No sweat," Mr. Quinn said. "Feel free."

"When is the hearing?" Alex asked.

"You worried about it?"

"I don't know. They going to send me up?"

"Up where?"

"The river."

"They might. But nothing's been scheduled yet. Usually takes a month, six weeks, two months, three months."

Mr. Quinn asked what he had been up to these days, how he had been feeling, and Alex, surprising himself as he spoke, surprised at his honesty, said that he had been reading a lot of books, and that he had felt pretty good, and that he had been working on becoming (he was succeeding, too, he had told himself, riding through the city on a bus that morning) a new person.

Mr. Quinn smiled. "Good," he said. "How's your father doing?"

"Fine. He's fine."

"Good. That's good to hear, too. I'll tell you what I want you to do. You just try to stay cool, and hang loose now, okay? You work on being that new person. And don't forget, don't be afraid to call me. See, I'm your man in City Hall. Nothing that passes between us goes elsewhere. You understand? They mess with you, they're messing with me. We'll go down this road together and if they send you off for a stint, don't sweat it—you know? I made the trip myself. Bad trip, bad scene, but I made it. Because I'm smart. And so are you. I can tell. You're so smart you even know it. You'll survive. Look at me. I'm here. You see, you keep your head looking that way, then if you don't get a trip, you're gonna feel *good*. Right? Okay. Now get outta here. And hang loose. I'll see you next week."

His father apologized. He asked Alex nothing of his visit to Mr. Quinn, but when Alex came in that afternoon he took two packages from the top of the refrigerator and put them on the table. Alex, surprised, retrieved the small package from under the tree. Standing at the table, they opened their gifts. His father liked the cigarette lighter. He flipped its top a few times, struck it to flame. He said it was sure something he could use. Alex's packages contained a new wallet, a fresh ten-dollar bill inside, and on a new key ring, a duplicate key to his father's Chevrolet. No toys, gifts for a grownup. Fixing them some spattering hamburgers for lunch, his father said he was sorry he hadn't made it home the other night, he'd had a few too many, and Alex was a good sport not to hold it against him. And Merry Christmas.

Saturday was always his father's best day. He was free from work, and Saturday night, like an adventure, waited. He spent the day preparing for the night, picking up the dry cleaning, bringing home the groceries, a bottle or two or three, bathing and shaving throughout the afternoon. His phonograph records played quietly throughout the apartment. As he dressed he carried a glass from room to room, sipping light drinks until he had a pleasant glow on, reddened and happy, until his eyes were as bright as the toes of his shoes.

He joked with Alex. Moving about, wearing suit pants and a sleeveless undershirt, the hair on his chest curling around the edges of cloth and up to his throat, he told stories of himself, of him and Alex's mother, Katherine, before the war—one of his phrases was "before the war" —taught Alex how to feint a light left in a street fight to expose, and with a right following, to explode the jaw of someone bigger but dumber, lectured on the dangers of hesitation, presented his drawn stomach for Alex to hit— "No, hit the son of a bitch, hit it!"—or his doubled-up, brick-sized arm muscle, which was as hard as hard soil. Or he lectured about massaging the scalp, working natural oils over the skull to the top, every day, never to go bald, demonstrating by pushing his fingers up the sides of his head into the proof of his theory, his thickness of wavy hair.

At last, in the afternoon, as the time to go was approaching, he slipped into a fresh white shirt, slapped a little something on his cheeks, carefully knotted a tie, perhaps buttoned a string of vest buttons, slipped into a silkily lined suit coat, and red-faced, glassy-eyed, happy, usually said, "Well, old pal, time to travel," and usually, at the door, nodded, or winked elaborately, and closed the door behind him.

Late this afternoon, for the first time ever, Alex had a drink with his father. At about dusk, using and admiring the cigarette lighter for the fourth or fifth time, his father asked him if he'd care to join him for a short one. Alex told him no, no thanks, and his father asked if he'd ever tasted the stuff. Sure, Alex told him, and his father said of course, of course, and nodded, and told Alex that the trouble with his family—his mother and father, but oh, especially his mother—was that they despised liquor so hard and fast, they put it up on a pedestal just a hair to the left of the fur pie between a girl's legs, which they despised just a hair more.

"What was her name?" Alex said. "Your mother."

After a moment his father corrected him, in a different voice. "Your grandmother," he said.

Alex said nothing.

His father was standing with his back against the counter. He finally said, looking up, "Elizabeth. Her name was Elizabeth."

He said nothing more about her—she had long been dead—and turned to the counter to pour another inch of amber-colored Seagram's into his glass.

A moment later, turning from the counter, returning from his momentary journey, he told Alex he did not mean to suggest that he start drinking. In case he misunderstood. He meant to do the opposite. Liquor—well, liquor was like rose-colored glasses, an easy way to live with yourself. Not that people who *didn't* drink were any better. Far from it. In fact, he wouldn't trust anybody who was *afraid* to drink any sooner than he would anybody who took too many.

He stood smiling at Alex now, and Alex returned the smile and said, "Okay, you talked me into it. I'll have one."

His father was tickled. He reached and slapped Alex's arm. Was he sure now? He shouldn't drink it if he didn't want it.

"I'll have one."

His father took down a fresh glass, poured in a half-inch or so.

Alex swirled the liquor as his father waited. Alex put the glass to his lips, looked down through the liquor, and then rolled his head back to take it all in a long swallow—all but a residue which immediately scalded his throat and his nasal system. His eyes welled. He tried glancing down to conceal the effect but could not stop the scalding in his throat. He blinked his eyes and they blurred; he wheezed the fire.

He swallowed the residue, as if swallowing two or three carpet tacks. He wheezed again. Blurry-eyed, he laughed a little, and his father also laughed and said, "Oh, son, Jesuschrist, what a world we live in."

Later, at sundown, entering the kitchen before they had turned any lights on, Alex was taken with a momentary desire to be out somewhere, to be with friends. It was the feeling of melancholy. Through the kitchen window and the window in the kitchen door, where the sun had been a large ball, there was now only the spreading of a winter orange, the black silhouette webbing of branches and wires and antennas, the haze of a December afternoon over housetops and chimneys and sooted snow caches.

Alex wished he had gone out for a walk. On a weekday, his father at work, he would have done so. He might have walked along Chevrolet Avenue, or he might have walked to the drugstore on the corner, to pick out a book, to sit at the counter, where he did not feel confined.

He had a second drink. Now the kitchen lights were on and this time his father added a squirt of faucet water. Alex sipped it slowly. He did not much care for the sour and warm flavor, and his father, watching him, weaving some by now, said, "Hey, don't drink that if you don't want it."

His father had a dishtowel tucked in around his waist, like an apron, and another, in the style of a cook, over his shoulder. Two T-bone steaks he had brought home were sizzling in a large black frying pan. Then, over a separate frying pan he cracked, and even as he weaved away some, his hands remained, carefully releasing four eggs—which in a moment he took up and placed carefully, sunny and unbroken, two each, upon each steak, and suggesting a bow, saying "Sir," he placed one of the plates on the table before Alex, and one before his own chair. Remaining a moment at the stove, he fried slices of bread in the juices and grease left by the steaks, and using the spatula, he then delivered a slice to Alex's plate, a slice to his own.

Alex did not feel relaxed. He might have been a little intoxicated. He sat thinking that this was his life, this. He felt the air of confinement in the apartment within the air of missing something. For a moment he even missed the detention home.

Following his father, Alex knifed a triangle of egg and steak, yolk and brown-and-red steak juices running together, forked it home on a corner of bread. Intoxicated? He did feel dizzy. He chewed, and looked over at his father. Curly Housman. A factory worker, a die setter. His father was a weekend dresser. On weekends, at a distance, he could pass for a banker or an executive. Sharkskin suit, vest, white shirt and tie, brown-and-white wing tips. Only within a couple of feet did the texture of his father's face become visible, the raw-plum flesh of his cheeks, his wormy lips, the coloration of his teeth, the film over his eyes. His mother's name was Elizabeth. His wife's name was Katherine. There were a few photographs—his father wearing a cap with a bill, a fuzzy narrow suit, standing near some Model A, holding some pretty woman, her face bordered with her hair, or with a cloth helmet, holding her to his side, or holding lightly the arms, or touching the waist, of his wife, Katherine.

Alex worked his way to the inside corner of the T, and ripped skin tissue from the bone. The food was absorbing the wooziness he had felt behind his eyes and ears, but a glow remained. He noticed that his father had not sobered at all. A glass of mixed whiskey and water stood next to his plate and he picked it up occasionally to sip. On the counter behind him, the pint, the torn plastic seal still lying beside it, was down to less than a couple of inches.

In a moment Alex said, "Pop, what was your father's name?"

Alex thought at first he had made his father angry. His father replaced his drink on the table. He did not look at Alex for a moment. Then he looked over and said, "Elizabeth," and he cleared his throat. "Your grandmother's name was Elizabeth. Your grandfather's name was Charles. Your mother's name was Katherine. Your father's name was William. They're all gone to you now. And your name is Alexander."

His father seemed to be smiling at him. His father's eyes were the pink color of gasoline.

Two

On a Wednesday, two days after New Year's Day, Alex returned to school. He had slept poorly during the night, in anticipation. Rising early, dressing carefully in the chilled bedroom—January was seeping in through the cracks—his muscles felt shrunken from the lack of sleep and wished to stretch. He washed and brushed in the bathroom. His hair, partially grown in, looked more weedy, more delinquent than on days when he had no place to go. The bathroom was warm. It was there, over the morning's silence and clarity, that he thought of the money.

Would they have forgotten? No, there was no way they could simply forget. Would they remember? He seldom remembered himself, and wasn't it possible they would seldom remember?

A small shock of terror had come to him, like an electric shock, thinking of the money. But it had passed quickly, as always. In the kitchen it seemed to be school which excited him, so excited him that he could eat nothing more than a tasteless card of toast.

There was his dollar bill, under the sugar bowl. Hesitant, he put the dollar in his wallet.

Outside, still running early, he walked along Third Avenue and did not stop to wait for a bus. The sky was almost dark; the streetlights were on, gray light above them. Snow specks blew, sparkling in the lighted spaces. In his new coat, packed warm, only his cheeks felt the bitter air. His ears felt hot, his eyes filmed; he was returning now.

He walked into the heart of lower downtown. He imagined that in payment now for denials in his life he had been granted an appreciative and poetic eye, this fluid eye. To passers-by, to cold figures before storefronts, in recessed doorways, he cast exhilarated notions that they had no idea what strange thoughts were surfacing in his weedy head, before his fluid eye. Irene Sheaffer. He imagined the two of them in a warm log cabin somewhere, or in a warm highway motel, and he imagined, walking now near the skidrow railroad corners of lower downtown, the handful of her fur, like the handful of a kitten's belly. He imagined her reaching to take him to her and repulsed by a birdshot scatter of pimples over his back. He laughed aloud; there was no birdshot on his back.

The school was ahead. No more than four or five stray walkers were in sight. The two barbershops were dark and locked. The dairy bars were lighted but nearly empty. Overhead, beyond the school, white was blending into gray, and into the dull chrome of winter, and no sun was visible. Nor was the school, as he had imagined, a sea of brick buildings and ball fields, gymnasiums and faces, books and knowledge. The school was a disappointment; he felt he had made a vague mistake.

The building was dark from the outside, for the classrooms were dark, but the corridors inside were dimly lighted. He walked toward the basement. The dry odor, the old tones of lights, brought the building back diminished, as if not a season had passed, but a generation.

A girl appeared. She wore a winter coat. Her face was familiar but he had no idea of her name. She glanced at

him just once, looking ahead to pass without speaking. He
had wanted to greet her, to greet anyone, and he nodded
slightly, but she was not looking.

He easily recalled his lock combination. He hung up his
new coat and straightened himself. He pulled at the triangle of white T-shirt exposed at his throat. His cheeks
were tingling from the January air. Taking up his notebook, he recalled placing it there, the two detectives casually around him.

Mr. Hewitt had not arrived and the room was dark.
Alex pushed the buttons to light the hanging globes. The
blackboard had been washed, all was clean and waxed.
He took his old seat. However much the nervousness remained, and the work ahead, the work undone, defied
achievement (it flared for the moment as impossible), he
told himself he was ready now, ready to try, to face all the
faces, for if they could do it, any of them, so could he.

The first tinny locker door slamming out in the corridor
preceded a girl entering the room. Janet Hamad, large and
dark.

Alex said "Hi."

She turned and nodded, surprised, going to the rear of
the room.

Another girl entered. Nancy Beach. She was slim and
quiet.

Alex also greeted her by saying "Hi."

She said the same, but as if in her sleep.

Alex felt foolish speaking, decided that was enough
and turned to his notebook. He rested his forehead in his
hand. The notebook startled him some. The gray cloth,
marked, initialed, doodled, embarrassed him. It was the
expression of another person, some fool. He turned its
cover, the dividers, a few, very few, pencil-written pages.
He would buy a new notebook.

More voices, footsteps, lockers opening and closing,
came from the corridor; one by one the others were entering the room. He kept his head down as if in concentration,

as his thoughts moved here and there, and back to the room, and away again. He imagined them saying to themselves on entering, "Well, look who's out of reform school."

He realized someone had stopped, was standing beside his desk. He looked up. Mr. Hewitt was looking down, smiling. He just barely nodded and moved on. Alex turned back to his notebook. He recalled sitting at the old desks in the classroom at the detention home, as if those classes had only been to pass time, as if this were the real thing. But a moment later, when Mr. Hewitt, in front, tapped his desk with a pencil, when the voices trailed off and the room settled to quiet, and Mr. Hewitt began explaining that he was still on vacation himself, even if it appeared that he was standing before them, that the gift he had received this year from Saint Nicholas was this ingenious robot device which . . . and as the class tittered with him and a boy in the room somewhere hooted, "I'm still on vacation too, Mr. Hewitt!" and the volume of their voices rose, Alex sank a little, in recognition of Central High School, and in recognition of himself.

One comment was made. From beside him somewhere he heard the voice of a boy: "Look who they let out of jail." It rang in his head, but he walked on as if he had heard nothing. There were no other comments and he realized at last that he did not know many other students, anyway.

He returned to his old classes, to his old seats. He exchanged a word or two here and there and entered no conversations. He looked ahead most of the time to avoid meeting eyes. He listened carefully. For the first time, however confused, he made pencil notes of assignments. At the end of each class he stopped by the teacher's desk and asked what he had to make up. The teachers told him to stop by after school or said they would give him a list the next day. Mr. Dorsey, American history, a line coach for the football team, shook his head, seeming to smile, and said, "I don't see how you can do it. The semester's practically over."

"I can try," Alex said.

"Listen, let me put it this way. I can't see doing extra work myself for an unexcused absence. You see? An excused absence is another thing."

"You mean I'm going to fail?"

Mr. Dorsey moved his lips but did not speak.

In gym class, his last class before lunch hour, Alex found that his socks and trunks and towel were stiff and odorous. Rather than dressing to go upstairs to the gym, where most spent the hour, he went to the swimming pool, swam and dove from the one-meter board, among the thirty or forty others there. It happened that Mr. Polletta, the varsity basketball coach, was on duty at the pool. He sat in the small spectator alcove, wearing his gray stamped T-shirt and khaki pants, his whistle necklace, his clipboard on his knee. Deciding to get it over at once, Alex walked up and said to him, "Is it okay if I come back out for basketball?"

Polletta closed his eyes; he pushed his glasses to his forehead, rubbing his eyes with two fingers. "Basketball," he said. He looked away, as if in thought. Then he pulled one side of his nose with thumb and forefinger, flicked something away, looked back at his fingertips, flicked again.

Alex, dripping, stood waiting.

"Dunno," Polletta said. "Season's almost over, you know. You been smoking?"

"No."

"Oh, well, I don't care. I guess you can work out. As long as it's okay with Mr. Varney. I'll tell you this, though, fella. I'm not very crazy about the idea. You mess around at all and I won't have you on any of my teams. You understand?"

Alex nodded. Turning, he walked away. Mr. Varney, a

much older man, the oldest of all the school's coaches, was the sophomore coach, and going to the sophomores was a demotion of a kind. Alex had been practicing with the junior varsity in the early fall. Still, five minutes later, dressed, he was upstairs at the doorway of Mr. Varney's office off the main boys' gym. Mr. Varney was sitting in a swivel chair, and when he looked over, Alex said to him, "Mr. Polletta said it was okay for me to come out for basketball if it was okay with you."

"When'd he say that?"

"Just now, in the pool."

Pausing, swiveling, Mr. Varney said, "Well, he's the boss."

"Practice tonight?"

"No, not tonight."

Alex stood waiting.

At last, swiveling again, Mr. Varney said, "Monday."

He saw Irene Sheaffer. Walking along the second-floor corridor, on his way to the basement, he saw that he was facing her. She was walking toward him. But for all his resolve to be friendly, to be direct and kind, he was too alarmed to speak. She glanced at him as if slightly alarmed herself, perhaps surprised to see him back, perhaps frightened. He smiled faintly at her, and she smiled as faintly in return. She passed and neither of them spoke. He walked on. All his determination about her seemed now to have been merely thoughts to fill his head as he lay along the corridor floor of the detention home. She was too human, here in the flesh, to be determined about. He felt a loss, and a sensation of affection for her.

The casseroles and milk and puddings and jellos in the cafeteria were bland compared to the hamburgers and Cokes and French fries across the street. But the cafeteria was pleasant. For the first time during the day Alex felt a relaxation. There was much talk and noise, a clatter and rattle of dishes and silverware, music broadcasting from a public address system. He recalled the detention home again, and felt the sense here—with a tunafish sandwich and a glass of milk—of an immense freedom.

Ten minutes later, proud of his discipline, he was in one of the small reading rooms off the library, his books from his morning classes before him on a large wooden table. He paused a moment before going to work. In spite of Mr. Dorsey, deciding on an inspiration to be above the man, he read the first two chapters in his American history book. They were short chapters, six or eight pages each, with maps and illustrations, but he also wrote out answers to the questions at the end of the chapters. He then read some five unillustrated pages into the text for general science. But without the laboratory experiments, and with the foreign words, general science made little sense. He closed the book and decided to grant himself a flunk in the course. He would do it over from the beginning next semester and double his efforts now elsewhere. He also looked over his notebook and course headings, not to calculate but to envision the order and spending of his time. On the first bell, never having worked during a lunch hour before, he re-entered the thickening corridor and walked with a faint measure of composure.

Geometry was a problem. He understood nothing of the work discussed and assigned. The terms—tangent, cotangent, sine, cosine—were frightening. After class, at her desk, Mrs. Leonhard shook her head in the manner of Mr. Dorsey, but without laughing, and told him she did not see how he could possibly catch up. He was too far behind. There was nothing for him to do but start at the very beginning of the text and read each chapter, and do all the exercises, memorize all the theorems and axioms, and come to her when he got stuck. But there were hardly three weeks left in the semester; she could not see much reason

for even trying. He told her he'd like to try, anyway—
what else was there to do? If he didn't make it, he'd be that
much ahead when he took it over. She agreed; she gave him
a library pass for the hour on a trial basis. He was to check
with her on Monday after school, and if she stopped by the
library during that hour, she expected to find him studying
geometry, not the *National Geographics*.

After school, in the gym, intramural teams had the
courts. Wearing his stale gym clothes, Alex went up to the
track which circled the gym overhead, and began trotting
around. After five laps he sat down on the edge of the oval
to rest, and rose again, almost immediately, to run.

Jogging five more laps, he sat—collapsed—down again.
He was perspiring now, sticky under his arms and down
his sides. The running and noise and whistles carried on
below. In a moment he was on his feet and running
again. He ran on and on. Coming to the end of ten laps,
stumbling as he slowed down, he walked a ways with his
hands on his waist, and sat down hard, breathing deeply.
His forehead and sideburns, his shoulders, even his shins
were covered with perspiration. Now he hurt and he was
feeling satisfied.

He sat on the side for several minutes as his breath
settled. He felt he was working the detention home, and
his own home as well, out of his system. This was where he
belonged, he thought. He was going to change. In time, in
this building, he was going to change.

On his feet, he set off jogging again. His legs were
heavy now as he picked them up and threw them forward
on the incline of the track, going a little faster all the time,
until he was past the sensation of falling down the hill of
the track from lack of momentum, until his feet were hitting the surface and leaving it again at once.

He lost count of the laps this time, perhaps ten, perhaps
twelve, and when he stopped, limping along a ways, he lay
down on his back on the flat surface beside the sunken
oval, to regain his breath. A moment later he heard foot-

falls on the track, but he did not bother looking up to see who it was. After several minutes he sat up. The boy circling the track was Jerry Hall. He went around, one lap after another. When he stopped, he came over and sat down not far from Alex. Neither of them spoke. Then, breathing hard, Jerry Hall said, "Hey, you see Cricket?" Alex shook his head no. "He was looking for you," Jerry said.

A moment later, his body heavy, Alex was running again. He picked up some speed, passed Jerry Hall a few times where he was sitting, and then Jerry Hall was no longer there. Alex jogged on, around and around, until he was so exhausted that, stopping, he had to hold the railing, and stay close to the sidewall, going downstairs to the locker room. Once there he sat for a time on the bench before his locker, before he reached down to work on his shoelaces. His feet, released of the wool socks, radiated.

His crusted towel over his shoulder, on pink and swollen feet, he walked to the shower room. Only a few others were about the locker room, and the shower room was empty. He turned on three separate showers so that steam filled part of the room and concealed him there. He spent perhaps twenty minutes under the water, soaping, squeezing three of the small bars of gray soap together, washing every inch of himself from his scalp to the spaces between his toes. The detention home was far away now. It seemed to exist in another country. He had sweated it all out and washed it all off, and he was back now. He had gotten through a day.

Leaving the shower room, drying himself, he looked in one of the mirrors. His hair lay washed down his forehead and did not look so ragged and weedy as it had that morning. As faintly as he had smiled at Irene Sheaffer he smiled at the face before him.

Only when he was dressed and back at the mirror to comb his hair did a memory of the wallets pick at his mind. His hair, rubbed dry and combed, looked weedy again. He glanced over at the janitor's cage, the wire enclosure where the janitor kept his brooms and carts and sweeping compound. Replacing his comb in his pocket, his heart thumping, drying his hands on a paper towel, he felt the need to return, to look. He walked to the wire cage. He looked in at the canvas pushcart; it stood filled with damp paper towels. He threw in his paper towel, and went on.

Three

The Dean of Boys wanted to see him. Mr. Hewitt whispered the message close to his ear the next morning, as homeroom was beginning. Alex took up his books and left, and walked through the empty corridor, upstairs to the first floor, down the hall to the dean's office. Entering the outer office, the dean's secretary said to him: "Sit down," and so he stood, leaning against the wall.

Two other boys sat in chairs waiting. Truancy, smoking on school grounds, swearing, talking back to a teacher —Alex had been there before. The first time, the dean, Mr. Gerhinger, one of the school's many former head football coaches on the administration, a gruff and bushy man of about sixty, had talked to him mainly of basketball, and baseball, for World Series time was approaching, and only as an afterthought mentioned Alex's smoking in a boys' lavatory. Mr. Gerhinger said the next time he saw him he wanted it to be on a basketball court, throwing in two-pointers, and they'd just forget they'd ever met in this office. The next time, when the issue was truancy, when a car was parked a block or so away, Mr. Gerhinger looked at him directly and told him that if he was going to be that kind of citizen, then they did not want him representing Central High School on the basketball team, or in any other way. Mr. Gerhinger issued punishment. The knowledge was generally accepted that football players could do little wrong. Athletes who got into trouble came away smiling; boys who played no sports were placed on probation and suspended for the same infractions. Cricket Alan, who cheated openly in classes, who terrorized many students and a few teachers, who was an all-conference and all-state linebacker, must have seemed only naturally wild to the old man. On Fridays before football games, in the rallies which Mr. Gerhinger led, he always called for the spelling of Cricket Alan's name, and the letters were roared from the mass of mouths, and Mr. Gerhinger, giving what he called "the old one hundred and one percent," roared them as well, to the point of wiping tears from the corners of his eyes.

When Alex's turn came and he was in the seat opposite Mr. Gerhinger's desk, the man spoke to the side, hardly looking at him. Alex was surprised by Mr. Gerhinger's anger, which was immediate. Mr. Gerhinger said he had just called him in to say that this was not his affair, not any more, that it was out of his hands, but as long as Alex was attending classes at Central High School, there were some things Mr. Gerhinger wanted very clearly understood. One was that he did not like this sort of thing even being talked about around here. As far as he was concerned, there was a place for individuals who broke the law and he believed that was where they should be. This was none of his business personally, but as long as Alex was there, in Central High School, he was forbidden to discuss his private affairs with other students.

Alex looked away. He felt both surprise and a growing anger, and he began seeing himself and seeing other things more than listening to Mr. Gerhinger. In the background he heard some words and phrases—*society* and *community* and *the courts* and *probation* and *taxpayers' hard-earned money* and *out walking the streets*. But Alex was thinking of himself, seeing himself simply standing up and walking from the room, or standing up and telling Mr. Gerhinger to go fuck himself, or giving him the finger close to his nose. But he did none of these; he sat watching himself do them until he realized the man was asking him a question and he looked over at him. "I said, 'How long will you be on probation?'" Alex gave no answer, said nothing. He sat looking back at the man almost calmly.

"Can't you talk?" Mr. Gerhinger said.

"Who's on probation?"

"What are you on then? What are you doing here?"

Alex sat staring at the man. He did not know what to say. He was surprised by the man's ignorance, but he was also confused by his own anger, by the hate he was feeling. He stared back and said nothing.

Mr. Gerhinger squinted. Leaning forward to speak, he raised a finger to point. He blurted the words: "I'll tell you one thing for certain, young man. The courts have their jurisdiction. We have ours. Any trouble from you. I don't care what it is. Any trouble from you and I'll see to it personally that you are suspended from this school. Permanently. That you do not set a foot on school grounds. Not ever. I have never been more disgusted by a student. Now you get out of my sight."

In the hall, walking along, Alex tried once or twice to laugh, or smile, and only sneered. He could not help feeling, at least partially, as he felt the man had seen him.

Classes that morning seemed to take place elsewhere. Even as he looked to the front of rooms, and paused, his mind was covered with other thoughts, other scenes which continued of their own volition to enact themselves. He caught himself elsewhere several times, returned, came down from fantasies of stepping forward to cut throats, to save lives, to run with footballs; he caught himself and told himself he would not stumble and fall because of someone as stupid as Mr. Gerhinger. Still, his urge was to walk away from the school, to break a few school windows from the outside—above all, it was to take another car and drive and drive. All that stopped him was an idea that Mr. Gerhinger would be pleased.

Later, he imagined himself transferring to another high school, and in some ultimate football game running touchdowns over Central High School, running like a cheetah, leaping twenty feet at a time, running sixty miles an hour, and in another scene he imagined himself cutting the old man's throat, slowly, with a razor blade between his fingers, with Mr. Gerhinger's eyes open and watching. And looking up again, he would see that he was in a classroom. A car. To be in a car, driving off into the country, to drive slowly into small towns, the radio playing, the heater running, to emerge and present himself as somebody before the eyes of some country high school. The cunning movement of watching for marked cars, for roof lights, antennas, mounted sirens—the idea was exciting for moments at a time.

He recovered some, settled down throughout the morning. In gym class—he had clean gear now—he went upstairs to shoot baskets. He stayed away from the three-man games, and shot around a basket where a few others were also just shooting around. It was the worst basket in the gym; at that hour, glaring sunlight fell directly over the backboard through the upper screened windows. He shot from the side, to avoid the sun, and most of his shots fell short, as if in the several months off, his arms had lost some of their strength. Shooting baskets quickly became tedious. Then, from behind him, someone said, "Man, Cricket's after your ass."

It was a boy named Bill McBride. Alex said, "He is? What about?"

"I don't know. But man, he's after your ass, I know that."

Alex shot again. Retrieving the ball, he heard Bill

McBride speak again, but in his movement, and in Mc-Bride's movement, he did not hear him clearly and did not ask what he had said. Alex shot a few more times, and after a few minutes he walked around the edge of the floor, lobbed the ball back into the bin, and went downstairs to the locker room. Without bothering to shower, having barely perspired, he dressed again, and even if it was ten minutes early, he left the locker room and walked into the empty corridor. Passing filled classrooms, glancing in a few doors, he walked to the basement to his locker, and exchanging his books for his coat, he went to the landing and left the building.

January. Even as the sun shone bright, the air was sharply cold and the ground was frozen. He walked on dirty snow paths behind the school, then past the maintenance building with its sky-touching brick smokestack, remembering again the day he and Red Eye and Billy Noname had cleaned the furnace room. He wondered if Red Eye was at BVS, if Billy Noname was still at The Lincoln Hotel. They seemed better places to be than this. They seemed more free, less lonely. Feeling numb in the cold, he walked among the backstops and uprights, the circular track, the rows of tennis courts. Far off, like a telephone ringing, the school bell rang. Lunch hour had started. Had he left the building to avoid Cricket Alan? He was not quite sure. In a moment, as if to answer no to the question, he stopped, and pausing to look over the snow-covered fields, he turned and started back. He found it difficult, walking back over the hard ground, to think very clearly or to sort things out. It was his second day back in school; already something was going wrong. He thought again of BVS and of The Lincoln Hotel, until he realized there was also something wrong in imagining, in wishing, that he were there.

He went again to the cafeteria. He knew Cricket Alan would not be there. But Alex was not hiding from him, he told himself. His evidence was that he had been there the day before, and that he had enjoyed himself. Still, he had no appetite and raised none passing through the line, and finally took a carton of chocolate milk, which he drank quickly and alone at a corner table.

Ten minutes later, his books in hand again, he was in the small side room of the library. Cricket Alan had not left his mind entirely. Against his presence, Alex tried to do his schoolwork. He wrote—the idea had come to him the previous evening, an inspiration at the moment to learn all the words in the language—*Vocabulary* across the top of a clean sheet in his notebook. He entered the first word he had intended to look up today, *correlation*, but he made no move to find a dictionary.

He could not study. Cricket Alan remained; Mr. Gerhinger's face raved mutely at him. He looked at his books and tried to read his way into them, but nothing came together. Several times, as if for no reason, not admitting any, his heart seemed to swell into his throat, and he looked up and stared at nothing. Looking back to the page each time, he could not find his place, could not remember what he had just read.

He heard Cricket Alan's voice that afternoon. Near the end of the day, going up a stairway in the flow of students, he heard Cricket Alan's voice rise from below, from the space under the stairway where boys gathered to talk between classes. Alex heard him say joyfully, "Not me—you'll never see me doing that," and going on, looking ahead, Alex realized that a sense of fear had enveloped him.

After school, in town, he stopped at a coffee shop on a side street. He had never stopped there before, and when, with his jacket unzipped and his books beside his feet on the ledge, he had sat at the counter for some fifteen or twenty minutes, he knew he was hiding. He had been hiding all afternoon, in his movements through the hallways, in his departure from the building. At last—the coffee shop was pleasant with knotty-pine walls and remained nearly empty—he thought, well, so what, if they beat him up, so what? All it would do was hurt for a while. Some blood and some bruises. So what? He could take it—he could stand the hurt.

He stayed sitting at the counter. He began to feel more loose than he had since running into Mr. Gerhinger that morning; before long he was feeling almost as free as he had the previous day. It was in this state, a few minutes later, thinking that he should do it now while his nerve was high, that he backed off the stool and walked over to an old telephone booth near the door to call Irene Sheaffer.

He had a vague notion of everything working out right somehow, of perhaps taking her to a movie that night, of her thinking it was sort of different to ride city buses rather than riding in a car, of their ending up in this deserted and pleasant coffee shop later in the evening, sitting at one of the old booths against the wall, where he could ask her if he could buy her a song, and would walk to the jukebox to insert the coins as she waited. In this frame of mind he found her number, wrote it down, and closing himself inside the dim booth, inserted his dime and dialed. As the phone rang, doubt rang with it. To the woman who answered, who must have been her mother, he said, "May I speak to Irene?" His voice surprised him.

A moment later her faintly familiar voice said hello in his ear.

"You're home already?" he said.

After a pause, she said, "Who is this?"

"This is Alex Housman."

"Ohh. Hello."

"Hi."

After another pause, when she did not speak, he said, "I'm in this place in town. This café. It's—fine. And I was just thinking of you."

She spoke gently. She said, "What place is that?"

"Oh, it's just this little restaurant. Coffee shop. I don't

even know the name. Only it's on Kearsley Street, and it's kind of out of the way. I mean, it's practically empty. In fact, right now I'm the only customer in the place."

"It sounds pleasant."

"It is, sort of. Ahh, listen, I hope I didn't embarrass you that day?"

"No, that's okay."

"I do some really crazy things sometimes. But I guess everybody does. Ahh—I was calling to see if you'd like to go to the movies? I know this is a crazy time to ask. But I just had the thought. I mean, I was here having a bite to eat and it seemed like a good idea."

"Oh, gosh, I'd love to. But I can't really. My mother and I were just going somewhere, to have dinner, and later I still have all my homework to do."

"Oh. You do a lot of homework?"

"Quite a bit. Do you?"

"I didn't use to," he said. He added, "Well," and then, "Suppose I call again sometime?" She did not seem rushed to be rid of him, but he was rushed to be rid of himself.

"I hope you do," she said.

"I'm sorry again if I embarrassed you that time."

"That's all right."

Some minutes later he was out on the sidewalk once more, walking. It was cold, most car headlights were burning in the dusk of five o'clock, and he felt even less desire now to go home to the empty apartment. Something besides emptiness seemed to reside there. He walked along, going nowhere, and then, just as he had been surprised by his voice, he was surprised now by a feeling of dejection. The sky overhead was covered with an orange fuzz, like a mold, the streets on the ground were dark, there were red tail-lights and headlight beams, and he walked with a sense of knowing no one, of having no place to go but to the empty apartment. He remembered Cricket Alan and he thought, all it would do was hurt for a while.

By accident he went to the city library. There it stood, its domed roof resembling an old mosque, its interior promising safety. Some old men sat reading newspapers near the front windows. The rooms, or the spaces created by the shelves of books to the rear on the main floor, were empty. In the first large space, he sat down at an old wooden table, and then to do it properly, rose again and removed his coat. He cautioned himself again against failing, against letting Cricket Alan or Mr. Gerhinger, or anything, make him stumble and fall, and quit.

Inspired to work, he made a list of all he had to do to catch up. He granted himself the F in general science but determined to pass everything else, including American history. In the few remaining weeks, if he maintained a steady pace, he could do it. Wouldn't they all be surprised. The library itself was a growing discovery—a secret and safe and pleasant place to work. Beginning with history, able to read again, he moved along page by page, efficiently, and when he finished a chapter he checked his list, and checked it again when he finished a set of questions. Two chapters gave him four now completed, four of thirty-six, a week's work in less than two days. By the time he started geometry he was feeling the satisfaction of work and discipline he had felt the day before. It was the first time he had ever done any homework at night; his mind was performing with unusual ease. He worked on, checking his list.

After the dinner hour people began to enter, standing to look at books on the shelves, sitting down to read. Around nine o'clock, carrying schoolbooks, a boy named Graham Webster walked in. Webster played varsity basketball, and Alex, glancing up from his geometry, saw him go to a table and remove his coat. Catching his eye, Alex nodded a greeting, and when he did so, Webster came over at once, smiling. Whispering, he asked Alex what the hell he was doing, studying? and said he was too, this was a great place to work and besides he couldn't work at home with his sisters there. He had three sisters, all younger. He asked Alex if he wanted to get a Coke later, and Alex said okay.

Webster returned to his table and Alex returned to geometry. He was surprised at Webster's being so friendly, but forgot him as he read and worked carefully, trying to understand every word, every theorem and rule, as if forever. On clean paper he worked the exercises at the end of each chapter. He had always been short on confidence in mathematics (the teachers and students seemed a secret cult) but he had never really tried, either, and now the exercises kept proving right. Deciding to show Mrs. Leonhard he could do it, using his compass and protractor, he drew careful triangles, added careful arcs and arrowheads, printed uniform 45° and 60° and 180°. He finished the first chapter, then the second, then the third.

There was Webster again, with his coat on. Alex was not ready to leave but he gathered his things. Webster had played for a suburban all-white junior high school and they had played against each other for several years, but that was all, and Alex was somewhat uneasy being with him. Alex did not say much. They walked up the street a block or so to a small hamburger-and-frosted-malt café.

They talked basketball. Webster said Polletta was an ass for sending him back to the sophomores. Polletta was a jackass in any case. Webster also talked about Mr. Varney, the old sophomore coach, and the junior varsity, and at last, surprising Alex, he said, "Did you play any ball out there at the reform school?" He waited for an answer now.

Alex finally shook his head and said, "No."

"What did you do?" Webster said.

"Nothing. Just work, that's all."

"You know what my old man said about you?"

Surprised that anyone's old man had said anything about him, and withdrawing further from the conversation, Alex said, more or less, "Hmm?"

Webster laughed and said, "I'll tell you sometime."

Later, back on the cold sidewalk, Webster offered him a lift home. Alex told him no thanks, he wanted to do some more work at the library. It was a lie, an old shame of where he lived.

He walked over to the library, anyway. But they were straightening chairs, eleven o'clock was closing time, and without removing his coat, he left again and walked back to the main street, to the bus stop. It was cold, and buses ran twenty or thirty minutes apart at this time of night. But he was lucky—after only a couple of minutes of standing back against the dark front of a dime store, a bus with its THIRD AVENUE sign lighted came along and he stepped over to meet its opening door at the curb. He sat shoulder to shoulder with his reflection then in the nearly empty bus, and settling some, he glanced back at the puzzle of the day. In spite of Mr. Gerhinger, of Cricket Alan, of Irene Sheaffer, he had the thought again that perhaps he was ultimately lucky, lucky to be out like this, to be alone during a pleasantly lonely hour in the city when almost everyone else was asleep, or talking, or listening to the words of others, words less rich than those he heard in his mind.

The apartment brought him closer again to earth. Re-entering the world it contained, the odor, the dust, the yellow lights, he felt he was not lucky at all, he was completely without luck. But then, at the kitchen table, working again on his geometry, he forgot to think of such things.

As he worked he discovered his hunger—he had hardly eaten all day—and he fixed one, then another, and then another peanut-butter sandwich. He drank about a quart of milk.

In the process he worked through another chapter of geometry, and into another. It was twenty to one. Still hungry, looking for cookies, crackers, anything, he flicked on the radio. He kept looking for food. But music was playing, and in a moment geometry was diminished to nothing, and then the cookies and crackers were forgotten, and the

music—perhaps no day had made him more ripe to be
taken by music—filled him as if transfusing his blood, and
he stood listening. He thought he understood, at last, why
the crazy girl at the detention home had embraced herself.

In the crowded corridor, at midmorning, he saw
Irene Sheaffer again. She was coming down a stairway at
the end of the corridor and for a moment she was above
the wavering of heads below. He stepped over to the wall
of lockers to avoid facing her in case she appeared within
the mass of bodies. From what he had seen of her, in his
glimpse, she had appeared calm, moving evenly and looking
ahead. She had also appeared forbidden.

The day passed slowly. He ate in the cafeteria again at
noontime, and worked in the library, and he tried to assure
himself that he was not afraid of running into Cricket
Alan. In the afternoon he left the exercises for four chapters of geometry with Mrs. Leonhard, holding on to two he
had also finished, and with the pass she gave him, went to
spend another hour in the side room of the library. He
tried to work into another chapter, but the rules and
theorems refused to catch for him now, even simple addi-
tion eluded him, and he passed the hour thinking and
worrying over things he did not care to have on his mind.

After school he found Mrs. Leonhard at her desk, looking over his papers, holding a sharp red pencil. He stood
waiting. When she finished, she looked up at him and said,
"Well, these look okay. What do you have there, another
four chapters?"

"No. Two."

"Let's have them," she said.

She took the papers and placed them upon the others,
but she did not look at them. She was looking at him. "Tell
me something," she said. "Did someone help you with
these?"

"No."

"They didn't?"

"No."

"That's a lot of work to do in such a short time. Six chapters." She kept looking at him and he hunched as if to say he guessed it was, knowing she was waiting for him to blush, or to give some sign of being guilty.

"You know," she said. But then she paused; her fingers down on the papers ran some in place. Her fingernails were long.

"You know, I know that all the old papers are out floating around. How do I know you did this work yourself? Do you see the problem? I'll tell you this. Whenever anyone cheats, it seems they go about it in the most obvious way."

Alex said nothing.

Looking at him again, Mrs. Leonhard said, "So let me ask you once more—did someone help you with these? I mean, it's all right to get help, that's why there are such things as teachers. But—well, did someone give you some help?"

"No."

She looked at him, studying him. She seemed so clearly not to believe him that he had a flash of doubt himself.

"You've learned your theorems then?"

"I tried."

"You *tried?*"

"I tried to memorize them."

In a moment she said, "Okay—what are they?"

He stood looking at her, and nothing came to mind; he looked down and tried to call them up, and saw nothing but a confusion of printed geometry pages.

"You might start with the first one," she said. "That's a simple one."

He finally shook his head. "I'm sorry. I just can't remember them right now. I memorized all of them. Last night—and I went over them again today. I sure didn't cheat. I just can't seem to think straight right now."

"Well, I'll tell you something. I'm sorry too. More than

you might think. Copying, turning in someone else's work —these are serious offenses."

"I didn't cheat."

"How do I know that?"

"How do you know I did?"

"That's not the point. If you did this work yesterday and today, how could you possibly not know the theorems?"

"I know them. I do. I just can't remember them right now."

"*All radii . . .*" she said. "*All radii of . . .*"

"Okay. Okay. *All radii of the same circle are equal.* That's the first.

"*All diameters of the same circle are equal.* The second.

"*If one straight line meets another so as to form adjacent angles, the angles are supplementary.*

"*If two adjacent angles form a right angle, the angles are complementary.*

"*If two angles are supplementary to the same angle or to equal angles, they are equal.* That's the fifth. That's as far as I've learned."

"Well, that's somewhat better," Mrs. Leonhard said. "Fine. I'm impressed now. But I'll still have to ask you to come in after school to take an examination. I'd like to do it right now, but I have to leave in just a few minutes. We'll do it on Monday after school. We'll cover the first ten chapters."

Alex returned to the same small café, on Kearsley Street. He did not intend, going there, to call Irene Sheaffer, but when he had sat at the counter some ten or fifteen minutes, and had drunk a cup of coffee, and perhaps because it was Friday and the sense of going somewhere and doing something grew in him, he backed off the stool and walked again to the phone booth. Even if his instinct was skeptical, there was a logic in trying again. This time he was going to ask her for a future date. It had not been smart, he thought, or fair, to call as he had, at four o'clock, asking her to go out a couple of hours later. He would suggest tomorrow night. Saturday. Perhaps he could use his father's car.

She answered the phone herself this time, and he said, "This is me again. Alex Housman. Ah, that was crazy, I guess, to call last night like I did. And I was just wondering if maybe—if you're not busy—if you would care to go to a movie or something, tomorrow night?"

"Ohh—gosh," she said. "I can't. Really. I'm awfully sorry. I've already made plans for tomorrow night."

A pause followed—he did not know what to say next— and then she added, "I really am sorry," and he believed he detected a desire in her voice to hurry.

"Oh, that's okay," he said. "I'll survive. You know."

"I would like to take a rain check."

"Fine," he said. "We'll leave it at that. Fine."

Outside the café, walking on the sidewalk, he thought how well she had handled herself, how kind it was of her to say what she had about a rain check, still managing to put him off.

Even as he knew it was out of proportion, he promised himself never to call her again.

Books, and the city library, were a bore tonight. He looked up and around the room often. He wished Graham Webster would show up, but doubted he would on a Friday. He also thought often, as darkness fell, of walking over to the café where he and Webster had stopped, to have some dinner, but he felt little hunger and remained sitting at the library table.

Geometry finally helped him. He raised some interest in solving a problem. The other problems allowed his mind to focus, and in time he was working once more without looking up. He worked through two chapters, and then a third, and then a fourth. Then he left the library for a break and walked over to the café. It was after eight o'clock by now and the difference of a Friday night was apparent in the noise on the streets, the people walking, the number of cars.

Later that evening, at the candy counter at the Fox Theater, from behind him, he heard Cricket Alan. He heard his voice and it was not in a dream. He looked into the gloss of candy; the voice had come from near the carpeted entry. He did not turn around. In a moment, with his candy in hand, in his coat pocket, he had to turn back. Cricket Alan was calm, almost friendly. He said, "Hey, Housman, where you been, man?"

"Nowhere, just around," Alex said.

"Well, I heard you were out of jail, but I haven't seen you. You know. How you doing?"

"Okay. How about you?"

"Egh, you know. Same old stuff. Say, man, when you gonna give me that money?"

"What money?"

"Come on, man, you know. I'm collecting for everybody. I'm the collection agency. Next week? Two weeks? —how's that? We make it two weeks? Okay?"

"Listen, I don't know what you're talking about."

"Awh, come on, come on, Alex. You know. Sixty bucks, right? Double indemnity. Okay? Two weeks? Okay, man? Then everything'll be fine again. Okay? You think about it. Looks like a good flick, huh?"

Four

On Saturday night, at a roadhouse north of the city, close to Shiwasee, his father told him a story of his wife, Katherine.

He—Curly—was juiced. Leaving the apartment, their rough plan had been only that Alex drive him somewhere, that he use his own key and act as chauffeur. Alex assumed he would get out along the way, in town, and his father would go on alone, as he did every weekend. In town, when Alex asked his father what he wanted to do, his father—he had already sipped two or three times from a pint in a paper bag—told him to go on, to keep going straight, he knew a spot out on the highway where they could get a cup of coffee.

Leaving the city, passing under a new overhead divided highway, continuing north on old two-lane Route 22, his father asked him what that bird at the courthouse, Mr. Quinn, had said to him this time. Nothing much, Alex told his father. Just some more forms to fill out. The hearing might be in a couple of months, he told his father, and no, he wasn't too worried about it. Did he think they should get a lawyer? his father asked him. Alex said he didn't know. His father said he didn't know either. He was still afraid it might do more harm than good. The way he figured it, they had to look innocent and they'd look a helluva lot more innocent without some slick prick speaking for them.

Without looking, Alex saw his father take another sip.

He told his father then that Mr. Quinn had told him to take seriously the idea of being sent to BVS.

It took his father a moment to understand; Alex tried to explain that it was a scheme to protect him, because there was a chance it could happen. Then, if it did, it wouldn't be so bad, and if it didn't, it would be a good surprise.

His father sipped again. He agreed. Something like that could hit you like a ton of fucking bricks if you weren't ready for it. And not only that. There was something else he could be goddam sure of. Nobody else was going to worry about him. Except for his old dad. If he let them, if he gave the sonofabitches half a chance they'd bury his ass. And they'd just go on about their business. Did he understand? He was the only one who could look out for himself, and if he kept his head on straight they couldn't touch him. Not with all their vocational homes and training schools. They couldn't touch a goddam hair on him.

They drove. Far into the country, perhaps fifteen miles north of the city, his father gave him directions to slow down and then to turn into an uncrowded parking lot next to a roadhouse tavern called TWIN GABLES. Leaving the car, walking back across the parking lot in the cool darkness, under moonlight, his father stopped to remove his bottle, to drink, and Alex stopped and looked away as if his father were taking a leak.

Inside, in a knotty-pine, uncrowded tavern, the bartender, among the mirrors and lights and bottles, knew his father well enough to call him Curly. The barmaid did not know him, and because of Alex's age, on her directions, they had to go on into the dining room, another knotty-pine room, which was filled only by the lighted face and belly of a jukebox and sets of empty tables and chairs. The tables had orange-and-white checked tablecloths, salt and pepper shakers.

The barmaid followed with her pad, but the kitchen was closed. His father reached for her arm and touched her elbow and she pulled back angrily and said, *"Hands off!"* They managed to order—pretzels and Coke for Alex, pig's knuckles and water for his father. The air of danger was around his father. He sat large and bleary, red-eyed, squinting a little, his hair in oily ringlets. The barmaid's words had also stabbed into Alex, and although they raised mainly a fear of his father's response, they raised an image as well of the two of them sitting there silently, each of them filled with an unusual anger.

Alex looked away from his father, avoided his face. Then, knowing his father was rising from the table, he looked at him. But his father was only walking to the jukebox, trying on the way casually to inspect a handful of coins. He weaved some in his passage, and Alex looked away again, his heart straining. He heard a coin hit the floor and still he did not look. And he thought, yes, they would send him to Lansing—where had he found the vanity to think they would not?

Sad country music—"Slipping Around"—began to play. His father sat down at the table again, and his anger over the barmaid appeared to have passed. The music filled the dim room, playing, it seemed, out in the bar as well, and they did not talk for a time. The barmaid came with their order. Alex glanced at her but she kept her own eyes down. A moment after the woman was gone, Alex glanced over at his father, and his father, looking at him, winked elaborately. He smiled. The record finished and was lifted away—his father was saying something about barmaids wanting to be Sunday school teachers, and Sunday school teachers wanting to be barmaids—and another record, placed down, delivered a deep-throated lament:

> *"Summday yew'll call ma naim*
> *An ah won't answer*
> *Summday yew'll reach for me*
> *Ah whon't be thair . . ."*

His father was talking again, and Alex looked away, with little desire to pay attention. He knew that his father was talking of his mother, speaking of her as *your mother,* and saying among other things, oh, she was a whore, all right, and although it was nothing new to call her a whore, it was new to say, as he did then, that she always wanted it from a stranger, any stranger would do, he said, until he was no longer a stranger.

> *"For you've grown tired*
> *Of all the love I gave you*
> *But someday you'll wish*
> *That I still cared . . ."*

Alex noticed that the water glass his father was lifting to drink from was amber-colored. He had not, not even on the periphery of his vision, seen his father pour from the bottle in his suit-coat pocket. Then he noticed a bubble of saliva appear and disappear at the corner of his father's damp lips, and he noticed the broken-vein fragments high in his cheeks, and the pebbled gray hide of the pig's knuckle untouched on the plate. Alex seemed to glimpse the man himself in a new and sudden way, and he asked him, over the din of the music, if he meant he had met her here? right here in this place? although he was sure he had understood correctly the first time.

> *"When your hair has turned*
> *From gold to silver*
> *And your eyes are dim*
> *By passing years . . ."*

His father told him that he wasn't a stranger exactly. But he hadn't seen her in four or five years. And there she was, perched on a stool out there at the bar with her legs crossed. This was when Alex and Howard were still at Mrs. Cushman's place. She was with some bird, but whoever he was, he must have gone to the toilet or somewhere. He always had figured he'd run into her sometime or other, and he figured it would be a collision of some kind, but then when it happened it was calm and quiet. He just stopped and they looked at each other. That was all. It was like running into an old girl friend, or a long-lost sister. He wasn't mad at her any more. That was all long gone. And he could tell she wasn't mad either. So he just stepped over and said "Hello," and asked her how she was doing, and she said "Hello, Curly," and said she was doing well enough, how was he doing?

This guy, whoever he was, his drink was there on the counter, and so he wasn't going to sit down, he was just going to say his hellos and farewells and go on about his business, but then—and she did look a little down in the dumps—she looked at him and asked him sort of in a whisper if he'd go back outside and wait for her in the parking lot.

Okay. Okay. He turned around casually and walked back outside. He stood out there for a while—it was warm out—taking in the air, and waiting. And he more or less had the idea that it had always been going to come to this. It had happened finally, and there was nothing to it. They would just quietly take a full turn around and everything would be right side up again. It was his turn now. Everything had always turned out the wrong way, just by accident, and here just by accident it was going to turn back the other way. First off, he'd forgive her for running off like she had—they'd never mention any of it again. Then they'd drive out to Mrs. Cushman's and pick up the two of them. Him and Howard. And then they'd all of them make a real go at it. She'd have had her fling—and that was all right—he'd had some himself, and now they'd be a little smarter than they'd been before and they'd work like all hell and make themselves a pretty good life.

Well, a minute later she came out. She came walking along, carrying her purse and cigarettes and things right in her hands. And by now he didn't care if this bird came running out after her or not, because she was his now and that was it—wasn't nobody going to take her away. So they slipped down along to his car—it was the old '41 coupe

—and they stopped there a moment next to the car. There was the moonlight, and she always was a beautiful woman, and she smelled good enough to eat. He'd never forget that moment, standing there, smelling her. He touched her, just lightly, put his hand to her waist, and she kept looking back over her shoulder at the door and each time she turned her head her waist turned under his hand, and he felt the silky stuff of her dress slide back and forth.

They slipped into the car then and drove away, and when they were down the highway a ways and nobody was following, she sounded more like herself. She said, "Curly, you son of a bitch, how are you?"

They drove into town. He figured he wouldn't ask her any questions about anything, that if they had a chance at all it was to let things just fall as they might. Anyway, it sure was something. You know, she'd been his wife. They'd lived together for three, four years. And they never really had any trouble or disliked each other, they'd just gotten all screwed up from living too hard, and then the war came along at the worst time.

Anyway, there they were, driving along like that, and she seemed as young and pretty as she ever had. And he felt about ten or fifteen years younger himself. And she wanted to go to his place. It was her idea. It was his idea too, but he had figured on waiting awhile, but she wanted to go there right away. She'd never been there, or even knew where it was he lived—that was when he had the room down there on Stevenson Street—but that was where she wanted to go. Either there or to a hotel. So of course he knew that was all she wanted, just to go for a little ride for the night.

But then, back at his room, it didn't seem that way. She wanted to have a hot time, that was for sure, and that was fine with him, but there was something else, too. He wasn't altogether sure what it was, but there was something else. Anyway, they had about as hot a time as anybody ever had. It was more, much more, than just a second

honeymoon. She said it was just about the best time she'd
ever had. And of course she wasn't any amateur.

They finally got to talking. And they kept on talking.
Talk was pretty easy in the dark like that, especially when
you've got things to talk about, and they had plenty. Of
course he got pretty crazy talking himself. Only—he meant
everything he said. Poor Katherine. She'd gotten herself
all fouled up with this bird they'd left out there on a toilet
stool. She said this guy wouldn't let her go, he wouldn't
hardly let her out of his sight for a minute. (He could
sympathize with that.) Anyway, he wanted her himself.
He wanted her back. He wanted to start again. He wanted
to go out there and pick up the two boys and start over
again. And he told her so. He told her he had to have her,
and they had to get back together, and he even told her,
because he figured he knew how she was put together, that
she could slip out every once in a while, if she had to have it
that way, to get her plumbing flushed, and he'd do the
same, and they'd never mention it to each other. He even
told her he'd kill this guy if he had to. And he wasn't joking.
He was sober, and he'd decided he'd do that if he had to. Of
course, it was a pretty hot night. Only she wouldn't say yes
or no. He even carried her down to the bathroom, and gave
her a bath, washed her all over like a baby, but she wouldn't
say.

Then she had to go. Only she wouldn't say where to or
why or who or anything about it. Of course, like it always
does, the dawning had to come, and he knew it even if he
didn't quite want to believe it. Here he'd decided to go
ahead and kill a man, he'd really decided to do that if it was
necessary, and she wouldn't even tell him where the hell
she lived. She wouldn't even tell him the name of this guy
he was going to kill. And she wouldn't even give him her
goddam telephone number. Well, she did agree to meet him.
She said if he went down to the cocktail lounge of the
Hotel Detroiter that Tuesday night, Wednesday night,
whatever it was, he'd find here there. So, fine. He said he'd

meet her, and they set a time. He had to work that night, but that didn't matter. This was too important to let work get in the way. Then she wouldn't let him drive her anywhere, either. She insisted on a cab, and he walked down to the corner to call her one.

Killing people—missing work. Could Alex believe such nonsense about his old dad?

Well, fool that he was, not only did he call in sick that day, but he got all his money together and went out and bought himself a new suit of clothes. And he got himself a trim in the barbershop. He even went down to that hotel ahead of time and rented a room. For him and his wife. And he rested. And he had some raw eggs so he'd be in fine fiddle for the night to come.

Like somebody said, there's one born every minute.

And, of course, when he finally got there—early—he waited. And waited. He really didn't expect her to show at all. Deep down he knew right from the beginning that she wouldn't show. It was like drawing to an inside straight. He knew he didn't have a chance and there he was, throwing away his time and his money. And making a fool of himself. And then, one hour and a half, two hours late, she came walking into the place. She was all slicked up in her fancy clothes, and everybody in the place was stealing a look at her. She had about the niftiest little ass he'd ever seen on a woman. And that threw him a little.

They sat down in a booth and began to talk. They talked on and on. And what do you know? She said she thought maybe he had a good idea. She wasn't sure. But maybe it was a good idea. She'd been around a lot, and she was ready to try something different. Maybe. Anyway, they sat there and talked until the place closed, and then they went up to the room. It was way up on the eighth or tenth floor or something, and they were having themselves a big time. They were both so oiled they could hardly walk straight. But they were happy, and they had themselves a hell of a good time.

A couple of days later they met again. Same time, same place. Another workday. He called in sick, and went through the whole routine again. Only this time he wasn't so worried about it. She was late again and it didn't matter. And they got juiced again. They really got juiced. Only this time she didn't want to go up to the room, she wanted to go out. So they went down to some of those old skid-row, honky-tonk joints on Water Street. They drove down in his car, but when they came out of one place they went to another, and then to another, until they were both so drunk they didn't either one of them know where the hell they had left the car. They ended up in a chili parlor, and then in one of those old movie theaters, and then in another chili parlor, and anyway, pretty soon it was getting to be daylight, there was the sun coming up and the birds were tweeting and they were so drunk they couldn't hardly walk. And they still didn't know where they'd left the goddam car. Anyway, they knew they had to get off the streets before they got arrested, so they got into a cab.

And it ended right there. In the taxicab. They got into a fight with the cabdriver. Or he got into a fight. Which she started. She got to bullshitting with the cabdriver, mainly all kinds of things pretty rough for a woman to talk to a cabdriver about. But then, she was drunk and she didn't care, and was just giving this guy a line. She told him for two dollars there was something she'd let him see— the subject of which he was not going to tell Alex—and the cabdriver, the son of a bitch, he pulled over to the curb and stopped, and reached back his two dollars. Well, that was enough. All hell broke loose in the taxicab. He hit the son of a bitch so hard in the head that his hand was sore for weeks afterward. For months. Anyway, he and the cabdriver had a hell of a fight right there in the taxicab, in the back seat and the front seat and in between, and when he finally got out of there, and got out on the sidewalk, there she was, two or three blocks toward downtown again, and running like she hadn't had a drop. Well, he was a

drunk son of a bitch, but he wasn't that drunk. So that was
it. He never did get to kill anybody. And he never made it
out there to Mrs. Cushman's to pick them up. That was it.
He didn't see or hear of her again for three or four years,
until she turned up married to Ward out there at the lake,
when she came back to pick up little Howard.

Back in the apartment, "Paper Doll" played on
the phonograph. His father weaved in from the kitchen and
sat down on the couch. Alex was sitting in an armchair
across the room, watching. He was tired, worn out, but he
did not feel sleepy. It was about three o'clock in the morning. Within a moment, except that he still held his glass
nearly upright, resting on his thigh, his father looked like
he had passed out. His head had fallen; his chin was on his
chest, and his eyes were closed. Alex thought about going
over and taking the glass from his hand. But he did not. In
an unusually clear decision, he decided to let it fall, and if
it was going to spill, to let it spill. His father slipped some
more to the side, but the glass slipped less. Alex looked
away from looking at him. He did not feel angry with his
father for giving up Howard, nor did he feel hate, but he
felt a disappointment with the man, sad, touched with a
faint disgust, a faint recognition. He realized where his
father had been going all these nights, all these years,
dressed up in his new suits and topcoats and accessories.

Alex sat quietly in the chair. The record finished and
started again. He had never been out and stayed up with
his father this way. The waste suggested seemed larger
than the waste of the night itself. Perhaps it was a horror
suggested. At The Lincoln Hotel, he thought, at this hour,
he would be asleep in his bunk in the dormitory. In only a
couple of hours he would get up and dress, and make his
bed, and wash his face, and then, as the sun was rising,
have breakfast in the dining room. There had been a
chilled and empty loneliness at The Lincoln Hotel, but

there had also been promise on the horizon, and he had cared, he had even enjoyed washing the pots and pans, for the chance to dream of the future, and to hear music in his mind. But there was no promise in this room.

His father, slumped at the end of the couch, had hardly moved. Alex, in the chair, was going in a direction opposite from slumping. He was growing more nervous. Once he felt the need to be up, to move, to do something, the need expanded quickly. He panicked slightly with tension before he got to his feet. Going to bed made no sense, and here, as if in his father's shadow, in the apartment, within the pressure of his father's music, there was the sense of suffocation and confinement. Leaving the record playing, with no destination other than the cold air, he took up his coat and slipped outside through the kitchen door.

The air, as he walked down Chevrolet Avenue, woke him some. He drew into himself for warmth. His father stayed on his mind. The green luminescent hands of a clock in a dark window showed that it was twenty after three; the sidewalks were empty and the concrete felt frozen and harder than usual under his feet. The air, highlighted by streetlights, was marked with a fine cold haze. There was momentarily no reason for anything, as if this dark and lighted street lay in Poland or Bulgaria or Hungary or anywhere, and it did not matter. A couple of cars passed, one a police cruiser, going the other way, which slowed almost to a stop as it approached. He saw both faces looking him over. His old fear of the police made his heart catch for a moment, but he walked on as normally as he could, and heard the cruiser, in a moment, accelerate lightly away. The detention home. However much it was a prison, it seemed a warm refuge now. Even washing dishes seemed a refuge. He saw himself standing over the deep sinks, scrubbing the pots and pans and metal pitchers. It was breakfast, when the oatmeal tubs were easier to clean than the casserole and scalloped-potato trays at other meals. He had slept through the night. The water was hot, his sleeves were rolled to his muscles, he was scrubbing and rinsing and the steam was rising, and the crazy girl passed and brushed against him. Why then and not now? he thought. Why, standing over those sinks, was music so near, and why did promise lie out over the fields somewhere, and why, so alone, had he been so strong?

Even though it was past three-thirty in the morning, there were a dozen or more people along the counter and in the booths at the Coney Island. Most of them were drunk. Alex sat at the counter drinking coffee. From a booth behind him, two middle-aged couples were talking, he realized, to him and about him. He sat as if he did not notice. (A sexual tease came from one woman, "He is cute, isn't he, I bet he's never even been kissed, let alone you know what," and a motherly touch from the other woman, "Ah, I'm sure he's got himself a nice little girl friend," and from the other woman, "I don't care what he's got, that's still what I'd like to get close to, I'll tell you," which raised their laughter lightly, and one of the men said, "Wul, go ahead and ask him, it don't make a shit to me, I'll just find myself some nice young pussy pussy," which raised their laughter higher, and the woman said, "What you gonna do when you find it?" and the laughter came hard and loud, and the man said, "Wul, what do you think I'm gonna do?" and the woman said, "I sure wish I knew," and the laughter exploded this time.)

Finishing his coffee, Alex left without looking at them. He sensed a fight coming. ("See, now you chased him away," he heard behind him as he walked to the cash register.)

Outside he walked toward home again. On the wide streets and sidewalks of downtown, besides himself, a yellow cab was going away, past the Hotel Detroiter; across the street what appeared to be only a black and rumpled overcoat, headless and footless, was weaving along, going away also.

Four bells rang from the sky somewhere.

He went on. The street and sidewalks of Third Avenue were deserted. He thought, at last, of leaving this town. To be a soldier, in uniform, to be on a ship at sea. They were of the world itself; the possibility of escape was startling.

Five

He was late and the locker room was empty. The quiz in Mrs. Leonhard's room, easy enough, had taken twenty minutes. He was changing clothes now, and from overhead came the thumps of feet and basketballs. The thrill of playing basketball did not come to him.

He did not hurry. Sitting on the bench, he dressed his feet, carefully smoothing out his heavy wool socks, tightening the laces of his white basketball shoes. The laces and shoes were dirty. He recalled how just a year ago, in junior high school, he had washed his shoes before games and laced in a special pair of green laces. Often on a Sunday evening (while his father slept, as he had yesterday) he washed his shoes by hand in the bathroom sink and stretched the tongues to dry. Basketball had been a thrill then. In their green satin trunks and white jerseys with satin letters, and their green satin, hooded but never zippered, warm-up jackets, they dressed as carefully as girls going to a dance. The wall between the girls' and boys' gyms was folded away, the bleachers were unfolded from the two sidewalls, and the glass backboards were lowered from the ceiling and locked into place. They came out to shoot around nervously, to avoid looking directly at any faces in the rows of faces, until the moment when they returned to the bench and the five of them pulled their jackets over their heads (the jersey never fit him tightly enough, always sagged at the underarms) and the two black-and-white-striped referees appeared from somewhere with their whistles hanging from their necks, one carrying the clearly pebbled game ball.

Rising from the bench, he heard a whistle blast overhead. He closed his locker door. He shook out his legs. He began to feel a pleasant spring and lightness in his legs and feet as he walked.

Practice was under way. Mr. Varney and the sophomores were at the far end of the gym. Alex stopped and stood watching. They were in a drill, running on one blast of Mr. Varney's whistle, stopping on another. Alex wondered if Mr. Gerhinger knew he was there. No, he could not possibly know. Alex shook out his legs again. He still had not decided, finally, to be there. His naked arms and legs were goose-pimpled, and his heart had begun thumping, not in any thrill of playing basketball, but in doubt of belonging here.

Stopping the drill to start another, Varney noticed him. He shouted, "Hey, let's move in here. Let's go. Where you been? Come up here late again, you can forget it."

Three lines were forming at center court. Alex walked down the floor and joined the nearest line. No one spoke to him, nor did he speak to anyone, and although he did not look at the floor, he looked ahead at nothing, to avoid eye contact.

The middle line was shooting; the two outside lines were rebounding and passing off. Alex followed along, in an outside line, and inevitably his turn came. Feeling conspicuous, he ran out and went up to take the rebound from the board, to pass off, to pose a second as if blocking. He went on then to the end of the next line.

On his turn to shoot he paused a little and broke quickly, but the other two fouled their passing exchange and the play was automatically canceled. Alex went on to the first line again without touching the ball. He tried consciously then to loosen up, to feel right. For a moment he seemed not even to be here, but to be in the locker room imagining he was here.

The next time the boy who cleared the board threw the ball to him poorly, too hard, too high, off the timing of his stride. He stopped automatically, as if to go backward, going straight up from a rubber-toe push. In a quick and lucky maneuver, he returned the ball with a finger pass to the third man, catching his stride and saving the play— the man went up to score—and the little sensation of something well done went through him, and must have gone through some of the others too, for a couple of them remarked softly, "Good pass."

In line again, Alex rocked forward on his toes. For a moment the old desire to play, to run and shout, to win, came to him. It appeared like an old friend.

On the next turn, he gave them a fancy shot. He did not know why, nor did he plan the shot beforehand. As his turn was coming, he held the line back, held it through the two or three shots before him, back close to the center line, with his speed building in him, and when he broke, quickly, he got his legs right and hit an old rhythm, and for a moment it was as if he had run a step back into being his self of a year ago, and taking the pass at about the free throw line, a shot he had studied and practiced perhaps a thousand times, he went up, up consciously more than forward, but also forward, laying the ball out as if to shoot but drawing it back and turning, drawing in his knees as he made a turning movement through the air, and as he came to his peak of height and thrust, and began falling away, he released the ball, lofted it over his right eye, back over his head, going on to hit the floor almost flatfooted in under the basket as the ball struck the backboard, and going on backward to get his balance, he saw the ball make its whip through the net. Hoots, some clapping, remarks followed. He started for the end of the next line, unable to look at anyone, and unable not to smile some, and nearby the whistle shrilled.

They moved to the side, off the court. Alex felt high now, too high, and tried to conceal the feeling. He stood holding his arm muscles, rocking on his feet again, willing his face muscles to stay still. Laughter, perhaps tears, wanted to escape, and he turned his face down to release the pressure. Still his eyes watered. Varney was talking before them, and then, picking them out, he began calling names. After eight or nine he said, "Housman."

Alex walked out onto the court with the others, but there was little talk. Varney told the players on the first team to remove their shirts. They would be skins. Alex was on the shirt team. Varney took the skins a little to the side, talking to them softly, pointing here and there, at players and around the gym. They all stepped over then to take their positions, as Varney instructed the shirts to use a zone defense. It meant the shirts were about the third or fourth team. Alex took his position as a guard. Varney held the ball and they tensed for the jump.

Varney lofted the ball; the two centers followed into the air after it.

The ball, tipped, came toward the skin on Alex's side, and they both went up after it, Alex jumping wildly, more than wildly, hipping the skin player as he grabbed the ball from the air, tearing it away from any possible hands, and passing it at once, two-handed, far downcourt, leading a runaway shirt who had to spurt to reach the pass but then went up easily to score a lay-up shot, and Varney's whistle came cutting the air immediately and he was jabbing a finger in the direction of a skin and shouting, "You have to stay between your man and the basket! You have to stay between your man and the basket!"

"I thought we'd get the jump," the boy said.

"You thought!" Varney shouted. "You're a guard!"

The skins moved down, to put the ball in play, and the shirts, already in their zone, were laughing. They were not supposed to score at all against the skins. Alex moved his arms and legs nervously and circled around in his position. Someone called from the side, "You can do it, shirts," and laughed. Alex found it difficult to wait and kept moving; he walked over near the other guard, and circled around him, whispering in passing, "Let's beat the shit out of them," surprised himself at his wish to win, walking over the center line downcourt then as the skins were finally putting the ball in play and starting upcourt.

Alex flagged his arms, and his legs as well, all over a skin who had received the ball and was trying to pass off. When the skin passed, Alex caught the ball on the instep of his foot, and sent it out of bounds. Varney called, "You forwards, get back down here and help out." The skin was trying to put the ball in play and Alex followed him, waving his hands close to his face, getting as close to the line as he could, trying to use his head to block the man's view as well, and he knew, the second the man faked to one side of him, where the ball was going, and intercepting it close to the floor he was off, scoring an easy shot straight in, and this time some applause came from the side, and some hoots at the first team, and several shouts: "Four-nothing, shirts. Four–nothing, shirts."

Alex motioned the other guard down, into a quick press. Moving before the man who was trying to put the ball in play, he again started waving his arms and legs, moving his head, and again, faking, the man telegraphed his release of the ball and threw it almost directly into Alex's hands, and taking one dribble directly backward, Alex jumped, and in the moment of going up, located the basket, shot and scored an easy shot off the board, and came down immediately on defense again, throwing his arms up, crowding the line, waiting for someone else to retrieve the ball, as the others on the side were shouting, "Six–nothing, shirts—six–nothing, shirts," as Varney once again cut the air with his angry whistle.

"Keep the press on," Varney said, going on to whisper

sharply in a huddle with the skins, pointing here and there, jabbing, hissing instructions to one face and then another.

The skins all stayed downcourt this time to put the ball in play, and the shirts stayed with them. Again, before Varney lobbed the ball to the man, Alex was before him on the line with his arms high and his hands waving. The skin backed off a step and passed high, over Alex's jump, what was intended as a high pass to their center, but then a shirt was there as well and the two came down, each trying to pull the ball from the other's hands, and Varney again came shrilling among them with his whistle. "See what happens when a team gets hot against you? See what happens? You fall apart! Jump ball! Come on, let's go!"

They lined up around the circle. Varney lofted the ball, and the skin got the jump clearly this time and tipped it behind him to another skin. The boy, under the basket, began pivoting some, looking to pass downcourt, and Alex, moving in quickly on the boy's blind side and completely around him, ripped the ball almost violently from the boy's hands, sending him off balance, and as Alex went back again, toward the basket, Varney, blowing his whistle, was calling, "Jump! No basket! Jump ball!" He added, "You see what happens when someone plays against you? You get rattled! You collapse!"

Alex thought it was a good steal, but it did not matter. He moved into the circle and crouched in position. He was shaking now. The other boy was a full head taller, several inches broader. Alex doubled way down, set himself there on his toes. Varney held the ball in one hand—he was fixing his whistle in his teeth with his other hand. Alex knew then, decided, what he was going to do: as the ball was lofted he did not spring up but on an angle directly into the boy's shoulder, glancing him out of position and balance, and out of the way, so the ball was his to tip, tipping it to the side to a shirt. But the shirt, a lanky, clumsy boy, shot at once and his shot fell short, missed the basket entirely, and was taken from the air by a skin. The shirts backed off and Alex, with them, back-pedaled downcourt for the first time to cover his zone.

Even though the gym was cool, perspiration was running down his sideburns, and down his legs and back. Still, however crazy he felt, he did not feel winded. As the ball came down, passed to a man on his side, he went after him crazily, agitated him with the agitation he felt inside, stayed with him, on him, as if connected by an invisible axis, waved his hands over his face relentlessly, so the boy could hardly see where to pass the ball. The boy became irritated and tried to use his dribble to break away, and Alex only moved with him faster and stayed closer, keeping his hands waving in the boy's face until he finally pitched the ball away, threw it too high, and it was taken from the air on the run by a shirt. The shirt pulled up, though, at center court, to wait for the others to move down. Alex dropped back from having broken away, to help bring the ball down. Again, from the side, the others were shouting, "Six–nothing, shirts."

Alex received a pass outside the foul circle, and when the forward made no move, he passed back to the other guard and followed behind him across the court. Varney was shouting at the skins, "Get after the ball! Get after the ball!" A couple of skins came out, and Alex, receiving another pass, seeing a chance, however poor, to get around his man, turned dribbling directly down the center toward the basket, directly toward the jam of bodies there, aware that it was a foolish move. Managing to get in two dribbles, arms going up everywhere before him, he jumped to get rid of the ball, threw it so it missed the basket and board completely, and fell into someone on the way down, hitting the floor first with the side of his foot, then falling as the whistle cut the air again close-by. Varney did not call a foul; he said, "Housman, outta there. Outta there."

On his feet again, Alex walked off at the end of the court, favoring his right ankle each time he let weight press on it. He heard Varney call "Play ball" behind him

and then, in a moment, Varney's gray sweat-shirted arm
came around his shoulder, turning him away from the
scrimmage and from the sidelines and toward the door to
the locker room. "You okay?" Varney said. "You feel
okay?"

Alex did not know what to say, found it difficult to
speak, anyway, and nodded yes as Varney said, "What's
with you? You okay?"

Varney stopped and released him then, in the corner of
the gym. Alex, breathing hard, looked at Varney, and
looked to the floor, and looked at Varney again, breathing
fast, his lips curled open. Varney said, "Listen, you better
go down and take your shower. You try to settle down
some. You can't go at a pace like that. What's the matter
with you?"

Alex shrugged, to say that he was all right. Varney
shook his head and turned to walk away.

Downstairs in the locker room Alex sat on the bench
before his locker, still breathing fast and raggedly. He
sat this way for perhaps five minutes. At last he pulled his
shirt over his head, but ran out of energy again and let the
shirt and his hands within it fall together in a limp tangle
between his legs. For no more than a second or two he felt
a child's sense of despair, of being lost on a strange street.
He saw that he had gone a little out of control upstairs in
the gym.

Varney promoted him to the first team. Varney
seemed to like him. Several times in drills and scrimmages
he complimented Alex, calling out, "Now, that's the way to
do it!" Still, the others did not approach him, nor did he
approach them. He dressed and showered as they did, and
occasionally exchanged a few words with someone or answered a question, but he knew none of them well to begin
with and the distance only gradually diminished.

Varney surprised him then. On Friday, during the

scrimmage, Alex and two others were replaced and told by Varney to go to his office. He followed them in, and closing the door, he told them they were being shifted to the junior varsity. The semester did not end for another couple of weeks, when the two or three seniors, creating the spaces, would graduate, but they were to report to Mr. Polletta over in the other gym for practice on Monday.

They took the news calmly. They went immediately down to the locker room, without speaking to one another, to shower and dress, to wait for Monday.

On Saturday night Alex went to the city auditorium to see a game against Bay City Central. He was there by six-thirty, to see the preliminary junior varsity game. By eight-thirty, when the varsity game began, the auditorium appeared to be full. A circular building, a memorial auditorium, it offered some nine thousand permanent seats and was the location of the annual AC Spark Plug Easter Concert, the circuses which came to town, the Harlem Globetrotters, the occasional auto shows and expositions. Not for the junior varsity, but for the varsity game, the lights around the auditorium were dimmed so only the basketball court was lighted, a solid rectangle of lights, hazed in its upper strata. Then these lights were dimmed, and to applause which must have thundered often beyond the walls and out over the cold city, one at a time, picking them up at the side with a spotlight and following them to midcourt, the starting players were introduced, as well tonight as three graduating seniors.

He had not told his father of his promotion, but he had mentioned it to Mr. Quinn that morning. Mr. Quinn's response had surprised him. Actually slapping his desk, Mr. Quinn said it was fantastic news. He said he had decided that Alex should find himself a part-time job, that he needed something concrete to impress upon the judge that he was serious and capable, and so on. But there weren't many jobs available, mainly paper routes and grocery sacking, a few weekend jobs, so basketball was

perfect. The hearing, Mr. Quinn told him, had been scheduled. He had known last week, but not wishing to worry
him, had not told him. It was still far off, on Saturday,
April 23, at 9 A.M. They would receive a formal "invitation" in the mail, which would give them the room number.
But he was not to worry. The judge would be a man named
Flynn who was so-so, but he was not to worry. The important thing was to build up his record in the weeks they had
left. Basketball was perfect.

Alex did not worry, not this night. Nor did his impression on a judge fill his thoughts as he watched the game
below. He thought of himself. Since perhaps the age of
eleven or twelve, when he had first begun to wander here,
he had dreamed of playing under the hazy auditorium
lights. He had the desire not necessarily or entirely for
any glory, nor for anything like teamwork or character
building, which Mr. Gerhinger liked to define. His reason
was more simple: he wanted to hear his name on the loudspeaker. He wanted to hear his name enough times, neither
he nor the rest of them would forget it completely.

On Monday afternoon, rather than running drills
to warm up, they ran patterns. The varsity was at one end
under Mr. Polletta and his assistant, Mr. Anderson; the
junior varsity was at the other end, under Mr. MacPherson, the junior varsity coach. Basketball, simple with Mr.
Varney, was complex here. Mr. Polletta spent most of his
time with the varsity, but he walked to the other end
occasionally and shouted, "Get off your flat feet, Myers!"
or "Move, Davis!" or "You clod, Gibson! Ten laps—get
moving!" and Gibson would head for the stairway leading
to the overhead oval track.

Alex spent most of his time standing and watching.
Mr. MacPherson gave him and the other two new boys
some instructions on a chalkboard on the side, and he
talked to them individually sending them in, but left them
on the court for only a minute or two at a time.

Another man, someone Alex had never seen before, also stood on the side watching. He was tall, perhaps six-six or six-seven, gray-haired, and he wore a white shirt with the sleeves rolled and the tie removed, and suit pants with the cuffs turned up once to reveal a pair of worn but expensive-looking white basketball shoes—shoes which had an impressive and professional-looking fine red line of rubber exposed evenly above the soles. After perhaps forty minutes of running patterns, Mr. Polletta whistled and called them together, and introduced the man. Mr. Cobb. Mr. Joe Cobb. He had played professional basketball for seven years with the Fort Wayne Zollner Pistons. This was his son—Mr. Polletta pointed to a boy who had been practicing with the varsity—Joe Junior, who was transferring to Central at the semester break. Mr. Cobb was going to give them some instructions and tips on fundamentals.

Mr. Cobb, standing before them, next to Mr. Polletta, said loudly, without hesitation, "Okay, give me a single line out here. Everybody. Line it up. Down the center. Let's have a ball."

Someone threw him a ball and he walked to the end basket, the ball hanging from his hand like a volleyball.

They ran lay-ups down the center. Mr. Cobb rebounded each shot, and either gave a comment or motioned the next man on, and fed the ball. He was loud and friendly; he fired hard passes. Often he said to someone, "What's your name, son?," and given the name, said, "Myers, you can go twice as high as that. Go *up*, son. Use your height." Or, "Drew, that was a good shot but anybody who can jump at all will put it right down your throat. Use your height, use your body. And you have to go *up*—not forward, *up!* This is a game of height. Height and speed." Once he asked a boy what his name was, and as everyone laughed he said, "Okay, Cobb—but you can jump higher than that. Get off your feet!" And once to Alex, firing a skidding bounce pass which Alex took on the run, he said, "Hey, that's the way, that's a ball handler."

During scrimmage Alex stood back with the others.

The JV's and varsity were interchanged, but neither his name nor the names of the other two new boys were called. Downstairs in the locker room Graham Webster said to him, "I see you made it," and later, walking into the corridor together before separating to go to their lockers there, Webster said to him, "You looked pretty sharp out there. So did that guy Cobb. Man, that guy knows what he's talking about. You know what? That's the first time all year I learned anything. Just from some of the things that guy said. Polletta—all he does is bitch."

Basketball began filling Alex's life. He thought about techniques and he imagined situations. And he imagined the auditorium. In practice each afternoon after school he ran the patterns with the junior varsity, ran hard, learned the moves, kept alert, but waited above all for the drills in fundamentals with Mr. Cobb. Mr. Cobb had established his authority. Even Polletta asked him an occasional question, or stepped over to confer with him quietly. And Alex believed that Mr. Cobb recognized his abilities, imagined him saying to Polletta, "What about this guy here?" In the scrimmages each night his name was yet to be called, even as a late substitute when it seemed nearly everyone had been worked in. The substitutes moved in and out, starters went back in, went from red to blue and back again, but his name was not called.

Mr. Cobb was as hard on his own son as on anyone, usually harder, letting no mistakes pass. Alex, trying hard to make few, running with all his quickness, jumping, had fantasies, however elusive, of being Mr. Cobb's son himself. He worked in the drills for the man's compliments, and so they came. Once, in a one-on-one drill, Alex scored with his left hand, the other boy, moving backward, getting his legs twisted trying to stay with him in the fake-and-hand shift from right to left; Mr. Cobb's remarks— "Beautiful move! Good Lord!"—seemed so excessive to him that he blushed going on to the next line. It was another shot he had practiced many times in past summers. At the end of the next line Clarence Blue, a Negro of six-

six who was the star, the scorer, said to him, "Man, you a whiz."

Still, it was Polletta's team. When he took over for scrimmage, Mr. Cobb stepped back and stood on the side with the gang of players, to watch and listen. One night in the locker room, in the confusion of getting dressed, Clarence Blue said to him, "How come Polly don't let you play? Man, you a ballhawk. You make a tough guard."

On Thursday, Polletta stood before them with a sheet of white paper in his hand. "Now, don't be disappointed," he said. "Those of you who aren't on the traveling squads this week. This is a new semester just coming up and we still got a lot of ball games left to play. When we play at home, most of you'll be able to dress for the games. So just keep working hard, because you got every chance left to get moved up. We can only play five at a time, that's the nature of the game, but everybody's got a chance. And don't any of you get too complacent because I won't hesitate to replace you with somebody who isn't. Hustle. That's how we play. That's how we win. That's how you make my team. Now let's get to work."

He had the paper in his hand; he had flapped it some as he talked. He walked over to a cork bulletin board and left the paper there, under a thumbtack. No one knew which names had been left off, and Alex, going on to practice at one end of the court, realized no one was going to walk over to see, not now.

For the first time Mr. MacPherson called his name among the first ten to take the floor. He went out self-consciously to take his position. He wondered if his being called meant his name was on the list, and thought it must. They began running the patterns. He passed, ran, ran behind the pass, backed away, passed and followed and blocked. He called the patterns then, raised his fingers and called them out sharply, and when MacPherson called him off, he had been in perhaps ten full minutes. He had not played that long altogether all week. Glancing over, he saw Mr. Cobb standing at the bulletin board, reading.

The session of fundamentals with Mr. Cobb was brief, the scrimmage longer. Mr. Polletta harangued more than usual and paid less attention to substitutions. Mr. Cobb's son was called in, as he had been every night. Alex sat on the sidelines, used a ball to sit on, and watched. Except for Graham Webster and Clarence Blue, he realized, hardly a person had spoken to him. This included Mr. MacPherson, who spoke often to the JV's when they ran the patterns, and called to them by name in the drills and scrimmages. Alex was afraid they knew, or sensed, that he was poison to Mr. Polletta. Still, he thought, he had only been there a week, and they had been practicing together since last fall. He sat on the basketball, watching. Once, turning, scanning with a finger, Polletta paused for a fraction of a second on him (Alex's breath seemed to pause) before going on.

At last the scrimmage ended. Alex was afraid to look at the list. He was afraid, especially, to look at it with the others standing there. He stayed back, and then carried the ball he had sat on slowly over to the bin. He pitched it in, certain it would bounce out, and when it did, he walked slowly to retrieve it. He walked over the floor then, toward the list. Five or six boys were still there. Most of them, probably those who were certain to be listed, had gone down to the locker room. The coaches were also gone. Two of the boys left as he walked up, and from over and between the shoulders of those remaining he read down the two lists. His name was not there. He read the lists again. No, his name was not there.

He turned then to walk away. He was surprised. He had not known until that moment how badly he had wanted, or needed, to see his name on the paper.

Mr. Quinn mentioned the hearing again. He said he had asked for a report from the school on Alex's work for the first semester. This report, together with another he would ask for later, would be submitted at the hearing. How was he doing in school? Was he catching up at all in any of his classes? Alex explained the flunk he had granted himself in general science, the flunk Mr. Dorsey had granted him in American history, and the chances he thought he had in English and especially in geometry. Mr. Quinn made some notes, and then, more conversationally, he asked Alex how he liked school. Did he like it? Dislike it? Did the work have any meaning for him?

Yes, he liked it, Alex told him. And, yes, he thought the work had meaning. And, yes . . .

But Mr. Quinn, watching him, looked amused, and Alex laughed outright at himself. He knew in the moment of glancing at the man that both of them knew he was lying. School did not have any meaning for him. Geometry, the only subject he had given himself to, was only a puzzle— it did not mean anything that he knew of. Still, he did not say that to Mr. Quinn. He did not say anything. He merely sat there, more or less smiling.

"Son, here you are—come in, come in, I got some news for you."

His father, in the kitchen, was in the glow of his Saturday drinking. Alex removed his coat. "What's that?" he said.

"*Romance*," his father said.

Alex, surprised, hung his coat over the back of a kitchen chair.

"You had a call," his father said. "A young lady. With a sweet voice. She said she'd call back. But she wouldn't give her name. That sounds like romance to me."

"You asked her name?"

"I only asked who was calling."

Alex said nothing to this. He was pushing a hand into a tight pocket of his blue jeans as if looking for something, looking to the floor. *Irene Sheaffer*. For the moment no one else came to mind. Then Eugenia Rodgers appeared and disappeared. *Irene Sheaffer*. Glancing up, he saw that his father had turned away. Perhaps his father had noticed that he was embarrassed. But then, carrying a carton of hamburger from the counter to the enamel side of the stove top, his father looked back and said, "Well—what's her name?"

"How should I know?" Alex said. He did not want to be teased, not now, nor did he want to reveal his confusion.

The idea that Irene might call back came home to him. The telephone was there on the counter, not five feet from his father at the stove. He paused a moment before stepping around the table and going to the bathroom.

He closed the door behind his back. He stood holding the handle; he wanted to squeeze his eyes shut but held them open. *Irene Sheaffer*. He was certain it had been Irene. But the knowledge that she would call back kept rising; he felt an old shame of his father, of where and how they lived.

Stepping over, he flushed the toilet. He washed his hands. Nothing helped. One moment he was simply going to ignore his father—he would go out and wait and take the call boldly when it came. The next moment he was going to slip out and run to the drugstore to call her first. The next moment, the most relieving, he imagined himself on the street, alone, walking, or hiding in a movie theater.

In the kitchen his father was molding hamburger patties and laying them in a frying pan. It was their Saturday routine. His father stood with his back to him, wearing a towel tucked in around his waist to protect his suit pants. He was partially dressed already to go out for the night. He did not look back when he had finished with the patties, but Alex knew that he knew he was there. Then his father said, "Two? Is that enough?" Turning back, he said, "Son, I didn't mean to make you mad. I should know better. I'll tell you one thing, though. Girls are just people, too."

Alex sat down at the table.

"You know what I mean?" his father said.

Alex nodded yes, he knew, but he did not look up.

"You used to be good company for a drinking man," his father said. "Before you started courting the ladies." Alex stood up again. He was more confused than angry. Taking up his coat—although not sure yet of deciding to do anything, sure only that the idea of the telephone ringing terrified him—he said, "I have to run down to the drugstore." He glanced at his father for an instant and saw a thin smile, a look of helplessness, on his father's face. He looked down to connect his coat zipper. His father had been looking directly at him. Alex turned, and as he left he heard his father say, kindly, "Take care now, son." The words reached out to the cold air behind him.

Something had happened during the road game on Saturday night, something to do with a boy named Larry Turner, some incident which took place either in the restaurant after the game, or in the bus on the way home, or in both places. Whatever it was—Alex overheard bits of it here and there—it had to do with water in a plastic bag breaking in someone's lap and it was funny enough to compel Alex to laugh himself at their laughter. His response was perhaps doubly unusual, for as he dressed to go up to practice, still bothered, or bothered again, by being there now and having been left off the list, it occurred to him that the reason was the cars. They were true. He had not thought of them in some time. A car thief.

Running the patterns with the JV's, he committed several errors. He was afraid the listing had damaged his confidence. Or he may have been rattled as well by a remark Cricket Alan had made to him that afternoon. In the corridor, hearing his name called, he had looked back and Cricket said, "You saving your pennies, man?" Not then, but moments later, he saw how serious Cricket Alan was. The wallets; they were true, too.

Whatever it was, he hoped, during the scrimmage, standing to the side, that tonight would not be the night Polletta finally put him in. He avoided looking at the man, and moved along the sidewall somewhat out of the way. He was leaning back against the wall, watching the play, when someone stepped up beside him. It was Mr. Cobb, seeming as tall and broad as a giant. Mr. Cobb said to him, "You're not Curly Housman's boy, are you?"

"Yes," Alex said at last. "Yes—I am."

"You are? Well, your father sort of works for me, too. Has—for years now."

Alex said nothing. He stood staring at the play out on the court. Aware that the man was standing beside him, he did not look at him once. Nor did he look, in time, when Mr. Cobb walked silently away, although the man had to pass directly before him. And it was not Mr. Cobb who angered him now, it was his father.

On Tuesday afternoon Alex quit the basketball team. He had not planned beforehand to quit, and when he did, within ten minutes, as if he had run away from home, he felt a miserable doubt. He had decided over the weekend, in spite of being left off the list, to earn his way back.

The incident was surprising. He made an error. It was not even entirely his fault. Running a pattern, a boy he was supposed to pass to turned the wrong way and Alex's pass sailed straight into the hands of a defenseman. From the sidelines, as if from the air above—it was the first time the man had spoken to him—came Polletta's broad voice, "Housman, you learn that at the juvenile home?"

No one laughed. Alex did not look at the man, nor, for the moment, did he look anywhere. He would have ignored the remark, and he tried, but he was unable to stop himself from reddening.

He took a pass, passed off, ran to his point. But he found it difficult to look anywhere or at anything very directly. As if of its own will, his face kept angling slightly down, his neck seeming to stiffen in that position. His mind carried on a flurry of thoughts of Polletta, of Mr. Cobb, of Mr. Gerhinger. A moment later MacPherson called his name and he left the court and walked to the sidelines.

He stood there. He still found it difficult to look around at anything. He glanced at the pattern being run, and hardly saw it. He tried to stand as if nothing had happened, and he may have given such an appearance. Certain that he did not stand a chance, certain at least during the moment of turning, of deciding, he turned and began walking away over the floor. He had quit now, in this moment, and it was final. The whistle blew behind him—it must have marked the end of running patterns—and the shrill declaration made the skin over his shoulders ripple. He did not look back, or change his pace, although twenty or more feet remained to the door and he believed they were all looking at him.

Downstairs he did not go directly to his locker. He walked back through the locker room to the area of sinks and urinals, as if he had only gone down there to wash his hands. He turned on a faucet and reached his hands under the water, and rolled them together. He glanced up at himself in the mirror; a light gloss seemed to be over his eyes; he made a vaguely silly face at himself.

Cupping his hands under the faucet, he raised them full of water to his face and splashed water into his eyes. He turned around and walked back to his locker. He tried to focus on one thing at a time, on the color of his locker, on the ventilation slits, on whatever was directly before his eyes.

Mr. Polletta had the final word. In gym class the following day he walked up to Alex and said, rather softly, "That's the end of organized school sports for you at Central High School." Turning, he walked away again. Alex did not look after him.

Six

"What's her name?" his father said. "Why you keeping it a secret?"

It was almost funny now, after a week, funny that his father had not forgotten.

"How should I know her name?" Alex said.

"Can't you even guess?"

"I don't have any idea."

"I bet," his father said. He went on fixing the hamburgers. A record was playing on the phonograph, the music spreading through the apartment from the living room. Jimmy Wakely and Margaret Whiting were singing "Slipping Around." Every few minutes, after a pause and a click, they sang it again.

Alex had not said anything to his father of the basketball team, nor did he plan to. He had told Mr. Quinn that morning that he had decided to give up basketball because it really led nowhere and it took up a lot of time he should give to his schoolwork. If Mr. Quinn was surprised, or disappointed, he did not say so. He told Alex he thought he should pick up a part-time job then; the charges against him could sound pretty serious and they might as well use whatever ammunition they had.

Alex decided on a paper route, a morning route of the Detroit *Free Press.* The only other jobs available were packing and carrying out groceries Friday night and all day Saturday and Sunday, or wrapping meat at a downtown meat market Friday nights and Saturdays. Mr.

Quinn, making a telephone call, had received a nod *yes* from Alex that he could stop by the circulation office at eleven o'clock that morning, and another nod *yes* that he could start the route sometime during the week.

Mr. Quinn had also asked him, when the paper route had been arranged, where he believed he was headed in this big world. What did he want to be? Did he have any idea what kind of work he'd like to do?

Alex had tried to think seriously of an answer. Being someone—not anyone—was an assumption, a fantasy, he had always carried with him. But trying to think of what he'd like to be, he could think of nothing. He recalled some of the notions he'd had of himself, but they were so obviously impossible they would be disheartening even to mention. He had to say that he did not know what he wanted to be.

Mr. Quinn told him not to sweat it. He'd think of something. One of these days he'd see what it was he wanted to be. Draftsman. Mechanic. Salesman. The important thing, Mr. Quinn told him, was to decide, not to just fall into something by accident.

Cricket Alan was standing near the end of the center aisle in the locker room. He was talking to someone. Others around the locker room were undressing and dressing for gym class. Alex felt a sweeping over of gray when he saw Cricket Alan. But he continued along as if all were normal. Cricket had turned his head and they glanced directly at each other. Neither spoke. Alex went on, and after a few steps, turned into the row of his locker. Cricket, at the time Alex turned, had been eight or ten feet away, and Alex heard his voice, almost friendly, behind him, "Hey—Housman."

Alex could not remember afterward exactly what he did next. Somehow he turned back, perhaps numb with knowledge, and Cricket had stepped over to the head of the row to face him. Alex saw him there, saw him smiling in a friendly way. Some others were behind him, watching quietly and not smiling. Others appeared from the sides; some were partially undressed, some fully dressed.

"You owe me money," Cricket said.

The admission was too humiliating for Alex ever to make to another, and he said at last, in a stranger's voice, "No—no, I don't think I do."

"Sure you do. You owe me sixty bucks."

"How do you figure?"

"Oh, come on, man." Smiling just slightly, Cricket stepped closer. The faces came closer with him, but stayed behind.

Alex heard some movement behind his back, or sensed movement, but he did not turn to look. He stood still.

"When are you gonna *pay* me?" Cricket said.

Alex stood looking at him. Cricket continued, just slightly, to smile. "I don't know what you're talking about," Alex said, the voice still not his own.

"Ohh, man," Cricket said.

Alex said nothing. He stood there.

He only glimpsed the fist when it came—he had seen Cricket's facial expression tighten slightly—and he was hit squarely on the side of his mouth, under his cheekbone, driven, knocked sharply into someone behind him and into a tinny wall locker. He stumbled but did not fall, nor did he let go of the books in his hand. Regretting the words even as he spoke them, he said, "What was that all about?"

Immediately he was hit again, as if in darkness. He went down this time, glancing off the lockers and into legs which were backing away behind him. He fell into the space between the bench and the wall of green metal. His books were left on the floor as he picked himself up.

Cricket did not rush into him, but he stepped closer again. Alex was on his feet. He felt no more pain than an itch on his upper lip, as if a fly had landed there. He tasted blood on that side of his mouth and touched the flesh inside

with his tongue. He stood there; everything seemed perfectly clear. He saw some of the fist coming this time,
coming from the same place, and turning his head, raising
his hand, it only glanced off his forehead, and hurt more,
instantly, than the two direct blows.

From behind Cricket someone screamed in a sharp and
sudden panic, "Kill that son of a bitch, Cricket! Kill him!
Kill him!"—a scream which aroused Cricket and he came
on in an immediate rush, with both fists. Alex was hit on
the other side of his head, over his temple, and was pushed
with the movement slamming back into the lockers. He
had managed to grab one of Cricket's arms, had a grip on
the forearm, but the other fist came thumping, wildly, over
and over, mainly into his raised shoulder, but also into the
side of his head, and over his ear, until he caught the flying
wrist and held, and kept holding, although Cricket
thrashed into him trying to break free. Cricket stopped for
a moment—Alex held tight—and in a sudden jerk, Cricket
tried to snap free. Alex held on. Someone began urging
them out into the center aisle, where there was more room.
A hand touched Alex's back, as if to gingerly guide him
along, but he still held Cricket's wrist, knowing that if he
released an arm, a fist would slap immediately into his face.

In the wider center aisle, where there was no bench, in
a confusion of people and their words, Alex released his
grip and he and Cricket separated. The others were getting
back out of the way. Alex raised the back of his wrist to his
mouth, touching the thickening itch over his lip, and
glanced at the blood on his wrist. His temple, the top of his
head, on that side, throbbed in the direction of his eye as if
he had bumped into a door.

Faces, half-dressed bodies, hairy legs on the ends of
benches, eyes over shoulders. Cricket had his fists up now,
and he came at him boxing, tucking his chin, thrusting and
weaving his shoulders, slowly pedaling his fists out front,
until, as Alex drew up his hands, Cricket's fists came flashing out, one catching him solidly over an eye, rapping his

head back and jarring his neck, knocking him off balance
back into the separating bodies, and down again, sitting
down hard on the floor as much from tripping over feet as
from the blow. He put one hand on the floor and sat for a
moment, blinked his eye and pushed himself up.

As he raised his fists again and began to crouch,
Cricket came charging, swinging wildly, into him. Being
hit and overrun, he tried grabbing at Cricket's arms again,
failing to catch anything, and Cricket went stumbling
down beside him. On an instinct, as if to cut into him, Alex
came around with a foot with the thought of toe-kicking
Cricket in the head, in the face or ear, but his timing was
all off and he missed, banging loudly into the locker.
Cricket pushed himself to his feet in a rush.

They faced each other again. Alex raised his fists and
got off his flat feet this time, and then he was pushed,
suddenly, violently, by two hands thrown on his back, a
voice behind him hissing something he did not clearly understand, pushing him directly into Cricket, who tried to
hit him, trying to back off as Alex grabbed into him. Alex
got a hold again, and tried to keep his face covered as
Cricket backed away and jerked his arms to get free. The
same voice that had screamed before screamed again,
sounding strangely close to tears, "Kill him, Cricket! Kill
that son of a bitch! Kill him!" Then—and he was so tired
it was almost for the hell of it, frightened some by the
voice, feinting the clinch—Alex exploded his own fists with
all he had, and hitting Cricket in the forehead, and in the
forearm, he went past him.

Again they faced each other. Cricket was almost smiling now, breathing heavily through his smile. Alex's shirt
was torn—part of the sleeve hung from his forearm behind
his fist. Cricket came swinging at him, punching, and
missed as Alex backed away. Cricket, hesitating, continued his vague sneer and smile, his nostrils flaring as he
breathed. Alex wiped his knuckles over his lips and realized
they were raw and wet on that side—they felt like broken

grapes—and he whistle-spat blood-strung saliva to the floor, and had to look at last and reach with his fingers to break the strand free, looking up again almost at once, when he was hit over his eyebrow and forehead, knocked back again among the others to a sitting-down position on the floor. Looking ahead now, he saw Cricket through a blur. He merely looked ahead. He raised a hand, palm forward, to say he quit, he was beaten. Not viciously, but enough to hurt, he was kicked, from the rear, kicked in his hipbone. He did not look around. He sat there, looking to the front at nothing.

He did not quite listen to anything. Legs were moving around him, and voices were talking, and still he sat there. He thought if he stood up he might be knocked down again. But it was not fear which caused him to remain sitting. It was something associated with the humiliation, as if to gather more might leave less. Voices were above him and around him as if he were not there. Legs stepped past him. Then he heard Cricket's voice say, *"I want that fucking money, man."* He had not looked to see if Cricket remained or had left, and he did not look up now.

The longer he sat there the more difficult became the moment and act of rising. He felt lost, and the feeling grew. Remotely, elaborate notions came to mind, ideas of winning, of defeat, of honor and dishonor, of life and death. Still, he sat there. Increasingly it was as if a veneer over him had been removed, as if he were skinned, and that if or when he rose, he would not quite be anyone any more, as if Cricket had taken something crucial away with him.

He began to check and double-check his wounds, as if preoccupied. He touched the side of his hand to his split lips and looked at his hand. He repeated the exact movement and looked again, as if in concentration, while in his mind nothing happened very clearly. He wiped the smear of blood-saliva over his pants leg and touched his fingers to his other eye and looked again. His eyebrow hurt and felt tender, but his fingers came back dry. He touched his nostrils and his thumb cracked away small amounts of nearly dry blood. He probed his tongue inside his lip and the flesh seemed wet and a numb distance away.

"Hey. Are you okay?"

He paid no attention.

"Hey?" the voice said.

Without looking, he raised a middle finger toward the voice.

"Screw you then," the voice said.

Time passed strangely. He may have sat there five minutes, or ten, or more. When he finally pushed himself up, he did not look to see if he was being watched, not even on the periphery of his vision. Nor did he know what to do; there was the thump overhead of feet and basketballs. Gym class was going on. He felt, painlessly, without his skin, without a veneer either of skin or clothes.

He made his way to his locker. Once he was there he realized there was no reason to open it. He paused a moment, and invented a reason. He opened the locker and took down his towel, and using a handful of towel, he daubed around his face, touched his lips, his eyebrow. Then he found a use for the towel: he emptied a lower mouthful of dark blood into its folds and laid it at the bottom of the locker.

A moment later he left. He walked, casually and slowly, his head partially down, from the locker room out into the first-floor corridor. The corridor was silent; he knew without looking up directly that it was empty. Classes were going on around him, through the glass of closed doors.

In a seldom-used boys' lavatory in the basement, he used paper towels and cold water to pad and nurse and wipe his face. He avoided looking up in the mirror. Once when he did, the face he saw made him look down in humiliation, working along until the feeling passed.

The flesh was torn inside his lips on one side. It was bleeding there now, and the numb feeling was fading. He kept spitting long droplets of the warm-tasting liquid into the sink, keeping the water running to blur the red to pink and wash it away. Still the blood flowed, seeming to fill the space between his lower lip and his teeth. He tried to tuck a fold of wet paper towel inside, but everything, teeth, lips, gums, hurt more sharply now and he had to tear the paper towel several times to make it fit, when it seemed to do no good.

As if from a distance, avoiding his own eyes, he glanced in the mirror again. His face was discolored, reddish, over one side. The most painful sights were his lip and eye on one side. The lip was swollen high, toward his nose, making him look harelipped; his eye was red and partially closed, his eyebrow bulging some.

Removing his coat from his locker, keeping his face down, he left the building by the end door. The sunlight outside was weak, and the air was warm for January. He walked toward the side streets, circling away from the bus stops, on his way into town. He wished to be nowhere now but at home in his bedroom with the door closed and the lights turned off. He wished to be there immediately, to hide in bed, but knew he would have to wait until his father had gone to work. He could not go back to school, and the thought of what might happen for not going was too frightening to consider. He imagined a police cruiser returning him to the detention home. He imagined the fields there covered with snow. Several times he stopped to lean over and release blood from his mouth to the crusted snow remains along the sidewalk.

In town he went to a movie theater. Before him, as he sat down, off in the depth of the screen, five or six horsemen were preceding their dust in a valley. They rode on, and for a moment they came close to riding into the theater itself, and stopped, the horses rearing and side-stepping as the men looked around. The cowboy in the center, a hat string loose in the V of his throat, was Richard Widmark. Then they were far off in the valley again, preceding their roll of dust, and from nearby, behind a rock surface, first the rifle barrel, then a painted hand gripping the rifle, entered the corner of the screen. The horsemen came on. Alex, trying to study the movie, used his handkerchief as a receptacle. The blood kept filling inside his lower lip, like warm coffee he could not swallow.

Book Four

Withdrawal

One

Alex spent the night where he had thought he would be the safest, closed in his room, concealed in his bed. But most of the night he lay partially awake, growing fitful. In this state an idea came to him. It was too late now, he thought. The only moment when he could have acted had passed.

The idea infected his mind. Once it was there, thought of anything else, even of the idea itself, was difficult. The pang was more distressing than had been any splitting of his flesh. Something in him seemed thereafter to be separating, a separation perhaps similar to the line of a fault running for hours, or days, through the skull of the earth. He wished only to withdraw deeper into the pit of himself, against the belief that he had lost his pride. What else did anyone defeat when he defeated a person?

At five or ten minutes to six that morning, he was standing on the corner of Garland Street and Seventh Avenue. The streetlight here lighted only a side of the small residential intersection, and he stood back on the sidewalk in the dark. He had to take on the paper route he had agreed to take on. He was waiting for the regular boy who was due at six. His fear and humiliation were slighter here. They remained, but remotely.

He paced occasionally and slapped his gloved hands together. Wind was sweeping in the branches and the temperature was down from yesterday. He had worried about the paper route over the weekend, having to be out in the cold every morning, having to walk a mile just to begin, but now that he was there he did not mind so much. Not this morning. The city seemed to be asleep and he felt momentarily hidden in the darkness. A question he had been unable to answer during the night—*What should he do?*—did not press so much upon him here.

His pillow had been bloodstained where he slept. In the bathroom he had seen the matching stain at the corner of his mouth. His lip remained swollen. His left eye had swelled up so that it was little more than a line of eyelash, a column of hairs growing from a plum. The skin on that side of his face was a similar color. He had tried to brush his teeth, to brush away a taste of sedimentation in his mouth, but it had hurt too much to separate his jaws. He brushed only across the front. For an instant, before the mirror, he had looked into his one opened eye, and the humiliation had come up again. But looking down to concentrate on washing his hands, sloshing water back and forth in his raw and tender mouth, the sensation had receded.

He had his coat collar around his ears, and his hands, inside gloves inside his coat pockets, were warm. His nose and cheeks were cold, but he was not entirely uncomfortable. It was quiet. Everyone in the world he knew was probably in bed, asleep. During the night he believed that he had to do something. There was no alternative. Such notions as running away, and suicide, and several methods of killing Cricket Alan, to his face and to his back, with weapons, with speeding automobiles, had passed his mind. Now these too had receded. It seemed for the moment there was an alternative. If he worked hard, and if he was lucky, there was still a chance there was something he could be. He saw it not as a compromise but as a point of light on the gray horizon. Mechanic? Draftsman? Salesman? There were still chances. He paced the sidewalk, slapped his gloved hands loudly together.

It must have been six-thirty before the boy appeared, walking sleepily, on the dark sidewalk. They did not introduce themselves to each other. The boy said, "Whatta ya say, man," and Alex, between the painful hinges of his jaws, said, "Whatta ya say," and followed the boy to a bundle of newspapers he had not seen before, lying beyond a fire hydrant.

Alex carried the papers. The boy showed him how to fold, and as they walked along he pointed at houses, at porches and side doors, at mailboxes and doorways inside warm and odorous and poorly lighted apartment buildings, and Alex delivered the papers. By seven there was light enough to read the papers if they wished, but they did not, and when they ran out of papers, where the route ended in lower downtown, it was twenty minutes to eight.

Now he had to go to school. He hurried, walking, worrying, along the way. Only when he was next to the school grounds did the idea of entering the building seem impossible again. He considered walking back to town, going once more to the movies. But the twenty-four-hour theaters were depressing and he left off thinking of them. He was afraid to skip school. He was afraid of being picked up by a police cruiser and returned to the detention home. Mr. Kelly would not even look at his face this time. He would lock him in the upstairs corridor.

He entered the school. He entered late and intentionally missed homeroom in order not to face Mr. Hewitt. He believed he could get away with missing homeroom. He retrieved his books from his gym locker in the empty locker room, but did not leave his coat there. When the rooms were ready to empty for the first class, he was waiting in the corridor, and as the rush of students came out, he immediately entered his first class, Mr. Dorsey's room. He sat with a hand visoring his bad eye and some of his swollen lip, and looked down as if doodling.

Students began walking in. He heard them and did not look up. When the room seemed full, a slight shock came to him over where he was, and the fear and humiliation rose again.

He did not glance up even in the slightest way. The visor of his hand all but covered one side of his face and he stared directly down his palm at his desk. Whispers, even silence, affected him. Still, he did not look up, even when he was certain someone was looking directly at him. He asked himself what in the world he was doing there—how could he have been so dumb? The detention home seeing, at the wood.

Mr. Dorsey was talking. Alex, sitting perfectly still, tried not to listen. He concentrated on the surface of his desk, trying to study the lines in the wood. Only a few minutes later he heard his name called. He could not quite believe it. He made no move.

Mr. Dorsey talked some more, and there was his name again. "Alex? Alex, don't you hear me?" Mr. Dorsey laughed lightly.

Alex did not answer, nor did he look up; he stared, unseeing, at the wood.

"*Ohh, Alex?*" Mr. Dorsey sang. "Are you here today?" The class laughed again, lightly.

Alex continued to stare down. His face and neck felt warm with blood, but he did not look up, nor did he move. In a moment Mr. Dorsey was talking again, and the class went on its way.

At the ringing of the bell, Alex rose to make his way out. Moving quickly through the corridor, keeping his face angled down, he left the building by the nearest exit. He paused outside the door in the cold, and on a sudden fear of being caught, he started away. Then, and his mind was working in a similarly rattled fashion, he hurried, half running a few steps, then he walked some, and again he was running. His eye felt cold, exposed in the light.

Some ten minutes later he entered the near-empty hollow of a movie theater. There, in technicolor, over the screen, Indians stepped their ponies, bareback, through shallow water, and soldiers and long-skirted women moved within the walls of a log fort. He tried to allow the story to take him, but it did not. His thoughts, and his eye, were there for a moment, and then they were elsewhere, and then they returned to the screen. He realized, in a moment, that it was the same movie he had seen the day before.

He returned to school the next morning. He knew he had to. There could be no possible excuse for not going. Mr. Gerhinger would suspend him. Mr. Quinn would shake his head no, and say he was sorry, buddy. They would not allow him to walk the streets; they would call him an *incorrigible;* the judge would send him to Lansing.

The discoloring on his eye and the side of his face had given way slightly to purple. He could see better today; the swelling had also gone down over his lip. Walking the last several blocks to school, growing nervous again, he forced himself to go on, to get through the day by ignoring everyone, by keeping his face averted as much as he could, by staying entirely to himself.

Throughout the day he expected to be called to Mr. Gerhinger's office, to account for missing most of yesterday, but he was not called. Only one teacher questioned him, Mrs. Kaplan, his English teacher, and when he responded by saying he had run into a train, she said, "I guess you did," and she added, "I think some of you live in another world."

One incident occurred. Late in the day, on his way through the corridor, a girl he knew, or her voice, for he did not look at her, hissed "Chicken" at him, and he was surprised at her venom, for he barely knew her, and she was a small and pretty girl.

Mr. Quinn, laughing, said, "Jesuschrist, man, what happened to you? You get hit by a car?"

"No—no, I got in a bad fight."

"I'll say. Where? Why? What happened?"

"Oh, just something stupid. It was nothing."

"Who'd you get in a fight with?"

"Just this guy at school."

"Hasn't he got a name?"

"Alan. Cricket Alan."

"Oh. I know him. I mean I've heard of him. Seen him play football. What was the hassle?"

"Nothing really. Nothing very important. Just a small disagreement."

"About what?"

"It was just something about this girl."

"Yeah? Who does she love? She love him, or you?"

Alex gave no answer and Mr. Quinn said, "Okay, forget it. What have you been up to worthwhile?"

"Nothing worthwhile. I missed a day or so of school this week."

"You did? That's bad. We can't have any more of that."

"You know," Alex said. "I think I'd be better off if I quit school. I could get myself a job some—"

"No, no, no. No chance. We have to get through this hearing. What would you do? Wash cars? Sack groceries? No, you don't want that. I mean, I know it can get rough. You get punched out, you miss some stuff, okay, you want to throw it all over. I understand. But you can't do it. There's nothing else for a sixteen-year-old kid to do. Especially you. Besides, you can't let them knock you off the track like that. You're too smart. And I mean that, too. I'm an old hand at this stuff. Just a couple weeks ago you were doing fine. So you get punched out? Who cares? I don't care. What do you care?"

"I don't know," Alex said. "I just guess I do."

The spaces below and above his left eye turned an ink color. Ink crescents. The purple over his cheek spread into dull yellow. The swelling went down. He avoided his father over the weekend by staying away from the apartment. He checked each time before he entered to be sure his father's car was not there, and except to sleep he did not stay long. When he had left the apartment and walked a block or two, he did not mind being out. But on Sunday night, a few minutes after he had taken off his coat in the kitchen, he heard his father on the stairs, coming up.

His father looked a little tight; he said, "I hope the other guy looks as bad as you do."

Alex did not laugh. He thought about lying, about saying "He really does," but he could not say it. Nor did his father say any more. It was as if he already knew.

His eye turned the color of yellow clay, almost a normal color. The crescents faded. Still, in school, perhaps from habit, he kept his face generally averted from others. He searched out, subconsciously, the places others avoided.

If someone entered the side room of the library during lunch hour, he did not glance up from his desk to see who it might be. He visored his eyes when he read, making believe he was engrossed in his work, although seeing as many images in his mind as he saw paragraphs on paper. Leaving the table in the library, gathering his books, he acted out the role of a working student, looking anywhere except at people, as if in concentration on the work in his mind.

Now in the mornings he delivered the newspapers alone. He was under way before six, and before seven, the canvas bag empty again, he was in the Coney Island in lower downtown. He usually had a breakfast of coffee and doughnuts and a glass of milk. He read his extra copy of the Detroit *Free Press* and alternately kept an eye on daylight as it blended upon the street and through the windows. He imagined he was one of the factory workers himself, sitting there not with a canvas bag, but with a metal lunch pail and a thermos, and at peace.

One morning he glimpsed a woman in a yellow nightgown pass a window. He saw no more of her than the draping of her gown, but he knew she was not sheathed and protected within the folds, and he imagined embracing her all over herself, all over her house.

Perhaps a policeman, a half-dozen factory workers, a bus driver, a lone airman, sat around the U-shaped counter over coffee and cigarettes, or over a morning paper. Alex spent an hour or so at the Coney Island each morning, reading and thinking, and watching the street, the unseen presence of the sky, its color lowering into the canyons of the city buildings, the buses and taxicabs passing, seeing occasional snow flurries, or seeing in the reflection of windows across the street the red-streaked reflection of the sky. A couple of weeks had passed and his eye had almost entirely returned to normal. Only a shadow remained. He believed, at least in these pleasant early hours, that he was coming along well enough.

School, after the Coney Island, was a different world. Most of them had dressed carefully and colorfully for the day. They talked a lot to one another, and made movements and gestures. Walking among them, sitting in the classrooms most of the day, divided against himself in their company, he did not enjoy his own company as he did in the morning. But he believed he was getting through.

Mr. Quinn told him to forget the first semester, to write it off as something that had not happened, and to go to work on the second semester. After all, he had missed three fourths of the classes. To pass geometry, as he had, was practically a miracle in itself.

It was the first Alex had heard of his grades, for they would not be issued in school until the following Monday. He had flunked everything but geometry.

The hearing, Mr. Quinn reminded him, was four Saturdays away. That was plenty of time to show that he could do the work.

Irene Sheaffer called him that afternoon. He was sitting at the kitchen table, adding and marking figures in his collection book. His father, back from doing his Saturday chores and shopping, was within his process of dressing, of preening himself, sipping small drinks, preparing, building up to going out for the night. After his visit that morning to Mr. Quinn, Alex had come home and spent most of the day lying on the couch covered with the old Indian blanket, dozing, walking occasionally, dozing again, trying several times to read the newspaper, having little interest, going no more than a paragraph or two, and dozing again.

When his father had come in from shopping, and called to him from the kitchen, he had made believe he was sleeping and did not move. Thereafter, lying there, he had been depressed with his sloth. Even if he pretended, he did not sleep. He had the thought that this was the way people lost their senses, that it began with the impatience he felt within himself, and led to a point of losing control. Still, he lay there, and when he finally got up and went to the bathroom to wash his face, to brush his teeth, perhaps to renew himself in the water, it was already dark outside. He was sitting at the table, and his father had just walked into the kitchen, when, over on the counter, the telephone rang.

He and his father looked at each other. The telephone seldom rang at all and had timed itself perfectly now. It was startling in the quiet. In its authority, pausing as if to draw in another breath, it rang again.

"Must be for you," his father said.

Alex sat at the table. The telephone rang again.

"Son, answer the phone. That must be for you."

Alex stood up. Feeling somewhat blind, he went around the table to the counter, to the phone, as it was ringing again. He picked it up. Doing so, he turned his shoulder and back to his father. "H'lo," he said.

He barely understood her first words, only that it was she. Then his father's hand was on his shoulder and he turned to see his father looking at him strangely. Then his father whispered, just audible, "Son, get a hold of yourself." His father gave his shoulder a very hard and affectionate squeeze and smiled. Alex could not help smiling slightly in return. As his father moved around him to leave the kitchen, he reached back quickly to take his drink from the table.

Alex was trying to catch up, trying to understand what she was saying. He knew she had said something about her calling him, about the "rain check," and she had also indicated that she knew of the fight ("I heard about the trouble you had") and now she was saying something about her mother, of having talked it over with her mother, and he realized at last that she was calling to ask him over for the evening; she mentioned two other names, she mentioned a game called *Scrabble,* that he was probably awfully good at Scrabble . . .

At last, in the silence, he said "Fine," and again, "Fine."

"Okay?" she said.

"Yes—okay."

He stood there for a moment when he had replaced the receiver. He was confused and perhaps somewhat delirious. He imagined his father at the far end of the living room, his foot up on the radiator before the window, looking down on Chevrolet Avenue, and his impulse was to go to him, like a child, to apologize, to exclaim something, to joke, but he was still not sure what had happened.

His father returned to the kitchen. He struck a match with his thumbnail and lit the burner, to begin the hamburgers. He did not say anything to Alex or look at him for a time. Alex was back at the table. Finally his father said, "That wasn't so bad, was it?" He added, "Now that it's over."

Alex said nothing.

"Well, what do you say?" His father was smiling happily.

Alex laughed, trying to check himself from laughing again, foolishly, but then they were laughing together, lightly and foolishly, and his father turned back to the hamburgers. Alex, finding it hard to sit still, rose again and went to the bathroom, where it was easier to laugh.

The hour and a half, two hours, passed. Alex was alternately happy, perhaps incredulous, and then angry, sullen—disturbed with Irene Sheaffer for causing him this desperate view of himself—thinking it was crazy, he had been fine before she called, he had been fine—hadn't he?— and now this. He kept wondering what she had heard.

His father left first. He asked Alex again if he was fixed okay for money. He asked again, for the third or forth time, if he was sure he did not want to use the car. Alex wanted the car, but for reasons he did not clearly understand he had said no the first time, and he kept saying no. He wanted somehow to go alone, on the bus, and walking. At last, in his overcoat, ready to leave, intoxicated by now, his father said, "What's your little girl's name, son?"

Alex hesitated at first. The confused anger came to him again, but he did not know if he was angry with himself or with his father. She was not his girl. Then he said, "Irene," and a warm sensation came to him from using her name, answering such a question. But immediately he felt he had jinxed himself, or that his father had congratulated him for some feat he had not accomplished. His anger only rose; he felt simultaneously that his father was intruding with his drunkenness, and that he was being unfair with his father.

He looked down, waiting for his father to go. He heard the door being opened. He felt the cool air pass into the kitchen. But then his father was talking again, saying that Irene was one of his favorite names, and one of his favorite songs was about a girl named Irene. Alex knew, without looking, that his father had all but stepped back inside to talk.

His father continued. Alex stood half listening, half thinking. Then, to lash out at his father, he looked up and said, "Do you know a man named Cobb?"

His father cocked an eye, in intoxicated surprise. "*Who?*" he said.

"Cobb," Alex said. "Mr. Cobb! Joe Cobb!"

His father was perplexed, slow in answering. "Why, sure," he said. "Sure. You mean the big shot at the plant?"

"His son plays basketball."

"Oh? Is that right? He any good?"

"I'm better," Alex said.

"I bet you are."

"I am."

His father said nothing. Alex looked up and they looked briefly at each other. His father looked somewhat confused, but then he said, "Son, suppose I give you a lift where you're going?"

"Oh, no," Alex said. "No, no, that's all right."

"Well," his father said, and then, "Well—I guess I'll be on the road then. You keep your nose clean now, y'hear?"

The door closed; he was gone. In a moment Alex heard the car start below. He heard the uncertain, heavy acceleration which told on his father's drinking, and he heard the car back around, and pause a moment, and accelerate heavily again before starting forward. In the living room, he turned off the phonograph. *Scrabble? Patty and Dave? Connie and Dave?* She had told him the names, but he did not know who they were. He tried to think of something else. He wondered again what she had heard, and realized that whatever it was, it was something he did not want to know.

The night air, when he left the apartment, was face-burning cold and chilled the dampness around his neck and ears where he had washed. He walked along the Third Avenue sidewalk, past the stadium, past gas stations and closed stores. He intended to walk at least into town, to give himself time to warm up, to feel more calm before boarding a bus. But he had never gone like this to a girl's house, and he did not warm up. Still, he went on, boarding one bus to ride a distance in its quiet lighted space, transferring to ride another, east from downtown into a residential district.

He had not minded the solitary bus rides, but as soon as he stepped down to the sidewalk again, a two- or three-block walk to her house, he knew he could not do it. He did not belong there, he told himself. Still, even though he knew it was hopeless, he walked toward her house. Here was the same street he had driven through in the Buicks and Chevrolets. How could she ask him to do something like this, to come to her house? He was sure her parents did not know about him. Still, although cautiously, he went along the icy residential sidewalk. He stepped along until he saw her house ahead, saw the porch light burning, when he stopped. The porch light was an apricot color. The street itself, like the houses, was almost new, the trees here and there were not large. He did not feel the concealment he felt near Chevrolet Avenue among the buildings and busy streets and noise. He remembered all the times he had driven past her house, mornings, nights, quiet Sunday afternoons, in hope of her somehow appearing and ending up in the front seat beside him, of his driving her somewhere. He paused for a moment. When he turned to walk back, he believed he was being strong. He believed it most of the way into town.

As if in a dream, but also on a flight of affection, from a telephone booth in town, he called Eugenia Rodgers. He anticipated himself talkative with her, and she with him, talkative and honest and pleasant. But when he had her on the line she became either frightened or angry, would not believe it was he, and when she did believe it, or admit it, she asked him what he wanted, why he was calling, and when he said to her, "I was just thinking of you, is all— I just wanted to see if you'd like to go out and pick up a car with me," she did not laugh. She said, "I think you're sick," and hung up the receiver.

Walking again, he tried to laugh away her incredible response, her uncalled-for anger. But he could not laugh very easily. He told himself to make believe he had never made the call, to make believe it had not happened. Within an hour or so, his face highlighted still again, among others, by flashing over the screen, the call seemed not to have happened.

Two

Lights came on in a house beside him. It was Monday morning, no more than five-thirty, as early as he had been out, and he was on his way to the bundle of newspapers on the corner. The house, the first-floor apartment where the lights came on, was a special house. The woman who lived there was apparently divorced. Her name was listed in his collection book as Mrs. Kesten, but she lived alone. He also peddled a dress shop over on Detroit Street where she worked, a formerly large house on the edge of downtown converted to pastel showrooms. Collecting there the previous Friday after school, Mrs. Kesten had called to the woman who owned the shop, "There's a man here to see you," and had smiled warmly at him, dressed in silks and frills, painted and perfumed. The night before, at her own apartment, she had not been at all flirtatious, but as he stood before her in the vestibule and she held her purse to her belly to look for coins, the smell of perfume about her and about her doorway had made its impression. Most doorways released a smell of food cooking. Was perfume an invitation?

At the corner, working with his wire cutters to unleash the tight cross wires, he lifted the stack of papers into his bag. Lifting the strap over his head to his shoulder, he prepared to start off. But he hesitated. Then he walked in the direction of her house, peddling his route backward.

Her entire first floor was lighted. As he came close to being before her house, he slowed his pace. He stopped at the head of the driveway. The air was warmer this morning, perhaps thirty degrees, and moist, and completely dark. Already, merely stopping, he felt he had stepped over a forbidden line, sensed that someone might touch him any moment on the shoulder and ask him what he thought he was doing.

He began automatically to fold another paper, and stopped on the crackling noise folding a paper made. The lights reflected down the side driveway from several windows and revealed the moisture in the air. The lights from her living room, from partially drawn shades, were an orange-and-brown color. The lights beyond, from rooms he did not know, were yellowish white. He imagined her there in her pink underwear. He avoided admitting to himself that he had stopped.

The house was six or eight feet higher than the sidewalk, and he stood looking up. He could not decide. He saw no movement, no passing of shadows. He wondered if anybody was watching him from a dark window. But he was sure he could not be seen. It was too dark under the trees. He was sure everyone in the houses around was in bed, and asleep. Or he tried to think he was sure. He took a couple of steps up the driveway then, without consciously deciding to do so. His foot had stopped on an uncomfortable stone in the gravel, but he did not move. He was at the edge of light. He stood there, stood still for a moment.

A part of his mind closing, he stepped quietly up the driveway. Hair at the back of his neck rose some; he approached the first window.

It was her living room. It was fully exposed, an old, high-ceilinged room with dark furnishings. It looked empty. He thought she must light all her rooms from fear. He went on, stepping around the light as much as he could to approach the next window. It was a dining room. It was also empty—but as he looked he saw something which heightened the pitch of his excitement. At the end of a short hallway, across the dining room, a line of white was visible under a closed door. A white bar. He backed more into the shadows and stood watching. It had to be her bathroom, and with the door closed, she had to be inside.

The five minutes or so that passed before the door opened passed like ten or fifteen. He thought several times that he should get out of there, that he was in enough trouble as it was. But he noticed how the sky was black, the roof lines invisible where the previous day their outlines had shown against a deep-blue sky. It was too dark as well to see the silhouettes of branches. Then, without sound, the door opened and Mrs. Kesten was there. He drew his head back slowly. She stood in full view in a light-beige nightgown. She had opened the door to leave, or perhaps for air, for now she leaned close to a mirror. She touched a finger to the inside corner of her eye and looked at her finger. Her movements were without sound. She wiped her finger into the folds of her nightgown and did not look away from looking at her eye in the mirror. As quickly then as she had appeared, she was gone. She turned to the rear of the house, going out of sight.

He paused for a moment. Then he started to walk, trying to stay in the shadows, although moving recklessly, around to the back of the house. A light from a rear window made only a dull line at the bottom. A Venetian blind was closed, and covered all but an inch or so. He stepped along quietly, and crouched so that his bag of papers rested on the ground. He saw only a blur. Then he lifted the bag, and duck-walked several steps closer. He could not see until his forehead lightly touched the glass; drawing his head away, he saw her. She was at the other end of the room, to one side, her back to the window. There was an unmade bed next to the window, and a dresser with a mirror to which she walked just then, again without sound. She removed something from the dresser, perhaps a piece of jewelry, a ring, which she placed back on the dresser again. She removed the nightgown. She lifted it from her shoulders over her head, becoming naked on the way up, and pulled it away from her hair to one side. Turning slightly, she threw it back onto the bed; he glimpsed one side of the front of her.

She was leaning forward, close to the mirror, touching a finger to her eye again. He stared; she blocked her own reflection in the mirror. On the side of his mind he was telling himself that this was a moment like no other. She was not perfect, the flesh of her thighs was slightly mottled, there was a stubbiness about her without her shoes. But this was a moment.

Several seconds passed before she leaned back from the mirror. She turned then and walked almost directly toward him. He did not move, although he feared her somehow seeing his eyes at the bottom of her window. She came so close that he saw little more than a swaying motion of flesh and hair. He saw only one leg then, from her knee to about her waist on one side, and as several pieces of clothing were laid soundlessly on the bed—a dresser must have stood just beside the window—he saw what he had hoped to see.

She walked back to the dresser. She had a brassiere in her hands, and she reached her arms into the straps, watching herself in the mirror. The brassiere was multiflower-colored, like the top of a bathing suit. She raised both hands behind her back to fasten the straps, her shoulders going forward. She hefted herself once in both hands; turning, she checked her profile in the mirror. The moments were improving.

Piece by piece, moving about the room, from bed to mirror and from dresser to mirror, she dressed. He watched her brush her hair several strokes. He watched her powder her face, and touch fingertips of perfume under her chin and around her neck and ears, and he watched her blacken her eyelashes and eyebrows, and fix earrings to her ears, and a bracelet to her wrist. His leg muscles and knees, his kneecaps, were aching by now from crouching, but he watched until she was completely dressed. It wasn't until then that he looked over his shoulder and saw that the sky had become more visible, a deep pencil grayness had washed in. Sound, as if his ears had been plugged, returned. Frightened for the first time, he backed away and straightened up. His legs were stiff, and as he moved back around the house, and down the driveway, they did not work quite right and he made noise in the gravel trying to hurry.

At the sidewalk he could not remember if he had peddled her house or not and withdrew a paper which he turned stiffly tight, and delivered, lightly, in a slide over her porch. A fear of actually being caught came to him then, against which, for the moment, he was unable to think. He went on, peddling one house after another, and nothing happened. No police cars came pulling up, no men came running from houses. In time, over on another street, he began to feel that he was safe. But he was suffering from what he had done; a stranger seemed to be within him, walking within him, making him uncomfortable. He looked away, trying to avoid the stranger, and he tried to avoid admissions and observations about himself. He hurried on to the Coney Island to check the clock there against the amount of light in the sky.

Seeing Irene Sheaffer again was inevitable. He did not see her in a school corridor, as he had expected and tried somewhat to avoid; he saw her one afternoon after school in the crowd at the bus stop. She was standing in front of him, looking the other way. He thought at first about turning and edging his way back out of the crowd and walking away, but he did not. He glanced at her often, as if each glance were the first. It warmed him to look at her—her profile when she turned her head, her hair which glistened a sable color in the low winter sunlight. But it

was as if over a distance, over a span of intervening time
and experience, although no more than three or four days
had passed since he turned away from her house. She
excited him, and her presence caused him an amount of
pain. When the students separated some, he stepped an
inch or two closer.

As she moved to board a bus he edged forward again,
to board the same bus before the doors closed off the flow.
With the shifting along the aisle and jumping for seats—
he did not try for a seat—they both ended up standing, and
he moved until he was next to her in the packed aisle, although not facing her. He felt her presence, but he did not
look at her. He imagined she had seen him as well and was
intentionally looking away herself. The bus was moving
along now. Once as it swayed he knew the fabric of his
coat had passed over the fabric of her coat, and it was like
the moment of an incomplete dream.

At the transfer point downtown he left the bus in the
flow behind her, in the confusion of others pushing their
way from seats into the aisle. Without deciding consciously
to do so, perhaps subconsciously only to continue the warm
moment, he walked behind her, at a distance, across the
street. When she boarded a waiting bus there, the same bus
route he had taken the night he went to her house, the
sensation spread over him as he stepped aboard, as he
followed her, separated by others, into the crowded aisle.

He did not look at her, or look for her. He made believe
even to himself that he had a reason to be there, a place
to go only coincidental to her. Holding an overhead bar, he
rode along, swayed along, and looked to the side of the bus
at nothing. He remembered how, as a fifth- or sixth-grader,
he had followed one girl or another home after school,
tagging behind, perhaps sneaking up to pull hair, or to
tease. Not altogether sure what it was he was doing, he
had nevertheless ended up several times with Kathleen
Sullivan or Marcia Lewis or Barbara Brown alone in a
garage or under a porch over touches and embraces and

kisses and rubbings, and a similar and remote sensation was over him now. He knew she was there.

When the bus pulled up at her stop, he still did not move his head or even glance toward the rear door, but he listened to its accordion opening and knew when she was stepping down, and stepping away, as the door closed again. For a moment, as the bus was leaving the curb, he still did not look. When he did, he saw there were empty seats all along now; he was the only one standing. Stepping to the rear, looking through the large rear windows, through a brown-spattered film, he saw her. Already more than a block behind, she was turning the corner of her street, a slim girl, walking. He still did not take a seat. Several blocks later he reached to pull the cord, and stepped over to wait by the door to be ready. He stepped down into the cold air then, and crossed the street to wait for another bus back to town. He made believe, even to himself, that he had just gone somewhere, that he had had somewhere to go.

He saw her again the next day, by accident. She came into the side room of the library during lunch hour. Glancing up from his work, he saw that it was Irene, but she had not noticed him. She walked across the room to a corner of several orange vinyl easy chairs and a low table. She sat down. Her manner, her movements, were as if she believed she was alone. Placing her books on the table, she sat back in the chair with her notebook at ease in her hands, to read.

He was perhaps twenty feet away, sitting in a straight-back chair at a wooden table, next to the wall. He was looking at her; he still had not moved. She sat at an angle, almost in profile. She had crossed her feet at her ankles. He looked at her legs, where they were exposed. Her ankles were small, her calves only slightly curved. She was a thin girl, mildly curvaceous. Looking at the faint points of her breasts, he tried to imagine them bare—imagined, elusively, small and upright lemon halves. A multiflowered brassiere. No, her brassiere would be pink. The hair on the back of his neck moved some again. He imagined her small seat, in panties, no larger than Mrs. Kesten's flower-covered cleavage.

She was not very well known in Central High School, for mainly the girls who were well built were known. She was slight; she was perhaps fifteen. He stared at her. At nineteen, or twenty, he thought, she would be beautifully shaped. Then, as if sensing his presence, she turned her head. She looked directly at him, and immediately her face reddened.

So did his own.

She neither spoke nor smiled, nor did he. She looked frightened.

He wanted to speak, and he seemed any second about to say something, but as if caught, he only looked at her, at her face looking back at his own. Then she looked away, back to her book.

At the last second he thought she was frightened by him. He looked at his books, thinking explanations and apologies to her—*I didn't mean to scare you*—but he heard her walking then. Looking up, he saw she was already at the door, opening it quickly and leaving without glancing his way. The door closed behind her, with a soft hiss.

He stood up in order to leave himself. He had no thought of following her, only a desire to be free of something in the room. He tried to stay calm; he tried not to care. But his stomach was knotting and he wanted to move to lessen the pressure, to stop it from growing. He walked out, and walked in the corridor toward his locker, toward the basement. Passing the recessed doors to the girls' gym, music from the noon-hour dance rose and fell, and it was as if the world was behind doors.

He was called on in class that afternoon to read aloud. He turned red and performed poorly. He had never blushed so severely in class before. When his name was called, his mind seemed to stop working. As he read, aware only that he was reddening more every second, his breath did not work right, and the words, which he picked from the page one at a time, rose like balls thrown in the air which do not fall again.

He dialed Irene's number that night. He was in the kitchen. His homework lay on the table untouched, and he was not altogether sure of what he intended to do. It was about five minutes to ten. He had been trying to think, within a general nervousness, and the idea came to him that if he could call her and apologize for not showing up, and for frightening her, then he could calm down and start thinking clearly again. But when the phone was answered, almost immediately, and he recognized her voice, he said nothing. She said "Hello?" a second time, and still, standing at the counter, holding the receiver to his ear, he only listened. For several seconds there was the sound of the open line.

Kindly, she said, "Who is this?"

A moment later she said, "Please answer—please say hello," and she sounded so friendly, so curious, that he smiled within to himself.

"Please?" she said, almost humorously. He replaced the receiver then, in its black cradle.

The following evening he dialed her number again. Like other acts, it was one he knew he should not commit, as if he were sinking away. But he was in the kitchen alone and he wished to hear her voice. When a woman answered, he hung up. He waited several minutes and dialed again. This time it was Irene, her voice higher-pitched, and more shy, but she gave only a single "Hello?"

He held the receiver and felt a distant comfort; he knew that she was nowhere but on the other end of the line, that the line ran across the city, from his ear to her own. But then, saying no more, she replaced the receiver.

.   .   .

Late in the day, the next afternoon in school, someone came up beside him and he saw without glancing all the way that it was Irene. She said, nearly whispering, "Did you call me last night?"

He tried to speak politely. "Did I do what?"

"Did you call me?"

"No."

"Are you sure? Because I think you did."

"Call you? Why should I do that?" He avoided looking at her, as if he had to look ahead in order not to bump into someone.

"You know what I mean," she said. "You called but you didn't say anything."

He said nothing. Nor did he look at her.

"If you did," she said. "I wish you wouldn't do it any more."

He knew in a moment that she was dropping away from walking beside him. Still, he did not look; he walked on.

It was midevening that same night, around seven-thirty, when he dialed her number. He had done little more since arriving home from school than sit at the kitchen table. He thought about her and knew he should not call. But then he took up the phone.

She answered herself, and she almost said "Hello" a second time, but checked herself. For a moment she said nothing. Then she said, gently, "I know who this is."

He listened.

"I know it's you," she said. "And I know you followed me on the bus the other day."

He said nothing.

The click came then, the buzz following, as she hung up the phone.

.　　.　　.

He slept poorly, and in the morning he was out so early that his bundle of papers was not yet on the corner. He stood around several minutes, waiting, then he walked back down the block, quietly, his canvas bag hanging limp from his shoulder, and he knew from a distance that Mrs. Kesten's windows were still dark. The sky was clear this morning, or this night, a translucent blue salted with stars, the air sharply cold. The wind chilled his ears and nose. It seemed to warm him, however, to walk past her house; at least he stopped thinking of the cold. He had told himself this was something he should not do again. But he knew within that he would go once more to kneel at her window.

He turned back before reaching the next corner, before exposing himself under the streetlight. Walking back, he heard a truck, and then it came around the corner from the direction of Detroit Street. It was a two-ton flatbed truck with lights overhead on the cab the size and color of oranges, with bright sweeping headlights. It barely stopped under the streetlight, its gears brayed, shifting—his bundle must have been thrown out the back—and then it came roaring on in his direction, with no fear of being seen or heard, of disturbing the people sleeping in the dark houses. Close to a tree, among many large trees, he used the turning of shadows to conceal himself, and he tried to think of something to say, some excuse to give, if the truck pulled over.

He loaded his papers slowly, to give her time. But when he started down the street again, her house remained dark. He peddled the houses before her house; he stopped a moment at the head of her driveway. He touched his pockets, as if stopping to look for something. His heart was pounding. He fished the wire cutters from the bottom of his bag, and taking a few steps up the driveway, laid them carefully on the ground. *I was just looking for my wire cutters; they must have caught on a paper and fallen out.* He did not much consider the illogic of looking for them behind the house. He returned to the sidewalk and walked on. He did not peddle her house, but he peddled as many of the nearby houses as he could, disrupting his pattern completely. Some twenty minutes passed, and at last, coming around the corner of Garland Street again, it was hard to believe. The lights were on. The orange color was there again, shining toward the sidewalk.

He approached carefully. He walked up the driveway, actually looking for his wire cutters, and seeing them, left them on the ground. At the dining-room window he saw the bar of light under the bathroom door. He stepped back to wait. He could have stepped farther back, but he wanted to keep his view through the window. He was too much of a single mind now to worry. Before her windows, it was as if there were these two women in his life, with no need to distinguish between the two. and the stranger was within him again.

Three

School days. They became more uncomfortable, the hours longer, the time in classes more tedious. Sometimes his stomach drew so tightly into itself that he had to squirm, change positions almost constantly, or rise and ask permission to go to the lavatory—a brief walk in an empty corridor. Occasionally, perhaps in the quiet lavatory, he had thoughts which were nearly lucid. One of these was a suspicion that school and classes were not very different from the detention home. The conditions were better, but school seemed to be a deceit of some kind, a confinement so large it was hard to see. Imagining himself on a ship, slicing through a warm ocean, or walking in a foreign city, was enough to make his eyes film and to make him believe his life was foul and unfair. His larger thought was that he had somehow been eliminated as a human being.

Another day, after school, he saw Irene. She was waiting again in the crowd to board a bus. He managed, at a distance, to board the same bus. He was not sure how he could go about it, but his intention, his hope, was to somehow make things right, to apologize in some way, and to withdraw.

At the transfer junction in town, he left the bus in the stringing out, some fifty feet behind her, but then he lost her. Had she not turned onto the main street he might have crossed the street to the next bus stop and found she was not there. But rather than going directly home, she had turned walking into the afternoon thickness of downtown.

Down the street, he saw her. She appeared in a separation of people on the sidewalk. She was with a boy and girl; they stood in a triangle near the curb. The movement of people was squeezing just slightly to the left to pass around them, and Alex had no space or time himself to angle any farther away. He looked to the front as he passed, as if not seeing them, and he only sensed their presence as he went by. But no more than two or three steps beyond, he felt her eyes on his back, even if they were not. He felt her eyes looking after him, without any comment in their glance. He had the thought again that something was wrong. Something was wrong. He walked against the wind, and crossed the street at the next corner to walk with the wind pushing his back.

In lower downtown, on an impulse, he bought a ticket and entered one of the old twenty-four-hour theaters. It was the Civic, near the river, near some pawn shops and taverns. The marquee announced: *Fun in the Sun/ From*

Sweden. He was no longer thinking of what had just happened, nor had it left him. He slipped into the flickering black and white theater, as if safe there, to hide in the darkness for a time. But it was there, in the theater itself, with nudes, filmed only from the waist up or from the rear, playing badminton, playing cards at a table, walking in a garden in pairs, that something in him came apart at last. His stomach, almost at the moment of sitting down, was boiling with the old tedium and agony, which, as he sat there, made him tighten and release his abdomen and groin, as if to find a way to breathe. He sat, shifting in the seat, for several minutes, until his mind and his body became so tense with the sensation that he leaned forward and took his head in his hands, and then he suddenly rose and turned to leave the theater.

The following ten or fifteen minutes passed in states where he saw the city, the world, with an eye of panic, and alternately, where he saw himself, alas, as a mean and worthless son of a bitch, invulnerable, and cruel, and saying to himself, *I don't give a shit, I don't give a shit, they can go fuck a duck,* believing he desired not the detention home but the fierce world of the penitentiary. He had known, leaving the theater, that he was going after a car. Whatever his sense of wrongdoing, he felt an attraction, he felt compelled, after a hunger, to do it.

There was still daylight, a weak winter sun, and he squinted, walking along. He looked away from two or three stray passers-by, and at midblock he turned into a short alleyway, between the buildings. Wine bottles and pints, pints in paper bags as wrinkled as the old hands which had laid them there, lay along the sooted alley, under some metal loading doors, among patches of weeds and dirt, of black snow. A warm exhaust of kitchen smells was broadcast over the end of a building, and for the time of passing the door, he went weak and closed his eyes once.

Turning from the alley, he walked along the tracks which ran behind the buildings. The oily river flowed off beside the tracks, flowed on toward the complex of factories where his father was working the second shift. More bottles lay along the tracks, between the ties, broken pieces of glass oiled and dusted brown with the chipped stones.

Passing between buildings again, he came out into lower downtown. The sidewalk here was crowded with people walking by, with bar and diner smells, with cars and buses. He stopped, paused for a moment at the edge of the sidewalk, looking the people over.

The front wheels of the white Oldsmobile were turned into the curb. A ring of keys was hanging from the ignition, from the darker half of the dashboard. Even at sundown the dashboard sparkled with its touches of chrome and dark glass. His ears held a faint singing; his heart was beating. Traffic on the street was heavy, just as the sidewalk was crowded with people. Walking past the car, stepping over next to the building side, he looked back and looked it over between the people passing. It was long and white; it was a Ninety-Eight.

He walked back past the car again, and did not look at it this time as he passed. Glancing to the windows of a jewelry store, he saw the car's reflection from behind him, or part of it, for the store was narrow and the sweep of the body passed beyond both ends of the glass. Past the jewelry store he turned into the doorway of a men's clothing store, where he stood for several minutes looking at suits of clothes on mannequins, and at shoes on thick carpeting. He glanced through a thin reflection of himself in the glass, until he decided to move. He turned around and walked evenly from the doorway. He was walking to his car now. As he passed between bumpers into the street he was nearly smiling to himself.

He opened the door and slid in upon the cold and squeaking black leather seat. Reaching, he turned the handful of keys; the motor roared smoothly. However silent its hum, it indicated with its starting that it was large with power. He had to jockey the wheels only once to enter the

long blunt nose into the line of traffic, and then, pressing
the accelerator lightly, he was driving. He pushed some
buttons until heat began to blow over the carpeted floor.
The warm air soothed him. He used the brakes and they
worked well; the car was tight and quiet. He drove on
through the early lights and heavy evening traffic of the
city.

At a red light, where he was the first in line, he shifted
to N and tested the accelerator. Then he pressed it, and
kept pressing until the 300-odd horses were running and
roaring in place. The motor squealed, the body trembled
like an airplane. He felt like a stallion himself, rearing for
the moment erect.

Leaving the city, on Highway 23, as the sun had gone
down, he turned on the headlights. Then he made the car,
with its headlights sparkling, pressing the taut pedal,
whistle over the highway at sixty, at seventy, at eighty
miles an hour. He streaked past cars almost soundlessly,
leaving them behind. He remembered a time, standing at a
crossing with his father, when a great blue diesel engine
with its line of cars came rocking by at fifty or sixty miles
an hour, and his father threw the engineer an old railroad-
man's highball, and high in his small window the man
waved, saluted, and the train went on, and then it howled,
and it howled again, in the rhythm of its clatter.

Driving became pleasant. Occasionally it was as if he
were on a train himself, as a passenger, and did not have to
worry about anything. He drove the white car through the
dusk, the falling of darkness, and on.

He stopped at a drive-in restaurant, on the outskirts of
Saginaw. It was an old and expensive drive-in, the central
building made of stone and glass, the lot crowded and filling
with cars. When he had finished his light meal, a hamburger and a strawberry milk shake, and started the car,
checking the rear-view mirror, he saw something which
overwhelmed him with enough fear to make his hips and
his bowels suffer a shock. Directly behind him, having

backed into a parking space, was a state police car. Two troopers, in their Stetsons, were in the front seat.

He looked away from the mirror. He sat still, closing his eyes automatically. He did not know at the time that he was panicking, but later, seeing the alternatives he could have chosen, he knew that he had. He did not even think, although it might have been his best move, to sit there and wait for them to leave. He saw two choices: either to leave the car and walk to the men's room, wherever it was, then to walk away, into Saginaw, or to go on and back out as naturally as he could, hoping they would not notice him. His mind was rattled as well with other ideas—fingerprints on the keys and buttons and dials, on the door handle, hitch-hiking, walking—and with the idea that he was taking too long, that the motor was running, he decided then to go on as he had started, on the logic that it was his natural movement and he had already started it. Glancing at the mirror again, he touched the accelerator to begin backing out. He glanced back and forth, from mirror to fender.

He made two mistakes then and immediately after each one, he saw that it was an incredible error. First, backing out, trying not to back around so far that he would be directly in front of them, he stopped and shifted, and going forward, discovered he had not backed around far enough to clear the fender of the next car. Drawing near, he shifted to R again. Then he made his second mistake. Backing in front of the police car this time, he glanced to see if they were watching. They were. Both faces, under both hats, were looking directly at him.

He shifted to D and started rolling carefully forward, approaching the exit into the street. He was afraid to check his mirror. He stopped before pulling out—right led to Saginaw, left to the dark highway and home—to check the traffic. He glanced at his mirror then, and decided simultaneously to head for home and that he had had it, for the headlights of the police cruiser were on.

Entering the street, he reached to turn on his own

lights. He did not look at his mirror now. He was afraid to look. He was begging and praying that they would not follow, and certain they were coming after him.

He drove along. He held the steering wheel in both hands, and sat upright and forward on the leather seat. He was trying to gain a good speed without going too fast, but with hardly stomach enough to glance at the speedometer. He may have been doing ten miles an hour, or twenty, or thirty-five. He had to look back again. Barely moving his head, he glanced to the mirror on the door. He glimpsed the police car. He glimpsed its side, the insignia on the door, as it came into the street behind him.

He prayed that it was coincidence. He prayed that they had coincidentally finished their meal—and knew with certainty that they intended to check him out.

He had a block or more on them. He glanced often at his mirror now, glanced, looked back to the front, glanced, looked to the front. They seemed content to follow him at a block or so. Only one car was ahead of him; beyond it were stoplights, green on the corner and hanging green in the center. Then the green flashed to yellow. The car ahead, its exhaust smoking suddenly, sped on and passed under the yellow light. He looked in his mirror again. They were coming on. Surely they would pull up beside him; surely they would look him over. The question was whether or not they would signal him to the side.

The stoplight was red now. As if it would help, he was edging toward the shoulder, completely afraid to stop or turn onto an unknown street. He believed he was without alternatives. If they stopped him, there was no question of what would happen, of where he would be taken. His only alternative, he believed, was to go.

He glanced at the mirror again. They were half a block back, aimed toward coming up beside him at the light. Then, and in spite of his inability to think very clearly from one point to the next, he did calculate passing right then just in front of a car entering the intersection, hoping to leave it stopped in front of the cruiser, and he did not ram the accelerator but pressed it steadily to the floor, and for an instant the Oldsmobile's front end, the long hood, seemed to rise as the wheels were spitting gravel and snow, whatever was on the shoulder, and then the wheels caught, and the other car was already stopping, but not quickly enough and he had to turn out a sharp quarter turn, to screech around the car, clearing its bumper by perhaps two feet, rocking down the highway before he had all four wheels straight, moving forward with the thrust, with the squealing sound again, of a jet engine.

Looking in the mirror now, he saw no headlights behind him. He could guess only that the cruiser and the other car had gotten confused trying to get around each other. He pressed the accelerator harder, even though it was all the way down, on the idea of getting farther away, gaining distance while he had the chance.

He passed a car. Glancing at the mirror, he saw the car's headlights fall away behind him. He stayed up over the steering wheel, reading the way ahead, releasing and pressing the accelerator now against the dangerous, shrieking speed, thinking that if he could gain only three or four minutes he could ditch the car, wipe it off in a hurry, and run, fly like an animal into the darkness, into the woods, the countryside.

Checking the mirror, both mirrors, with quick glances, and checking the speedometer once, seeing the dial floating in red between 105 and 110, and then checking the mirror again, he saw the cruiser, or saw its flickering blue light, for it must have been a mile back. When he looked ahead again, his heart leaped and he pulled his foot from the accelerator. The road was curving to the right. He slammed the brake only once; he went around the curve on two wheels, sliding out into the other lane. Returning his foot to the gas pedal, pressing again, he decided he'd have to run without looking back, in the hope that they were doing eighty to his hundred.

Still, he looked again in only a moment. Going down into a valley almost as if falling, passing two more cars, blaring his horn perhaps ten seconds, he looked in the mirror as he was coming out of the valley and saw the blue light, and felt that he was gaining, gaining quickly, knew that he was gaining, and he felt a sudden hope on the chance of an actual escape.

Braking, sweeping around another long curve, he studied the road ahead and decided to keep his eyes there. He had to release the accelerator some now and then, and several times he pressed the brake. But every chance he had, he pressed the accelerator all the way to the floor again, on the idea that he was getting away for this reason, that he would escape in this way, by gaining every second, every inch.

There was a junction some distance ahead, a Y junction with the right side going home, the left to Detroit. He knew a cruiser called by radio might try to pick him up there, but he also realized that if he could gain enough distance to make his choice unseen, he had a fifty-fifty chance of the cruiser guessing the other way. The danger was that the state police knew that too, and cruisers called by radio might already be approaching the junction on both highways.

He checked his mirror again; he did not see the blue light. He pressed the accelerator almost continuously, touched the brake occasionally and pressed the accelerator again. Once, without hesitation, as if he were dribbling in a basketball game, not even touching the horn, he passed a car which was passing a car, sweeping into the north-bound lane and streaking by.

He kept thinking of the junction ahead. And he thought the cruiser had surely radioed in, and it seemed his best hope was that it would take another cruiser longer to get there than it would take him. The danger beyond that, whichever way he went, was to encounter another cruiser.

In only moments he saw the first sign signaling the junction. Quickly there were more signs, and he released his foot from the accelerator, coasting down to eighty-five, and eighty, and seventy-five. He decided to gamble then, knowing he was within a quarter mile of making his turn, of the gas station and some other buildings at the junction. He decided to pass the junction within the speed limit, not to pick up another cruiser which was not looking for him in the first place. He kept checking his mirror, but the blue light did not show. He swept around to the right, toward home, doing fifty in the 45 MPH zone, feeling as if he were walking. Getting beyond the gas station, perhaps another quarter mile, he pressed the accelerator again, and the Oldsmobile, the front end rising, rocketed, jetted on once more.

Again, for the view ahead, there was only darkness. No headlights were coming on, although it was hard to tell how the highway curved and dropped and when the changes might appear. By now the gas station was over a mile back. He thought that any moment the cruiser would be deciding which way to go. And he thought if the road did not curve or dip soon, the cruiser would see his taillights, but almost immediately he was both curving to the right and going down. Looking quickly to his mirror, he saw only darkness. A car passed him going the other way and again there was darkness before him.

He began looking for side roads, thinking this was his chance. He missed the first one, going too fast, and afraid to back up so far, he gambled and slowed down to thirty-five and thirty miles an hour to look for the next one. He hit the brake pedal almost at once. Turning onto a two-lane paved road which was dark and empty, he pressed the gas hard again until he was moving between sixty and seventy, scattering bits of gravel, until the road had curved several times. At the next crossroads he turned again, turning left this time. He decided to circle back to the city, to stay on these back roads and keep driving until he was there, anywhere in the city, or near the city, and then to walk home, to stay off the main streets.

He drove on, turning often by instinct more than calculation, trying to make his way in the right direction. He passed an occasional car or pickup truck, and farm houses strung out from each other, and an occasional gas station or country store. Then, once, lights were ahead, and he saw he was coming into a small town. He braked until he was doing thirty in the 35 MPH zone, then to a speed under twenty-five, and there was a local sheriff or deputy, in his dark car in a dark gas station, the exhaust curling gray. Alex did not look as he passed, nor did his heart seem to beat again until he was a block or so along and saw in his mirror that the car had not come after him.

Leaving the small town, he realized he did not even know what town it was. He checked the gas gauge for the first time and saw he had over a quarter of a tank, nearly a third. He drove on.

He was not sure at first that it was the right city. He had come upon houses on a dark road, until there were houses in blocks next to each other, until he was not driving on country roads but on neighborhood side streets. He started looking for street signs, for anything familiar. Then the street he was on ended, his headlights spreading out over a field, and he knew it was Beecher Park, a baseball diamond where he had played some years ago. He was home. The city zoo was to the left ahead, on—and it was a coincidence—Lincoln Road. Eight or ten miles to the right, into the country again, was The Lincoln Hotel.

He pulled over to the curb on a dark side street and turned off the motor and lights. The car settled and he paused a moment, looking around. He had no handkerchief, and using a piece of paper from his pocket, he began wiping wherever his fingers might have touched. He wiped over a second time, and then a third time, reaching around in the dark car. Using the paper then to open the door, leaning away from the dome light in case he was being watched from a house window, he slipped out and closed the door again. Standing close to conceal his hands, he wiped over and under and inside the chrome door handle, wiped hard, and balling the paper into his hand, into his pocket, he stepped over to the sidewalk and walked in the direction away from home. At the first corner he turned back the other way. There was a wind along the street and he kept his head down.

Ten minutes later, on Lincoln Road, he boarded a city bus for the long ride downtown. He looked only at his reflection in the glass beside him, and through his reflection at buildings and stores and gas stations along the way. He felt secretive toward people he saw, and they appeared at ease and naïve. In town he deposited the ball of paper into a trash container. The paper gone, and in the city again, he felt some relief. He walked. As if he had escaped, he began reading the names of movies and movie stars on the city's white-lighted marquees. For moments at a time he felt like himself again.

Four

The weather on the morning of the hearing was disappointingly cold. It was Saturday, April 23. Several warm days had lowered upon the city before this. The remains of soot and sand-filled snow had melted, there had been an occasional balmy afternoon, and grass here and there was making its change from brown to green. The air this morning, although sunny, was windy and cold, the temperature was down to perhaps thirty degrees, and the previous days seemed a withdrawn promise, a false spring.

Alex and his father drove through town to the courthouse well ahead of their nine o'clock appointment. They

were quiet and polite with each other. In the building itself they waited in the corridor outside Mr. Quinn's office.
They stopped to sit on a bench there because his father
made a gesture that they sit down, and Alex made no
mention of Mr. Quinn's office waiting room. He felt ushered
and silenced, however much the day seemed to be his, by
the authority of his father, of Mr. Quinn, of the judge.

A sprawling black woman sat on the same bench, a
thin, frog-eyed boy beside her. Alex and his father sat
knee to knee. Alex, stiff in his white shirt and tie, his
sports jacket and slacks, his polished shoes and freshly
combed hair, placed his hands on his thighs. He was still
cold from not having worn a topcoat, not owning one. At
a bench directly opposite was another woman, white, a factory badge from AC Spark Plug on her purse strap. She
was smoking a lipstick-marked cigarette; a lipstick-
marked girl, thin, sat beside her.

His father, unlike himself, sober as he was, began to
talk with the two mothers. He said, "I guess they'll learn
something today, won't they?" Almost in unison the two
women said, "I'll say," and, "They surely will." His father
said, "I suppose we'll all learn a thing or two." The women
nodded and within a moment the three adults were talking
of the cold weather, and bravely, strangers to their children, of life itself, agreeing with the notion that everyone
made a few mistakes along the way. The black woman
told a story that she had read, in *Reader's Digest*, she
thought, of a mother somewhere, in the state of Washington, she thought, driving a truck to the prison to say good-
bye to her son and then to drive his body home herself when
he was hanged, or electrocuted, she wasn't sure which it
was, but that poor mother waiting in her truck, she knew
when her boy was going, she could feel it just like it was
herself. Alex's father said, "That's why they got us here
today," and the women looked off or down in silence.

When Mr. Quinn came out, Alex felt a mixture of pride
and shame over the presentation of his father, pride for his

appearance, his dress—factory worker or not, he carried his expensive hound's-tooth topcoat, and silk scarf, blood-colored, over the arm of his expensive suit—and shame for the exposure he felt as his father's son. He flushed then with embarrassment and anger, for, as if still talking to the two women, his father responded to Mr. Quinn's introducing himself by saying, "We're all set if you are," offering to shake hands, reaching his hand out, holding it there as Mr. Quinn shifted a manilla folder to free his right hand, and shaking hands, Alex thought, as if he had met someone in a bar.

Alex walked behind the two men down the corridor, squeezed from a threesome, but at the elevator door they separated to let him enter first. They rose two or three floors in the silent box, and stepped into another corridor. Mr. Quinn nodded to the right with the manilla folder and Alex walked in the front this time. Mr. Quinn stopped at an oversized wooden door, which he opened gently, and when he glanced in, he stood to the side and held the door behind his arm. He nodded yes for them to enter. Alex walked in first, his father behind him. He paused just inside until his father was beside him. Mr. Quinn came around as if they had entered a church and ushered them with silent head motions to two ordinary armless wooden chairs in the center of the room. Alex felt a point of pressure in his bladder. He had to urinate now, but he was afraid to say so.

The judge had been reading and he had raised his eyes alone as if looking over glasses, although not wearing glasses. The Honorable Charles R. Flynn. He gave a slight nod. The greeting was so uncertain and the protocol of Juvenile Court so unknown that both Alex and his father ignored it. The judge kept his eyes on them as they sat down. When they were settled, seated at least, and Mr. Quinn was stepping to the side, the judge said, "Excuse me just one minute, please," and returned to reading some papers he held in his resting hands. Mr. Quinn took a seat to the side, fearlessly scraping the chair legs over the floor. Alex, feeling as if he had taken a seat on a stage, moved his knees closer together, to contain the pressure in his bladder. He held his head straight and did not look around.

He had expected the judge to sit at an elevated bench, and to wear black robes, as in the movies, but the man wore a dark suit and sat at a desk. There was a flag on a stand behind him, and ferns and broad-leafed plants on tables, and shelves filled with dark-covered books. His desk, in the foreground, was as large as a small bed. The flag, glossy nylon, fringed with brass-colored strings, seemed an assurance that black robes or not, an authority was there that could impose punishment.

In time, in the silence, as the judge continued so slowly to read whatever it was he was reading, Alex looked down and stared at his hands in his lap. He tried to read their topography of veins and lines and hairs; within a moment he was only staring. His father had warned him that morning as they dressed that nothing would be funny or easy, and it was not. His father had also promised to be with him, to stick with him, but for the moment, if only a couple of feet away, Alex felt he was out of reach. He thought of the white Oldsmobile, and felt a flash of panic, which he tried to conceal by not moving.

He glanced to the side, at his father. As if they were schoolboys in the principal's office, Alex thought darkness might be made light on a secret smile. His father sat looking ahead. Alex knew his father had seen him on the periphery of his vision and for a moment he felt lost.

The judge began at last by explaining, in a monotone and not very clearly, that this was a hearing, but the court had the authority to impose sentence, and if they wanted they might be represented by counsel. He reviewed the charges against Alex, charges which did not recall a sense of the crimes but a sense of the time itself. The judge did not say Alex had stolen, he said he had "unlawfully driven away" fourteen automobiles. Looking at the papers before him, he mentioned the switched license plates, a spare tire from one car Alex had traded, wheel included, for three dollars in gas, the Chevrolet sedan he had damaged in the amount of "three hundred nineteen dollars nineteen cents," an unforgettable figure, and a woman's coat from one car he had given to "Miss Eugenia Rodgers, aged fifteen, G-five-twenty-seven-forty-three Birch Road, Shiawassee Township, whose mother, Mrs. Jean Osborn, notified police . . ."

Alex sat all this time looking at his hands in his lap. He held his back straight and sat straight, not to present what had always been called defiance. There were hundreds of lines on his hands. They looked as fine as the far-off branchwork of winter trees. He felt the pressure mount again in his bladder.

The judge continued. He was talking now as well as reading, explaining that the spare tire had been recovered and returned to the owner, as had the coat, that the owner of the damaged Chevrolet in a signed statement to the county prosecutor had decided not to bring suit for damages which were covered by his insurance policy . . .

When the judge stopped talking, Alex looked up and saw that the man was looking at him. "Is this account complete?"

"Yes sir."

"Nothing withheld?"

"No sir."

"What do you have to say for yourself?"

Saying this, the judge looked down and began turning over some of the sheets again on his desk. But he was listening. In a moment, without looking up, he said, "Go on."

Alex had no planned alibi, but he had often imagined giving some credible explanation of himself. Now, as if out of breath, he said, "I don't know."

The judge looked up and looked directly at him for a moment, and looked down again. When he spoke now it was without looking up from the papers. "Why did you do these things?" he said.

Alex still did not know what to say. He said, "I'm not sure. Just to show off, I guess." He thought he would anger the judge but the man did not look up; he continued looking at the papers before him. In a moment, still looking down, he said, "Mr. Quinn, has your office anything to offer?"

Mr. Quinn stood up to speak and on his first remarks Alex looked back at his hands. "This is a simple pattern of divorced parents," Mr. Quinn said. "A lack of guidance and example in the home, and a drinking situation in the home."

Alex tried not to listen; he looked down at his hands again and made no attempt to glance at his father. He understood now what he did not quite understand before, that it was not the crimes they were really interested in, it was the way they lived. Mr. Quinn went on speaking of "the mother," and "the brother," and then of "Mrs. Cushman's," calling it "a rooming house for children looked after by a woman confined to a wheelchair," and of his "history in school," that he was "bright and adaptable," that he "has learned over the years to see to most of his needs, takes care of his own laundry, keeps his own room, fixes many of his own meals," and then of his "progress since his release from the detention home," that he was "up early now every morning to take care of a Detroit *Free Press* paper route . . ."

When the judge spoke, when Mr. Quinn had finished and stepped back to his chair, it was again without looking up. He said, as if to the papers on his desk, "Mr. Housman, what is your occupation?"

"I work over here at the Chevrolet, in Plant Four," his father said. His father's voice was diminished, slightly off key. Alex sat looking down again.

The judge said, "What type of work do you do, sir?"

"Die setter," his father said.

"How long have you been employed at the Chevrolet?"

"Close to nineteen years."

"And before that?"

"Well, that doesn't count close to four years I spent in the army, and before that I worked for the railroad, back in Kansas. But that's when I was a youngster, a young fella."

Alex sat looking down. It was not the language—*a youngster, a young fella*—which he had never heard his father use before, it was the telescoping of his father's life. Was this all? Was this what all the stories amounted to?

"Mr. Housman," the judge said. "Can you explain why your son has gotten into this trouble?"

His father was slow in answering. After a moment he said, "I'm not entirely sure. Things have always been more or less hard on us—"

The judge interrupted. "Well, how do you feel about this?" he said. "Your son says he was showing off, now you say you're not entirely sure. That's not saying very much, is it? I'd like to know how you feel about this?"

"That's a hard question," his father said. "I think they were awful foolish things to do. I hold myself more to blame than him. We have a family car, and we could have worked out a way for him to use it. I don't think he's done anyone near as much harm as he's done himself."

"Well, sir, there was damage in excess of three hundred dollars. There was untold inconvenience suffered. The law was broken. Just to mention a few things. Which do in fact cause harm to someone, do they not?"

"Yes, yes, they do. I just meant to say he also harmed himself. I mean, he hasn't gained anything from this—"

"No, he hasn't, has he," the judge said. He stared directly at Alex's father for a moment. Then he said, "What of this drinking situation, Mr. Housman?"

His father did not answer.

"You better see to it," the judge said.

In a moment, looking down again, the judge began

to write. Alex glanced at his father, but his father sat
looking to the front. The judge continued to make nota-
tions, occasionally lifting a loose sheet and turning it over
on its face. Alex felt at last that he had to speak or he was
going to wet himself. "Excuse me, please," he said. "I have
to go to the lavatory."

The judge looked up but said nothing. Mr. Quinn said,
"I'll take him, sir," and rose from his chair.

Alex did not look at his father. He followed Mr. Quinn
across the room and through the door. In the corridor Mr.
Quinn said, "It's right down here," and Alex followed.

"Nervous?" Mr. Quinn said.

"Yes."

"I wish I could tell you something, but I don't know
what to say. I wouldn't worry too much, though."

Alex said nothing to this, and then Mr. Quinn said,
"This is it right here. You go ahead. I'll wait out here for
you."

Alex opened the door, which had MEN painted in peel-
ing black on old frosted glass, and walked in. The room
was clean, and there was an association of the detention
home. There was also a slightly warm smell, like that of
hard-boiled eggs. He stepped up to one of the urinals. A
window, to the side, was opened a slice, and the cold air
was also strong enough to smell. He looked to the left, at
the booth, but saw no shoes, no trouser folds, on the floor.
He was alone in the room. At the sink he ran water on his
hands. He dried them on rough paper towels. There he was
before himself in the mirror; a new white shirt, sewed-in
collar tabs not quite concealed, a new necktie, his wool
sports coat.

He turned from the mirror, and stood there. His father
had not left his mind. It was not an image of his father
which was with him, but a feeling, the feeling perhaps of
being of the same flesh.

His father had stopped him that morning in the kitchen
when they were ready to leave, and taking his shoulders

in his hands, had said to him, almost politely, "I want you to remember this now. You're still young. You still have your whole life before you. You have it, and it's yours to live, no matter if they send you away for a while or not. You try to understand that. I don't know what else I can say, or what advice I can give you, except that. If they send you away—that's all right. I've thought about this. It won't matter to the size of your life. You have to understand that. It might even make it bigger. Just so you don't let the sons of bitches get to you. You have to understand that. If you don't let them, then they can't touch you. You see what I mean? They might try to rip your guts out, for nothing. I've been around a few judges, and a few jailhouses, too. Well, fuck them and their automobiles. You see what I mean?"

Alex had not quite seen what his father meant until now. It's funny, he thought—and he did not mean it was funny at all, but that it was so strange, he knew no word for it. They could not stop him, or break him by sending him away. They could not do that at all, if he did not let them. He did not know what it was, only that it was there, within him now, as if in his fierce and sober words that morning his father had hammered it in to stay.

For a moment, standing yet in the center of the room, he felt that he was going to weep—not in misery, but merely from the certainty of being there that moment and merely being alive. He did not weep; the door opened and Mr. Quinn looked in and said, "Hey, you okay?"

Alex nodded.

But Mr. Quinn, entering the room, said, "Awh, buddy, what's the matter?"

Alex thought he appeared composed, but speaking, his word came out in a surprising whisper, in an ascending pitch. "Nothing," he said.

"Awh, listen, really," Mr. Quinn said, whispering himself. "I don't think he'll send you away."

"Oh, it's not that," Alex said. "It's not that—I don't

care. I don't know—what a nut I am—I just felt like I was
going to blubber like a baby." He wheezed, laughing simultaneously, unable to help himself. He glanced up at Mr.
Quinn, and down again, to look away from Mr. Quinn
seeing his face.

"Oh, well, hell, go ahead and blubber," Mr. Quinn said.
"I know how you feel. Jesuschrist anyway. I'm about to do
it myself."

Alex laughed, through his wheezing and sniffling, and
looked at Mr. Quinn. Mr. Quinn was not crying but he was
smiling an awkward smile. He shook his head once. "Awh,
man," Mr. Quinn said. "Sometimes I don't know what it
all means." He wiped the corner of each eye with the back
of his thumb knuckle. "None of it makes sense to me half
the time. All I know is we better get back there or he'll send
both of us to Lansing."

Alex nodded. He stepped out and they walked back
through the corridor. When Mr. Quinn opened the door this
time, he nodded to Alex, as if secretly, to say something.
The judge looked up, glanced at them, and returned to his
papers. Alex sat down in the chair beside his father.

After a moment, again without looking up first, the
judge spoke. He said, "No attempts to sell the cars or any
parts thereof?"

Mr. Quinn answered. He said, "Just the one tire, sir,
which was recovered."

The judge made another note. He looked up this time.
"Alex," he said. "Would you please rise and step forward?"

Alex rose and stepped to within four or five feet of the
desk.

Looking directly at him now, the judge said, "I'm
placing you on probation until the date of your eighteenth
birthday. Are you aware of the terms of probation?"

"Yes sir, I think so."

"Are you aware that I could as easily order you confined
to the State Boys Vocational School for a similar period?"

"Yes sir."

"Are you aware that if you fail to maintain the terms of this probation, you may be so confined, by order of this court, at any time during this term of probation?"

"Yes sir."

"Do you fully intend to comply with the terms of this probation?"

"Yes sir."

"Is there anything you wish to say?"

"No sir."

"Mr. Housman, would you please rise?"

His father stepped up beside him.

The judge said, "Mr. Housman, are you aware of your responsibility concerning the terms of this probation?"

"Yes, I am."

"Is there anything you wish to say?"

"No."

The judge looked down again and made another notation. Then he said, "This court is no longer in session."

Alex and his father stood in place a moment before they glanced at each other. But they did not smile; there was no feeling of victory, or of release. Then Mr. Quinn was with them, as before, directing them with a slight hand motion to follow him across the room again and into the corridor. It was like leaving a room without saying good-bye.

Down the corridor to a point beyond hearing, Mr. Quinn said softly, "That wasn't so bad, was it? He can be tough at times."

Neither of them answered. They had stopped before the elevator doors, where Mr. Quinn pressed the button. Alex stood staring at the doors, as if to concentrate on something else. The doors were unpolished, the color of lake water.

They rode down without a word. At the second floor Mr. Quinn held the elevator door a moment as he stepped out. He said, "Alex, I'll see you at about three-thirty on Thursdays, right after school. Your curfew is ten on school nights, midnight on Fridays and Saturdays—and it's nothing to take lightly."

The door closed. Alex expected Mr. Quinn to say something in parting to his father, perhaps give him a left-handed apology for what he had said about his drinking, but Mr. Quinn said nothing. He and his father continued down within the hum of the elevator.

Outside the courthouse they walked along the sidewalk in the sunlit cold air. Alex followed his father, in single file, for others were coming toward them, entering the building. There was a light wind, enough to swirl the vapor of Alex's breath and to cause his eyes to run at the corners.

Walking along, Alex looked at his father's back, at the sweep and fabric of his overcoat. He realized that his father overdressed, and unexplainably, he realized why. He heard once more the diminished voice in which his father had summed up his life. He looked again at his father, as if to be sure. The blood-colored scarf covered the back of his father's neck; high on one side, it ruffled his hair. They edged between two parked cars, walking along.

Five

One evening, a warm evening in late May, Alex was sitting at the counter of a diner in town when he was surprised, remotely, by a voice behind him somewhere. He looked over to the door. Three Negroes, two young girls and a boy, were entering. The boy, seeing him, smiled and said, "Hey—say, man?"

"Hey, how you doing?" Alex said.

The boy, smiling, went on with the two girls, heading for a booth, and Alex turned back to the front. It was Herrick Herford. The King.

Alex sat smiling to himself, wanting to go over to The King, to talk and joke with him. The King with two girls. There was a logic in it somehow. The three of them were loose and laughing over there now. Alex was immediately attracted to the girls, to the extra girl, imagining, in spite of the taboos and perhaps partially because of them, a foursome. With them, it seemed, he might somehow become free of himself and so move into the night. They would talk easily, and joke easily, and seriously, and before long he might be admitted with them into some pleasant layer of spring fever. Out on the streets, in the balmy spring air, they might stand on their heads on grass somewhere, in darkness, and he might tackle one of the black girls, or give her a ride on his shoulders.

He sat with his back increasingly aware of the three behind him. He heard The King's voice several times, and he heard the girls laughing.

He sat there. Then, not knowing quite how to approach them, he slipped back off the stool. He gripped his glass of Coke in his hand. Calmly, he turned and walked toward the booth. They did not see him, or look up, until he was standing beside the booth. Then the three of them were looking at him at once and he said, politely, "Join you?"

The King pushed over to the side of his seat, saying "Sure," and Alex sat down. The two girls sat looking at him, almost smiling, but they said nothing. Alex said to The King, "How you been doing, man?"

"Good," The King said. "Good. You know. How you doin?"

"Okay. Fine. On and off."

They all sat silent again. Alex wanted to talk about the detention home, and Red Eye, and Billy Noname, but was afraid The King would not like it mentioned. "What's with the Hotel these days?" he said.

"Beats me, man. I ain't been out there, and I ain't goin out there no more."

Alex did not know what to say. Finally he said, "Where you headed?" He glanced to the side, at The King, but wanted to look at the girls.

"Goin to the show," The King said.

Alex nodded.

Then The King said, "This here Laura. An' Carolyn. Man, I don't recall yo name."

"Alex."

"Yeah. Oh yeah."

"Hi," Alex said to the girls.

They nodded, smiling, but still did not speak.

"What show you going to?" Alex said. He imagined the four of them sitting in a dark theater, in deep cushioned seats, one of the girls sitting beside him, eventually finding her hand.

"Palace," one of the girls said.

"What's on?" Alex said.

"Ghost picture," The King said.

The girls laughed lightly and there was silence again. Alex thought if he was going to say anything he had to say it soon, but one of the girls said, "What is yo name again?"

"Alex Housman."

The girl was smiling. Alex thought her eyes caught his own. He said, going warm all over, "Want to make it a foursome?"

No one answered. They were glancing at one another; then The King said, "Man, we got somebody to meet, you know?"

"Oh," Alex said. He tried to indicate that it did not matter.

They sat silent again. Then The King began moving; he said to the girls, "We gonna be late we don't go."

Alex slipped out and stood up so The King could slide out. The girls also edged out.

"See you now, man," The King said.

"See you," Alex said.

The girl who had asked his name glanced at him. She said, " 'Bye."

He sat back down as they made their way along the aisle and over to the cash register. The girl who had spoken was last. She was carrying her jacket, and her blouse, satin purple, was not tucked into her skirt. Her waist was small and long, her seat narrow and erect.

A while later he was on the sidewalk himself, walking along. Store lights and most car headlights were on, but darkness was just falling upon the city. He walked slowly. Sometimes he stopped, stood back against the front of a drugstore, to watch, but moths and insects were thick around the warm glass and he soon walked on again.

There were no classes the last day of school before summer vacation. A pleasant mood prevailed throughout the rooms and corridors. The expanse of summer air, the expanse of choice, was there at last—following a final homeroom meeting and a final general assembly. The endless school year had ended.

Alex went about the routine this morning of turning in his books and locks, of packing his gym bag in the stifling locker room. In the lines, and in the assembly in the auditorium, he overheard remarks of a gathering to follow at Long Lake, of rides, of swimming, of six-packs. He was content and strong, he told himself, to be leaving now and not to be going there.

In the final assembly the last speaker, Mr. Gerhinger, gave an emotional farewell to the graduating seniors. Mr. Gerhinger's emotion did not affect Alex, but when the man spoke of the future, of the new football season coming next fall, and the football team coming, the new victories, Alex felt a loss Mr. Gerhinger had not intended.

Alex happened to speak to Irene Sheaffer. There was no mass outpouring of students but a general drifting away, and Alex, leaving the building, walking to where the two sidewalks from the two front doors converged at the street, met her. She was waiting to cross.

He said "Hello," and she said the same.

They stood on the curb as several cars and a bus passed, both of them looking to the front. It was the place, Alex recalled, where the police car had parked, where the students had to flow around the front of the car.

The street clear, she stepped from the curb to cross, as did he and a few others. He was beside her. "Did you do all right in school?" he said.

She said, "Yes," politely.

He was not sure if she was afraid of him, or embarrassed to be seen with him, but he wished to show her that he was all right now, that he carried no bad feelings, no childish splinters of the heart. "What are you doing this summer?" he said.

"Oh, nothing. We may go up north."

"Well," he said—they were across the street and he knew he should leave her side—"I hope you have a happy summer."

She said nothing. Looking ahead, as they came among others and separated, he walked on. He walked along the sidewalk, conscious that she was behind him, and however taken he was with a desire to look back, however strained the view from his eyes, he kept walking.

Book Five

Summer Death

One

Alex took a job as a caddy at the Country Club. It was late June. School had been out ten days. Or perhaps it was two weeks—the warm days were already running together. Mr. Quinn had made the arrangements by telephone. There were no other summer jobs around the city. From lower downtown, the Country Club was a long bus ride to the east end of the city. A walk of a half mile followed, back along a curving gravel road where new cars, the drivers looking elsewhere, sped by. The road entered an oasis. There were pastures and wood lots marked with ponds of clear water, with fresh loam, with crescents of raked sand the color of women's face powder.

He carried an occasional single, an occasional double, in a twosome of ladies, in a threesome of men. He spent half-hours lofting pennies to lines in dirt outside the caddy house, waiting for his number to be called over a speaker. The caddy house, as marked and dirty as the upstairs corridor at The Lincoln Hotel, was the size of a one-car garage. It stood beyond the parking lot, out of sight of the clubhouse and the aqua-sparkling swimming pool, out of sight of the row of earthen-colored tennis courts.

Something of the Country Club reminded him of his mother, even though he hardly knew her. It may have been the flash of clothes, or the drinks, or the voice-play between men and women.

A sign on the Pro Shop screen door announced: CADDIES NOT ALLOWED. The sign delivered a sting. So did the call by number—to hoist the strap of a heavy leather bag, umbrella attached, filled with cosmetics, clubs, balls, shoes, over his shoulder. Golfers pretended he was not there, looked past him and talked to each other, told stories as if they were alone. The heavy bags compressed him downward, so he felt like a coolie, while the golfers stood upright and swung their clubs.

He disliked women golfers less than men. He imagined he was performing a manly service for the women. The men issued small orders and reprimands—"Please mark the ball"—when on arches turning ninety degrees the white specks slapped distant leaves, ricocheting, disappearing into jungle.

The women wore white blouses and khaki skirts, and ankleless socks, while the men wore tangerine and lemon and turquoise costumes, and tassels on their shoes.

Sometimes, in the morning when it was quiet, carrying a single or a double in a twosome of ladies, he removed his shoes and socks, and rolling his pants legs, waded into the sandy water hazards to retrieve a dubbed ball. The women found it impractical to waste the valuable balls so readily. He found the water and the exchange pleasant. He usually picked up two or three more balls in the process and pushed them into his pockets. And he usually thought of his brother, Howard, for they had waded for golf balls most of the last summer Howard spent in the city. They waded in the oily, murky Flint River, while these Country Club water hazards, the rippling water clean enough to dive into, to frog-swim over the bottom, the white blurs all around, this golf-ball-hustler's paradise was off limits.

One return from the job, a mild return, came in the evening when the day had ended. Taking the bus back into the city at first darkness, stopping, sunburned, to have something to eat at a lunch counter somewhere, perhaps partially listening to a night game from Detroit, the bat cracking and the throat of the night crowd rising from a fly-specked radio—occasionally at this moment he felt a reward of having worked, the authority of a working man.

Rain in the morning was the finest of pleasures. Rain drops beginning to rifle into street dust, to splat black upon asphalt and to ping upon tinny cars—a farmer standing on his soil may have had a similar feeling. He rested his red and tender shoulder on rainy days. He often sat for a long time in town, at daybreak, reading the morning paper, looking to the street and air outside, at people passing with newspapers or plastic kerchiefs on their heads, the rain spattering, his shirt wet and sticking to his shoulders.

One morning, perhaps four weeks into the summer, within a heavy thundershower, he made a decision. He had stopped to fold a supply of papers under the doorway overhang of an unopened gas station. He stood looking at himself as if from above. The summer was without promise. The future was without promise. The idea of returning to school was impossible; he knew he should leave this town. The navy, the army, the marines, the air force. The only problem was his father.

He may have been persuaded by the storm. The rain, warm and heavy, came on and off. It was filling the air, assaulting the pavement, making the asphalt deep in spattering water. He stood perhaps a foot from the drip line, up on a curb. His thoughts were not new. The same ideas had come to him before, and then as now they had made his heart hesitate with an excitement of escape, even of adventure. But now he had no day in court to worry about; now he was only weeks away from being old enough. And alas, it was not a mere thought this time, but a decision. He decided.

He stood there. The fact of his decision frightened him. Immediately he was filled with relief, and with doubt. In only a matter of weeks he could be on a vessel of some kind, slicing through the warm green ocean. He seemed more alive in the scene he imagined than he was standing here. There seemed a promise that away from here, in a moment like this moment, the strength and youth and rage of himself he had never released would make its way free.

He and Howard searched for golf balls that summer not with their eyes, but with their toes, naked toes, feeling the bottom, pressing into muck, hoping to avoid glass, rolling objects in a search for those which rolled evenly, reaching down, trying to keep an ear out of the water, retrieving a ball, or a stone, with their finger-tips. The water in the river was mud-brown in color; rainbows of oil-slick flashed in the frog hair along the sides. However murky the water, once they had been attracted by the gamble it offered, they went to the golf course nearly every morning of the summer. It was no more than a fifteen-minute walk, downstream from the complex of Chevrolet factory buildings and their apartment on Chevrolet Avenue.

Most golfers used old river-balls to hit across the water, and the balls they found were usually cut or waterlogged or cheap brands, and only rarely did they find a white

U.S. Royal or Titlist. Occasionally in the velvet muck they found balls which were two-thirds black, unreadable and dead, which may have lain in the river for years. Still, there was an excitement each time golfers came up on the bank to tee off. Alex and Howard stood to the side, hoping to see the balls topped into the river, marking the spot, watching for another ball to be hit, or for others to tee off, and then plowed their thighs through the water, to search quickly with toes for the downed ball before someone else found it.

When the golfers had loaded their carts and come down the bank to cross the long footbridge, which was made of rope and wooden planks and swayed a little, they left the river and waded up to the edge of the grass to meet them. They laid out their collection of balls, and if the golfers stopped to look, they named their prices, pointing—"Ten cents, fifteen, two for a quarter, a quarter each, thirty-five for each of these." With some more coins in their soaked pants pockets, and the remaining golf balls stuffed back in, they returned to the water, to wading and watching for new golfers to appear on the opposite bank.

One afternoon, a day which was extremely hot even wading in the river, a morning when the air was motionless and the temperature was in the nineties, Howard, shirtless, his dungarees rolled above his knees, dove from the footbridge into the water. He paused on the edge first, until he had Alex's attention, and the attention of three or four other boys wading, and expanding his chest, squealing something, he sprang and entered the water headfirst. He swam under water ten or twelve feet, as if in the YMCA swimming pool, and came up. Someone, a black kid, yelled, "Hey, that water's rancid," and Howard called back, "It's good—you just have to spit the turds out," and he disappeared underwater again, and swam a distance downstream, and surfacing, called out, "I wanna go swimming, screw it!" and he rolled and began swimming underwater upstream.

He climbed to the bridge and paused again, and this

time jumped high into a cannon ball, and splashed water
back over the bridge, water which looked clean and transparent in the air. There were more remarks of "slime"
and "carp" and "crap" and "turds" and "toilet paper" and
still he kept swimming, going underwater and coming up
again, and swimming on his back, until he stopped once,
and stood up, the water around his chest, and said to the
rest of them, "It's not dirty. It's just muddy."

Before long Alex and the black kid and another white
kid were diving and cannonballing from the bridge, swimming and returning to the bridge to hoist themselves up,
dripping, to sit on the edge a moment and to dive again,
as if they were at a lake in the country and lifting themselves from green water to a floating raft. Three black
golfers teed off, and one of them called out, "You kids is
crazy, that stuff is poison." Still they swam, the black kid
did a cannonball, they all did cannonballs, and when the
three men came over the bridge they stopped to lean on
the ropes for a moment, to watch, and one of them said,
"Shoot, I swim in dirtier shit 'n that when I was kid."

It was one of these afternoons, returning from the golf
course, that their mother showed up for the first time. They
had not seen her since the few early visits she made to Mrs.
Cushman's. Nor did they have any idea why she was there.
Over seven years had passed. Her car, a new Pontiac—
they did not know it was her car at the time—was parked
in the yard behind the apartment building, and her scent,
the smell of perfume, greeted them immediately on entering the kitchen door. No one was in the kitchen. They had
come home to eat, to go back into the summer day, but as if
startled by the unusual odor, they stopped there. "Pop?"
Alex called out. "Pop? Are you here?"

In a moment his father came into the kitchen. "Your
mother's here," he said. "Come in and say hello."

"Who?" Howard said.

More than surprise, Alex felt a curiosity. He hardly
remembered what she looked like.

She appeared then, in the doorway which led to the living room. She said "Hi" to them. She presented the aroma, faint but everywhere, of violet or lilac. They only looked at her, without speaking. She stood smiling. Alex was so overwhelmed by her, by her pretty face, the dark trimming about her eyes, the faint dust of rose over her cheeks, her shining lips, that he could only smile in return and found almost nothing to say, and forgot at once, when he did speak, what words he had just used. Howard said nothing.

They went politely into the living room. There was a magic about her, about her smile and the presence of her body which occupied the space of the room. She asked them some light questions: How had they been? What grades were they in now in school? What had they been doing this summer? They answered with partial and foolish answers, as if ashamed, saying they were fine, and they were in such and such a grade, and they had been just fooling around, looking more at each other when they answered than at her. They did not know what to call her, nor did anyone tell them. Nor did they know what to make of her visit, and when she was gone, just minutes later, Alex and Howard, as if left speechless, said nothing to each other of her having just been there.

Their father had to change to go to work, and Alex and Howard fixed sandwiches and left, walking to the park this time. But once they were there, they did not join any game. It was as if they had just seen an automobile accident or a fight, and rather than play in a game they sat on the grass at the side, in the shade, and they treated each other with unusual consideration, as if they were frightened by something.

They stole a case of beer that night. It was another night when even if the sun had gone down and the sky was dark, the temperature seemed to fall only a degree or two, from perhaps ninety to eighty-nine. Fan propellers hummed on floor stands in tavern and store doorways, and overhead in apartment windows, sweeping back and forth. They were passing through an alley behind a row of stores when they saw a heavy wooden door standing open. Within, in a dark room lighted only from another interior doorway, were stacked cases of beer. Out on the street, on Chevrolet Avenue, it was the Auto City Beer & Wine Takeout. Howard went to the end of the alley, and in a moment, peeking in the doorway, Alex stepped in, just one step, placed his hands in the end slots of a cardboard case, lifted the heavy case and carried it out.

By the time he was at the end of the alley, the case was pressing against his thighs. Once there, Howard took one end and they turned walking down Third Avenue, entering the relative darkness under trees, passing before houses with short lawns. Walking quickly across streets under streetlights, they carried the case to the golf course. There, sitting in darkness on the edge of the footbridge with their feet hanging toward the flowing water, the deep skylight coming from among branches far overhead, they opened the flaps on the case and removed bottles to see what they had. "Goebel's," Howard said.

Alex used a key to pry open the first bottle. He worked for perhaps five minutes, the bottle hissing foam at the edges, before he sprang the cap free and the suds shot out. When the arch settled, he drank. "Ooh," he said.

"How's it taste?" Howard said.

"Shitty."

"It'd probably be better if it was cold."

"It couldn't be any worse. Here, have some."

Howard drank. He lowered the bottle at once and exhaled. "It tastes like piss," he said.

Alex, taking the bottle, drank again. Drawing his arm back, he threw the bottle high and long downstream into the darkness. When it splashed, he said, "Christ, did you hear that fish jump?"

"That was a big turd that jumped," Howard said.

Alex found a way to uncap the bottles reaching to the

understructure of the bridge. He opened two this time, handing the first one politely to Howard. This beer was less foamy, and Alex said, "I guess it's better if it's not all shook up."

They sat drinking.

"We'll probably get polio from swimming in the river," Howard said.

They sat, sipping the warm beer. "Polio doesn't hurt you," Alex said.

"How do you know?"

Alex did not answer. He lay back on the bridge, his legs still hanging down. He tried to drink this way, but spilling some beer over the sides of his face, he sat up again.

In a moment he said, "I wonder what's with her?"

"Who?"

"Her. Our mother."

"Beats me."

They sat sipping the beer, and then Alex also threw this half-full bottle downstream into the water.

"Those are worth two cents, you know," Howard said.

"You think so," Alex said, and taking the case not quite angrily in the crook of his arm, he pushed it into the river.

"Wha'd you do that for?"

Alex gave no answer; he knew none and sat there confused.

In a moment he said to Howard, "Throw that shit away."

After a pause Alex heard beside him the swing of Howard's arm, and the space of silence before the bottle splashed.

The following week she came to the apartment again. Alex and Howard were in and out that morning, and although their father said nothing of the visit, it was clear that something was happening. Rather than going about the apartment in his undershirt, he bathed and shaved, and dressed in suit pants and a white shirt opened at the throat. She drove in around noon, and he held the door open to let her into the kitchen.

There was the aura of perfume again, of her presence. She smiled and shook their hands this time, but they stood and talked only a few moments in the kitchen before they left. In this time she said to Howard, strangely, "I bet you'd like the lake, wouldn't you?" She looked only at Howard. Their father stepped in then with two drinks, ice cubes in the amber oily liquid, and said to them, "You two run along now so your mother and I can talk." Shying away, saying good-bye, they left.

They looked over the Pontiac in the yard. All the windows were rolled down and it looked cooler within the dark upholstery than out in the shade. They circled the car and looked in at the dashboard.

Out on Chevrolet Avenue they walked down the shady side of the street. The street was somewhat busy, the factories ahead, the rail crossings, in the rumble of noon hour.

"What do you think she meant by that?" Howard said.

Alex said he did not know. He felt an unusually strong sensation of jealousy, or fear. He felt he was to blame for something and did not know what to make of the feeling. He treated Howard with unusual kindness throughout the afternoon, throughout the evening. He shared what coins he had, and he shared what candy he bought, and he spoke almost in apology.

Howard could get into the basketball games at the park only during off hours, through the afternoons and the dinner hour, before cars began pulling up to park on the street, and men and boys came over to sit on the grass to put on their sneakers. One evening, a day or two after their mother's visit, Alex and Howard were shooting around at the near-deserted court with a couple of other boys when a boy named Jack Lafond showed up and they started a game. Jack Lafond was tall and very skinny, perhaps six-two or six-three and weighing no more than a hundred and forty or fifty pounds. He was a poor basketball player and he ruined almost every game he was ever in by causing someone to quit or causing a fight. Still they played, perhaps thinking this time would be different. But tonight he started picking on Howard. (Once, at gunpoint, with an army .45 pistol he had found somewhere, Lafond had held two younger boys at bay in a garage, through more than two hours of a Saturday morning.) Now he was grabbing Howard's shirt occasionally from behind, holding it when he tried to run, and he began placing his hand over Howard's head when he tried to jump, laughing, ignoring and disrupting the game.

He and Alex began trading bumps and hips under the basket, jumping into each other, backing into each other with elbows flashing. The others kept saying, "Come on, let's play ball, for Christsakes."

They played some. But Lafond continued to pick on Howard, and finally, jumping for the ball and striking immediately into Lafond's hand above his head, Howard bit his tongue. He ran, kicking at Lafond, swinging his fists at him and crying some as Lafond side-stepped and back-stepped, laughing. It took a moment for something to snap in Alex, but then it snapped, and he went after Lafond himself, furious and for the moment almost in tears, moving directly after him. He grabbed Lafond, taking him from the side and the rear as he was back-pedaling, taking him in both hands at his elbows, lifting all but his toes off the ground, and walking him a step or two as if moving a railroad tie, threw him, heaved him with all his strength over the asphalt court, hissing, "You keep your hands off him!"

Lafond rose to fight, but he hardly stood a chance. Alex was possessed with a desire, even a passion, to literally break Lafond's bones, to make him bleed, to crack his skull, to end his life. He lost all control of himself for a moment or two, running after Lafond, stalking him, ducking his swinging fists, taking some blows around his neck and shoulders in an exchange of clawing and hitting and grabbing at Lafond's face at the end of his long neck. Then, in a maneuver where Lafond was trying to contain his fists and he was trying to get Lafond in the face, Alex leaped up on him, up on his side, and got an arm, his left arm, locked immediately around Lafond's neck and both legs locked around his midsection, discovering, still in his outrage of fury, as Lafond staggered along top-heavy under his weight, grabbing at Alex, that his own face was protected directly behind Lafond's head and that Lafond had no way to stop his right arm, his right fist, which he began cracking wildly into Lafond's forehead and cheek, into his ear and against the upper part of his head, sometimes hitting Lafond's raised hand or wrist, striking over and over as fast as he could whip his fist in and out, so Lafond seemed undecided each second between using his hands to claw at Alex's grip or to cover his face.

They staggered around, Alex riding him, squeezing his waist with his locked legs, squeezing the boy's wild neck with his locked arm, squeezing more tightly every time Lafond tried to dig into his forearm, or reaching back, tried to claw at the back of Alex's neck with his fingernails. Alex kept pounding his right fist into Lafond's head and face, trading on Lafond's madness with a fury of his own which was much faster, striking like a jackhammer.

Lafond might have fallen, to land on Alex and break his grip, but apparently he did not think of it. When they did tumble to the ground it seemed to come from Lafond's knees giving way, so they sank, collapsed, into a pile. Alex came down to the side of Lafond, still swinging at him, trying to get in every possible blow, at the same time pulling wildly and violently to get his legs and his caught arm free of Lafond's weight, to get his body balanced, to get

to his feet again. But as he pulled loose, Lafond did not
follow but lay there, his knees drawn, and although Alex
knew Lafond had quit, he struck at Lafond's head several
times as he tried to cover himself with his arms. Lafond
was saying, "Hey, that's enough. Enough. I quit. Back
off, man, I quit."

Alex backed off and stood waiting. He was panting. He
suddenly felt the scratches over his arms, and over his
neck, down his back and up into his hair. He did not trust
Lafond and expected him to get up and feign exhaustion,
and try to hit him. He stood poised and ready, however
foolish he might look.

Lafond, on his feet, held the side of his face with one
hand. He laughed lightly and made a joke of the fight. "I'll
get your ass next time," he said. He was nearly smiling .

Alex still did not trust him, but Lafond turned then and
started walking away and said, almost politely, over his
shoulder, "See you guys."

Alex sat down to rest. The others made comments of
congratulation and went on to shoot baskets, and Alex
found it impossible not to smile or grin foolishly. "That
dumb son of a bitch," Howard said, standing before him,
laughing very lightly but with great pride, so Alex found
it impossible as well not to laugh, or perhaps to gurgle,
with the ecstasy of having won.

A day or two later, she came again. It was mid-
August by then and school time was approaching. As the
four of them stood in the kitchen, their father explained
the reason for the visit: Howard was going to live with
his mother at the lake. Alex, unable to compose himself, to
have a chance to understand, stood still and speechless for
the moment as if he had lost his breath. He went through
the apartment with them, helping Howard pack his things,
smiling painfully, even saying several things to him—

"You sure are lucky to be going out to the lake," and, "You better promise to come and visit us sometime." But at last his cheeks began to hurt and wrinkle, and his eyes began to blur lightly, and he looked away from looking at any of them. In their bedroom closet he helped Howard separate his sports gear, and he spoke to him without looking at his face, trying to make his voice sound normal. But his breathing would not come right. Before long he was unable to contain himself any further and he turned as if on his way to the kitchen, speaking to no one, and slipped outside and closed the door quietly, and slipped down the stairs.

He ran along then, ran against losing control of himself. Out and around the corner, where the summer day was carrying on, knowing he was losing control, he turned into the alley where they had stolen the case of beer. He made it fifty or sixty feet along before the first eruption came from his throat, and he turned into a space between buildings and leaned, facing a concrete block wall, his arms over his head, and gave way to the spasms which kept surfacing and relaxing. He wailed as he tried to stop them, until another one rose and his back and shoulders jarred and trembled.

Perhaps an hour later, the tears dried around his eyes, he was still in the space. He was sitting on the ground now, his back against the wall. He looked down at the line of washed pebbles under the roof line and picked some of the small stones out to drop again or to toss lightly away. He did not think of much of anything, and he seemed to have recovered. The earlier frightening thoughts of Howard not being there any more, not going to school, not eating breakfast, not playing basketball, thoughts which had been incomprehensible, did not come to him now. Rising at last, he made his way out of the alley the other way, not to be seen.

He circled and went to the park. With two or three others there, he shot baskets. One moment he talked with someone as if all were normal; another moment he moved and shot the ball poorly, and silently, as if he were alone, as if his vision were strangely out of line.

As evening came he went to the movies. It may have been the first time he had ever gone to the movies alone, without Howard. Still, he did not think very clearly of Howard. It seemed that something had happened, and now it was over, and there was nothing to do. He tried not to think of it. Shame rose in him when he remembered the tears. Tears were childish. But when he came close to thinking of Howard again, of realizing what had happened, he was taken with a misery so strange that he turned his head down and closed his eyes. A moment later, when the thought had passed, he looked back at the screen, to watch the movie.

Two

"Permission is possible," Mr. Quinn said. "But it's still something I want you to think about. I want you to give it some hard thought. The army can be a tough place, you know. And I want you to promise you won't decide for at least a week. You go sit on a stump somewhere and put it through your computer. You understand what I mean? And you also need your father's permission, you know."

Alex continued to caddy at the Country Club. But clear daybreak, the broadcast of horizon sunlight in the morning, began to promise only dry and miserable labor, hours of being sun-blinded in the whiteness while others oiled and creamed themselves for a time, and swung their clubs in propeller circles, and went on to the dapple-shaded veranda to drink their frosted drinks. The idea of leaving the city kept him going.

He thought often of Howard. He wished, if his illusive future was going to arrive, to see Howard again before he left, and at last he wrote him another letter. On a morning when the sky was gray and doubtful, and a light wind was blowing, even if only a couple of separate raindrops had passed his eye, he sat at the Coney Island hoping for a storm to blow up and excuse him from caddying. Before long, sitting there, he was writing an imaginary letter to Howard. Then he walked over to the city library, to sit down and write an actual letter. The letter he had written in his imagination was filled with humor, and perhaps affection—he had to contain his laughter and tears at the counter—but the note he finally composed was more direct. He wrote:

> *Dear Howard,*
> *How are you? Did you get my letter sometime back? I'm okay now, in case you wondered. I did okay in school. I'm caddying this summer at the country club. I would like to come out there for a visit. Is that okay? How about in the next week or two sometime? How about you writing me a letter to say if it is okay? Then I'll get Pop to drive me out. I'll race you across the lake underwater. Okay?*
> *Alexander the Great*

No rain fell this morning, but he still did not go to the Country Club. When he had mailed the letter he returned to the library, to look at magazines. He thought of school. The thought may have come on the gray and somber air. It was the first time he had recalled the building and the crowded corridors and cafeteria since leaving in June. In

September the world would begin once more in those rooms and he wasn't going to be there.

Howard's letter lay on the kitchen table. A week had passed. It was after ten o'clock in the evening and Alex had just come in from having seen a single-feature movie in town. The letter lay alone, without any note from his father, and the envelope itself looked odd, for the return address showed the name, *Howard Connell*. Alex only vaguely remembered that Connell was his mother's married name. So Howard had changed his name.

> *Dear Alex,*
>
> *It was a real surprise to hear from you. Can you come out on Saturday July 15? I asked mother and she said okay. Can Pop drive you out and pick you up on Sunday? There are all kinds of things we can do. I can run the boat by myself now. I'll see you when you get here.*
>
> *Howard*

Alex heard his father whispering his name that night, trying to wake him. When he raised himself on his arm, squinting, his father whispered, "Son, what was the letter from Howard about? Anything special?"

To the blur of yellow, the black silhouette, Alex said, "Oh, he wrote to invite me out for a visit."

"To do what?"

"To visit. Out at the lake. Next weekend. Can you drive me out?"

"What's this now? Whose idea was this?"

"I was just going out for a visit. To see Howard. Just over Saturday and Sunday."

"Oh, son . . . how did this happen? Why don't you come on out and talk to me for a minute?"

Alex left his bed, and in his underwear followed his

father out to the kitchen. Alex sat at the table as his father
placed a teakettle of water on the stove. Cracking a match
to light the burner, his father turned back. Still nearly
whispering, he said, "How did all this come about?"

"Oh, I just wrote because I wanted to go see Howard,
is all. And he wrote back and said to come out this weekend. That's all."

"Well, why do you want to go out there?"

"I just want to see Howard."

"Oh, well, son, I don't know. Do you think you should
do that?"

Alex, surprised at how seriously his father was taking
it, said, still through the cobwebs of his sleep, "I was just
going for those days, is all. He said it was all right. What's
wrong with that?"

"Well—we haven't seen them in a long time. Don't you
think it might be better to just leave well enough alone?
What brought all this on, anyway?"

"I just wanted to see Howard."

"Well, I think that's fine for you to see Howard, but
I don't know about going out there and staying overnight.
That means I'll have to drive out there twice. I think—"

"I can hitchhike," Alex said.

"Oh, son, try to understand. You know we've never had
anything much but trouble with those people. I just think
it might be wise if we stuck pretty much to ourselves,
that's all."

Neither of them spoke for a moment then, until his
father said, "Well, let's let it rest for now. You better go
on back to bed. Or would you like some bacon and eggs?"

"No, no thanks," Alex said. "I'm not hungry." He hesitated, thinking of telling his father about the army, and
decided to wait.

A boy named Mickey Elliot agreed to peddle his
route on the Sunday he would be gone. But on Saturday
morning, when Elliot had promised to walk around with

him to learn general directions, he was over forty minutes late. Alex sat on the curb, enjoying the warm air and the freedom from the golf course, folding and sacking his papers. His father had still not agreed to drive him to the lake, but he believed, without worry, that he would. His only worry came from the vague anticipation of seeing Howard again. When Elliot came wheeling along Garland Street at last, on a bicycle, Alex only smiled nervously at him and said nothing of his being late.

The apartment was still quiet when he returned. Bravely, he entered his father's bedroom, and stood a moment at the foot of his bed. His father lay sleeping on his side; the shade over his window was highlighted by the morning sun. His father, lying asleep, looked human and without strength. At last Alex pressed his father's foot to the side. "Pop?" he said. "Let's go. It's really warm out."

His father roused around and opened his eyes. He looked over at Alex, and he did not look unhappy.

"I'll get some breakfast while you get up," Alex said.

"Where the hell you going in such a hurry?"

Alex only smiled.

"You're sure determined, aren't you?" his father said.

Alex packed his gym bag—toothbrush, comb, underwear, socks—and then sat waiting in the kitchen. He checked his money. His father did not want anything to eat, and Alex, waiting, had a second bowl of cereal. He checked the clock again; it was ten minutes to nine. At the bathroom door, which was opened about an inch—water was running within—he said, "Hey, Pop. Come on. It's getting late."

"Okay, son," his father said. "Hold on. I'll be out in a minute."

In the kitchen, feeling worried now, Alex checked his things over again. He then cleaned up his mess and wiped the table. Back at the bathroom door he asked his father if he was sure he did not want some eggs. His father said no and asked him to put on some coffee. When the coffee was perking, Alex returned to the bathroom door. He heard water running in the bathtub and he said, "You taking a bath?"

His father said nothing for a moment; then he said, "That's what I'm doing."

Fifteen minutes later, when his father came out to the kitchen for the first time, barefooted and wearing clean underwear, he drank quickly, standing up, a half cup of coffee. Rinsing out the cup, he immediately put some ice cubes in a glass and fixed himself a drink. Alex looked away. Without speaking, taking his drink with him, his father left the room.

The next time he came to the kitchen he was wearing the powder-gray pants to his summer suit and his black-and-white summer shoes. He was still in his sleeveless undershirt. Fixing himself another drink, he looked over at Alex and said, "Can you tell me why you want to do this?" His voice was gentle and serious.

"I just want to see Howard," Alex said.

His father looked at him for a moment. Then he raised his glass and drank.

The next time he came to the kitchen he was dressed. He fixed himself another drink. Turning to Alex, he smiled. "Okay," he said, "Let's hit the road." He finished his drink and placed the glass on the table. He wheezed lightly, and wiped his lips with his hand.

Taking up his gym bag from the floor, realizing his father was already showing his drinks, Alex was filled again with the strange worry. He led the way, out into the heat, down the back steps.

His father continued to drink all the way to the lake. They said little more to each other. His father fell into a mood that was not at all like his usual drinking moods. Neither drunk nor sober, he seemed at a distance. Alex sat quietly; he took a pint from the glove compartment the first time it was asked for and handed it to his father. His father smacked his lips lightly and said "*Ahhh!*" each time he drank. He kept the bottle, opened, in the crotch of his legs. Alex glanced at him once. His lips had taken on a damp color; his cheeks and neck were growing raw-plum–colored. Alex sat worrying, smelling the waves of whiskey. Oddly enough for this moment, he saw why his father always bought pints rather than fifths. They were easier to hide; they fit easily into the glove compartment, into his lunch pail. Alex glanced at his father's profile again. Feeling afraid, he looked down the highway.

They drove over the country, by-passing Shiawassee. His father knew the way. When they came to the tavern, to the sunlighted gravel parking lot, he pulled in, and stopped, in almost the same place where Alex had stopped the Buick, and sat a full minute in silence before he turned off the ignition. Five or six cars were lined along the front of the tavern, facing its windows. The dirt road beside the tavern, leading down to the houses and lakeside cottages, was rust-colored. Finally, opening the door, his father said, "You wait here. I'll see what's going on." He got out of the car, but he paused again. Then he looked back in the car window. "Son, this is pretty dumb," he said.

Alex said nothing. He glanced at his father and looked straight ahead again.

He watched his father walk over and move between two cars opposite the door of the tavern, passing into and out of the glare from their hoods. The glare knifed into Alex's eyes. When he refocused, his father was at the doorway, rocking forward from his toes slightly as he cupped his hands to light a cigarette. His balance had swayed from control. Alex looked away. When he looked back again his father was gone, the screen door was closed.

Alex looked at the channel of water where it appeared beside the tavern. It ran along beside the road, a couple of hundred feet away. He could not see the dock, or the red gas pump, but the dream he had carried with him all week —of visiting Howard, of fishing, riding over the water in a boat—came to mind, and left again, like the glare of sunlight. The smell of lake water in the air, slightly cooler than the air from behind and smelling faintly both of fish and pine, floated by.

Alex left the car after a moment and walked down to the dock. He thought Howard might possibly be there, but he was not. White suds were washing back and forth in the weeds at the edge of the water, and an unidentifiable fish lay on its side in the wash, gray and bloated. The smell was stronger here, as if the lake itself were alive. The dream of swimming and fishing flashed through him again. It seemed he had only to get rid of his father, that once his father was gone, the sweeping surface of water would present itself completely. In front of the tavern again—the car remained empty—he looked over at the screen door and smelled the damp and stale cigarette coolness that came from within. He saw nothing beyond the sunlighted gray fabric of the screen.

He was sitting in the car when his father came out. With detachment he watched him waver just slightly into the side of one of the cars, clearly losing his balance this time. He continued, obviously trying to appear in control of himself, a man in a handsome summer suit walking over gravel and raising powder around his black-and-white shoes. Alex looked away.

In the car, his father sat still again. A couple of ringlets of wavy hair had fallen over one side of his forehead; he was deep red-colored now, his shirt collar looking fluorescent-white around his neck. Finally he spoke, but said only, "Your mother and Howard are down to the house. You go ahead on down. I'll be heading back."

Something had happened in the tavern. Alex had expected something to happen, had expected it all morning, but still, he was surprised. An image of his mother's husband came to mind, although he had yet to set eyes on the man.

"You go on now," his father said. "They're down to the house."

Alex knew he should not ask questions, but the words came out. "What about you? Aren't you going to see Howard?"

Quietly, without anger, his father said, "Son, the man doesn't want me to go down there."

Alex said nothing to this. He sat looking ahead. He remembered a morning when his father had come home with an eye so swollen that it was completely closed. A touch of the fear he had felt that morning came back to him.

His father spoke again, still softly. "It's a one-story house, white, about a half mile down—on the right-hand side." Then he said, "You want to stay?"

"We're here," Alex said, feeling immediately that he was trading this weekend, this little possible enjoyment, for something intangible and all out of proportion.

His father nodded. "You go on now," he said. "Have yourself a good time."

Alex paused. Then he took his bag in hand and opened the car door. Outside he eased the door shut again. Bending down, he looked in through the window at his father. Their eyes met as they had few times before. His father was neither smiling nor not smiling. His eyes were pink. Softly, he said, "Slam it, son."

Alex reopened the door—the lock had not caught—and slammed it. He looked through the window again. "You coming after me tomorrow?"

"Course I'm coming after you. Go on now and enjoy yourself for a change. Catch some fish."

Alex still paused. "Are you—okay?" he said.

"Okay for what?"

"I don't know."

"Why'd you say that, then?"

"I don't know."

"What do you know for sure?"

"Oh, quite a bit."

They looked at each other, smiling faintly over themselves, over the humor of being father and son. Then his

father winked. With a slight head motion he waved Alex
on his way.

Alex straightened up and turned. He set off walking,
over the gravel toward the dirt road, listening for the car
to start behind him. When he had gone a distance and the
car still had not started, he wanted to look back, but knew
his father would be watching him, gauging him in his intoxicated and sentimental way. Go home, Alex thought.
He continued walking, his legs seeming to cover little
distance. He looked back then, suddenly, and although the
windshield was covered with a reflection from the sun and
he could not see in, he raised his hand and waved. He looked
long enough, if his father was there, for his father to wave
back.

He walked along the dirt road. As he came opposite
a cove of water on his right, houses began to line the
shore. Then it was like a street in the city, with houses
crowded next to one another and across the street from one
another, but there were more shrubs and flowers here,
many flowers in bloom, sunlighted, and the aroma of the
lake water, and far off, an insistent hum of motors furrow-
ing the lake's surface. At last, where the houses and road
turned across the view ahead, at the turn, stood a single-
story white house. He realized he was trembling.

Someone was in front of the house, on the grass that ran
down to the water. It was Howard, he knew it was Howard
—but he could not make himself look long enough to be
sure. He went on to a door at the back of the house, out of
Howard's view, an attached garage between them, and
rapped his knuckles lightly on the glass storm door which
covered a closed wooden door. He did not knock again, and
waited a full two or three minutes. The doors, the house,
stood silent.

Working up his nerve at last, or perhaps losing his
nerve, trembling, he walked back around the garage. There
was a gate. He felt like a strange boy on the block entering

the yard of a boy who had always lived there. His vision felt awry, as if he were glancing away from something without moving his head.

"Hey—hello," he said, his voice off key.

Howard was doing something over a wooden box. Turning to look, he did not speak.

"What're you doing there?" Alex said.

"Well, look who's here," Howard said.

Alex was vaguely shocked by Howard's appearance—the change and growth that had taken place. Still, his face, and a vein of his voice, were recognizable, as though his features had remained nearly constant while his face had grown longer and thinner, while his voice had blended deeper. "It's me," Alex said, and walking over, he seemed to look away, at the ground, to the side, his face asserting its own foolish control.

"I wasn't sure at first," Howard said. "You sure have changed a lot."

"So have you."

"Boy, does your voice sound different," Howard said.

"You should hear yours."

"Boy," Howard said. "I didn't think anyone could get any uglier but you managed all right for yourself." He finished his line weakly, laughing uncertainly, as if he had been rehearsing its delivery all week. When Alex joined him laughing, smiling, he laughed harder.

"What are you doing?" Alex said. "What's that stuff?" He indicated the box, a handful of dirt Howard held in his hand.

Howard let the dirt, along with several night crawlers, fall back into the box. "This is my worm box," he said. "I been gathering some worms, in case we want to go fishing. I got over three hundred." He replaced a cover on the box, and then nearly whispered, "Listen, we should get away from here in a hurry or I'll probably have to clean the garage or something." He began moving toward a small white dock and a boat tied there, and Alex placed his bag beside the worm box and followed. "Where's Pop?" Howard said. "In the house?"

"He already went back," Alex said, nodding over his shoulder, feeling a slight heart shiver. He thought about saying something of his father being sorry not to see Howard, and expected Howard to say something, but neither of them spoke.

On the dock they were awkwardly silent with each other, looking at the boat and the outboard motor afloat beside them, getting in each other's way once. "Can you run this?" Alex said. Howard nodded yes, and lifting a rope over a post, gripped the boat and presented it for Alex to climb in. Alex stepped in and the boat gave on the water and he almost lost his balance. Howard laughed, and Alex, sitting down, also laughed. "Where's—Mother?" Alex said, nodding toward the house.

"Probably still asleep," Howard said. He was crouching on the dock, hand-sliding the boat along the dock.

"Shouldn't we go see her?" Alex said.

"Nah, we'll see her later," Howard said. He pushed the boat away from the dock, drawing himself in beside the motor.

Alex had a feeling that something important had been left unsettled, but he sat on the wooden seat, watching Howard work with the motor, and said nothing. Within a moment, on the third pull of the rope, the motor's sputtering caught, and Howard turned and looked past Alex to the open water.

Howard kept his eyes over Alex's shoulder, looking ahead, and Alex looked at him directly for a moment. He seemed no larger than the motor he now controlled. He was thirteen. In a moment he turned his eyes to Alex and smiled, proud of himself, of his lake, of running the boat. Alex smiled back, and not thinking to do so, he winked. Concealing a minor embarrassment, he looked away again —over the motor's roar there was nothing to say—and shifted around to face the front. It had been a detached wink, called from a wandering mind, touched with love. He felt of age, father to the child. With the warm sun coating his back, he looked ahead, over the open water, but seeing an endless distance within, seeing his father.

Later, without warning, Howard turned the handle to full power. The motor roared with the noise of an airplane, the front of the boat leaping, slapping the water once like an opened hand, as Alex, thrust back, grabbed the sides with both hands in order not to tumble backward. Alex turned to see a wind-whipped smile on Howard's face. They left a deep churning V behind them now, the water spraying, spattering up from both sides. In the roar, the acceleration—they were skimming, bouncing over the surface of green water—something of the promise of the week came home to Alex.

They swept out into the lake in a circle, banged over their own waves. They stopped once and bobbed for a moment in their wake. Later Howard shouted over the motor that they had to get gas, and crossing the long mouth of a cove, they entered a channel. Howard still drove the boat forcefully through the water, leaving boats tied along docks on the two sides bobbing. Alex held the sides of the boat. In a few minutes, down the channel, he saw the back of the tavern coming into view. LAKESIDE TAVERN was painted in black on the pink stucco. He knew it was possible his father was still there, waiting around. His father had done those things—had come around the ball fields when he was supposed to be at work. Once, playing baseball, Alex had noticed from his position that his father was over on the street, sitting in the car, but when Alex slipped over between innings to see him, his father told him it was nothing, told him to go back to his ball game, and drove off a minute later.

Alex glanced around at the bank and at what he could see of the parking lot as they approached, but he saw no one. Howard cut the motor then, the boat sank its belly into the water, and they sputtered up and stopped, as the motor stopped, beside the red gas pump. Alex, holding the dock side, tied the rope over the post. Howard said they had to get the key first, and started up the bank toward the rear of the tavern. Alex lagged back, until Howard turned and said, in invitation, "Come on."

Howard waited, holding the back door open. They passed through a small dark room filled with beer cases and folded tables, and opening another door, came into the cool tavern behind one end of the bar. The man down the bar had to be Ward Connell. He stood opposite a small gathering of men. Alex had imagined him to be small, or wiry, or homely—a stubby sailor—but he was tall, taller than his father, and younger-looking. He wore a short-sleeved sport shirt and looked very sober. He said "Hi" to Howard, and glanced past Howard to Alex. Alex stayed back in the doorway and waited as Howard and Ward talked to each other. He was strangely bothered by the man's youth and height. He imagined his father entering the bar in his gray suit, his black-and-white shoes. He wondered how they had talked to each other. Had they talked right there with those other men listening and watching? The images which came to mind were not pleasant, as if that hard stomach of his father's and his bricklike arms were strong only for him, as if here in this dark building, where it counted, they had gone soft.

He noticed Howard and Ward both looking at him as Howard was talking, and he noticed also that some of the men along the bar were looking his way. He thought they must know he was the son of the man Ward had talked to ("Ward, listen, I got my boy out here in the car . . ."). He thought they looked too long not to know something. He made no move, but all his fear and shyness sharpened to a needle point and left him, and he stood looking directly back. For a sudden moment it was like the night at the dance, in the sweeping colored lights, when given a word, he could have waded into them.

Howard made no introductions. Leaving Ward then, he came back to Alex with a ring of keys. As he came to Alex, passing and going first through the doorway, Ward called out behind them. "You guys want some pop, help yourself."

Alex decided he would have no pop. If his father had been behind that bar, he thought, he would have come over to shake hands and make him feel welcome. His father *was* a kind and generous man, he thought. In the small room, where Howard was lifting the iron handle of a wooden freezer door—laughter came from back in the bar and a knife point rose in Alex's chest as the laughter rose— Alex said, "No, I don't want any."

Howard ignored him and pulled out two bottles. "Sure you do," he said.

Down on the dock Howard handed Alex one of the bottles, which he took, Hire's Root Beer, as Howard worked a jackknife from his pocket. Alex hesitated, and wishing at once, even as he was doing it, that he had not, he heaved the bottle perhaps fifty feet out into the channel. The bottle hit in a splash and disappeared. Beside him, Howard said kindly, "What's the matter?"

"Nothing."

"What did you do that for?"

"I just didn't want it."

"Why you so mad?"

"I'm not mad. Forget it."

After a pause, Howard said, "We can go play shuffle-board later. If it's not too crowded."

"How about going fishing?"

"It's too late now," Howard said. "Wait'll later. Fish never bite this time of day."

Howard, his bottle of Hire's opened, placed on the dock, unlocked the pump and knelt to pump gas into a red can on the floor of the boat. He looked up, and he and Alex looked at each other for a moment, and then he looked back to his pumping.

Alex sat in the boat as Howard ran back to return the

keys. Howard was gone so long that Alex imagined them whispering about him. He thought of his father again. He imagined him driving back to the city, on the highway, alone. He imagined him back in the apartment, alone. It was the first time he had ever seen, or felt, his father's consuming loneliness. He was relieved that his mother was not in the tavern when they first arrived.

They knew no words of apology, and Howard, returning, offered the driving of the boat to Alex, which Alex accepted. He guided the boat back along the channel toward the open water of the lake. He had thought all week of a moment like this, driving ahead as if he were only going from one place to another. Howard, looking back over his shoulder, said, "Hey, give it some gas."

Alex turned the handle. The motor roared; the front of the boat rose, pointing up. But nothing beyond the noise and the slamming movement of the boat seemed to be happening. Alex felt little excitement. Howard was shouting; he motioned down with his hand.

Alex did not slow the motor. He held the handle tight and looked ahead, around the side of the boat, as if he had not understood Howard's signal. Howard stopped waving and held on, partially standing, looking ahead himself. The boats along the channel rose and fell in their wake.

Entering the open water, going a distance, Alex's feeling of rage sank away. He turned the handle, and abruptly, the boat settled into the water. Howard looked back at him. Alex smiled, and Howard smiled in return. The motor stopped; they bobbed quietly in a vacuum of sound.

"I forgot what a crazy bastard you are," Howard said.

Alex laughed a little. "You better drive," he said.

In the afternoon, back at the house, Alex met his mother. She smiled at him. Her deep voice surprised his memory with recognition. "What happened to Curly?" she asked him.

"He had to get back," Alex said, feeling a shiver.

His mother was wearing a silk housecoat and drinking coffee standing up. She said nothing more of his father. She looked him over and said he was certainly growing up. She asked him how he had been getting along, how school was—he was in the eleventh grade now, wasn't he? He gave short answers—he was fine, he'd be in the eleventh next year—wondering if she knew about the cars, about the juvenile home, his probation. Going to her bedroom to dress, she called back to Howard to fix him and Alex some lunch. Howard called back that they had already eaten, and he nodded to Alex and they slipped out quietly and escaped in the boat, back to the tavern, to play shuffleboard.

There were more people in the tavern now, including a couple of women. Music was playing on the jukebox. This time Ward said "Hi, there," and Alex said "Hi."

The tavern was cool, a dark place lighted at midday. Everyone seemed to know everyone else. They seemed happy with the day, or with the summertime. Howard taught Alex how to play shuffleboard and Alex tried to pay attention. But as they played he felt that Ward was keeping an eye on him. He did not think why, only that he felt out of place. When a group at the bar laughed he wondered if they were laughing about his father, if the men who had been there earlier were now telling the story to the women of what Ward had said to this guy.

Alex saw the air of comfort in the place, although it was their comfort. Glimpsing his life back in the city, from this distance, he saw a world which was drab. He also saw that his father, back in the city, would be dangerous today, and it seemed this was the first time he had ever understood why.

Howard was an expect at shuffleboard and beat him at every turn. Alex did not mind. From his distance, exchanging remarks with Howard, his mind was satisfying itself with thoughts. Nothing was altogether clear, however—he was having thoughts of the city, of freedom, of the factories, their apartment—until he realized that the threat he felt from this place, from Ward and those strangers, was not of their making but of his own. Why should they care about him? It was not they; it was his father. Any moment he might enter through that screen door, red-faced, dressed in his expensive clothes, his hair in ringlets over his forehead, carrying his air of danger. Alex watched as Howard slid another of the weighted discs along the powdered surface.

He did not recognize his mother when she first came in the front door of the tavern. Then the recognition was overwhelming; she looked as she had the times she came to visit. She wore a shining summer dress, or a springtime dress, a ruffle of something white outlining a deep V down her throat, and make-up, dark lipstick, faint powder and high-heeled shoes. People along the bar turned on their stools and called to her, called her Kathy and Katherine and looked happy if she spoke to them, happy to see her. Alex felt a remote pride that she was his mother, that she was so attractive. She talked to several people along the bar, laughing and throwing her head back, stopping several minutes with some and a moment with others, until she was at the end of the bar and ducked under to come up on the other side. Another man was working with Ward, an older man—Alex had not noticed him before—and Alex heard him say to her, "How's my sweetheart?"

Alex looked at her occasionally from the shuffleboard. He wanted to look at her and was afraid he would be noticed. After a while she came over. She told Howard this would have to be their last game—it was getting too crowded. She looked at Alex and smiled warmly, and asked if he was enjoying himself. There was a scent of flowers about her, and a slight rustling of her silk dress around her legs. He nodded, and he even smiled; music from the jukebox allowed him not to speak.

In the evening, when the sun was down and the boats had left the lake, after a meal of potato chips and root beer in the empty house, they went fishing. Alex asked

Howard if he ate every night like this and Howard nodded with an embarrassed smile that he did. Alex himself was in a melancholy mood in the quiet house. Feeling fatherly, he asked Howard if he didn't ever fix himself a meal. Howard said, "Sometimes," and Alex thought it was a lie.

Howard was not allowed to take the boat on the water after dark and they fished from the bank, using the nightcrawlers from the wooden box. Facing the house for the light from the windows, Howard showed him how to hook two of the long worms onto the hook so they made a gob, and tentatively at first, Alex reached for the worms.

They caught dozens of bullheads. They fished just off the bank in the shallow water, catching most of the bullheads before they were hooked, throwing them back on the grass at once, on Howard's instructions, shaking them loose, leaving them to flop in the darkness. Others they unhooked by holding them underfoot, avoiding their horns, using pliers to take the hook from their small grinding teeth and throats—some of the bullheads squeaked faintly —catching still others almost at once on the same gob of worms.

The air grew completely dark, but they could still see the red-and-white bobbers on their lines reflecting the house lights behind them. Alex enjoyed himself now for more than a few minutes at a time. He was without any fear. When he felt the line go taut, felt it pull and tremble, bending the rod, zigzagging and cutting water as the fish took the bobber down into the blackness and out of sight, there was nothing else to think about.

The night air remained warm. Fish thumped now and then behind them on the grass, and the frogs and insects around the edge of the water were singing, buzzing, croaking in a continuous hum, as if to fill the air, to deny any space for thinking. Lights from other houses and cottages ran over the water, along with occasional voices or music or laughter. Near midnight they kicked the fish back into the water, kicked them because Howard said they would stick their fingers with horns if they picked them up. Howard said the bullheads were tough fish and could do something special with their gills to stay alive for hours out of water, but they did not count or watch to see if any of the fish failed to swim down into the water.

Alex was pleasantly tired. Before going to sleep, lying on a cot in the small bedroom off the kitchen he shared with Howard, he had the thought that he had gone on to start a new part of his life. He had a vision for a moment of himself being above his father's confusion, of having passed through it as a stranger, of leaving the city soon. Howard lay in his own bed opposite, in the dark room. They talked some, softly, of school, of teachers, taking turns telling stories. Howard asked him no questions about the cars or the juvenile home. Alex would not have minded, as if he had turned a corner on those times as well.

But voices woke him during the night. They raised him from full sleep to half waking. He recognized after a moment the strange bed with its damp smell, and remembered where he was, realized they were not the voices of his father, his father and some woman he had brought home. There was a line of dull white along the bottom of the bedroom door. The voices were close-by, from the kitchen, and he lay listening.

There were four or five of them. Laughter was around everything they said. Alex looked across the room toward Howard's bed, but heard nothing, could see nothing in the darkness. He had an idea they were both lying there awake, listening, thinking, both of them somehow caught this way. He considered whispering to Howard, considered talking to him to somehow straighten out in their own way this confusion that had them listening in the dark, and afraid. But Alex was not sure of the idea, nor sure of Howard, nor of himself, and he could not bring himself to speak.

There were both men and women in the kitchen. Alex knew Ward's voice, although he had only heard it once or twice, but his mother's voice sounded different. He listened to her tell how she and Em Lewis had decided to open a whorehouse with the dock out there lined with red lights. They all laughed as she talked. (Was Em Lewis a man or a woman?) Every time she used the word "whore," although his father used language much stronger than that, Alex felt a slight shock, and felt himself shiver. He lay still and listened, or did not try not to listen, until the people left. He listened then to Ward and his mother talking farther away in the house, talking more casually and without laughter, and he listened for a time thereafter to the wandering of his mind.

Waking at daylight, he recognized again the sheets and the room. The voices from the night, as well as Howard's and his own when they were catching bullheads, were like voices in dreams and difficult to play over in daylight. Birds were singing outside now, and far over the lake, after a moment, he heard a lone motor approach and pass, moving beyond hearing. According to the way he guessed the time in the morning at home, by the sun and the feel of the air, he thought it must be no more than five or five-thirty. He worried about his paper route. Mickey Elliot would not be up yet, would not finish before ten or eleven o'clock, would miss perhaps a dozen houses.

He rose quietly from the cot, in his undershorts and T-shirt, and stood there. He looked over at Howard. Howard lay with his eyes closed, holding his pillow. His upper lip and nose were curved up against the pillow, and his T-shirt was yellowish-looking against the gray, wilted sheets. He was asleep. Alex could see and hear the rising and falling of his breath. Howard was underweight; his arms, out over his head, were too small. Alex had no thought of talking to him, waking him, not in the daylight, which held none of the intimacy the night had held. Alex looked at him, gauged him again, and for a moment he was unable to look away. Howard Connell.

In the kitchen Alex crossed the linoleum floor on his bare toes and looked through the glass panel of the kitchen door. The dirt road that ran back to the tavern was empty, its surface lightly coated with dew. He thought of the full day to go. Waiting for his father. Would he come to the house? What would he and Ward say to each other now?

On his way to the bathroom, he saw something that made his heart actually jump. They were naked. Their bedroom door was open and they lay asleep, in a tangle, naked. He seemed to glimpse Mrs. Kesten for a moment. He went on to the bathroom, but once he was there he was unable to urinate. Standing back, leaning against the cool tile wall, he let out a deep breath.

After a moment he went back, eight or ten steps through the quiet house. He looked in their bedroom door. They had not moved. He stared at his mother, at the woman who happened to be his mother. He looked at her as if Ward's body was not there. He looked at her breasts, which were large and full-looking where they lay upon her ribs. The nipples were a black purple and darker than her hair, almost the color of her lipstick. He wanted to keep looking, but he imagined them opening their eyes now and catching him. He walked over, into the kitchen, and stood for a moment. The linoleum was cool on his bare feet. He thought he could hear their breathing behind him. He could hear his own.

Passing their door again, he glanced in and saw that they had moved. They continued to sleep, but their bodies had shifted. His mother was entirely visible now. He paused just long enough in passing to look her over again, to look at the powdery and deep smoothness of her flesh against the darker hairy background of Ward. Going on, thoughts were moving in his mind with the ghostlike and wavering diffuseness of weeds seen deep in the green water from the boat. He thought of his father. He thought of Ward telling his father not to go to the house. He thought also of Howard and of his mother, or saw them, not knowing what it was he was thinking. For a moment then, the things in his life which had been confusing seemed to be rising from the confusion, seemed to be focusing into clarity. But the moment blurred quickly.

In the bedroom, Howard was still sleeping. Alex looked at him again. And he very nearly looked away, turned to climb back into bed to let the day carry him along and work itself out. Then the knowledge came to him. Howard Connell. Howard Connell was not his brother.

He left the bedroom again. He passed their door on his way to the bathroom and glanced in to see them sleeping as before. When he had finished in the bathroom, he paused a moment, trying to decide whether or not to flush the toilet in the Sunday-morning stillness. Then he flushed it. He held the handle down as if to prolong its gushing-sucking roar, as if to announce his knowledge to them all. He thought of his father, and closed his eyes for a moment.

When he came from the bathroom, their door was closing its last several inches. They must have known he had seen them. He was not disappointed by their knowing.

Howard continued to sleep. Alex's gym bag was there by the foot of the cot he had slept in, but when he had picked it up and decided to leave, he almost grew confused again. Then he could not move quickly enough. If they stopped him now, if he had to wait the full day for his father, the day looked as long as the entire summer. He decided they would not stop him, he would not allow them to stop him, and he felt strong. He would run if he had to, or fight; they would see.

When he had dressed, when he had packed his things into his bag and quietly drawn the zipper, and at last looked over, he noticed that Howard was watching him. Howard lay with his eyes open, looking frightened.

Howard said, without condemnation, with worry, "Where are you going?"

Alex paused, looking at him. "Home," he said.

"What's the matter?" Howard said.

"Nothing," Alex said.

"Why do you have to go home?" Howard said. His voice sounded close to breaking.

"I don't know," Alex said. "I don't know—I just feel like it."

"Don't you want to go fishing again?"

Alex hesitated, looking down. Looking over at Howard, he said, "No. Not now."

They looked at each other for a moment, both of them trying, it seemed, to hold on and not to lose control.

Alex spoke again; his voice was clear, although high. "I'm going to join the army," he said.

Howard said nothing.

Alex did not know what to say. Briefly, for no more than a second, he thought his eyes were glossing over. But he knew how to stop the feeling. He said to Howard, "Listen, I'm going. But I'll see you sometime. Soon. You go back to sleep." He opened the bedroom door, looking away from Howard, and stepped out. He closed the door behind him, carefully and not completely. Stepping over to the kitchen door, he began feeling confused again with doubt, thinking he should stay, he should go back. He seemed to see a deeper loneliness in Howard's life, in spite of his motorboat and his lake, than in his own.

The air helped. It was warmer without than within. He walked along the carpet-soft dirt road. The dew from the night had left a velvet texture over the powder of dirt and he concentrated on breaking the texture with his footprints. In a moment, some distance away, he heard a truck pass on the highway. Its tires sang. They sang louder than the truck's motor, for a long time, until he was not sure if he still heard them or not. He walked faster. He tried to make his mind think of something, of anything, and thought of the city, imagined his papers lying on the curb untouched. He thought of his father. He imagined being there in the city, and remembered how quiet and hot it was on Sunday afternoons. He imagined his father asleep in his bedroom, with the fan on his dresser sweeping back and forth, back and forth, so slowly.

He passed the tavern. The gravel parking lot was empty of cars and stale-looking with litter. He thought of Ward, without thinking of anything much in particular. He walked along on the shoulder of the highway.

Maybe this afternoon he would go to a movie. Yes, he would. He wished he were there now; he sensed the feeling of hiding in the cool darkness and giving himself over to the world on the screen. In the afternoon the Coney Island would have its windows opened to the sidewalk, the grill just inside the window lined with rows of pink glistening hot dogs, the baseball game from Detroit coming over a radio. He felt homesick for the city at the same time that he feared its tedium.

Was Ward Howard's father? Maybe. But no, probably not. It did not matter to Alex, not at all. He recognized in himself that his father was his father; the certainty was faintly humorous and faintly sad.

At a crossroads, at an old country Sunoco station, he tried to call his father. Standing at a wall phone, he felt inhibited by a man sitting behind a greasy, littered desk. There was no answer. He let the phone ring, far off on the kitchen counter, seven, eight, nine, ten times, intending each time to hang up and letting it ring once more. It was just as well; at least he had tried. At the same time that he felt pity for his father, he did not wish to talk to him. Back on the highway he walked, listening for cars and each time one approached he stepped onto the soft shoulder to lay out his thumb and walk backward. Each time a car stopped to give him a lift, he ran after it.

The drugstore on the corner of Chevrolet Avenue had not opened yet. Morning doves were hooting; stacks of wired Sunday papers stood against the front of the drug-store. Passing between the buildings, he saw that the car was there. He wondered, for the car and the unanswered phone were bad signs.

His father was there. He lay on his bed in a fetal posi-tion, on top of the covers and still wearing the gray summer suit and his black-and-white shoes. The room was already warm from the sun through the window. Alex stood and watched for a moment, as he always did, to determine the rise and fall of his father's breathing.

In the kitchen, quietly, he wrote a note and propped it against the sugar bowl.

Dear Pop,
   I'm back. You don't have to go get me. I have
to go take care of my route. See you later.
                                          Alex

He had no intention of looking after his route, although he was sure his bundle of papers lay yet on the corner, and that Mickey Elliot lay yet asleep. By the clock in the dry cleaner's window it was twenty minutes to seven.

Along Chevrolet Avenue the doves, perched on the wires overhead, were still hooting. He realized their hooting rang only in the silence of the factories on Sundays. He thought of Howard, but their voices of only an hour ago were like the voices from the night—he did not recall what they had said exactly. It was as if Howard was gone now; as if he knew how to keep him at a distance. There was no way to understand, nor was there anyone to blame. There was only the immediate silence, like the silence of the factories.

The Coney Island in lower downtown was cool within. The dark old guy behind the counter greeted Alex for the first time in the months that he had been stopping there mornings. He said to him, "Hello there, Curly," and Alex looked over at the man without speaking.

Three

Alex did not return to the Country Club for a week. He carried on negotiations with the recruiting sergeant in town. He sat around the park at times, and shot a few baskets. On Saturday, after paying up at the circulation office, he went home to explain his plan to his father. He found his father in the kitchen, having breakfast, and said to him, "I'm going to enlist in the army."

In a moment his father looked at him. "You are?" he said.

"Yes, I am."

His father sipped his coffee, and then he said, "What about school, son?"

"I decided not to go back."

His father was silent. Then, more affected than Alex had anticipated, he said, "I always hoped you'd finish school."

"You—you didn't finish, did you?" Alex said.

"No. No, I didn't."

"What—how far—?"

"The ninth grade," his father said. "But then, not many went any farther in those days. Why don't you want to go back to school?"

"I don't know. I just don't like it any more. I can't take it."

His father stood looking at him. "Did all this business last year make it hard on you?"

"I guess it did."

"I'm really sorry about that."

"Well, no, you don't have to feel like that. It wasn't your fault."

"Oh, it was my fault all right. That old judge knew what he was talking about."

They were silent again. Then his father said, "I'd sure like to see you finish school, son. You sure you can't go back and finish up? Jobs can be pretty hard to get, you know, if you don't have yourself an education."

"You—you did all right," Alex said.

His father only smiled and shook his head once, softly.

"When would all this take place?" his father said.

"In August. On my birthday."

"What about Mr. Quinn, and your probation?"

"They'd have to give me permission, too. But I think they would."

"Yes, I'm sure they would," his father said. In a moment he said, "You really mean it, don't you?"

"Yes," Alex said.

"You've gone and grown up on me, haven't you?" his father said. He looked at Alex a moment, before raising his cup to drink.

Alex waited, and then he said, "Well?"

"Is there a hurry?" his father said.

"No."

"Have you thought about this at all?"

"Yes."

"You really thought about it?"

"Yes."

"It's a big thing, you know. You might never see your old dad again."

"Oh, I'd be home. I'd be home a lot."

Still his father paused. At last he said, "You let me think about it." Then he winked lightly, as if to apologize. He raised his cup to drink again.

.   .   .

Graham Webster was on the asphalt court shooting baskets. Some younger boys were at the other end, but otherwise the court and park were nearly deserted, as they often were on weekends. Alex shot baskets leisurely with Webster and they talked of basketball and Central High School. Webster said he planned to make the all-conference team next year, and the year after that he planned to go to the University of Michigan on a basketball scholarship. Alex shot baskets without much skill or style. There was already a space between himself and this past world of his. The thought of school did not worry him any more with the threat of exposure, for he had decided not to return, not ever. But he felt a fear, deeply, of making a mistake.

He and Webster decided to go to a root-beer stand over on Dupont Street to get a drink. Webster had his car parked on the street bordering the park, and as it happened, when they came to the street along a path through the trees and stopped for some cars to pass, there was Alex's father in the second car, and seeing Alex, he pulled over to the curb ahead of them.

Alex, slightly confused, waited at first, and then started walking toward the car, but by then his father had gotten out and was walking back. He was dressed now, in his powder-gray summer suit and his black-and-white shoes, and his face was only slightly red. "Whatcha doin?" he said.

"Just shooting some baskets," Alex said. "What are you doing?" He was embarrassed and smiled almost constantly.

"I'm just on my way," his father said. He also smiled, but more affectionately. For a moment neither of them spoke, as if they had nothing to say. "So this is where you play basketball?" his father said.

"Right down there," Alex said. "Would you like to see it?"

"Sure, let's see it."

Awkwardly, silent again, Alex walked down the path between the shrubs and trees, his father following. Webster stayed back.

At the opening Alex said, "That's it."

His father looked over the deserted asphalt court. "You're pretty good at this, huh?" he said.

"I've put in a lot of hours," Alex said.

They were both still smiling lightly, but not at each other. Then his father said, "If I were your age I'd join the army myself. That's what I'd do."

Alex said nothing. His father turned then and led the way back along the path to the street. Webster was standing there, and Alex knew he should introduce them to each other, but he did not know quite how to do it. His father said, "Hi, there," to Webster, and then to Alex, "You fixed okay for change?" Alex said that he was, and his father said, "Okay, I'll see you later on," and nodding, he walked off again to his car.

Across the street in Webster's car, Webster said, "Who's that dude?"

"Oh, that's my father," Alex said.

"He sure is dapper, isn't he?"

Webster's car was an old Ford, painted only with a gray primer. The motor and the exhaust were loud; taking a corner to go up the long Dupont Street hill, Webster said, "My old man drives me bananas sometimes. You know? Do this, put this away, why didn't you do that? Jesus, it can be a drag, I tell you."

Alex said nothing, feeling at the moment a loyalty for his own father. At the root-beer stand he and Webster left the car and stood at a counter where they were served through a sliding screen. Webster went on talking. His plan, he said, was to get a scholarship, so he figured that rather than working his ass off now at some two-bit slavery, he was going to play basketball, and that way, what would he make on a scholarship—four thousand? five thousand?—for a couple of summers' work. Only, his old man didn't see it that way. All he believed in was work. He figured if he had to suffer to earn his goddam money, then by God you had to suffer, too.

Webster went on talking, and Alex looked away. He glanced at the cars passing in sunlight on Dupont Street. He thought again of the unusual kindness his father possessed. He thought of him off driving in his car now. He thought of Howard and of his mother. He glanced at the cars passing.

"Where to?" Webster said. "I'll give you a lift."

"Oh, nowhere—I'm just heading home."

"Come on, I'll drop you off."

"Oh no, you don't have to do that. In fact, I was thinking of going back to shoot a few."

"You sure?"

"Sure."

As Webster drove off, Alex walked back to the park. He walked through, past the fenced-in and deserted tennis courts, and out the other side, past the basketball court. He was so accustomed to telling lies in shame over where he lived that he made his direction automatically.

In the morning he found his father asleep at the kitchen table. He was sleeping with his head on his arms. Alex was going to slip by him to go and peddle his route, but his father looked up at him. Alex went about fixing himself a slice of toast then, and he said to his father, "Can I fix you some coffee?"

His father gave no answer. He sat up some, but then his chin fell to his chest. In a moment, from behind him at the counter, Alex heard his father begin to mumble.

His father was so drunk that he was on the verge, Alex knew, of falling over and passing out again. Alex watched him for a moment. His father's neck seemed made of rubber, of rubber so soft that he could not pick up his head again. "Would you like some coffee?" Alex said more loudly.

At last his father got his head up, angled up. He only squinted at Alex. He looked unconscious, with his eyes barely opened. He said nothing. A moment later, when Alex left, telling his father he had to go, his father did not look at him and he still had not spoken.

Outside, in the air, Alex felt some of the relief he always felt getting away from the apartment when his father was in that state. He did not return when he finished his route. He went only close enough to slip his canvas bag under the bottom step. He spent the morning at the park, and the afternoon in an air-conditioned theater. When he returned, expecting to find his father either asleep, sleeping off his drinking, or perhaps awake and still drinking, he found neither. The car was gone and the apartment was empty. The kitchen was dirty with ashes and the remains of his father's drinking. They were old signs. It might be a day, two days, four days, before his father returned.

Going to sleep those nights in the empty apartment was a problem for Alex of stopping himself from listening to sounds which had always been there anyway. His father might come in at any moment. He might be dangerous; he might be sober. The Chevrolet whistles gave no outline to his movements. If he was moving.

He did not return throughout Monday or Monday night, but on Tuesday afternoon, returning to the apartment, Alex could tell that he had been there. There were no discarded clothes or evidence of sleep, nor was there any evidence of his having eaten. The evidence was in the bathroom, an unflushed toilet, a strand of toilet paper over the edge of the toilet bowl. He was alive.

Alex did not clean the kitchen. Nor did he wash his own dishes, but stacked them unrinsed in the sink or left them dirty on the counter. He took care of his paper route, and he spent time at the park shooting baskets or lying in the shade on the grass. He went to the movies every night. The city and the apartment both had a haunting quality, those days and nights, of a wind always in the background, raising slight noises as it blew.

On Friday night, at last, coming home from town, Alex saw that the car was there. It was parked in its old place, and the kitchen light, burning above, raised a star on its hood. Alex approached the car first, trying in the dark to see inside. The window on the driver's side was open. He whispered, "Pop?" Still he could not see and he opened the door to bring on the dome light, to see that the car was empty.

Upstairs he entered the kitchen carefully. The apartment was still. The kitchen was untouched. Stepping through the rooms quietly, he found his father was in bed asleep. In the partial light from the door he could see his father's form there, under the covers. He must have been cold. His clothes lay on the floor next to the bed and there was a body odor over the room. Alex reached in and softly closed the door.

In the morning, coming home from his paper route, he found the door to his father's room still closed. He left again, and returning at midmorning, found the door still closed. The apartment remained cool yet from the night. The air was better. He saw how clearly his perceptions and feelings were entwined with his father's condition.

Alex was taken with an urge to see the kitchen clean, to see it polished and sparkling. His father had always initiated the cleaning sessions, but removing his shirt now, down to his T-shirt, getting some music on the radio, getting a blue fire going under a teakettle of water, removing rags from under the sink, Alex went to work.

He felt a desire both to have the cleaning job finished before his father came out and also to have his father join him in the work, to do it together as they had in the past.

At those times his father got him working by perhaps slap-boxing—"Come on, tough guy, let's see your stuff, come on"—so they ducked and bobbed and danced around the kitchen for a moment, jabbing, feinting, Alex getting some slaps in and off his father's sandpaper cheeks, receiving a few on his own, until his father said, "Okay, okay, let's see how fast you can wash these dishes—come on, everybody has to be a dishwasher sometime."

He was working, singing lightly but too seriously to himself, when he turned from the stove and saw his father in the doorway, watching him. As if shocked to be caught singing, Alex stopped, but it was his father's appearance that had shocked him. He looked like an old whiskered man coming to stand and smile a moment in the doorway of a hospital room. He looked shrunken from loss of weight, and he was pale, a faint pink and a faint blue spread over gray. He said, "That's a good job to get done."

Alex had intended, in the manner of his father, to put his father to work, but he abandoned the idea. "Hey, let me fix you some bacon and eggs," he said.

"Fine," his father said. "Fine. That's a good idea. And some coffee, too. I'm going to take a bath, and shave, and I'll be out in a half-hour or so. How's that?"

Alex began removing things from the refrigerator and cupboards. There was no bacon, and on the run he went out and down the street to a small grocery store. Returning, on the sunlighted sidewalk, he was shocked once more by the fact of his father's condition, by its contrast with the warm summer air.

His father looked better over breakfast, but only a little. He was shaved, dressed now in a white shirt open at the throat. He had red cut marks around his throat from shaving, and his hands trembled steadily as he ate. Still, however weak and gray, he looked stronger than before. At the end of his meal, drinking his coffee, he said to Alex, "Listen, son, I'm sorry about this. I shouldn't give my troubles to you."

Four

The polished army sergeant at the recruiting station told him he could take a GED test, to earn a high school equivalency certificate. If he passed, in the eyes of the army he was a high school graduate and eligible to make his choice, guaranteed, of army schools: radar, tele-type, clerk typist, motor vehicle maintenance, construction drafting, engineering drafting, medical lab technician. There were a hundred possibilities, and the range of worlds was not without excitement. Was it possible that he could make drawings for the construction of a bridge and go out to see bulldozers and generators and cranes put it to-gether over a stream? Here in the city, outside the recruit-ing office and within the odors of roasting peanuts and diesel exhaust from the city buses, it was not a small dream.

Days passed. A gray-haired lady in her forties began having his number called nearly every morning at the Country Club. She was a suntanned and large-breasted woman, almost frail except for the thrust of her blouse. She smoked steadily and swore often. "You laugh," she said to him once, turning from a topped drive, "and I'll wrap this goddam club around your sweet neck."

Her face and arms were copper-colored. Standing be-side him, having to wait, she sometimes raised her elbow and placed it on his shoulder. Her breast, if she moved or turned, would touch against the muscle of his arm. The pressure and give through the fabric told him that her breast, firm-appearing, was watery. Sometimes she would hold herself against his muscle for perhaps a moment.

At last, the third or fourth time she leaned against him, on a fairway within the overlapping shadows of trees, he willed his arm muscle to harden so it pressed back against her. She stood looking ahead as well and he believed she was returning the pressure. His lower abdomen and loins were unrolling pleasantly. He willed his arm muscle harder. She did not move. There was quiet out over the fairway before them. A moment passed. Then she lifted her arm and stepped away. She stepped over to her ball. She reached to flick away a strand of grass. She swayed her feet into place, and hit, and walked on without looking at him.

The unrolling sensation did not go away. He tried to catch her eye. He looked at her, at her calves, her arms, the extension of her blouse. He walked close to her. Once when they stopped he stood overly close to her. He felt a desire to touch her and he came within an inch, within half an inch, of touching his hands lightly over her arms, over her shoulders. She said nothing. Another time he picked up her ball and washed it and held it for her, and she caressed his fingers lightly taking it, and stepped away. She did not look at him. Nor did she raise her elbow to his shoulder again. They moved along. At the end of the round she handed him three dollars extra as a tip, and looking up at him at last, she said, "It's too bad, isn't it?" and she turned and walked away, returning to the privacy of the clubhouse.

However ashamed of his feelings for the small woman, he fantasized taking her in among trees, within the cover of bushes. But it was not the bushes alone which occupied him. It was a more continuous feeling, an infatuation. Throughout the day and night he felt he had been a fool for not taking her when she seemed to have offered, for not touching her, or reaching his arm around her, for not kissing her, embracing her head in his hands and stabbing his erect tongue to the base of her own.

The next morning, even as rain dripped down, he went to the golf course. He spent the morning sitting in the caddy house. But she did not have his number called. Nor did anyone else; nor did any other caddies report. He sat looking through the coverless remains of *Saga* and *Male* and *Motor Trend* magazines. Rain dripped down over the opened doorway and the speaker remained silent, although lights were on through the trees over in the clubhouse. He left at last and walked in the drizzle back along the gravel road, imagining her coming by in a car to pick him up. In town he spent the afternoon before magazine racks and in dime stores, glancing at women in their profiles and movements, listening to their voices. He thought of Irene Sheaffer. He thought of Mrs. Kesten, and of his mother.

The following day, under a fresh sky, he returned to the golf course. He was certain, as if through a mutual chemistry, that she would have his number called. But she did not. When his number came over the scratchy speaker, at the right time, and he went over, it was for a foursome of businessmen. Waiting at the first tee, and along the course, passing and crossing other parties, he looked around, but did not see her.

Another morning, when his alarm went off, rain was pouring down. The window sill and the floor beneath were covered with water. Rain spattered on his undershorts and legs as he removed the screen and lowered the window. He looked out for a moment. The rain was brown and heavy; he could hardly see across the street.

On his way to the bathroom he noticed an odor of fresh cigarette smoke on the air. His father was up. Alex dressed, in mild alarm, before going out to the kitchen.

His father was bleary and gray. He had still not recovered from the long binge. He looked up at Alex with that unusual smile on his face. The sound of the rain was louder here, for the kitchen door was opened, the lower half of the screen saturated with water. Alex stepped over to close the door, but his father said, "No, no, leave it—let it rain." His father's face looked shrunken, his eyes shining pink, but he did not sound intoxicated.

"How you feeling?" Alex said.

His father only smiled lightly. Then he said, "Sit down a minute, sit down and talk to me."

"I can't—I have to go."

Alex fixed himself a slice of toast in silence. He ate the toast standing up, together with a small glass of milk.

His father said, "Can't you sit down and talk to your old dad for a minute?"

"My papers will get soaked," Alex said.

His father only smiled lightly again.

Alex left the room and came back with a jacket, which he slipped on quickly. He took his canvas bag from the back of a chair, but then his father was standing up.

"You leaving now?" his father said.

"Yes."

"Can't you stay and talk for a minute?"

"I have to go," Alex said.

Alex was surprised again by his father's appearance. His face looked dusted with ashen make-up, but he did not sound at all intoxicated. He kept trying to smile. Alex had never left before like this when his father asked him to stay. He wanted all the more to be out in the refreshing rain.

"Shake?" his father said. He was raising his hand.

Alex was surprised. He said, "What for?"

"Just for the hell of it. That's all. Come on, shake."

Alex hesitated. Then he raised his hand.

They shook.

His father squeezed his hand hard and held it. Looking at him, the light and strange smile over his gray face, he said. "Do me one favor, will you?"

Alex said nothing.

"Will you?" his father said.

"Okay."

"Remember your old father from a better day."

"Please don't talk like that."

His father ignored this; he was pushing something into Alex's jacket pocket, saying, "Don't look at that." Alex did not look. He knew it was a roll of greenbacks. He stood a moment and then left, feeling awkward as he went down the steps in the rain. But immediately, walking between the buildings, he felt relief to be away. The rain spattered quickly through his jacket and shirt to his shoulders, and out on Chevrolet Avenue he stepped back and stopped under an awning. He wiped water from his face and from the back of his neck. He tried not to think of his father, not to see him up there in the kitchen.

The morning, the entire day, became dissonantly sunbright. At midday the sun was clear and red, although the ground remained damp and puddled. Alex was at the park shooting baskets with Graham Webster. He did not care to be shooting baskets. He shot poorly, and missed, with awkward coordination. It was as if there was nothing else in the world to do, and he was beyond any desire to play basketball.

When he first arrived at the park, someone had said to him, "Some kid was looking for you," but he had paid little attention. He had not considered Howard. But later, when he and Webster were passing among the sunlighted and wet bushes on their way to the street, someone was entering on the path the other way. It was Howard.

Howard stopped, seeing Alex, and Alex also stopped. Howard, as if pleased with the surprise of himself, stood smiling, waiting for Alex to speak first. Alex saw Howard before him, and he was aware of the sunlight flashing on the damp leaves, but he did not speak. Something within him had frozen. His skull felt drawn tight. He was aware that Graham Webster had stopped ahead on the path and was looking back. Howard broke the momentary silence, saying, as if to reprimand him, "Well, hello!"

"Hello," Alex said.

Howard, thrilled enough with his surprise to be close to either laughing or crying, said, "Well, how are you?"

"Good," Alex said, and there was silence again. Alex did not know what to say next; nothing came into his mind. Then the words "What are you doing here?" came out.

Howard, underfed, brown from the sun and the lake, said, "Ohh, I just happened to be out for a stroll," and he added, with unsure intensity, *"What do you think I'm doing?"*

In only a moment Alex was going on with Graham Webster, and Howard was going on the other way. Alex seemed to be in a trance of some kind, following Webster out and across the street to his car. Barely able to think, he could not recall clearly, nor could he stop trying to recall, the remarks he had just made to Howard. The very last had been, *I'll be seeing you then.* Even before that, Howard had stopped his continuous smiling, as if understanding that something was wrong. An expression familiar from their years together had come over Howard's face, an expression of alarm. He had turned his head awkwardly to the side for a moment, and stepped around Alex on the path, when Alex said, *I'll be seeing you then.* Just as Alex had glimpsed the wet sun-flashing leaves, he glimpsed Howard's face, a flashing over his eyes.

Several minutes went by before Alex was struck by what he had done. He and Webster drove up Dupont Street to the root-beer stand. As if unaffected, Alex carried on some conversation along the way, an exchange over being thirsty. Then they were standing at the counter, opposite the sliding screen. In a clear voice, Alex ordered his drink. But glancing about, moving his hand to flick at a fly absorbed on the sticky wood, he discovered that his physical movement was as dissonant as the day. His strength had felt partially numb, and now something was melting away. He looked out over Dupont Street. He saw cars passing. Suddenly the world seemed to fall from under him.

His hand had stopped before the fly. He glanced at it through a blur. He looked out to the street again, and he seemed to believe that if he thought of nothing he would be all right. He managed to get his hand into his pants pocket to remove coins. He tried to steel himself against himself, to see nothing, to think of nothing. But he saw Howard once more, on the path among the glistening leaves. The sensation of falling came within him again, and he had difficulty placing the coins on the counter and removing his hand again.

He saw a quarter, a penny, a nickel lying there.

Then his heart filled and he began walking off, walking over the gravel toward the street. He heard Webster call from behind him, "Hey, where you going?" and he waved a hand to leave Webster there, and passed into the street, crossing before and behind cars, seeing them in the blur, breaking into a trot partway across and trotting on down the opposite sidewalk toward the park. But he seemed to cover too little space, as if moving on a treadmill, possessed with the horror of himself, with a horrible disbelief, and a horrible belief, of what he had done.

He did not find Howard. He went through the park, walking and half running. He looked over the tennis courts, where a few people sat on the benches and a few people played, and he looked over the pair of Ping-Pong tables, and over the basketball court. Going through the bushes on the path again, he looked up and down the street. Howard was not in sight. Five or six streets led into the park, and he could have left in any direction. Alex imagined him going away, walking, perhaps riding a bus by now. He leaned against a tree then, leaned on his shoulder, with little idea of what to do or what to think.

His father had gone to work. He had picked up the apartment before leaving. Like the storm, his binge had lasted only through the night. Alex sat for a time at the kitchen table. He seemed neither to have stopped thinking of Howard, nor to have continued thinking of him. He could not quite recover. A couple of hours had passed by now. On a thought that Howard might somehow be in the apartment, he went through the rooms and looked in the closets. He sat at the kitchen table again, or on the couch in the living room. One moment, merely despondent, he tried to believe he could write a letter, a long and serious letter, or he could make a phone call, or, when he was calm again, he could go out to the lake. But in another moment, seeing Howard as he had appeared he knew that no apology, no explanation, was possible. He sat around. When the horror rose in him again, he squeezed his forehead almost violently with his fingers, or squeezed his eyes shut. He tried to blame his father, and a moment later he aimed a mad and nearly tearful outrage at Graham Webster, as if in his presence he had been ashamed of Howard.

At about first darkness he began to recover. He had not, when dusk filled the rooms of the apartment, turned on any lights. Standing at the screen door in the kitchen, or at the screened window looking down at Chevrolet Avenue from the living room, near the fresh evening air, he had begun shedding the feelings of outrage and slipping into moods deeper in self-pity and melancholia. As the apartment filled with darkness, he came up with an idea. He decided to take, to borrow, his father's car and drive out to the lake, on the chance of seeing Howard. With lies, he thought, or with the truth, or with nothing at all, he might apologize. Or he might merely drive by.

Leaving the apartment, he walked along Third Avenue to Stevenson Street and down the Stevenson Street hill to the lot where his father parked his car. The unlighted parking lot was along the river behind the stadium. Cars were parked in long rows on gravel, across the river from the blue-lighted windows and the yards of Plant 4. Alex walked, searching two rows at a time, intending to leave at once—he had never taken the car this way before—to be back before his father's shift let out. But when he had found the car, on the bank facing over the river, and had got in behind the wheel and closed the door, reaching to insert his key, glancing up, he saw someone, a man, silhouetted on a single railroad trestle, crossing the river toward the parking lot. Alex watched the man for a moment; he shivered with a slight shock of recognition.

He sat there. He was not sure. But he knew it was not at all impossible that it was his father. The man continued through the pattern of light and dark cast by the trestle's framework. Where the trestle curved in its wide sweep to the right, the man stepped over the tracks and ties to the left, keeping on a line with the dark car. Alex sat still. When the man crouched to let himself drop from the trestle to the ground, going out of sight, Alex knew from his movement that it was his father.

In a moment, still a silhouette, his father came up over the crest of the bank, no more than thirty feet from the car. Alex began unrolling his window, confused with fear and resignation, and announced himself, whispering, "Pop —is that you?"

His father was startled. Pausing, stepping up to the driver's side of the car, he whispered back, "Alex?" and added, "What are you doing?"

"I was just going to borrow the car for a while."

His father stood there in the darkness, looking toward the opened window.

"I planned to get it back on time," Alex said.

"That's all right," his father said. He was not angry, but mystified. Still whispering, he said, "Scoot over a bit— or stay there, I'll go around."

Crossing before the front of the car, his father opened the other door, the dome light flashing on for only a second, and sat in the front seat beside Alex. Alex did not want to look at him.

"You want to use the car?" his father said.

"Yes."

"Where did you want to go?"

"Nowhere. Just for a drive. I was just going to take a drive in the country."

"Sounds like a good idea," his father said.

Still they sat there.

Then his father whispered, "I have to get right back. I only have a minute or two."

"You don't need the car?"

"Oh no, no."

"Is this your lunch hour?"

"No, no."

They sat quietly. Hesitant, in the same hoarse whisper, his father said, "You know—I keep a old jug out here sometimes—so I can have myself a little snort now and then . . ." He seemed not to finish. Then he said, "Sit tight here a second."

His father opened the car door, the dome light flashing again, and Alex thought at first he was getting out to take a leak. Then his father was in front of the car, working the hood latch, and Alex sat looking at him. They could not see each other's eyes in the darkness, but Alex felt they saw, for the moment, into each other. The hood came toward the windshield, and went down again. His father glanced around; he had something in his hand.

In the car again, his father said nothing. There was the familiar paper-wrinkling of the sack to expose the neck of the bottle, then the motion of raising, tipping the bottle no higher than his nose, and the exhaling of a little fire when he had swallowed, the sweetish odor spreading.

From beside him, far away, Alex heard his father say, "You might have gone off and I'd be out here looking for my old medicine."

Alex sat there, sat still. He felt no anger now. He seemed to feel nothing, unless it was a dying away in resignation. Nor did he care if he hurt or insulted his father. He paused, and with only slight nervousness, he opened the door and stepped out. He said nothing. His father did not speak. By the time he was around the car, his father was rolling down his window, as if to call to him, or to ask what was wrong.

Alex walked steadily, expecting his father to speak. But no sound, no voice came from the dark space of the car window. He walked along between the rows of cars.

Five

On the outdoor basketball court, now after all the night games throughout the city, throughout the summer, the championship game of the men's division was being played. The two teams were mainly black giants six-three and six-five and six-seven, three or four white giants among them, and everyone knew they were approximately the varsity teams from Michigan at Ann Arbor and Michigan State at East Lansing. They presented astonishing speed and strength and skill, fighting under the baskets with elbows and shoulders and backs, throwing sprays of perspiration in attempts at a loose ball, snarling their breath . . . and they delivered breath-catching razzle-dazzle, as if they had eyes in their backs and sides, as if the ball had eyes, stopping within the stampede, driving, jack-knifing upward, hanging calmly, momentarily in the air, and firing, making the net whip from twenty or thirty feet.

Green wooden bleachers had been set up on the sides of the court, but they were filled, and Alex stood in a crowd at the end, watching between shoulders. As if to deny himself, when he had watched for a while, he side-stepped back through the crowd and walked across the park. Music came from a square dance on the tennis courts, and the park was alive with its rhythm, and with people, couples strolling, young girls in pairs, boys racing and tackling one another over the dark grass. The floodlighted rectangles of light were hazy where they blended into the sky overhead. Alex walked among the people. From behind, the crowd at the basketball game exploded regularly with applause as baskets were made, and settled again. Something in the action on the court, and in the music filling the air, kept making Alex's throat try to fill, as if in awe of no less a phenomenon than mankind, in awe of existence.

The tennis nets had been removed and the three fenced-in courts were covered with several hundred circulating, unfurling and entwining dancers. Women swirled in gingham gowns and swirling ruffled petticoats, and men in short-sleeved shirts and Western shirts circled in and out and missed notches in the gearwheel dance turnings with shy abandon. They all looked red and happy-faced, stepping back and bowing, greeting their partners, and promenading left and dosie-doeing, following the deep Western serenading voice of a man in the center. The man stood on a wooden platform, the musicians with their fiddles around him, and he may also have been a champion come to town, keeping the microphone nearly touching his mouth however much he moved, stomping his foot on the hollow boards and perspiring, closing his eyes and swaying away and back, possessed with the music, stomping his foot in time with his bottom-of-the-river-throated voice, delivering the rhythm, *allemande right, and a dosie-doe,* as the hundreds of people swirled, as the music reached high into the dark air and escaped over the city.

Alex left the wire fence after a time and walked on again.

Over the grass beyond the square dance, within trees and hanging lights, reaching back into a darkness of great pine trees, were scattered tables. People sat on folding chairs or on the ground around the tables, older people and younger children, the remains of their cake and ice cream littering the tables. Along the side parallel with Dupont Street was a row of tables end to end perhaps a hundred feet long, covered with white paper, gray-haired ladies still serving pieces of cake and scoops of soft ice cream and paper cups of coffee. Two uniformed policemen stood at the end of the row near the street, but there were no fights to break up, nor any thefts, nor were the gray-haired ladies concerned with money, for the food was free.

Alex returned and stood at the fence once more to watch the swirling square dancers. He thought he saw Irene Sheaffer dancing and an immediate wind seemed to pass over him. The caller's foot went on pounding with the fiddles, and she circled into view, and out of view. He knew by now that it was not Irene, but he chose to continue believing that it was, as if she had blossomed over the summer into this long and smoothly shaped woman, as if in that vacation locale of hers she had grown brown and her breasts had swollen.

He stood watching for her to appear and disappear. Almost imperceptively he had begun tapping a heel in time with the caller's stomping foot, as the music began to possess him as it seemed to possess the others. For a moment as he stood there he might as well have been within the high-wire fence himself, dancing the dosie-doe, and a-promenading left and all around, and bowing to greet his partner, until, again, as if over the display of mankind, or perhaps in his failure to be a part of it any more, his throat tried to fill and he walked on.

He left the park this time, not even returning for the crowning of the black champions. As he walked away on the street, the caller's voice still came after him, together with the fading rhythm of the fiddles and the harmonicas, the shoes scraping over the cement.

A mile away the two-story doors of the factory buildings had been rolled open to take in the cooler night air. From the interiors came a sparkling of blue and orange arc torches, and grindings, and insistent machinery hissing and sliding and sliding back. The earth trembled lightly underfoot with the factories operating. The smell of oil was warm, mixed with warm coal smoke and sulphur fumes.

A bell began clanging before him. A diesel locomotive with a dim light, a yellow eye, was rolling between yards, crossing the street. He stood and watched it coming his way on a curve. The engineer was in the high porthole, leaning out at the waist. The side of the locomotive was blue, streaked with oil and dirt. The iron wheels threw up sparks, and the tracks depressed and rose as the wheels turned. The blue body rolled past him as gingerly as an ocean vessel, and rolled on.

The guardrails came up and he walked over the glistening tracks. At the top of the hill, at Chevrolet Corners, the doors of the taverns were also opened. Country music came through the screen doors and seemed to hang in the air before the red-neon–bordered windows, and along the street.

His father was back down there in Plant 4. Or perhaps he was out in the car, looking over the hood and over the river. Or perhaps he was inside the hammering factory, in the can, raising a bottle no higher than his nose, in a secretive and urgent sip. How could he do anything other than what he did? Wasn't there something foolish about such a man dancing with abandon?

Chevrolet Corners. Only six or seven of a dozen bars remained, and only a couple of the old cafeterias and chili parlors. He and Howard used to walk down here evenings. For some years, years ago, a man had lived around the Corners named Whitey Canada. His father had told him stories about Whitey Canada and he had once seen the man's picture in the paper. His father told of having seen him handle six policemen who were trying, in a doorway and on the sidewalk before a tavern, to arrest him. His father said that Whitey Canada was the toughest man he had ever seen, and he was not a large man.

Alex's birthday fell on a Saturday. There was no celebration or attention given to the day, nor was any expected. But for the first time on a birthday he thought he experienced a change. Out over the land, it seemed, a world was open to him now, as if he had turned twenty-one and come of age. Seventeen. He was old enough, without breaking any laws, to leave school. He was old enough, with permission, to enlist in the army. He was old enough to leave home.

More from boredom than from a desire for the money he had returned again to caddying at the Country Club. Finishing his route in the morning, rather than returning to the apartment, rather than spending time at the park, he found it more pleasant to take the bus out to the edge of the city, to walk along the gravel road, to walk through the green oasis silently with a golfer or two. And he felt less bothered now by the turquoise swimming pool, by the tanned girls, for his negotiations with the recruiting sergeant had become plans, and promises, and he felt that the future was impending.

His father was working steadily again these late days of August. Occasionally Alex left the golf course after a morning round and stopped to see the sergeant, or to talk with Mr. Quinn, who had cleared his way legally to make the move. Alex went about most of these tasks without mentioning them to his father. The days passed. His father had yet to go with him to the recruiting station to sign the papers, and his father perhaps did not yet understand that he was going to leave.

On a Sunday night Alex asked for permission to use the car on Monday, to drive over to Lansing to take the GED test. If he failed the test the army would still take him, but he would have no high school certificate, nor any choice of those army schools. He was worried about the test one moment, not worried another. "We're supposed to go down on Tuesday to sign the papers," he told his father.

His father said nothing.

"You—you said you would sign for me, remember?"

"Yes, I remember."

"Will you?"

His father appeared to be trying to smile, and Alex looked away. He heard his father say, "Of course I will, son. If that's what you want me to do. I'll miss you though, I won't deny that."

"Can I take the car?"

"Oh, sure, the car. You take the car. Don't worry about that. I'll give you some money for gas. And if you're not back in time for me to go to work, that's all right, I can walk over."

Alex kept glancing around. He had not expected a moment as awkward as this. His father had turned to look through the screen door. He waited a moment. When his father did not turn back, he left to go to his bedroom, as if he had something to do.

Later, into the night, he was awakened by his father's voice in his bedroom doorway. If his father had been drinking, he gave little sign. "I think what you're doing is a good idea," he said. "It'll be good for you to get away from here and see some of the world. Meet some new people. You might even pick yourself up a pretty good trade of some kind. Just so you come home and see your old dad sometime when you get a furlough. Will you do that?"

"Yes—I will."

"I was thinking, I might even take a drive sometime to see you. You know, if you're not stationed too many miles away. We'll go out and have ourselves a drink or two together."

"Sounds fine," Alex said.

After a moment his father said, "What is this test tomorrow? They gonna see how smart you are?"

"No, it's just to see if I should be a high school graduate."

"Well. You better get some sleep, then."

"Yeah."

"We'll have to write us some letters," his father said.

"Sure, Pop."

In a moment, quietly, his father closed the door.

On the way into Lansing, Alex drove by the State Boys Vocational School. It was nearly downtown, a green tree-spotted campus with large ancient brick buildings far back from the street. A double line of perhaps twenty boys in herringbone uniforms was marching from one place to another near the buildings. There were no fences here in front, but many of the upper windows were covered with heavy wire. He thought of Red Eye. Life itself seemed to flare from the ground to the sky. He was wearing a stiff white shirt, and a tie, and in spite of the season, his wool sports coat. On an impulse, he threw his package of cigarettes into the bushes near the sidewalk.

At a stone building near the capital he found the room with the right number, and within, removing his jacket, he sat at a table and filled in spaces and calculated numbers on the forms a middle-aged woman kept walking over to place before him. After some three hours the woman took away the last booklet and paper, and told him to wait again in the outer room. When she returned he stepped up to a counter to listen. She mentioned some figures and said he had done very well. She would forward the test scores by mail. According to the army he was now a high school graduate.

He had lunch in the city. It occurred to him that he had never been to the state capital before, nor had be ever crossed a state line. He sat at a counter in a busy restaurant and felt certain, with excitement, that this city was different from his own.

Driving from Lansing, in order not to drive past the vocational school again—he had a haunting fear of being stopped because of the cigarettes—he went another way and happened to drive past the campus of Michigan State University. Along the way, almost suddenly, the people and the style of clothes had changed. There were young men and young women walking on the sidewalks and sitting on the grass under trees and pumping by on bicycles, tanned and wearing short pants. It was another world, one he had never seen. He saw a young man and woman holding hands and carrying butterfly nets. They were not chasing butterflies, only carrying the nets, and he tried not to laugh, but could not stop his eyes from filling.

Beyond the campus, on another highway, he headed for home. At last, as he drove, he removed his tie and worked his way out of his jacket. With air blowing through the car, and the radio playing, he drove on. He smiled to himself over his high school certificate. Had he tricked someone? Life itself flared again, out over the highways and rivers and cities, curving over the land.

Sullivan's Recreation was a dark second-floor pool hall which covered perhaps a quarter of a city block. A row of large windows lined the street side—old men usually sat there in high chairs looking out—but the windows appeared dark at night, for the hall was lighted mainly by the hanging shaded lights over the tables. Alex and his father happened to stop at Sullivan's when they went out on Saturday night, at his father's suggestion, on the occasion of Alex's leaving home to join the army.

They began a game of straight pool. But his father was already partially intoxicated—he had been sneaking sips from a bottle in his pocket—and before long he was sitting in one of the high spectator chairs, sipping from a paper cup, watching Alex shoot by himself. Alex worked his way around the table, glancing now and then toward his father, although his father's face was above the light and in shadows. "This what you do when you go out?" his father said.

"Sometimes. Not much any more. I used to."

He shot again. He felt self-conscious walking around the table and shooting.

"Who do you shoot with? You shoot by yourself?"

"Usually," Alex said. "Not always." He shot again, and surprising even himself, drawn to his father's warm tone, he talked as he moved around the table. "Whenever I play by myself," he said, "I always start to cheat a little, so what I do is I make believe I'm in a game. And I always stick right to it. What I do is I make believe I'm two different people. And I keep score. When it's one guy's turn, I'm that guy, and then when it's the other guy's turn, I'm that guy."

He was lying a little. The imaginary games were true, but they usually took place within fantasies of his having stepped forward from the crowd to play Willie Mosconi, or some champion from out of town, with the stakes being death to the loser, or the life of Irene Sheaffer to the winner, a life he managed never to lose.

"Tell me," his father said. "What do you want out of this frigging world?"

Pausing, Alex said, "I don't know." Shooting, standing upright as if to study the table, he said, "I'd like to have some fun, I guess. Do something exciting." He reached over the table and shot, cracked the balls together again.

"You will," his father said. "Just don't be afraid to use your head. Because you've got a good one. That's about the best advice I can give you. Be smart. And be brave. That is, if you're sure you want to go through with this."

Alex said nothing, to indicate that he was.

. . .

They stood for a moment as three men of the world, the sergeant, and Alex and his father. His father wore a suit, and white shirt and tie, and his black-and-white shoes. His face was red, and his eyes were pink and floating, but he did not appear unhappy, only sentimental. The sergeant had introduced himself and they had shaken hands. The sergeant had said to his father, "Now I wish I was young enough to leave home again," and his father had said, "Well, once may be enough." For a moment the two men had been like mothers trying not to fuss too much over a boy's celebration.

"Shall we get this over with?" the sergeant said. "I got the papers all ready here."

Leaning over the desk, holding the pen and going through a slight warming-up flourish, his father signed his name. He hesitated, as if to read his own name over, and stood upright.

He and the sergeant shook hands again.

The next morning Alex went out and found his father at the kitchen table.

His father said " 'Morning" almost soberly, but he also winked. He wore one of his khaki army shirts with the sleeves rolled, and denim work pants, and his oil-soaked work shoes. The old smell of the factory was about the room—as if his father had worked overtime, deep into the summer night, and was relaxing at the kitchen table, as if it were a moment from the past.

"How you doing?" Alex said. He went about fixing a stand-up breakfast.

They were silent for a time. Alex stood over the toaster, waiting.

"How you fixed for cash?" his father said.

"Fine," Alex said.

"Can you spare a ten spot?"

"Sure. Let me—"

"I'm just kidding. Just wanted to see where your heart is this morning."

Alex only glanced as his father rose, and returned to watching the toaster. He was not sure if his father was drunk or sober. He had seldom seen him drunk in his work clothes, and he had seldom seen him up and sober at this hour.

"Here, son," his father said behind him. "Hang on to this for me."

Alex turned and there was the familiar roll of bills. "No," he said, not looking at his father's face. "No, you keep it." He glanced up then and there was the familiar glimmer over his father's eyes, the strange, nearly shy smile.

He turned back to the counter to butter his toast. He ate without looking back. He knew his father was looking at him.

"Hey, pal, shake hands," his father said behind him.

"No," Alex said. "No. I don't want to." He turned to leave, not sure why he was angry, nor why he was leaving abruptly. He felt certain his father was drunk now, but when he glanced at him there was the faint smile. Still confused, Alex went on through the screen door. His father said nothing more behind him, and he said nothing more. Nor did he look back. But by the time he was on the ground, walking between the buildings, he felt a desire to go back, to make things right again by saying something friendly.

That afternoon at the Country Club, Mr. Quinn, playing as a guest with another man, had Alex's number called. Walking over to the pro shop, Mr. Quinn called to him, "Hey, Alex Housman, over here," and Alex called back, "Hey, Mr. Quinn, what are you doing here?"

"I'm human," Mr. Quinn said. "Can't I take an afternoon off sometime?"

Mr. Quinn was in a twosome but he had not hired Alex.

Alex had been called to caddy for the other man, to whom Mr. Quinn introduced him. The man offered his hand, saying, "Hello, Alex," and they shook.

At the first tee, Alex took up Mr. Quinn's golf bag—it was canvas, turning brown, holding only two woods and a few irons—and heading down the fairway, Mr. Quinn kept chasing after him and saying, "Come on now, let me carry that," and Alex kept saying, "That's all right, I carry doubles all the time," walking on, keeping a step away from him. At last Mr. Quinn said, "Okay, okay, corrupt me, I don't care."

Along the way Mr. Quinn talked with him some, walked with him and asked him how he was making out, how was it going with the recruiting sergeant, and did he make any dough working out here, and what is that, a six- or an eight-iron shot? The other man was apparently a lawyer. At a sand trap Mr. Quinn said to him, "You better warn me of my rights before I go into that thing." The other man wore ice-blue slacks and a matching ice-blue polo shirt, crossed golf clubs stitched over the pocket, fluorescent pink golf tees inserted like cartridges at the waist of the beltless pants. His shoes were black-and-white, like Alex's father's shoes. But there was a difference.

At the end of the first nine Mr. Quinn came walking from the veranda with two bottles of Pepsi-Cola, one of which he handed to Alex. The other man followed. They stood for a moment, the two men talking, and then they sat on the grass under a tree. Alex knew they had come out there to sit because he was not allowed on the veranda. They sat talking for a long time then, perhaps for an hour. Alex answered their questions, proud to be included. The dapper lawyer asked him how it was caddying for the ladies, and Alex told of one woman always pressing her jugs against his arm. The lawyer asked who she was, and Alex said he'd better not say.

"These old gals," the lawyer said. "They know you're a stud at sixteen or seventeen, but you seldom know it yourself."

"It's one of life's tragedies," Mr. Quinn said.

It was nearly dusk when they finished eighteen. The lawyer paid him, and Mr. Quinn tried to pay him as well. He refused. "No," he said, walking away. "Forget it." Mr. Quinn still came after him with a folded greenback or two in his fingers. "No," Alex said, adding happily, clearly, "Never! My pleasure!"

Mr. Quinn stopped and called to him, "I'll owe it to you."

"What do I need it for?" Alex called back. "I'm rich."

"You're nuts!" Mr. Quinn called.

Alex walked past the deserted swimming pool, over to the gravel road, pleased enough with himself to smile most of the way.

In the apartment then, at twilight, Alex found his father's body. He knew when he looked into his father's bedroom what had happened; he knew even before he noticed a rifle lying on the floor; he knew, immediately, from the dark circle on his father's white shirt, over his heart.

He may have known even a moment or two before this, for the car had been in the driveway, although his father should have been at work, and the apartment, when he entered, would have been unusually quiet if his father was home and drinking. There had been other signs of something being wrong: the roll of bills still lay on the table, and a glass and a half-full bottle stood on the counter, and the kitchen light was on, but no music was playing, there was no sound at all. For some reason Alex had at the time opened the refrigerator door and looked in, as if he were hungry, but he could not remember afterward what he had seen there.

He stepped into the bedroom and over to the side of his father's bed. He looked at the man. He looked at his face. For a moment there was no passage of time, or of breath.

His father never slept in that position. He lay on his

back, his eyes closed in the dimly lighted room. He had washed and shaved, and he was dressed in the pants to his powder-gray suit, and his white shirt was without a tie, open at the throat, and he had his black-and-white shoes on, as if ready to go out for the evening. The deep-red spot over his heart had already dried. The spot was not as large as a man's fist. Alex could never remember later if he had seen a hole in the dark spot, in the shirt, or not. Even so, at the time, as if it were his duty, he touched two fingers to the spot, felt the dryness of the stained fabric, but he did not notice or touch any bullet hole or any larger giving of space.

For reasons unknown to himself, he also closed the lid over one of his father's eyes. Released, the lid moved slowly back. Whether the skin was warm or cool, he did not notice. He then touched his father's wrist, picked it up as if in imitation of something he had seen in a movie, and tried to feel his pulse. His father's hand was heavy. In just a moment Alex laid it down again. His father lay still. Alex knew that the man had left now; he knew that he was gone.

Turning, undecided about leaving or staying, he looked at the rifle lying on the floor. Just visible in the shaded space, the barrel and stock of the rifle were shining. He looked down at the rifle. His father must have gone out to buy it, for they owned no rifles. The barrel looked blue; the stock was polished. He looked at his father again. He must have sat on the bed, the rifle turned to his chest, and when he squeezed the trigger he must have lain back or fallen back, and let the rifle drop from his hand to the floor.

Alex stood quietly in the kitchen, next to the wooden table. He did not know quite what to do. For a moment hardly a thought or a feeling seemed to rise within him. Then, for a moment, a visionary and strange moment, as if none of this were true, he felt a desire to see his father, to seek shelter within his father's strength against something troubling and frightening and unknown.

He glanced around the kitchen, lighted at twilight. He stood there.

Outside, in front of the house, he stood on the sidewalk for a moment. A car passing had its lights on in the dusk. He went up the steps then to the landlady's front porch and knocked on her screen door. He glanced around as he waited, down Chevrolet Avenue toward the valley of factories and railyards, and at the cars passing in the street. Across the street the floodlights over the gas station were on, although the sky was still blue above them. Mrs. Lovejoy was looking at him through the screen door.

"My father's dead," he said to her.

"What?"

"My father's dead. He shot himself."

He hardly knew Mrs. Lovejoy. She was a woman in her sixties. His father had always stopped by to pay the rent. She stood looking at Alex now; then she unhooked the screen door to let him in.

"Is he upstairs?" she said.

"Yes."

She left him sitting in a chair in her living room while she went to the kitchen to use the telephone. He sat in the chair for some twenty or thirty minutes altogether. She returned to tell him that she had called the police, and sitting down in a chair opposite, she asked him if he felt all right. He told her yes.

She said nothing more. He sat there quietly. The moments passed. He was aware that the circumstances excused him from offering conversation. He sat thinking of the people he knew. He thought of Howard and wondered what he would think. He thought of Irene Sheaffer. He thought of Mr. Quinn. He thought of others, and of other things. He had a feeling that he should not think of such things or people now, and a feeling that it did not matter.

At last two uniformed policemen came to the door. Mrs. Lovejoy spoke softly to them, before they came all the way into the living room. Alex rose from his chair as they entered. The policemen were polite. One of them asked his name and spelled "Housman" to himself as he wrote it down. He wrote down a couple of other things before he said, "Which way upstairs?"

They went out through Mrs. Lovejoy's back door and up the exposed stairway to the apartment. The sky was dark by now.

"I'll have to ask you not to touch anything," the policeman said.

The two policemen preceded Alex into the bedroom, one of them turning on the overhead light. Mrs. Lovejoy stood back.

"Where did the rifle come from?"

"I never saw it before," Alex said.

"What time did you get here?"

"About a half-hour ago."

"When did you leave?"

"This morning."

"Where were you today?"

"I was working out at the Country Club."

"What do you do there?"

"Caddy." Alex thought of Mr. Quinn and decided not to mention him, because of the suspicion his being on probation might arouse.

In a moment the policeman said, "Let's go back out here," indicating the kitchen.

"What was wrong with him?" the policeman said to Alex.

"He just died," Alex said.

The policeman looked at him for a moment and then he said, "I'm going to call an ambulance. Do you have some place you can stay tonight?"

"Oh, he can stay downstairs," Mrs. Lovejoy said.

"Okay," the policeman said. "Why don't you go on down. We'll take care of things up here."

Later, downstairs, Alex saw a dull-red ambulance enter the driveway between the buildings. He stood at Mrs.

Lovejoy's screen door. She had turned on a couple of dim lamps in the living room behind him. He went out and waited on the porch.

In a while the ambulance came out again. He could see nothing but darkness through the window of the back door as it entered the street. The two policemen walked around to the front of the house and talked to him for a moment from the porch steps. They wanted to know if he would be all right there for the night. They told him they had taken his father to the Lothrop Funeral Home on Third Avenue. They asked him if there was someone who could help make arrangements, and as he told them yes, Mrs. Lovejoy also spoke up from her screen door to say that she would help. The policemen left in the squad car, going out of sight, as the ambulance had, down Third Avenue.

Alex remained with Mrs. Lovejoy in her living room. It was completely dark outside by now, a warm summer night. Cars went by on Chevrolet Avenue as usual. The sounds of the motors were more apparent down there, with an opened door facing the street. At last he stood up and said to her, "I'm going out for a walk."

She looked at him for a moment before she said, "Well, okay, that may be a good idea. When you come back, just ring the doorbell and I'll let you in."

He walked along Third Avenue. He walked past the Lothrop Funeral Home and glanced at its lighted windows. He tried not to think about much of anything, and as before, his thoughts passed calmly over Howard, and his mother, and Irene Sheaffer, and others, even Cricket Alan and Mr. Gerhinger. He decided to call Mr. Quinn in the morning, to ask for help. Everything was more quiet than usual; he felt contained within an invisible covering.

He walked into lower downtown. He walked along the lighted and busy streets. Cars and buses went by, and people passed him on the sidewalk; radio fragments of a night baseball game were in the air. He had the thought that he should notify Howard and his mother tonight, but knew he would not. His heart continued, as before, to tremble only mildly.

He went to the Fox Theater. As he sat in the cool, air-conditioned cavern, he was aware that something was different. He looked at the screen. He seemed to keep seeing through the screen to a world beyond. It was a world where his father appeared, and he appeared himself. The action on the screen interfered with his view of that world. But when his father came close, as if offering his hand, Alex felt frightened, as if something were interfering with the action on the screen. He tried to concentrate on the screen, to let the movie come to life.

In the morning, after sleeping poorly on the couch in Mrs. Lovejoy's living room, he left as usual to carry his paper route. Again, walking, he felt contained within an invisible covering. When he finished his route, he had breakfast, coffee and doughnuts and milk, at the Coney Island. He read his extra copy of the Detroit *Free Press*. The news did not matter; it did not matter if a team had won or lost. He was waiting to go to Mr. Quinn's office, a long wait, for it was still not seven o'clock. He sat on a stool at the counter, waiting, until a desire came over him to be at home again, if only to visit for a moment, and he rose to leave.

The apartment was still. The air in the rooms was cooler now from the night. If there was a covering about him, it began to disintegrate as he stood in the kitchen. He looked around then for a note, but found none. He knew that he was alone now. He walked into the bedroom. The spot on the bed looked purple and was larger than the spot on his father's shirt had been. Alex stood still and looked at it. For an instant the floor seemed to rush away.

Six

The army buildings were wooden and yellow, in rows everywhere, a maze of yellow buildings one or two stories high among clusters of trees. Soldiers in fatigues and soft caps walked among them, as did an occasional starched and polished sergeant in a yellow helmet liner or an officer in a red helmet liner. This was the Basic Training Center at Fort Belvoir, Virginia, home of the Army Engineers. It was mid-September now, and it was midmorning. The warm Virginia air was touched with an aroma faintly of autumn, perhaps of the sea, an air richer with moisture than the air of the Middle West.

Alex stood at a plywood counter in one of the single-story buildings. He wore a khaki uniform, with a necktie, and a khaki hat which he now held in his hand. The shirt and pants were slightly large, of heavy material, and his pants were bloused over boots dull with newness. He felt awkward in the uniform, wrinkled and bushy. He was a private E-1.

There were a dozen or so desks behind the counter, with PFC's and specialists and sergeants working at them, walking occasionally with papers in hand, or coffee mugs, but they did not look his way. Still, he knew they knew he was there. He also knew he should not rap his knuckles on the counter. But he was tired after the all-night train ride, a little exhilarated, it seemed, from having missed breakfast, and when another several minutes passed and no one looked his way, he rapped on the counter, louder than he intended: *KNUK KNUK*. The heads in the room turned. A master sergeant at a nearby desk, a man with a bulbous face, stared at him. "Wait outside," the sergeant said.

Alex waited outside, next to his duffle bag. His legs began to ache from standing, and he shifted his weight now and then from one foot to another. He had not slept well on the train. It had been his first train ride, and however quiet, it had not been a small adventure. Through the evening, leaving Michigan, he had sat next to a window. Into the night he had watched through the glass, and dozed, and weaved down the aisle many times as if going to the men's room, through other cars and back again, returning to watch the countryside, the house lights and highways, click by. Somewhere in Pennsylvania, at about three o'clock in the morning, he imagined for an instant that his father's reflection had looked at him from the glass, that he had seen the man smile.

His focus over the maze of yellow buildings had grown blurred by now. Perhaps an hour had passed. It must have been close to noon. His neck and back muscles ached and he rolled his shoulders, pleasantly, as he stood there. His eyes burned some from lack of sleep. Still, he felt an unusual strength, a tenuous vision of being there and being alive.

He stood before the building throughout the day. The clerks left for lunch and returned. They did no more than glance his way. Later in the afternoon he sat for a time on his duffle bag, resting the weight of his head in his hands, looking at the ground between his feet. His eyelids drooped occasionally and his head settled; he wavered for moments at a time over an endless sea, and seemed to awaken, and wavered again. For a moment he merely looked at the boots, at the two glossy bulbs of the toes before him. Lifting his head, uprolling his eyelids, he focused over knife-sharp fatigue pants, and over the sudden sunlight of a belt buckle, seeing at the top, more than face or feature, a shadowed space within a red helmet liner, a single silver bar. He lifted the weight of himself to his feet. He raised his arm and saluted. The figure saluted back, with style and rhythm. From within the shadow came the ascending words: "You stay on those two feet, SOLDIER!"

He stayed. He walked, strolled here and there, not far from his bag, from his envelope of orders and papers. His eyes itched now and he ground them often with his knuckles. He stopped once and stood looking away. Three weeks had passed since the funeral, and until this moment, it seemed he had not thought of it for several days. Nor did he now think of it very long—the tedious hours of waiting in the funeral parlor, the heavy aroma of the dying flowers, the silken casket. The only refreshing moment had been at the cemetery, the brief service there within the shade of some old trees, when he had tried to issue a private farewell to the man.

Through the haze over his eyes he saw the clerks leaving the building again. He stepped over to face the door, to catch the sergeant this time, but the sergeant did not come from the building. In a moment, from behind him, from the surrounding barracks, came the first scratching noises of a recording over a loudspeaker. He saw one of the speakers up under the eave of a barracks; he thought he saw the sound waves emitting. Off between the buildings he saw the two soldiers in fatigues stop walking and salute, saluting nothing but the sky. He, too, lifted his arm and held his hand over his eyebrow, throughout the wail of a trumpet. As it ended he again felt momentarily exhilarated, and foolish, and not unhappy over being there, and being alive.

The door opened and he turned to see the master sergeant, who said, stopping, "Oh for Christsakes."

Alex took his envelope from under the edge of his bag and followed the sergeant into the building. The sergeant shook the contents to one end and ripped off the other. He flipped through the papers. "Idiots," he said to the papers, shaking his head. Looking up, he said, "Listen, little soldier, they got you here two days ahead of your cycle. You go on and chow down in Company F." He waved his thumb over his shoulder. "Sack out there for the night. Try the Fourth Platoon. Or the Third. See Sergeant Rose, the platoon sergeant, big tall guy. Tell him I sent you over. And then report back here in the morning. First thing. Oh-eight hundred. You got that?"

Alex nodded.

"What the hell you waitin on then?" the sergeant said.

Outside, the envelope clipped inside his bag and the bag hoisted to his shoulder, Alex walked. But when he was past the first barracks building, in the direction of the sergeant's waved thumb, he realized he did not know where he was going. Wearily, he could remember only that he was supposed to eat somewhere, and sleep. See some platoon sergeant.

He tried a barracks. He wasn't sure. The sign next to the door said COMPANY G/2ND PLATOON. But nothing sounded right. He let the bag fall from his shoulder, opened the door, and dragged it in behind him.

Soldiers were moving around inside in fatigues and white T-shirts. They were polishing boots and cleaning rifles; others were walking by with brooms and mops, going to the latrine and back. Some looked at him, but only with a glance, and no one spoke. Several minutes passed. He was standing there, trying to decide what to do next, when a tall slim soldier, coming down from the upper floor, paused before him. The soldier's T-shirt was puckered and dark under his armpits. "Whatcha lookin for?" he said.

"The platoon sergeant."

The soldier said nothing for a moment. Then he said, "He's not around," and turned to walk away.

Alex spoke to the next soldier, one passing with a mess kit and a roll of toilet paper. "Say, where can I find the platoon sergeant?"

"Beats me, pal," the soldier said without stopping.

A few minutes later Alex dragged his duffle bag back

outside. The sky was growing darker by now, but the air remained warm. He let the bag bounce down the steps, and lifting it from the ground, hoisting it to his shoulder, he walked on. Beside him, behind the lighted windows, the soldiers were moving with mops and rifles and rolls of toilet paper. He wished he were inside working with them.

He walked past a mess hall where soldiers in muddy fatigues were in line at the side doorway. Within the lighted windows, other soldiers were eating at tables. The smell of coal smoke was in the warm evening air. He walked on. Some distance down the road, the barracks buildings were all dark and empty. The only light there came from the moon, off to the right over the rooftops, powdery-looking, leaving the roadway a dark tunnel. He considered the empty buildings, considered the soldiers who had used them, including his father, in World War II, the Korean War, and he glimpsed the simple swiftness of events.

He had walked perhaps a mile by now, and however slowly and wearily he was moving, he kept moving. He did not stop until he heard something on the dark road ahead. He lowered his bag to the ground and stood listening. The noise continued, growing gradually louder. When he realized it was coming in his direction, coming at him on the road, he pulled his bag beside him, over into a half-moon ditch, and out again, up an incline to the wall of a barracks. The noise came on, growing louder. In another minute it was close-by. Then it was beside him in the darkness, a body of soldiers, two or three hundred of them, running steadily in groups, their packs and rifles and helmets rattling and clicking in rhythm with their boots striking the ground. They were past in seconds, and he left his bag to step out and look after them. He felt as if a train had gone rocking by close enough to whip his clothes against his body. Somewhere in a dream, a nightmare of war, he had felt the same terror of movement in darkness.

Back at the wall he pulled his bag by the strap around

to the side porch of the dark barracks building. At the door he stopped from weariness to catch his breath. He tried to open the door. The knob moved loosely all the way around and failed to catch. He put his shoulder against the door and pushed, but the door remained tight. He felt suddenly so exhausted and weak that he slid slightly down the door and his hand fell limp from the knob. At last he lifted himself away and lowered to the porch, sat on the top step with his feet on the second and third steps. He held his head. He had never been so tired or sleepy. All that kept him awake was a sense of not knowing what to do next, or where to go.

Standing up a moment later he felt faint. In exhaustion he worked his way back down the steps and sitting there on the edge of the block of sidewalk he unsnapped the clip on his duffle bag and spread the canvas mouth. His overcoat with its wool liner was in a roll near the top. He pulled it out and did not bother to clip the bag again, but rolled over onto the clay and pulled the coat over his shoulders. Then, before him, he noticed the space under the small porch. He knew he should raise the energy to crawl in, but he did not move. He lay there, and in a moment the small problem grew large enough to disrupt his sleep. Was he big enough to make the move? At last, calling on what was left of his strength, he sat up. He clipped the bag this time, and as if his strength were increasing through use, he worked and pushed the bag under the porch, and worked himself in feetfirst beside it. He pulled in his overcoat to cover himself. He felt better now. In a voice similar to his father's voice, he said to himself, "Woof, all you spiders and bugs." With his head on his arm, on the sleeve of his khaki shirt, he went immediately to sleep.

He woke once, but only for a moment. With no idea of the time, he disappeared again into sleep.

Before dawn, soldiers double-timing on the dark roadway, going out, woke him again. He thought it must be around five-thirty or six o'clock. Coming out of the drowsiness of sleep, he raised his head and listened. He knew where he was; he felt calm now.

It was cooler moving from under the coat and from under the porch, but still a warm morning. First light was showing in the sky; a mist was in the dark air. He stood up and shivered and felt dry in the fall dampness. He straightened his uniform, brushing dirt from his sleeves and knees, wiping the tops of his boots on the backs of his pants legs. Stretching as he moved, he stepped over to the side of the building and pleasantly relieved himself. He could see the small reflecting pool he made in the clay and the steam rising. His eyes were softer now and more fluid. He could feel the moisture of the air in his nose, an oil of perspiration over his face.

With his bag packed and clipped, he lifted it once more to his shoulder and started walking back. Again there was a sense of not knowing where to go, or what to do next. But it mattered less now. He knew things would work out. His strength was coming around; a muscle-lined space of thirst and hunger was growing in his stomach. Ground level remained dark, but the sky was becoming blue with the approach of dawn.

Walking the mile back, near the maze of yellow buildings where soldiers were marching and double-timing in squads and platoons, he found a snack bar. A couple of sergeants sat at the counter, and a waitress, a tall thin woman, was on a stool pouring water into the top of a coffee machine. She had apparently just opened or just come to work; she wore a fluffed purple-flowered handkerchief pinned over her breast on a fresh white uniform. The snack bar was warm with coffee brewing and fresh bacon frying. Alex sat on a stool opposite the woman, and when she turned to him he ordered ham and two eggs and toast and coffee, and he asked for a glass of water.

She brought the water and coffee at once. Waiting for the ham and eggs, he leaned down the counter and dropped a quarter into the counter jukebox. He did not care if the music imposed upon the two sergeants or upon the waitress, nor did he care which songs played, pushing the buttons without reading them. It was his celebration of a night's rest, of the warm food cooking, of feeling strong this morning.

He sat humming a little to himself with the music—all country songs, it turned out—when the woman came with the plate of ham and eggs and toast. There was her white nylon, her movement before him, placing the dish on the counter, and he felt an urge to touch her arm.

Using a triangular half-slice of toast, he piled on a piece of ham and a piece of egg, and reached it into his mouth. Chewing, he glanced up and saw his reflection in the coffee machine. He looked over the blurred image of himself. He looked older there.

He worked on his meal. He was rested now, and his mind was clear. Back across the land they would be rising soon to go to school as the September day was breaking. Over his shoulder, through the windows, the sun had just come up.

Leaving the snack bar, he waited outside as the first rays of the sun touched the roadway. The ham and eggs and coffee had strengthened his body. He parked his duffle bag near the snack-bar door and walked here and there among the yellow buildings, watching soldiers marching and double-timing away with packs and rifles. His khaki uniform and his bloused boots seemed to fit him better, as if they were broken in by now. The light moisture in the sunlighted air was refreshing. He felt the anticipation of something new about to happen, and for a sudden moment he felt he possessed the wisdom and size of his father.

With linens and blankets and a pillow, he was assigned to a barracks. He was the first to arrive, and the sergeant, walking him over, told him to fix up his area and stay out of sight. He was still a day early. Others would arrive that night and the next day.

He chose a bunk upstairs on the second floor, the last bunk in a row. He fixed the crisp sheets as he had at the detention home. Thinking of the dormitory there, glancing back, he saw himself as a child at the time. He went on making the bed, straightening and tightening the heavy wool blankets. He calmly transferred his clothes from his duffle bag to a foot locker, and as if this were his home now, he opened windows on both sides to let in the fresh Virginia air. He looked out for a moment. In his mind again he saw the distance back over the land. He turned and sat on the springs of an empty cot. He saw Howard as a child as well, steering the boat over the surface of the lake, appearing on the path within the leaves. He sat still. For an instant the world seemed to turn before him.

Downstairs in the latrine he showered, and then he shaved. He had never shaved before, and for the experiment he welcomed having the latrine to himself. Mr. Quinn had given him a leather shaving kit as a gift and had suggested, helping him clear the apartment, that he take along his father's razor and razor blades and shaving brush. "Unless it bothers you?" Mr. Quinn had said, and not concerned at the time, Alex had said that it did not bother him.

He threw his father's last blade into a trash barrel and replaced it with a new one. The brush was dry from the weeks of nonuse, and soaking it under the faucet, he worked it into his bar of soap. He worked the lather over his cheeks. Then he realized that it did bother him to use the brush and razor. Still he continued. He pressed the bristles of the brush into the soap, and spread the lather over his cheeks, until he knew that he was afraid to look up at himself in the mirror. It seemed his father might look back at him from the reflection of his own eyes.

He looked up then, and for a moment he imagined the man was looking into him. He stood still. He felt a need to admit, to confess, if only to himself, the range of his cruelty

to Howard, and to his father. His admission seemed an
acceptance in some way of his failure and his weakness,
and it seemed also to come from him as a request to be for-
given. Against the trembling of his heart, he continued the
process of shaving. But his mind was not on shaving.
Glancing up again, he looked at himself. He believed he
felt within himself the emergence of his father, of his
father's large strength, his heart, and his weakness too, the
strength and weakness of them both.

He finished shaving. He rinsed the razor and brush,
and he rinsed the suds from his face with cool water. A
knick of blood appeared on his chin, growing slowly
dark. He looked down at the sink as he moved water on his
fingers from the faucet to the raw spot. He looked into the
mirror again. The cut had stopped bleeding. His cheeks
stung and looked red from the scraping razor.

Upstairs, next to his bunk, he dressed calmly in fresh
underwear and socks, and put on a new khaki uniform. He
was going to go out and walk across Fort Belvoir, to look
around. Standing at the window next to his bunk, he fixed
his tie. He looked through the window, out over the rooftops, over the warm air rising. The thought came to him
that here in the army, perhaps, they would call him Curly.

Downstairs again, in the latrine, he checked his uniform, his brass and tie in the mirror. He fixed his khaki
cap over his thickness of hair. He glanced at the eyes looking at him from the mirror. He looked aside and glanced
again, and he felt a new heart was beating in him now. In
a moment he was out on the roadway he had seen from
upstairs, walking along.